On Past Horton Creek

First Edition
Copyright © 2008

A *Sage River Press* Book

All rights reserved.

ISBN 978-0-9794670-1-1

For comments or questions to the author or to receive an excerpt of his next book, email
michael.lindley@comcast.net

On Past Horton Creek

The saga of the *EmmaLee* continues with this story of the undying power of love and conviction.

Michael Lindley

A *Sage River Press* Book
2008

On Past Horton Creek

ACKNOWLEDGEMENTS

With the release of my second book, the sequel to *The Seasons of the EmmaLee*, I have to again thank the many bookstore owners and buyers who have been so supportive over the past two years and who continue to support *EmmaLee* in its second edition. And to the many readers and book groups and librarians who have shared the story of the *EmmaLee* with friends and family, I am sincerely grateful. It has been a wonderful adventure in telling a story about a place that I love and about characters that have become all too real to me over these past months. It will be sad to say goodbye to them. I hope that you enjoy the continuing story of the McKendry's, of George Hansen and of Sally and Alex.

ML

All things truly wicked start from an innocence.

- Ernest Hemingway

This second book is dedicated to my wife Karen and children, Chase and Kristen, who have been more than patient and supportive in my time away from the family, hovering over the keyboard trying to find the right words, or traveling to meet with readers.

Chapter One

Only when you have a chance to rise above the physical world and stand apart from the life you've led and the people who have shaped your life, can you begin to see the ironic patterns in all of this. In passing on from your time in the here and now, off into the bright light of the eternal, it is so surprising to be able to look back upon your life with such terrible clarity and insight. As I looked down that day on the people I've known and loved, gathered in the small cemetery in Charlevoix to honor my passing, the memories swept back before me in vivid and often haunting detail.

How quickly our time on this Earth passes and yet, before us lies the promise of new hope and salvation, as well as the inevitable failings of those who will follow us. The generations continue on and the seasons return in their relentless progression.

Time is the ultimate irony.

***

Megan Clark felt the warmth of her stepmother's hand in her own. If there was ever a good day for a funeral, this must surely be one of them, she thought. The first warm day in June had arrived with just a trace of wind sending soft swirls out across the lake and a soft rustling through the tall pines in the cemetery. The midday sun moved high across the tops of the trees. The sky was a deep blue, unfettered by clouds and the air carried the scents of new growth in the summer gardens. The pastor spoke softly, sending words of comfort and hope to those in attendance.

Megan looked at the people gathered around her. Most were dressed in somber dark clothes. Many were looking at the ground in front of them in reverence. Easily more than one hundred people had come to pay their respects to their friend and loved one, George Hansen. At the age of eighty-

1

four, the man that she had come to know as *Uncle George*, had been found dead this past week in his fishing boat anchored down near Holy Island.

She noticed her stepmother Sally trying to hold back her tears as she looked over at the tall blonde woman who had come into her life six years ago during her first visit to this little lake town of Charlevoix, Michigan. She and her father had both fallen in love with Sally Thomason. His marriage to Sally had been held on the deck of their boat, the *EmmaLee*, a year later here on the waters of Lake Charlevoix. Sally had become a source of both strength and grounding for she and her father, helping them to always remember what is truly important in otherwise hectic lives. Things like their new family unit and the bonds that they had created together after so many tragic losses earlier in their lives.

Next to Sally stood Elizabeth Hansen, George's wife. Her face was pale and dark circles framed her moist eyes.

"Ashes to ashes..." Megan heard the pastor's words, but her mind was elsewhere thinking about her father.

***

"Damn it, Lou!" shouted Alex Clark. "I told you this was going to lead to nothing but a disaster!" He slammed the phone down on the cradle and turned his chair to look out the window of his office, eighty floors above Park Avenue in New York. He looked north out across the vast expanse of concrete and glass buildings rising up from the island of Manhattan. The green interruption of Central Park stood out in surprising contrast to the harsh edges and colors of the rest of the city.

Alex took a deep breath to calm himself and he struggled to keep his hand from shaking as he picked up a glass filled with more bourbon than ice. His brown hair was cropped close, a few random hints of gray beginning to reveal themselves and the once smooth features of his face were showing the strain of his years running some of the country's most successful internet software companies. The conversation with his business partner, Louis Kramer, was like a sharp blade cutting deep into his chest. *How could I have let it get this far?*

He pulled his cell phone from the leather clip on his belt. Pushing three buttons he listened as the phone connection was made. He heard the answer at the other end of the line. "Cancel the plane for tonight. I'm not going to Charlevoix."

***

Megan and Sally walked slowly down the sidewalk toward town. The summer traffic was already backing up in both directions on Bridge Street in the little business district, a narrow street lined with small shops and restaurants. Trees had been planted along the sidewalk every few yards casting soft shadows from the early season leaves. The west side of the street had been cleared for a park for many years opening up a spectacular view of the small inland harbor known as Round Lake. Megan could see the bright blue drawbridge up ahead, rising slowly to open the channel for boats to pass on the half hour in and out to Lake Michigan. Summer visitors and locals darted around the slow moving traffic to make their way across the busy street and down through the town. She could see the big boats at the docks along Round Lake. Other boats cruised slowly across the calm waters, keeping their wakes to a minimum. Large flocks of gulls swept over the harbor and the slightest smell of fish and gasoline fumes from the boats drifted on the air. The *EmmaLee* rested at anchor out in the center of Round Lake. At almost 180 feet of waterline, it dwarfed the other boats in the harbor. Its graceful white hull was gleaming brilliantly in the afternoon sun.

Megan had grown over the past few years into a tall and athletic body. She was a swimmer and gymnast in high school and her arms and shoulders were strong and well developed. Her dark brown hair was straight and cut at shoulder length, held back with a scarf rolled and tied behind her ears. She had her father's deep green eyes and the lines of her face were smooth and flowing. Dressed in a simple black dress, she had pinned an early blooming flower above her heart from the gardens up at Sally's house on the bluff. All her life she had heard how much she resembled her mother, particularly after she had passed away when Megan was only a young girl.

She felt comfort in Sally's arm around her shoulders. Megan turned and looked into her stepmother's face and could see the swollen redness around her eyes from her tears and grief. Only two years past 50, Sally had kept trim with regular walks in the city and along the beach when they were in Charlevoix and her face showed only the slightest hints of wrinkles along

3

the corners of her eyes. At times Megan wondered what their lives would have been like without Sally Thomason. What if her father hadn't found the old ship and brought it home to Charlevoix leading to the chance meeting with Sally whose family had owned the *EmmaLee* so many years earlier? Sally had helped to bring them both back from the heavy dark sadness of the loss of Megan's mother. Although she was only twelve at the time, Megan could remember their first meetings like it was yesterday. Sally had been a bright light that stood out in a crowd full of strangers they had met that first summer and as the days of their visit went by, Megan had felt a strong connection, not quite maternal, but warm and trusting. She had never called Sally, *Mother;* that was a space held in her heart for a woman that she had loved so deeply and even a young school girl's grief never fades completely, but Sally Thomason was, in so many ways, just as close and important in her life.

"I know how much you loved Uncle George," Megan said, putting her arm around Sally's waist. "I'm so sorry he's gone."

Sally didn't answer for a moment. Then she sighed and spoke softly, "Isn't this the saddest day. I feel so badly for Elizabeth. They've been together for so many years."

"I'm going to miss Uncle George this summer, too," Megan said.

They were across the street now from Sally's old art gallery next to the bookstore and the coffee shop. She had sold her interest in the business six years ago when she had left Charlevoix to begin her new life with Alex and Megan Clark. Her former partner, Gwen Roberts, had been at the funeral earlier and Megan had watched as she and Sally held each other in a long embrace after the service. Gwen had pulled a handkerchief from her purse and had dabbed at the tears flowing freely from Sally's eyes.

"It was nice to see Gwen today," Megan said. "Do you want to stop into the gallery?"

"No, I don't think so honey, not today. Let's get on down to the boat. I want to call your father and see when he's going to be coming in tonight."

"You know he really wanted to be here today, Sally."

"Yes, I know," Sally answered and Megan could sense the frustration in her voice. "I just can't imagine what would be so important that he couldn't get away from the city for the service today."

"You know Daddy, it seems the new business has just been getting crazier."

Sally didn't respond.

Ahead on the sidewalk up above East Park along the docks, Megan saw a boy walking toward them. She first noticed the sharp features of his brown face, then the long black hair, nearly down to his shoulders, that was brushed straight back and blew all about in the gentle afternoon breeze. He was wearing a loose fitting white shirt, untucked over a faded pair of blue jeans. His feet were barely covered with faded green flip-flops, and he walked with a comfortable and confident stride.

Sally noticed who she was looking at. "You remember Will Truegood, don't you?" she asked her stepdaughter.

"That's Will?" Megan answered.

"Yes, he seems to have grown a bit since last summer."

Megan felt her heart grow tight in her chest and her breath was hard in coming. It was that irritating reminder that she had yet to move beyond her adolescent shyness and awkward fumbling around meeting people. *When you turn eighteen, aren't you supposed to grow out of all of this old nonsense?* She saw a smile spread across his face as he spotted them. He came up and gave Sally a hug.

"Hello, Mrs. Clark. I saw you earlier at the funeral, but I didn't want to interrupt," he said.

Sally reached out to give him a hug. "Will, it's so good to see you, and you have to start calling me *Sally*. I'm feeling old enough these days."

He nodded and then turned to Megan and reached out for her hand, holding it firmly. "Hi Megan, do you remember me?"

Megan struggled for just a moment in answering, catching herself lingering too long looking at his face. It bothered her that her hands felt cold and clammy. "Hi Will, I didn't recognize you at first. You've grown so much since last summer."

Will just smiled back at her. He turned to Sally. "I'm really sorry about Mr. Hansen. He was a very special man."

"Yes he was, Will," answered Sally.

"You know, he's been a friend of our family for so many years, even back to my great grandfather in the 40's."

"How *are* your parents, Will?" Sally asked.

"Oh they're fine; they live up in Mackinaw now. My dad's working on a project for the State."

"The next time you talk with Jonas, you give him our best," Sally said. "I can remember so many stories that George and my father told me about your dad and his big brother Samuel."

"I'll do that," he said.

"What have you been doing, Will?" asked Sally.

"I just finished up my first year down at Michigan State. I'm working on my degree in Fisheries Biology," he said. "I'm off for the summer and staying out at the family's old cabin on Horton Creek."

"How do you like college?" Megan asked, thinking about her own plans for the fall and the uncertainty of it all.

"It's really a blast and I'm thinking seriously about the Masters program," he said and then he paused, looking at Megan. "You know, I'm not the only one who's grown a bit since last year."

Megan felt the warm prickles of a blush spread out across her face as she watched him look up and down her tall body. She realized she was still holding on to his hand and she pulled hers away quickly. She wasn't quite sure how to answer and couldn't seem to come up with anything appropriate to say.

"Will, it was nice to see you, unfortunately on such a sad day," Sally said, breaking the awkward silence.

"Thank you, Sally. Megan, it was nice to see you again. Are you up for the summer?"

"Yes, my dad had the crew bring the boat out last week and we're going to be up for most of the summer…maybe take a few short cruises when my dad can get away."

"Hey, that's great," he answered. He paused for a moment, seeming to think about what he was about to say. "Do you still like to fish?" he asked, looking directly into Megan's eyes without blinking. "You'll have to come out to our little cabin. The trout are really fishing well so·far this year."

"The trout?" she asked, wondering if he was asking her out on a fishing date.

"Yeah, some nice rainbows. I'll give you a call and see if you can get out."

Sally jumped in and said, "That would be nice of you, Will. It was good to see you.

He dipped his head quickly and then walked past the women, moving on down the sidewalk away from the park.

Sally reached around Megan's waist and pulled her close. "Looks like my daughter has already got the summer off to an interesting start." She laughed for the first time that day as they started down through the park to the launch that would take them out to the *EmmaLee*.

***

Alex Clark sat facing the senior partner from his law firm across his expansive desk, anxiously tapping a pencil on the smooth mahogany finish. The office was mostly windows, floor to ceiling, looking out over the city. What little wall space still available was filled with pictures of family and boats.

Anna Bataglia was dressed almost too casually in jeans and a sleeveless light blue blouse and she wore thin leather sandals over bare feet. She had been on vacation out at her beach house on Long Island and had only come into the city at Alex's urgent pleading. Her long black hair was pulled back and held with a thin white ribbon, soft curls cascading down her back. Her Italian heritage was evident in the classic features of her face and soft brown eyes that looked back at her client. Slight wrinkles that appeared when she smiled betrayed the years and the stress of her profession. She sat confidently in the plush leather chair, her legs crossed and a glass of red wine in her hand.

"Alex, you need to be completely straight with me. Is there anything else I need to know besides Louis pulling this bullshit with your CFO and your earnings reports and stock options? The SEC is going to have all your asses in a sling and I'm not talking about a slap on the wrist. There is no tolerance these days for any of this nonsense. Not only will your reputation be ruined, you will do time and the financial penalties could wipe you out."

"Thanks for those comforting thoughts, counselor," Alex said. He stood and walked over to the window, looking out across the city. "As I've told you, several months ago I noticed a number of things that didn't add up in the financial reporting to the Street. I met with Lou and our CFO, Littlefair and was reassured with some very credible documentation that the numbers were valid. The whole stock option thing, I haven't a clue." He turned back to look at Anna. "You need to realize that I have never been a numbers guy… sales, marketing, product development is what I do. I hire people to keep the books."

"The little evidence that I've been able to see so far from the Attorney General's office is pretty damn incriminating; inflated earnings forecasts and very questionable internal accounting across subsidiaries, and possibly back-dating stock options to the benefit of management." Anna put her wine glass on the desk. "I know that you and Louis Kramer have had a lot of success as business partners in the past. Have you had any reason to doubt his integrity?"

"I've always felt that I could trust him with my life, honestly," answered Alex.

"You need to think long and hard about who you can really trust now, Alex."

***

Sally sat on the aft deck of the *EmmaLee*. A breeze coming in off Lake Michigan through the channel into Round Lake caused goose bumps on her tanned arms and legs. The last few days in the sun had also brought the old freckles out under her eyes and across her nose. There were days now when she looked in the mirror too closely that she realized how quickly time's ravages can take their toll when you've passed your fiftieth birthday. Megan was down below in the galley helping the chef prepare a late afternoon meal. She pressed the speed dial button for Alex's cell phone.

He answered in two rings. "Honey, hello. I am really sorry that I couldn't get up there today for the service. How are you feeling? I know this has been a very rough day for you."

"I've been considerably better," she answered. "God, if I have to go to another funeral in my life…" She couldn't finish the thought.

"I hope you were able to give Elizabeth and her family my condolences."

"Honestly, I didn't feel the need to make excuses for you," she said with an edge.

"Sally, you know there are some issues coming together here. Lou has pulled some serious shit with our books and the Attorney General of New York is all over us."

"I just thought that you could take a day for someone who means this much to me," she said quietly.

Alex sighed deeply into the phone. "Sally, I was just getting ready to call you. I can't come up for a couple more days. I'm here with Anna right now trying to work out how we're going to put our case together for the Grand Jury."

"With Anna?" she said, her voice growing tense again. "Where is Louis? Why isn't he doing the work on this?"

"Right now, Lou Kramer is a big part of the problem and I'm not sure how much he can be a part of the solution."

"So where are you now?" she asked.

"I'm down at my office in the city. Anna and I have been going through the background on all this."

"I didn't know high-priced New York attorneys worked on Saturdays."

"I had her come in from the Island. We have to get prepared for this as quickly as we can."

Sally could feel an old sense of dread coming back from years ago and an ex-husband who always had some excuse for staying away. She tried to calm herself before speaking. "Alex, I'm sure you're doing what's best, just please try to get here as soon as you can. Megan and I need you to be here with us."

MICHAEL LINDLEY

"I'll be there as soon as I can," he promised.

Chapter Two

Jonathan and Emily Compton had been married here in Charlevoix about a year after the Second World War had finally come to an end. It was quite an affair on her father's big ship, the EmmaLee, right here on Round Lake. All the summer society people were there and Jonathan's local family and friends. It was a real contrast in cultures, as I recall. We had all been through so much together in those years before and after we returned from the War. Jonathan was so blessed to have had Emily there with him to see him through some very dark times for all of us. My wife Elizabeth and I remained the closest of friends with Jonathan and Emily. They were a wonderful couple together.

Emily finished medical school and her residency down in Ann Arbor and joined a family practice here in Charlevoix. Jonathan was able to finish school and received his engineering degree from the University of Michigan about the same time I was finishing law school down there. He worked for a couple of years for a boat manufacturing company down in Elk Rapids before he was ready to go off on his own. McKendry Yachts was formed back in 1950, and Jonathan and his company built some fine boats over the years. A few years later they would be blessed to have their first and only child, the beautiful little Sally.

We were all settling down into a fairly normal and peaceful existence here in the North. Then there was the summer of '52.

***

Jonathan McKendry steered the small fishing dinghy into the slip as George Hansen stood up in the bow to secure the lines. It had been dark for about an hour and the bugs gathered in furious clusters around the lights along the pier. It was late June and the big summer mayflies were out like a blizzard on most nights. There was a new moon and all of the forces of nature had come together to get the fish to feed with abandon. The stringer tied to the side of the boat was filled with trout and smallmouth bass. Heat lightning flashed across the sky out over the big lake to the west and the distant rumble of thunder could just be heard over the sounds of the comings and goings on the little Round Lake harbor. The smell of rain was heavy in the air.

"Hansen, do you remember how to tie a knot up there?" Jonathan teased as he watched his old friend scramble up onto the dock in his baggy shorts and old sneakers, a faded flowered shirt stretched out over his fully rounded middle. His sandy brown hair was trimmed short in a brush cut sticking straight up on top of his head and his face had a perpetual flush of redness in his cheeks.

"Yeah," George said, laughing, "a better knot than you tied on that hook that big bass still has in his lip down of the bottom of bay."

Jonathan laughed. "That must have been a helluva fish. He took me down like a freight train."

"You think every fish you hook and don't land is a monster. There can't be that many big fish in the whole damn lake."

They both heard footsteps on the dock and looked up to see Emily McKendry and Elizabeth Hansen coming down toward them.

"Well, look at this welcoming party," Jonathan said. "You're just in time to help clean the fish, girls."

"Not likely, McKendry," answered his wife. Emily was a year from thirty and in spite of the toll of medical school and residency she had retained much of the youthful brilliance in her face. Her light brown hair still curled naturally and she had kept it long over the years. In cut-off jeans, an old faded University of Michigan t-shirt and worn sneakers, she looked more like one of the summer kids up for the season than someone who had graduated near the top of her class in medical school just a few years earlier.

Both women sat down on the edge of the dock next to the boat with their feet dangling above the water, as the men continued to stow their gear and clean up the boat. "Boys, there's been a really bad incident in town tonight. Elizabeth and I were just downtown at the drugstore and we heard about it from Dr. Bailey's nurse, Gail. You know Jennifer Harris, Connor's younger sister? She was found in pretty bad shape down on the beach off Fisherman's Island tonight. Gail wasn't supposed to say anything, but apparently she was found passed out drunk up in the dunes and it appears that she's been raped."

"Oh no," said George, "is she going to be O.K.?"

"It sounds like it," answered Elizabeth.

Jonathan just looked at his wife in silence, thinking about his past dealings with the Harris family.

"Has she said who did this?" asked George.

"I guess not, or at least Gail didn't know," Emily said, standing back up and holding on to one of the big wood pilings that supported the dock.

"There's going to be hell to pay knowing the Harris clan," said George, "and damn if there shouldn't be."

***

The next morning, George was unlocking the door to his small law office on Park Street when he noticed someone coming up from behind him. He saw that it was Mary Truegood, a member of the Ottawa tribe of Indians whose family had lived in the area for many years. She had a little boy at her side, holding his hand. George had come to know her father Albert in the times following the tragic death of his sister Catherine back when he and Jonathan had returned from the War. Albert Truegood had ultimately helped to free Jonathan from being mistakenly charged with her murder.

She stopped beside him as he opened his door. "Mr. Hansen, there's been some bad trouble and I need to speak with you."

"Come on in, Mary, let's get some coffee going," George answered and then held the door for her to enter. "Who do we have with you here today?" he asked, looking down at the young boy.

"This is my youngest, Jonas," she answered. "I couldn't get anyone to watch him."

He offered them both a chair across from his desk and went into the small pantry next to his office to get the coffee pot going. When he came back out he noticed that she was fighting to hold back her tears. She was a woman who appeared to be approaching her fifties; streaks of gray were showing in her long black hair and hard lines spread across her forehead and down her cheeks. She was dressed in a long black cotton skirt and loose fitting blue and black checkered blouse. George noticed that she was wearing heavy work boots that seemed odd for a woman. Little Jonas sat next to her, his feet dangling above the floor. He had a small stuffed animal in his hands that seemed to be keeping him occupied. "Tell me what's happened, Mary."

"Mr. Hansen…"

"Please call me George."

"Yes sir. It's my oldest son, Samuel. Do you know Sammy?"

"Yes, I've seen him around town. Doesn't he work over at McKendry's boatyard?"

"That's right, he's been there for over a year and he works very hard. He's already received a raise from Mr. McKendry. He works on the hulls, but he's also learning to be an electrician."

"Yes, I do know Sammy. Tell me what's happened." The tears were flowing freely now and Mary Truegood reached for a handkerchief from her small brown leather purse. Jonas looked up at his mother with a frightened stare. George sat down across from her and put his hand out on top of hers. "Please, what's happened with Sammy?"

She managed to choke back her tears and then spoke with a frantic whisper, "Do you know the Harris girl? They're *summer people*."

George felt his heart sink. He just nodded.

"She's been badly hurt."

"Yes, I know. I heard about it last night."

"She told the police this morning that it was my Sammy, that it was Sammy that hurt her!" She almost wailed as the painful words came out.

"How did you hear about this?" he asked, trying to calm her by holding her hand tighter.

"They came to my house this morning. The police came to find Sammy."

"Did they take him away?"

She pulled her hand away to rub her eyes and blow her nose. "No, he didn't come home last night."

"Wouldn't he be at work this morning?" George asked.

14

"I called there, but he didn't come in today. He's never late, or absent. Something's happened Mr. Hansen."

George reached across his desk and picked up the phone. "Let me call my friend Jonathan and see if he's seen him yet today, or if he's heard from him."

"Mr. Hansen, my Sammy would never hurt this girl. You have to help us."

***

The night before, Connor Harris had stood with his father in the hall outside his sister's hospital room. He tried his best to calm the fury that kept rising in his chest. In his early 30's, he was prematurely gray and the skin on his face was pallid, his eyes sunken and brooding. The hospital was quiet and only an occasional nurse walked by on her rounds. The antiseptic smell of the place was thick in the air. They had received the call earlier that evening that his sister Jennifer had been brought into the hospital by friends when they had been unable to revive her during a party at the beach.

He and his father had immediately come down to the hospital. The first nurse that they encountered in the hallway tried to reassure them that Jennifer had just had too much to drink and was suffering from a terrible hangover. But, she was already beginning to regain some sense of where she was and she started to complain of various pains and discomfort. A doctor was called to examine her again.

When the doctor came out into the waiting area he had a stern look on his face. "We should step over into the hallway where we can speak privately." Connor Harris and his father followed young Dr. Bailey who was on call that night. Connor still walked with a slight limp from an injury he had received in a fight with Jonathan McKendry's brother Luke, years ago on a summer night on the streets of Charlevoix.

When they were alone and the doctor could speak freely he began, "Let me be very honest with you. I'm afraid that Jennifer has had intercourse this evening without protection. She's having trouble piecing together the events of the evening."

"I'm her father, Warren Harris. Who was she with!" the elder Harris demanded. He was slightly built and noticeably shorter than his son. A pinched expression on his pale white face seemed to come from some deep ailment or affliction that caused him constant discomfort. He had thrown a wool Burberry sports jacket on over a white golf shirt before coming down to the hospital. They hung loosely on him like a son trying to wear his dad's clothing.

"She doesn't seem up to talking about it right now, sir," the young doctor said, somewhat embarrassed.

"Well, she'll damn well talk to me about it!"

Connor followed his father down the hall and they entered the private room. Jennifer was lying on her back, apparently asleep. A nurse was checking a chart next to the bed. "Would you leave us alone for a bit?" Connor asked the nurse. She nodded and left the room. "Dad, don't you think we should let her sleep this off? I want to find out who this asshole is as bad as you, but she'll feel better in the morning and we can find out what's going on here."

"Goddamit, no!" his father said. His face was glowing red from the bad combination of high blood pressure and the anxiety of what may have happened. He walked over and leaned in close to his daughter. Her hair was in a scattered mess against the pillow. Her face had a yellowish pallor and darker circles spread out beneath her eyes, streaked with tear-stained eye makeup. The nurses had dressed her in a blue hospital gown. He placed his hand on her shoulder and shook her several times. "Jennifer, you need to wake up!"

After several moments of prodding, the young girl's eyes began to flutter and then they opened with a vacant stare. She moaned softly and said something indistinguishable.

Connor spoke up, moving over next to the other side of the bed. "Hey Jenn, what's going on here? You need to wake up and tell us what the hell is going on." She didn't respond. "Jennifer!" he said with more urgency. "Tell me who did this to you?"

Her eyes gained focus and she looked first at her father and then over at her brother.

"Oh shit," was all she could manage. "My head is going to explode."

Connor could smell the whiskey on her breath. "Jenny, just tell me what happened."

She tried to sit up some in the bed, but didn't make much progress. She let out a deep sigh and then tried to swallow. "I don't know."

"You sure as hell do, young lady," her father said. "How much have you had to drink?"

"Daddy, I don't know. I was down at the beach with Elaine and then some other kids came and then... I don't know."

The doctor walked back into the room. "We have some additional tests that we need to do, in case... in case something inappropriate has happened here."

"A few more minutes, Doc," Connor said.

The doctor nodded and backed reluctantly out of the room.

"Jennifer, who were these boys?" her father asked again. "You had better tell me now. You know I'll find out one way or the other."

Jennifer hesitated and then tried to speak, but just mumbled a few words.

"Dammit, girl, who was it?" Warren Harris demanded.

She turned her head into the pillow. Her father reached over and pulled her back to face him. She started to cry and let out a low moan. "Daddy, I'm sorry, I didn't mean..." she couldn't finish the thought.

Her father softened a bit, "I know, baby. I know you didn't mean for this to happen."

Connor looked up, noticing someone standing at the door. Sammy Truegood stood there with his hands in the pockets of his faded denim overalls. His thick black hair was cut unevenly and fell over his ears and across his eyes until he brushed it back to the side.

"What the hell do you want, boy?" Connor spat.

Jennifer struggled to sit up to look around her father. "Sammy, what are you...?"

"Who the hell is this?" Warren Harris asked.

"I heard that Jennifer had been brought down here and I wanted to check in to see if she was OK," Sammy said.

"Do you know this boy?" her father asked.

17

She didn't answer, seemingly confused about his arrival.

Connor came around the bed and walked the short distance across the room to face the young man. "You better tell me you weren't down at the beach tonight with my sister." He pressed in closer, only inches from Sammy's face.

"Yeah, I was with her and Elaine. We were swimming out at Fisherman's."

Connor grabbed him with both hands by the loose fabric of his shirt and pushed him hard up against the door jam. "Why you sonofabitch! If you touched my sister…"

Sammy pushed him away and Connor staggered back against the bed.

"I don't know what you're talking about. We were only swimming. I just wanted to come by to see how she was feeling," Sammy tried to explain.

A nurse walked in. "All of you need to be a little more quiet. We have other patients," she scolded.

Warren Harris walked over to her, keeping his eyes on Sammy Truegood, who was still standing in the doorway. "Nurse, you need to go find the doctor and tell him to call the sheriff's office, now!" he demanded.

"Daddy, please," Jennifer pleaded.

The elder Harris reached back to calm his daughter. "Honey, we will damn well get to the bottom of this," he said. He helped her adjust the pillow behind her head. When he looked back to the door, Sammy Truegood was gone.

Chapter Three

The month of June in the small resort towns of northern Michigan, holds the early promise of the coming summer season. As the weather warms and the days grow longer the wild flowers show along the edges of the woods and the first trout begin to rise along calm eddies of the creeks and streams in the late dusk of evening. Traffic and shoppers in the downtown districts begin to gather, building steadily to the arrival of the Fourth of July weekend when summer officially begins its high season. By late June the docks and boat hoists are in the water as summer families prepare for the long awaited season of swimming and boating. Along the banks of the tiny harbor of Round Lake the docks and piers fill with the magnificent boats of summer residents and weekend cruising visitors.

The *EmmaLee* rested serenely on the surface of the small inland harbor of Charlevoix. Other boats cruised by slowly admiring her handsome lines, taking pictures and pointing to various parts of the ship.

Megan Clark stood at the rail in the stern of the *EmmaLee* with a cell phone against her ear. She had changed clothes after the funeral and was dressed for comfort in khaki shorts and a New York Yankees t-shirt.

"Rebecca, is that you? Oh, I'm so glad you finally got in," Megan said. "You need to come downtown. Will your parents let you get away, or do you have to unpack?" She listened as her friend from Chicago, Rebecca Holmes, answered. The Holmes summered each year in their house out on Lake Michigan, just down past Charlevoix Country Club. "Well hurry, we're going to have dinner in about a half hour and I want you to join us. We have a lot to catch up on." Megan nodded as her friend confirmed the plan.

"O.K. great, I'll run the launch over to pick you up at the shopper's dock. We'll see you in a few minutes. Bye."

Megan clicked her phone closed as Sally came up behind her. "Is Becca in yet from Chicago?" Sally asked.

"Yeah, she's going to be able to join us for dinner."

Sally stood next to her stepdaughter at the rail of the ship. "That's great, honey. I spoke with your father. He has some business to deal with in New York for the next couple of days and won't be able to come up."

Megan could see from Sally's face how disappointed she was. "Sally, you know he'll come as soon as he can."

Sally just nodded, watching the steady parade of boats making their way around the *EmmaLee*. "I'm going up to the house tonight after dinner. I think I'll probably stay there for a night or two. You and Becca are welcome to join me." After her marriage to Alex Clark, Sally had kept her home up on Michigan Avenue north of town on the bluffs overlooking Lake Michigan. "I need to check in on the old place and I want to spend some time in my old studio to try to spread a little paint on canvas."

"Becca mentioned that she really wanted to stay over on the boat tonight. You know how much she loves it out here. Maybe we'll take a boat ride after dinner."

"You two go ahead and invite some other friends if you'd like." Sally looked up at the soft orange and red colors in the clouds coming in from Lake Michigan in the fading light of the day. "I just need a little rest and time to gather myself after the funeral today." She paused for a moment and her shoulders seemed to sag under the weight of the day. "It will never be the same up here without George around, honey. I wish you had come to know him as well as I did. He was the best friend of my mother and father...back before they were lost in the accident. He treated me like his own daughter all these years since. I feel like I've lost my father again."

Megan moved over and hugged Sally. She didn't say anything because she knew that nothing she would say could possibly help. She had only known George Hansen for a few years, but she had come to know him as family as well, and she held onto Sally and tried to help share her grief at his passing.

ON PAST HORTON CREEK

The Charlevoix Country Coroner, Jacob Henry paused for a moment before he looked up from his notes. His glasses were resting back up on his forehead. The few wisps of gray hairs still remaining on his head were pushed back as a result, leaving only his heavy and untrimmed eyebrows to break the cold impassive shininess of his face. Across from his desk sat the County Sheriff, Elam Stone, a middle-aged public servant whose ever expanding waistline had caused him to order new uniform pants annually for the past ten years. His hat sat on the coroner's desk, sweat stains spreading up from the leather band that wrapped around it.

"Elam, the autopsy reports on George Hansen seem to be pretty clear to me. The doctors down at the hospital that first worked on him after he was brought in declared *cause of death* to be coronary related. Since he had been dead for over three hours before they had a chance to examine him, they were really just speculating," the coroner said. He took particular pleasure in over-dramatizing the situation for the benefit of the sheriff. It was a small county and he had very little work that kept him interested. George Hansen was a prominent community leader who was found dead in his boat of what appeared to be natural causes. "When we got the body and had a chance to do a thorough examination and autopsy, we were a bit surprised to find lake water in the man's lungs. Most people who die sitting in a fishing boat of natural causes don't have lake water sloshing around in their lungs."

The sheriff pushed his hat aside and leaned his arms up on the desk, almost knocking over the cup of coffee that he had been served. "How does Hansen take a big swallow of water down his windpipe from the lake and then sit back in his boat and croak?" he asked with a sincerely puzzled expression.

"There are a few scrapes and contusions on his legs and arms that are concerning," the coroner answered. "It's possible that he fell overboard and then managed to pull himself back into the boat, scraping himself up as he did, and then died from the exertion of all that."

"I suppose," said Stone, still with a question in his voice.

The little Chris Craft runabout *EmmaLee II* cut through the slow rolling swells coming in through the channel from Lake Michigan. The varnished brown hull stood out sharply against the deep green water of the lake. Megan Clark and her friend Rebecca Holmes sat on the front leather seats, Megan at the wheel. They looked out across the vast distance of the big lake into the glare of the bright setting sun on the horizon. The sky was cloudless and glowed bright pink along the sharp edge of sky and water. Megan kept to the right of the channel, cruising slowly in the "no wake" zone, allowing other boats room coming in from Lake Michigan.

Rebecca pushed the hair back from her eyes, loose ends flying in the breeze over the windshield. "I'm glad that Sally suggested we take *Little Emma* out tonight," she said.

Megan looked in all directions for other boats as they passed the end of the pier. The big white lighthouse rose up above them on their left, the bright signal light passing around every few moments just beginning to show in the fading light. The wind out of the southeast had calmed to just a soft whisper and the waves coming across the bay were laying down to a comfortable light chop. "Yeah, I wish she would have come with us," she said. "She's really feeling pretty low with Uncle George and the funeral…and my Dad is being a jerk about some business deal."

Megan turned the boat off to the north along the shore, the low rumble of the engine rising as she pushed forward a bit on the throttle. She could see Sally's yellow house up on the bluff, just down past the big condominiums next to the pier. A few lights glowed on the first floor, but she couldn't see anyone moving around. The high dunes along the shore running up to North Point in the distance spread up into dark clusters of pines and cottonwoods. A couple walked along the shoreline, their dog running up ahead jumping into the water and barking at gulls.

She thought again about Sally and how close they had grown in the past few years. Megan's mother had died when she was very young and the memories of her passing from cancer were blurred, but still painful whenever those thoughts came back. Sally had been such a wonderful new addition to her life. She had come to love Sally Thomason almost from the first time she had met her as a little girl. All of their lives seemed to come together so naturally after that first summer in Charlevoix when Sally and her father had fallen in love, and then the wedding the next year. *The two of them have been so happy together these past years.* She had only noticed in the last few weeks that a tension was growing between them. The explosion of a fireworks rocket up ahead on the far shore brought her attention back to the moment.

"You'll never guess who I saw today," Megan teased.

Rebecca reached over the back of the seat and grabbed two Coke's out of the cooler that lay on the floorboard. She opened them both and handed one to Megan. "I can't begin to guess," she answered.

"Do you remember Will from last summer? Right at the end of August we met him down at that party in Boyne City."

"Will?"

"Will Truegood, his family is Native American."

"Oh sure, that Indian boy. Where did you see him?"

Megan winced at her friend's description. "He was downtown at the park when Sally and I were walking home from the service up at the cemetery. He wants to take me fishing."

"He asked you out?" Rebecca asked.

"It's not like a date. He just likes to fish and wants to show me the river out by his cabin."

"Girlfriend, you can't go out with him."

Megan let up on the throttle and the boat slowed, rising gently over low swells. She turned to look at her friend. "Excuse me, but I can go out with whoever I care to, but I told you it's not a date."

"What do you think Rick will have to say about you being seen with some local… and he's an Indian, for God's sake!"

Rick was Rick Brandtley, son of Oliver and Judith Brandtley from Grosse Point. The Brandtley family had made a considerable fortune many years ago as one of the primary parts suppliers to the big Detroit car companies. They had a summer home in Charlevoix just down the street from Sally's house up along the big lake. Megan and Rick had dated often during the past two summers. They kept in touch when they returned to school each year and had spent some time together at the Brandtley's home over Christmas.

23

Megan could feel her anger burning up through her chest. "Becca, I can't believe you. When did you become such a ....," she paused trying to stay calm. "Rick won't care if I go out with an old family friend to go fishing, and frankly, it's none of his damn business."

"Oh, I think he'll consider it his business, little Ms. Clark," her friend teased. "Have you seen him up here yet?"

"No, they won't be up until after the fourth," Megan answered. "Just relax. I don't know if I'll even see Will again and I'm sorry I said anything." She pressed the throttle forward again and the boat lurched out ahead up toward North Point. Megan tried to put Will Truegood out of her mind. She had been looking forward to seeing Rick again and spending time with him up in Charlevoix over the summer.

The two girls watched as a big twin-masted sailboat came around the point up ahead from the bay down in Harbor Springs. The low sun lit up the bright white sails of the boat, luffing softly in the light wind.

***

The big artificial mayfly landed softly on the calm water of the eddy pulling back behind the cedar deadfall. Only the slightest rush of water over the limbs of the downed tree could be heard in the quiet of the fading evening. The low light of the sun found its way through the heavy woods and cast a glare across the surface of Horton Creek. Will Truegood twitched the fly line and watched the fly move with a quick hop across the water. He waited, holding his breath, knowing that the drag on his line from the faster current near him would pull the fly out of the feeding lane for the nice trout he had watched rising for the past few minutes. The fly held its precarious position for a few seconds more. The sounds of the water and a light breeze through the trees echoed in his head. He leaned over, holding the rod out as far as it would go to prolong the presentation of the fly to the wary fish.

And then the water broke in the most subtle of takes as the trout sipped the fly from the surface, making only the slightest break in the surface of the stream. Will lifted the rod instinctively and felt the joy in connecting with the heavy weight of the fish. He pulled the rod low and away to muscle the fish out from the snags of the downed tree limbs. The fish ran hard to stay down in the cover of the tree, but Will put the heavy butt of the rod into the fish and pulled him back away from the trouble. The bend in the rod was hard and pleasing and he knew he was on to a good fish. He moved cautiously back across the river to the near bank making sure of every step as he played the fish in the loose sandy bottom that was intertwined with rotting downed tree limbs from past seasons. As he reached the undercut bank of the river the fish tired and came up to the surface, gasping for another reserve of energy to run again. Will slipped his wooden net under the fish and held it low on the surface to keep water moving through its gills. The trout lay on its side in the water surrounded by the net. Its green sides and brilliant orange belly showed brightly against the clear water of the creek.

Will let out a long breath. *Damn, what a nice fish.* He reached down and cradled it gently under its round belly. It lay there calmly, resigned to its fate, not knowing that it would soon be free to return to its cold recesses. He watched the fish lying there on its side, its gills moving rapidly to capture some flow of water and oxygen. He thought that it was the most beautiful fish he had ever caught, but then he knew that he always felt that way. He pulled the net down and away from the fish and watched as it regained its equilibrium and found new strength to dart away quickly from the clear sandy bottomed shallows of the river, back down into the dark protection of the cover of the deadfall.

Will Truegood moved back and sat on the bank of the river. He felt the pull of the current against his legs and the chill of the cold water press through his waders. The sun was a deep orange blinding light now through the low branches of the cedar and hardwood forest. Movement upstream caught his attention and he watched a young whitetail deer nose out from the underbrush across the river. It stepped downed cautiously into the current to take a drink. Will tried to remain still, but the deer looked up suddenly in his direction. He looked into the deep brown eyes of the deer only yards away and it seemed to accept the fact that the two of them were together in this place and that there was room for all who cared to be there.

The deer dipped its head back down to the water and took one more drink before it turned and jumped effortlessly back up onto the bank and disappeared into the darkening woods.

***

Sally Thomason sat on the familiar soft cushions of the wicker couch on the sun porch off the back of her house on Michigan Avenue. The water of Lake Michigan glittered in the late evening sun's reflections. The windows had been opened half way up to let in the cooling breeze off the lake. An empty sketch pad and pencil lay on the table in front of her. She noticed a small boat coming out through the channel from behind the pier and could see that it was her old Chris Craft runabout, the boat that her parents had given her those many years ago. She could see Megan and Rebecca sitting up front, enjoying the beauty of the fading day and the exhilaration of the boat ride.

She allowed her head to fall back and rest on the cushion behind her, letting out a deep breath and thinking back on the day's events. The loss of her dear friend George Hansen lay heavy on her thoughts. She knew that he was getting on in age, but it was still so hard to think about losing him… and then the earlier conversation with Alex. She was beginning to feel guilty about being so harsh with him. She knew how difficult this new situation with the business was and she was growing more worried that Louis Kramer had gotten them into serious trouble. But, she couldn't help but feel the awful weight of jealousy when she thought of Anna Bataglia, Alex's lawyer. She had met Anna on several occasions down at Alex's office and at receptions in the city. She was the type of woman who always seemed to know everyone in a room and hugged and kissed most like they were her closest friends. She would occasionally hold onto Alex's arm when they were talking in a crowd and Sally often noticed the lingering kiss on his cheek at the end of a party or meeting. She had no specific reason to believe that Anna and Alex were anything more to each other than close working associates and friends… *but, she is so damned beautiful!*

Her rapidly declining mood was broken by the sound of the doorbell in the front hall. She struggled to pull herself up from the soft escape of the couch. Most of the lights were out through the house and deep shadows from the setting sun played across the rooms as she made her way to the front door. She turned on the front porch light and opened the old stained wooden door and then felt the air get sucked out of her lungs.

Standing before her on the porch was Louis Kramer. His usual confident air was gone and she could see a panic in his eyes that was only thinly disguised by the immaculate styling of his hair and clothes. He rushed past her into the house without being asked.

"Louis, what in hell are you doing here?" she asked.

He just kept walking down the hall toward the kitchen. She followed him in and saw him opening the refrigerator door. "Do you have any wine? I need a drink, now!" he said in his heavy Texas drawl.

Sally came up beside him and pushed the door closed. "I want you to get out of my house, now!"

"Sally, I'm sorry." He put his hands on her shoulders, attempting to calm her. It wasn't helping. She pushed his arms away and stepped back against the far cabinets. "Sally, really I just needed to talk to you. You need to know what's going on here. Alex is freaking out on me."

"It sounds like he has every good reason. What in hell have you done?"

He opened the refrigerator again. "Can I please have a drink?"

She went over to the small wine cooler under the counter and pulled out a bottle of white wine without bothering to look at the label. She pulled a corkscrew from a drawer and handed them both to him. "Let me get a couple of glasses and we'll go sit down."

Out on the sun porch, Louis sat across from her and worked on opening the wine. Sally turned on a small lamp next to the couch. She watched in silence as he filled the glasses, thinking how little she knew about this man. Alex had always treated him as his best friend. *What could possibly have happened?* She had met him that first summer when Alex had come to Charlevoix. He had flown in on his plane late one afternoon, unannounced, just like today. Mary Alice Gregory, the wealthy summer professional divorcee, had quickly swept him away to the Florida Keys. They had been married a few months later. Alex had provided occasional updates that they were still married, but rarely together, as Mary Alice hopped around the world keeping close to her, always on the go, entourage.

Louis handed her a glass, the moist condensation from the cold wine already cool and wet in her hands. He took a long drink with his eyes closed, swallowed and then took another. He seemed to let the wine work its way down through his body, waiting for its familiar numbing effect.

Sally placed her glass on the table without drinking. "Tell me what's going on… now!"

Louis breathed deeply and then sighed. He leaned forward, resting on his knees. "Sally, this has all been blown way out of whack, honey."

"Don't call me *honey*."

"Sally, please just settle down a might, here. You need to know that this is all gonna be okay, but you need to get Alex to settle down some, too. He's got his lawyer bitch…" He stopped when he saw Sally grimace.

"From what I know, Alex is pulling together all the help he can get to save your company and both of you from going to jail. How could you do this to him?"

"I'm telling you, this is all going to work itself out," he answered. "The Feds are going way overboard on this. They're just trying to scare us. This guy in New York is a big asshole, trying to make a name for himself to run for office next year."

"I don't know how all this works Louis, but when the Securities and Exchange Commission and the State of New York come after you, they usually have a pretty good case," Sally said, picking up her glass and sipping the wine.

Louis Kramer sat back in his chair. "All I wanted to ask you is this. You need to talk to Alex and get him to settle down. He's got his attorney digging in to all this shit…" Again he paused. "He's having her firm go back through all this history that's not going to help our cause in the least. He and I need to work together on this, but he won't even talk to me. Can you please just get him to sit down and talk to me," he pleaded.

Sally looked into his eyes and again saw the panic. "If you've done anything to hurt my husband, I will personally help to see you rot in hell. Can I make it any more clear than that?" She felt the heat of anger welling up inside her.

"Please, just talk to him. I'm going back to New York soon. Just tell him that I want to sit down and talk this through. He and I can make this right."

"Louis, you need to leave."

He stood up and put his glass down on the table. "Okay, I'm headed over to spend the night with Mary Alice at her folk's place."

"Be sure to give her my best," she answered in a tone that showed no attempt to hide her distaste for his wife.

Chapter Four

The Ottawa Indians have lived in this part of the North Country for a thousand years, or more. The Odawa (Ottawa), the Ojibway (Chippewa), and Bodowadami (Pottawatomi) refer to themselves as the "Anishanabek", or "the Original People". The oral history of the ancestors of the Little Traverse Bay Band of Odawa Indians, or the Ottawa, teaches that their people lived far to the east along the Ottawa River, a tributary to the St. Lawrence River and Atlantic Ocean. They migrated slowly westward, settling in northern Lake Huron on Ottawa Island, now known as Manitoulin Island. Here the tribe split into the three major groups that they are known as today.

Wars with the Iroquois and other tribes eventually caused some to move on to the Straits of Mackinac and on down the Lake Michigan shoreline to what is now Emmet and Charlevoix counties. Other groups moved to the Detroit and Toledo areas, later being resettled on Walpole Island in Ontario and down in Oklahoma.

The Ottawa were well known as intertribal traders and barterers, carrying cornmeal, sunflower oil, furs and skins to faraway tribes. They were a migratory people, moving with the seasons. In the winters they would move to areas in southern Michigan where the climate was more tolerable. In the spring they would come back north, collecting maple syrup, fishing and hunting, planting crops and tending gardens to feed their families.

As the White settlements continued to encroach on their land, some continued west, finding their way to Oklahoma and Kansas, remaining there on reservations to this day. In the North, many of the Ottawa stayed and saw their lives change with the development of the area. As their land was taken away over the years, they moved from rural areas to the towns looking for wage labor to support their families. Through it all they tried hard to maintain the traditions and beliefs of their people.

ON PAST HORTON CREEK

In spite of treaties and agreements and promises of cooperation and goodwill, a clear divide remained between the White and Indian cultures through the years. Today, the "Original People" continue to struggle to find their place in this land that was once their domain. Poverty and alcoholism remain a threat to their place in society.

In more recent years, the arrival of preferred hunting and fishing regulations and the casinos and special gaming license privileges for the Indian Tribes brought new promise as well as new challenges to the Anishanabek.

In those earlier years when the Truegood family came into our lives, and even later as my life began to reach its final ebbs and flows, not all of us who lived in this supposedly welcoming community were as accepting of the "Original People".

***

Sammy Truegood tried to catch his breath. He had run from the hospital, all the way through town, on out to the familiar rocky shore of North Point. His family's home was just over the dunes, nestled in the heavy pines. He walked now along the shore of the point jutting out into Lake Michigan to the west and Little Traverse Bay off to the east. Right at the point, cutting into the shoreline, years of storms and erosion and ice flows had carved a small round inlet, only a few hundred yards across, protected by the heavy winds and waves from the big lake. In the spring his people came to catch the spawning fish that came back to the inlet. In the fall, they shot ducks that gathered along the shores of the calm waters.

He turned in along the shore of the inlet, walking in the shallows, not concerned with the cold water drenching his shoes and feet. A flock of geese rested calming on the water in the center of the inlet, occasionally dipping their heads down to feed on the bottom of the bay.

Thinking back on the scene in the hospital, he felt numb inside thinking that the Harris family believed that he would have done anything to hurt Jennifer. His mind was panicking with all of the possible consequences of his assumed crimes.

He thought back to his childhood when his uncle, who was 26 at the time, had been arrested and sent away to a penitentiary. He had been found drinking in the park in Charlevoix on the waterfront. Earlier that day a bank had been robbed down in East Jordan and they had described one of the robbers to closely resemble his uncle. When questioned that night in the park, the sheriff found $200 in his pocket that he had actually won the night before in a poker game. The bank teller identified him in a line-up and he was sent away.

Pushing through a line of low scrub brush, Sammy walked out along the rocky edge of the bay. At the end the path narrowed to a sharp point and then disappeared into the waves of the big lake, larger rocks breaking the surface out into the deeper water. The sky was growing lighter back behind him down towards Petoskey as the morning sun pushed up from behind the dark line of hills. He sat down just back from the high water of the waves and rested his back against a rotted piece of driftwood that had been washed up. He looked out north over the water to the point across the bay that led up to Cross Village and eventually to Mackinaw. Attempting to block out thoughts of Jennifer Harris, he tried to envision his ancestors navigating across this water in small canoes, carrying trade goods, or returning from battles. He and his late father had come to sit at this place on many occasions. He would listen to stories of his people and his family's past. The legends of his people had always seemed so magical and it made him proud of his legacy.

Thoughts of Jennifer kept pushing back. He had come across her and Elaine down at the long beach across from Fisherman's Island. It was getting on to late evening and the three of them had stripped down to bathing suits and gone swimming out to the small island. They had skipped stones in the calm water behind the island and walked through the narrow path to explore the old abandoned cabin that lay in a wreck back in the woods.

A few more summer kids had joined them as the sun was starting to set. A bonfire was made and bottles of beer and whiskey started to get passed. Three of the boys were friends of Jennifer and Elaine from previous summers. One named Andy seemed to feel particularly connected with Jennifer Harris and started to give Sammy a hard time about being there. He eventually left after overhearing not so subtle comments about his Indian heritage and *too much firewater*. On his way back from the beach along the trail through the woods, the three boys confronted him, including Andy Welton.

32

One had bumped him off the trail as he tried to pass and then the three of them turned to laugh at him. The one that had run into him had taunted him and said, *"Hey Chief, aren't you a little late for smoking the peace pipe back at the teepee."*

Sammy had quickly measured his chances in trying to retaliate against all three of them. He realized that the odds were far from good and he had turned and continued down the path, trying to keep his anger from tempting him to run back and take all of them on.

He tried to think of how he could defend himself if the family or the sheriff came after him. From Jennifer's condition in the hospital, he wasn't very confident in her ability to vouch for him.

A red-tailed hawk swooped down low from behind him and then plummeted into the water, talons extended. Flapping with powerful wings, the bird lifted up with a large lake-run brown trout in its grasp. Sammy watched it angle up and away, back to its nest somewhere in the heavy pine forest along the dunes. His father had told him many stories about the birds and the animals. He remembered an old tale of a hawk that had led a group of his people across the ice flows from Mackinaw when they had been caught in a heavy blizzard. The people had followed the hawk and its call through the storm. When they had reached the tree line on the shore the bird had flown up and perched on the limb of a tall white pine above them. The people gathered together to give thanks for the bird. The hawk had looked down upon them with its head cocked to one side, its shiny brown eye blinking in the light of the sun breaking through the clouds from the passing storm. It screeched loudly and then flew up and away back across the channel to the island.

What message did the hawk bring today, he thought.

Often finding release and solitude during long swims in the cold lakes of the area, Sammy rose and pulled off his shirt and pants and walked out into the waves wearing only a faded pair of plaid under shorts. Among the *Precepts* of his people was the commandment to immerse his body into the lake or river at least ten days in succession in the early months of the year, that his body would be strong and swift. The water was still icy cold in the early weeks of summer and the chill cut through his muscles to the bone leaving an aching sensation as his body struggled to adjust. When he was waist deep he dove out and under the next wave coming at him and his entire body felt the cold shock of Lake Michigan. He kicked and stroked powerfully to stay under the water and slowly he began to feel more comfortable. Finally he came up for a breath, choking for air, breathing deeply into his lungs. The water depth was just over his head and he had to stroke with his arms and legs to stay afloat.

As usual the cool fresh water worked, if only for a few moments, to wash away the day's burdens. He let his mind linger only on the water and the air and the beautiful stretch of beach before him.

***

Emily Compton McKendry led her husband Jonathan by the hand up the sidewalk from the drawbridge over the channel into Round Lake. Jonathan dragged reluctantly behind. Emily had her physician's jacket on and her wavy brown hair was pulled back behind her ears and tied with a narrow black ribbon. Jonathan was dressed in his daily work clothes of jeans and a faded wool shirt. His dark brown hair flared out along the edges of an old fisherman's cap and his face glowed with a permanent reddish windburn along his cheeks from his many years outside in the harsh climate. An early morning chill layered in over the town from Lake Michigan. Out over the bluff, Emily could see the big Great Lakes passenger ship, the *Manitou*, setting up course to make its way into the Charlevoix harbor. Passengers from Chicago, St. Joseph and Muskegon were traveling north on the elegant ship for their summer visits. Emily marveled again at how magnificent the old passenger liners were and how miraculous that they could actually navigate through the narrow channel into Round Lake. Jonathan, always more than engaged in great ships, stopped to watch the *Manitou* clear the channel breakwalls.

Emily grabbed his arm to get him moving again. "Jonathan, this will just take a few minutes. I really want you to see this house."

"Emily, we have a house…a perfectly good house," he objected.

"I've told you before, I have loved this place since I was a little girl coming up here in the summers. When I saw the *For Sale* sign go up last week, I just had to see it."

They reached the top of the hill and turned down along the lake on Michigan Avenue. The first house on the left sat back in the trees, a traditional two story Cape Cod with yellow wood siding and black shutters. The vast distance of the horizon over Lake Michigan could be seen off behind. The *For Sale* sign had been placed by the sidewalk.

"I know Jenny, the agent," Emily said. "There's a key under the mat." They walked up the front steps and Emily found the key and let them in. She turned on the hall lights and they made their way back towards the rear of the house. Immediately they could see the striking blues and greens of Lake Michigan through the broad expanse of windows along the back of the living room. To the right, an opening led out to a sunroom that was also wrapped in windows looking over the lake. They stood together looking out at the back lawn leading down to the edge of the high sand dunes that cascaded down to the lake.

Emily reached over for Jonathan's hand. "I really love this house, Jonathan."

He stood in silence for a while, enjoying the view with her. He knew that his wife could buy whatever she wanted. Her family's money was substantial and yet she rarely lived to excess and was actually quite frugal. He also knew that if she wanted this house, there was very little he would be able to do to change her mind.

Having come from a family that was always trying to just get by on the money his father made from the small marina and boatyard they had run down on Round Lake, and the modest amount of extra money that his mother had been able to bring in from working over at the Belvedere Hotel, Jonathan was still overwhelmed and uncomfortable around the incredible wealth of the Compton family. Emily's father, Stewart Compton, had retired recently from a long and successful career in the automobile business down in Detroit.

In their years together, Jonathan had found that in spite of her family's background, Emily was not the slightest bit interested in extravagant displays of wealth. They had lived quite simply in a modest home off Park Street. They had one car that she had driven since college, although he had to admit that it was actually quite nice; a sleek sport convertible that Emily had picked him up in on their first night out together back in Ann Arbor when he was recovering from his wounds at the Veteran's Hospital. He was driving an old truck from his father's boatyard and they still had the little Chris Craft runabout that her father had bought from the McKendry Boatworks back before the War. The *EmmaLee II* was his wife's most prized possession. She kept it lovingly protected in a small private boathouse down on Round Lake near where his family's old boatyard used to sit. Jonathan had actually worked to restore the boat before the Compton's purchased it and he and Emily had enjoyed many great hours together on the boat, including the first night they had ever made love, anchored down in Horton Bay.

More recently he had built a larger cruiser for them down at his boatyard. It was 30 feet in length and had two sleeping cabins and a small galley. They had made several trips up and down the big lake to ports like Mackinaw and Leland, often with the Hansen's. Emily's father's yacht, the *EmmaLee,* had returned after the war. Commissioned by the Navy at the outset of World War II, it had been used out east to patrol the coast for German submarines. The Compton family kept it up in Charlevoix again each summer. Jonathan had become good friends not only with his father-in-law Stewart Compton, but also the captain and crew of the *EmmaLee*. He had been cleared to skipper the boat when he was accompanied by the captain and he had enjoyed many wonderful hours on the great ship with Emily and her family.

His wife nudged him in the side. "So, what do you think?"

He focused again on the house and the incredible view. "I suppose that there's not much chance of me talking you out of this place?"

"Jonathan, I just want to know what *you* think."

"I think we should try out that incredibly comfortable-looking couch out there on the porch," and he took her by the hand.

She laughed and said, "We don't have time for any *funny business*. I need to get down to the clinic."

He pulled her down on the couch next to him with his arm around her. The morning light reflected softly against the kaleidoscope of colors in the gardens outside the windows. A cool breeze blew in through a screen door. Holding her close, he kissed her and then leaned back, looking deeply into her eyes. "I don't know about the rest of this house, but I see great potential in this porch."

She laughed and pushed him away. "Would you be serious."

"I'm *seriously* thinking that if you really love this house, and knowing how much I truly love you, and even though I haven't even seen the rest of this place, that it's just a matter of time before I'll just have to love this house… so, I may as well get started now."

"Honey, don't you just love it?" she asked, giving him a look that he knew he could never resist.

"Can I at least see the bedroom?"

***

Connor Harris sat in the office of Sheriff Willy Potts with his father. The old sheriff was nearing his 70's and moved slowly around his desk to take a seat. He settled back allowing his wide bottom to ease into the cushioned leather chair. His round belly pushed out over the shiny black belt that wrapped around his vast middle. His .45 caliber revolver was strapped to his side. He put his coffee cup down and looked across the desk at the two men. Taking a handkerchief from his shirt pocket, he dabbed at the perpetual sweat that broke out across his brow. "Sounds like we had a little trouble last night, gentlemen."

"It was more than a *little* trouble, Potts!" the elder Harris said. "It was my damn daughter, and I want that sonofabitch arrested now!"

"Now let's not jump to any rash conclusions here, Warren," the sheriff said calmly. "I know your daughter Jennifer claims that this Truegood boy took advantage of her, but she obviously had a lot to drink and I'm wondering what she really can remember clearly."

"I don't believe this!" Connor yelled, his face turning a bright red as his rage burned. "Are you going to bring this kid in, or not?"

"I've got some of my men out looking for him right now. We'll have a little talk with young Sammy and get his side of the story."

"Dammit, Potts! If this was your daughter, would you be moving so slow on this?" Warren Harris said, his face flushed with anger.

37

"Let's see," he said calmly, "my daughter stopped drinking entire bottles of whiskey and chasing boys down on the beach about 35 years ago."

This response only infuriated the two Harris men even more. Connor stood up quickly, knocking his chair back behind him across the floor. "Let's go find this asshole ourselves!"

"Unless you want to find your own ass in this jail, son, you leave this to me and my men," the sheriff warned. "Am I clear on this?"

Warren Harris stood up next to his son. Pointing at the nose of the portly old sheriff, he spoke in a low menacing tone, "You will bring this boy in and do what's right, godammit!"

They both turned and walked out of the office, slamming the door behind them.

Sheriff Potts picked up his coffee mug and took a long drink. He stood staring at the closed door. Shaking his head, he spoke softly to himself, "This is gonna be a damn mess."

Chapter Five

It was a morning of fresh promise. The sun had risen above the tree line across the shore of Round Lake. Low clouds and fog lying on the lake down towards Boyne were slowly dispersing leaving a clear brilliant blue sky. Joggers and early dog walkers were already out on the streets of Charlevoix. A late night patron of one of the town's bars hadn't made it back to his boat at the docks. He woke with a startled expression on the lawn of the park that sloped down to the small inland harbor. He rubbed his eyes and looked around in surprised confusion. One of the workers from the Harbormaster's office came over to help him up and get him back to his boat.

Sally smiled as she watched the man stumble down the hill toward the long line of big cruising and sailing yachts. She sat on one of the park benches at the top of the hill with a cup of coffee in her hand. The warmth of the paper cup felt good in the early chill of the morning. One of the larger sailboats that was kept each summer over at the docks near the Belvedere Club was backing out of its slip. She watched as the long shiny blue hull knifed silently back across the calm surface of Round Lake. A man was at the wheel pointing to a woman at the mast who was working to unfurl the mainsail. The boat turned and made a course for the drawbridge. Sally looked at her watch and saw that it was 7:25. The bridge would be coming up in just five minutes allowing the first boats to make their way out to Lake Michigan.

She thought back to the night before of restless sleep, worrying about Alex and the visit from Louis Kramer. She had only left New York two days earlier, but already she missed her husband. She was also terribly concerned about the problems with his business and the betrayal by his partner. She tried not to dwell on the nagging sense of jealousy about Alex's lawyer, Anna. *Come on, Sally.*

Motion to her left caught her attention. She looked over and saw a jogger coming down the sidewalk. It took only a moment to recognize Mary Alice Gregory. Their eyes met and Mary Alice slowed and then walked around on the lawn in front of Sally. She was rail thin and her deep brown tan was well revealed by short jogging shorts and a black sports bra. Her hair was pulled back from her face and held in a small ponytail. Sally struggled to be gracious at the interruption.

"Well, Sally Thomason. Welcome back for another summer in God's Country."

"Good morning," was all Sally could manage.

"It's nice to see you back in Charlevoix. I noticed the *EmmaLee* out on the water when I flew in to town the other day. Where is Alex?" she asked, looking around.

"He's still in New York. He'll be up in a day, or so." Sally tried her best to block old resentments and suspicions of Mary Alice and an affair with Sally's former husband many years earlier.

"Oh, that's too bad. Louie flew in last night and surprised me," Mary Alice said.

"Yes, I know. He stopped over to see me at the house." Sally couldn't resist letting the comment lay out there without explanation.

Mary Alice got a very surprised look on her face. "He what?"

"He hasn't told you about the problems with the business in New York?" If there was anything good about this whole mess it was catching this woman uninformed, Sally thought.

Mary Alice tried quickly to regain her composure and cover her first reaction. "Oh, I'm sure Louie has mentioned something about it. I just try to keep my nose out of all the business nonsense."

"Well, you might want to talk to him about it again. It's more than just a little nonsense. The company is being investigated by the SEC and Alex and Louis are in a lot of trouble." She couldn't leave it at that. "Your husband is apparently responsible for some very questionable decisions and bookkeeping."

Mary Alice smiled with a big grin to show that Sally couldn't possibly upset her. "Oh, I'm sure it's nothing serious with those two boys. How many fortunes have they made already?"

"Really, Mary Alice, this is truly a mess and your husband came to see me to try to convince me to have Alex help him."

Mary Alice was having more trouble trying to hide her displeasure at not knowing about any of this and particularly of her husband's visit to Sally's house the previous night. "Sally, you really shouldn't worry so. I need to get on with my run, but we must get together for drinks when both the boys get up here, don't you think?"

Sally couldn't hold back her irritation, "Didn't you hear anything I just said?"

Mary Alice dismissed her with a wave of her hand. "Really, I'll call you. We'll have you out to my parent's place. They had it remodeled over the winter and it's just lovely. You have to see it."

Sally just shook her head as Mary Alice ran off down the street. The alarm at the drawbridge sounded and the barriers came down. She watched as the two sections of the bridge started to slowly rise. The mast of the big blue sailboat soon made its way through the open channel.

***

Megan Clark walked up on to the deck of the *EmmaLee*. She brushed her hair back away from her face and rubbed her eyes to clear the hazy effects of a long night's sleep. She had a cup of hot coffee in her hand from the ship's galley. A blue New York Yankees sweatshirt covered her swimsuit, goose bumps breaking out on her bare legs. Walking to the side rail of the ship, she watched the morning coming to life on the quiet harbor. Small Zodiac dinghies with outboards buzzed about the bigger yachts at anchor. Fishing boats adorned with rods and baits flashing in the early sunlight, worked their way toward the channel out to Lake Michigan. The orange Coast Guard skiff cruised slowly around the perimeter of the lake, waving to early risers coming out on the decks of their boats.

Megan yawned and placed the coffee mug down on the rail and stretched her arms high over her head. She wondered about Sally and her night alone in the old house. She remembered the first time she had gone there as a little girl with her father. She had played in the backyard and run down the low dunes to the lake. Sally's paintings were displayed all through the house including the canvas of her daughter Ellen. Soon after Sally had married her father, she had sat down with her one day on her bed and shared the story of the tragic accident that had taken the lives of Ellen, as well as Sally's parents. The boat they had been cruising on had been lost in a bad storm off the Manitou Islands down near Leland. Megan could still remember the service that her father had arranged out on Lake Michigan near the Manitou's to honor their passing. That was the day that she recalled first feeling so much love for Sally Thomason.

Megan had lost her own mother to cancer just a few years before that. She had been only nine years old, twelve when Sally came into their lives. As the years passed she found it harder to remember her mother; the sound of her voice, what her hair felt like, what she liked to wear. It was a deep hole in her heart that Megan knew could never be filled.

She felt the sun on her neck and decided that it was warm enough to take a quick swim. Stairs had been placed at an opening in the rail with a small platform at the bottom for guests to arrive by boat, or for swimmers to easily get in and out of the water. She walked down the steps along the side of the big ship running her hands along white hull illuminated by the sun's glare off the water. At the bottom she stood on the platform and took off her sweatshirt. She didn't dare dip a toe into the water, knowing how cold it would be. This early in the summer you had to dive in all at once and let the shock take its effects quickly. She did just that, diving out into the green water. The cold was like a thousand needles biting into every inch of her skin, but she dove deep, marveling at the wonderful joy of being at the lake again after a long winter out East.

When her lungs were about to burst and the numbness in her arms and legs was almost unbearable, she turned for the surface, breaking through and taking a huge breath of air. The water on top, now warmed by the early morning sun, felt almost comfortable compared to the icy depths she had just endured. She kicked off away from the boat and began swimming smoothly across the calm water leaving a gentle wake behind her. Her years on the swim team in school were pleasant memories of good friends and fun trips to other private schools around the New York and Connecticut area. College now loomed in the fall and she was still undecided about continuing to swim competitively. The long hours of training before classes and then again in the evenings had been more and more difficult to manage.

She had been accepted last fall to three different schools, finally deciding on Dartmouth where her father had attended. With the excitement of high school graduation just beginning to fade, the reality of starting college in a few months was both exhilarating and frightening at the same time.

Noticing another boat coming near, Megan turned and started back toward the *EmmaLee*. She pulled herself up on the platform and used the sweatshirt to try to dry herself. Rubbing it through her hair, she turned and watched as a small runabout came towards her, moving slowly in from the direction of Lake Charlevoix. The sun's glare on the windshield prevented her from seeing who was driving the boat. As it pulled up to the big ship, it turned sideways and eased along the side of the platform. Megan could now see that it was Will Truegood and she smiled as she reached out to help guide the boat to a stop.

"Aren't you out a little early?" she asked.

"Aren't you in the water a little early?" he replied. "That water has to be 50 degrees!"

"Feels like 40," she said and laughed. "What are you doing?"

Will turned off the ignition to the boat, an old wooden runabout powered by an ancient looking green 20 horsepower Johnson outboard. Three fishing poles were leaned against one side, tucked under the middle seat. Doing a little smallmouth fishing before the sun got up too high. Soon as that sun touches the water, those little devils hide deep and get lockjaw."

"Is this your boat," Megan asked.

"Yeah, I keep it down at Horton Bay. I have a friend who lets me keep it there on the beach for free."

"Seems like a long way down from Horton Bay to go fishing."

"Oh, I've been out half the night working my way along the shore, hitting all the good ledges and holes. Thought I'd head out the channel to try the ends of the piers."

"Didn't catch much I see," she said, looking at the empty deck of the boat.

"I let 'em all go. Don't like to eat bass anyway," he answered, turning up his nose. "Hey, you want to come along out to the big lake? Should be calm for another hour or so before the wind comes up."

"You mean go fishing?"

"Yeah, come on. You got a license?"

She nodded. "I get one every summer to fish off the boat."

"Get some dry clothes on and let's get out there. Might even catch a summer-run steelhead. Crazy things will pull us half way across the lake."

Megan looked down at Will Truegood in his old fishing boat, sitting on a worn boat cushion, faded jeans with holes in the knees and a few other places. His long black hair was blowing loose in the light morning breeze. He kept brushing it back from his eyes. She was having a hard time looking away from his eyes.

Thoughts of her conversation the night before with her friend Rebecca about seeing Will and what her friend Rick Brandtley might think, raced through her mind for a brief moment before she said, "I'll be right back."

Ten minutes later Megan was sitting on the front seat of Will's boat as they motored slowly under the blue metal grid of the drawbridge heading out the channel to Lake Michigan. As cars passed overhead, a loud roar from the tires drowned out the rumble of the small outboard engine. Several people stood along the rail of the bridge waiting to see the big boats head out on the half hour. No one paid much attention to the old fishing boat.

The small boat cut through the smooth rolling swells coming in from the lake. They cruised past the Weathervane restaurant with its classic stone façade. The balconies and decks would soon be filled with the summer lunch crowd. A large cruising yacht was coming toward them down the channel, moving faster than the no-wake zone would suggest, pushing large waves out behind it. Will yelled out, "Hold on, this might be a little rocky for the old girl here."

Will's boat rose up on the first of the waves and then dipped quickly down the other side, nosing right into the next wave, taking on water over the bow. Will just laughed as Megan unsuccessfully tried to cover herself from getting soaked from the spray. Pushing wet hair away from her face, she yelled at the skipper of the cruiser, "Slow down you crazy maniac," but the boat was already gone.

The next two waves were more gentle and they continued on. Will just laughed again. "I don't think they even saw us. Probably a Bloody Mary cruise and they're already half in the bag."

Megan started laughing, too. "So much for dry clothes."

"Are you ready to fish?" he asked.

She nodded, looking around not quite sure what to do.

"Grab that rod there and start throwing that plug up against the break wall and then reel it back in fast." He reached over to show her which fishing rod and then helped her free the bait hook from the worn cork handle of the rod. Steering the boat with his knee on the throttle arm of the outboard, he showed her how to cast the plug and retrieve it.

Her first cast didn't release and the bait snapped back and hit the side of the boat. She looked at him helplessly.

"Take your finger off the line when you throw the bait," he said calmly.

She tried again and this time the bright orange plug sailed out beautifully over the channel landing right next to the metal break wall. Her eyes were open wide and she yelled in victory, "Now, how about that?"

"Well done. Well done. Now start reeling."

She turned the handle of the reel fast and felt the plug dive deep and pull back against the rod with a jittering motion that shook down through to her hands. In seconds the bait was back against the top of the rod and she cast again. The bait again fell with a splash near the side of the channel and she started reeling again. "How will I know when there's a fish on?" she asked.

"Oh, if it's a steelhead, there won't be much doubt," he answered.

Not two seconds later Megan yelped as the rod was almost pulled out of her hands, the tip arching down toward the water. "Ohmigod, what do I do!" she shrieked.

"Just let her run! Let her run!" The reel was singing a high pitched tune as the line flew out after the fish. The boat was nearing the end of the north pier and the fish was heading out to open water. "Don't try to stop her, Megan. We'll go after her."

"How would I stop it? It feels like a whale," she said laughing.

"Just hold on, she'll slow down." They cleared the channel and continued following the fishing line that was stretched out far ahead of them. Will looked around for other boat traffic and then sped up to chase the fish. "Reel just enough to keep the line tight. We don't want any slack," he instructed. "We'll catch up with her."

"Will, really, I've never had a fish like this on before; a few bluegills and bass off the side of my dad's boat, but this really feels like a whale!"

"You're doing fine," he yelled over the roar of the outboard. "Most people fish half their life to catch a steelhead. You just hooked up in two casts. You've got the touch, girl."

"Let's just get this thing in!"

Will slowed the boat and Megan began reeling faster to keep the line taut. Now she could really feel the throbbing pull of the fish as it dove deep and shook its head to free the hook in its jaw. She turned as Will came up behind her. Reaching around her, he grabbed the reel. "Let me check the drag." He turned the knob a few clicks.

She felt his arm around her middle and for a moment forgot about the big fish. He pulled back and reached for a net tucked on the side of the boat.

"Start trying to gain on her," he said. "Keep reeling until she tries to make another hard run."

Megan felt sweat running down her forehead and dripping off her chin. The drops fell on her bare thighs. She focused on the pull of the fish and reeling as fast as she could, stopping only when the fish ran again, or when Will told her to wait. She was surprised when the line went suddenly slack and she groaned thinking it was lost, only to see the fish fly up out of

46

the water 20 yards out from the boat. Its silver sides with a bright red stripe sparkled in the sun and water flew in all directions as it crashed back down in to the lake.

"Holy cow!" she yelled with a gasp. And then within just a minute the fish began to noticeably tire and she reeled even faster. Then it was along side the boat, lying on its side. Will reached over with the net and carefully slid it under the fish and then lifted it up out of the water.

They both yelled at the same time and Megan came over the seat and gave him a hug as he tried to hang on to the fish and the net. They both nearly fell overboard as the small boat rocked back and forth.

"Congratulations, Ms. Clark, on your first Lake Michigan steelhead."

"Oh, we don't have a camera," she said, looking around the boat.

"No, but we'll never forget this fish, will we?" he said. "Do you want to release her?"

"Yes, I want to do it."

They both leaned carefully over the side and Will pulled the hook barb out with a pair of pliers and then eased the fish out of the net, holding it behind the gills and down by the tail. He handed it over to Megan and he showed her how to work it slowly back and forth to get water and oxygen moving through its gills. "When will I know she's ready?"

"Oh, you'll know."

And then the fish lurched with a giant splash, getting them both in the face and was gone. Megan sat there in the bottom of the boat, her arms hanging over the side. The cool water lapped at her fingers and she could feel the slime of the fish as she rubbed her hands together. She turned and saw Will smiling at her. She took a deep breath and realized how drained she felt from the excitement of the chase and pull of the big fish.

"You fight fish pretty good for a city girl," he said.

***

Alex Clark ran out of the park up onto Central Park South and then past the entrance to the Plaza Hotel. He slowed at the next corner to wait for traffic to clear and then continued on, running along the curb to avoid the steady flow of people on their way to work. His gray sweatshirt was drenched dark around the neck with sweat and his face was deeply flushed and dripping. The city was coming back to life after the quiet of the earlier morning when he had started out on his run. He saw his coffee shop up ahead and slowed to a walk to give himself a few moments to start catching his breath. With hands on his hips he gulped in large breaths of air. He could feel the rapid beating of his heart through his chest and it gave him a warming sense of satisfaction that he had finished a good workout.

He walked through the doors of the small coffee shop, slowing to let his eyes adjust to the low light. The heavy aroma of coffee swept over him and then he saw his lawyer, Anna Bataglia, sitting at a table in the far corner. He waived and then stood in line to order his coffee. He pointed at her cup, suggesting that she might want a refill. She shook her head no.

When he joined her she made no effort to get up to greet him. "Morning, how was your run?"

"Great, now that it's over," he answered, sitting next to her at the small table. He took a long sip from his coffee, not caring that it was burning the inside of his mouth.

She pulled out a folder from her bag and set it down between them. "I wish I had better news."

Alex looked around the shop. There was no one near that could overhear their conversation. "Why am I not surprised?" He looked at her for a few moments trying to read her emotions. She was dressed for a day at the office, a crisp gray suit with a white shirt open at the neck. Her long black hair was gathered up on top of her head. He had become practiced in not letting himself get distracted by the striking beauty of her face. "Tell me that you were able to at least get a little more time to prepare."

She shook her head. "No, I'm sorry. We have to go ahead with the schedule of events they've already laid out. There will be a preliminary hearing in about two weeks."

Alex had an empty feeling in his gut, a feeling that was becoming all too familiar. "Have you talked to Lou's attorney?"

"They're stalling."

"Of course," he said, trying to remain calm. "Sally called last night from Charlevoix. Louis stopped by her house and tried to convince her that he had done nothing wrong."

"That must have been quite a performance." She took a sip from her coffee cup, holding it in two hands and letting the aroma work up into her nose. "We have to get to Littlefair," she said, referring to the company CFO."

"If we only knew where the hell he is."

"Well," she answered, "there are a lot of people out there looking for him, including the FBI and half the Attorney General's office investigators. I've got one of our firm's hired hands out on the trail, too."

"Until we get a chance to get Bobby Littlefair to open up about what in the hell they were trying to pull, I won't have a prayer in court. They're not going to believe I didn't know what was going on. If you remember, those Enron guys couldn't pull that crap and I sure as hell won't be able to."

Anna Bataglia looked back at him with an angry and insistent stare. The look in her deep brown eyes made him feel like she could see all the way through to his soul. "You need to step back and realize that your future on the right side of a prison wall is going to depend on your ability to believe *and* communicate that you are 100% fucking innocent."

***

Sheriff Elam Stone stood on the bridge leading across to Holy Island and looked south down the lake towards East Jordan. His mind was working hard to envision the day that George Hansen had been sitting on this quiet bay in his boat fishing. He saw the harsh reflections of the midday sun on the chop of the water. Two children ran in and out of the water down the bay on the lee side of the island. Their mother sat in a beach chair reading a book, seemingly oblivious to their activity. A few boats were anchored in the bay, no owners or activity apparent on any of them. Above him to the right the wind was lifting up off the big lake from the west and blowing surly gusts through the tops of the cottonwoods and maples. There was a pungent smell of decay in the slack water where the lily pads pushed up and the bottom weeds were already beginning to lose their battle for clear water and sun to the algae flushing out across the surface.

Stone was a simple and straightforward man. He had lived in this county his whole life, graduating from Boyne City High School and then moving on to college down in Traverse City. He knew that he wanted to be an officer of the law from the time he was a small child. In school he worked part time as a security guard to help pay for tuition, but also because he just liked being in a uniform with a badge on it. Family connections helped him get his first job with the

Sheriff's Department some twenty years ago. His hard work and good fortune in avoiding any serious controversy during his long career had allowed him to gradually rise in rank and pay grade and he was generally respected by those in the department.

He had found his career satisfying enough although the pace was slow and the cases often dull and mind-numbing. Kids partying too late and a few drunks out driving when they should be home in bed were the typical situations in his day-to-day. He often found himself daydreaming in his patrol car, sitting by the side of the road with the radar gun blinking at him as cars passed unnoticed. There had been some occasional excitement over the years. He had helped on a big drug bust in a condominium complex down in Mancelona. They had come away with several kilos of cocaine and five local bad guys sent away a long time for dealing. Then there was the bank robbery and hostage situation over in Antrim County. He remembered trying to calm his nerves and keep his shotgun from shaking as he kept it pointed at the front door of the bank with 20 other state, county and local cops. The guy finally came out when he ran out of cigarettes.

In his mind though, he knew that it was just a matter of time until he came across the ultimate case here in Charlevoix County. He couldn't help but think that there was a big case out there with his name on it; picture in the paper, commendations, admiring glances from the people around town.

All of these thoughts swirled through Sheriff Elam Stone's brain as he stood on the Holy Island Bridge looking down the bay. *How the hell does George Hansen end up dead in his boat down there with his lungs full of lake water?*

The Sheriff's Department lake patrol boat would be arriving any minute with divers to search the area around where the boat was found anchored with George Hansen's lifeless body.

Chapter Six

I remember our last trip together on the EmmaLee that summer in'52, like it was yesterday. Not long after, the Compton's sold the big ship and it was taken out east, not to return for over fifty years.

***

Jonathan McKendry stood in the pilot house with Emily and the ship's captain, Miles Roberts, his hands resting on the big wheel of the ship. He looked out ahead as he carefully steered the *EmmaLee* through the channel into Lake Charlevoix. It was just before noon on a Saturday and the boat traffic was heavy coming and going from Round Lake. Emily stood close holding on to his right arm, wind coming in from the open side hatches blowing her hair around her face.

Her father, Stewart Compton, came into the cabin followed by a crewman with a tray full of drinks. Emily reached for an iced tea and handed it to Jonathan to take a drink. The elder Compton held a chilled glass of whiskey over ice that was about half gone. "Where we off to, Skipper?" he asked.

"With the wind out of the northwest, the bay down at Horton will be dead calm and quiet and perfect for a picnic on the beach this afternoon," Jonathan answered. "We might even find some fish moving around near the creek late afternoon when the shadows come up."

Captain Roberts just nodded and smiled as he looked back at his boss, Stewart Compton.

"Sounds just fine, Jonny," said Compton.

"Daddy, did you see George and Liz come onboard?" asked Emily. "They joined us at the last minute when George decided he could get away from the office for a few hours on a Saturday."

"Yes dear, I said hello to them back in the rear of the ship. They were reading and drinking some cold tea."

"Did you hear that George has agreed to represent Sammy Truegood in that case with the Harris' daughter?"

Her father's expression changed noticeably and a flush of red spread quickly across his loose jowls. "How on Earth did George get involved with all of that?" he asked.

Emily came over beside him and put her arm around his big shoulders. "Daddy, you know that George has been friends with their family ever since Sammy's grandpa helped ..." She didn't finish the sentence, realizing that her husband Jonathan was listening and would be in no mood to let a conversation about the tragic death of George's sister Catherine ruin such a beautiful day. She had been Jonathan's girlfriend through high school. Soon after George and Jonathan returned from the War she was found raped and murdered out on North Point. Ultimately, Jonathan's own brother Luke was found guilty of the crime.

Emily looked into the eyes of her father for some sign of understanding, but he just glared back at her. It had taken considerable time for him to come to terms with how she had risked the reputation of their family in helping Jonathan McKendry when he had first been charged with Catherine's death. Over the past years he had come to know and love Jonathan, but it had taken time and the bitterness of that summer of the incident often touched on a raw nerve with her father.

"I just can't believe he's getting involved in something like that again," said Compton, taking a long drink from his glass.

Jonathan looked quickly over his shoulder. "Stewart, I've known Sammy Truegood for years and he's one of my best workers down at the boatyard. I don't have any reason to believe he could be involved with this mess with the Harris girl."

"Dammit Jonathan!" he said, a bit too loud. "The kid admitted he was down there that night with the girls."

Emily hugged him close again to try to calm him. "Daddy, please don't get so upset about this. George is a lawyer. This is what he gets paid to do."

Her father finished his glass and turned to hand it to the crewman standing behind him. He nodded to him to go below for a refill. "I don't give a damn what he gets paid to do! He should know better than to get mixed up in something like this again, particularly with *those* people."

Emily pushed away from her father and looked at him with a stern glare. She was about to launch into him about his intolerance for the Truegood's and their people when George Hansen walked into the cabin. Before her father could say anything she moved between the two men and gave George a kiss on the cheek. "Hello stranger, I can't believe we actually got you away from work for a few hours. I should take your temperature and make sure you're feeling okay."

George looked around the cabin and immediately noticed the strained expressions on everyone's faces and the tension hanging in the air. "Did I miss something?"

Jonathan continued looking ahead, piloting the ship out past the last red buoy in the channel and into Lake Charlevoix. "George, probably best to just drop it," he said, trying to diffuse the situation.

Emily jumped in again. "We're going down to Horton Bay. Won't that be grand, George?"

Stewart Compton turned suddenly and walked out of the cabin without saying anything.

***

Jennifer Harris sat down heavily on one of the chairs by the tennis court in the backyard of their summer house. Sweat rolled down her forehead into her eyes and dripped down leaving spots on her white skirt. She dropped her tennis racket on the ground and reached for a glass of lemonade sitting on a small table. Taking a short sip, she took a deep breath and closed her eyes, hoping the pain in her head would finally go away. She hadn't been able to take enough aspirin in the last day to calm the effects of the hangover and the night at the beach that had left her in the hospital. She was struggling to put fragments of memories back together and the guilt and fear at what had happened still left a dull ache in her stomach. Her friend, Elaine, was coming over after picking up balls on her end of the court.

"Hey Jenn, I thought a little exercise might help you, but you look like death," She sat down in another chair and reached for her drink sitting on the table. "That whiskey still has my head on fire, too," she said, rubbing the moist chill of the glass on her forehead and cheeks.

Jennifer slumped in her chair and laid her head back looking up at the high white clouds floating by overhead. She knew that Sammy Truegood had been arrested for having his way with her that night at the beach. Everyone she knew in town had heard about it and the whispers and laughs behind her back were growing intolerable. Her father was threatening to take her back to Chicago for the rest of the summer and she was beginning to think that may be best. She thought about Sammy and what he must be going through, but her anger for what he had done quickly took over any thoughts of concern for the boy. Lying in bed awake for most of the past night, she had tried to break through the dark cloud of empty memory of what had actually happened out on the beach at Fisherman's Island. All she had been able to piece back together was driving out there with Elaine late in the afternoon to get some sun and go swimming. She remembered that Sammy had come along and joined them for awhile swimming and then Andy and some of their other friends had come out and then everything else was gone from her memory until she woke up in the hospital feeling like her head was going to explode and her body had been run over by a truck. Elaine hadn't been much more help in putting the evening's events back together. She had nearly as much to drink and wasn't able to fill in much more of the detail. Looking over at her friend, she said weakly, "I think my dad may literally kill me if this hangover doesn't get me first."

Elaine reached over and took her hand. "You know honey, you're lucky we found you in the dunes and not floating face down out in the waves. God, I'm never going to drink again."

"How many times have I heard you say that?" Jennifer said, finally able to manage a weak smile.

"I haven't seen Andy since they let me come home from the hospital. I can't believe that you all found me out there in the dunes like that." Andy Welton had been her summer boyfriend since last year.

Elaine didn't answer, looking off across the tennis court at the lake through the trees.

"I'm afraid to ask, but did I have any clothes on when you guys found me?"

"Honey, it's okay, we got you covered up right away."

"Have you seen Andy? Has he said anything?" Her friend just shook her head no. "My mother won't even talk to me and Connor is spitting nails about this whole thing, but you know him."

Elaine stood up and began gathering her clothes and racket. "This will all be over soon and they'll send that asshole Truegood boy away. People will move on and forget."

"I'm too ashamed to even go into town, or up to the club. Everyone's looking at me like I'm the biggest tramp, or something."

"You didn't do anything wrong, other than drink most of a whole bottle of bad whiskey."

"Don't remind me," Jennifer said, putting her glass back on the table and reaching up to press on her temples. "I still can't believe that Sammy would do something like this."

"I'm glad that I passed out by the fire, or he might have come after me, too."

Jennifer looked at her friend and tried to find some comfort in her face. "Just tell me that none of this really happened. Wake me up!"

Elaine reached over and rubbed her shoulder. "Honey, this will all go away soon enough."

Jennifer heard the words and felt the comforting touch, but couldn't quell the fear that sent prickles through every nerve ending in her body. She tried hard to push back the thought that she might also get pregnant from what had happened. "I wonder if Andy will even talk to me?"

***

The *EmmaLee* eased around the point that protected Horton Bay from the wind and waves blowing down from Charlevoix. Jonathan and

55

George stood at the rail up in the bow, feeling the Captain power down the big ship to ease into the calm waters of the bay. George watched the heavy woods that lined the shore along the point. He thought back to the story of Nick Adams that he had read and Hemingway telling the story of Nick rowing out to the point with his girlfriend Marjorie and telling her *that it wasn't fun anymore.*

"What's going to happen to Sammy Truegood?" Jonathan asked.

George kept looking at the shore and the trees along the point. "I don't feel good about this at all, not at all," he answered.

"What does Sammy have to say?"

"You know I believe the boy. He tells me that he was there with the girls and that they went swimming and had a good time swimming out there near Fisherman's Island. He says that some more kids came down to the beach later that night and they had a bonfire and there was a lot of liquor getting passed around. He left them when he had to get back to town and he said that he ran into some summer boys on the way back through the woods."

"What summer boys?"

George turned away from the shore and rested back against the rail looking down the lake towards Boyne City. "Some friends of the Harris girl. They tried to start a fight with him. There were three of them and Sammy was smart not to get into it with them."

"Have you talked to Jennifer Harris yet?" Jonathan asked.

"No, Connor and her old man won't let me see her. God, Connor Harris can be such an asshole," George said, shaking his head. "Too bad old Luke didn't catch him a bit harder with that board that summer." George watched his friend wince and look away. Jonathan's brother Luke had almost killed Connor Harris that summer back before the War. And then those years later, when they had found that Luke was the one responsible for the death of George's sister, Catherine. They rarely mentioned Luke anymore and he regretted bringing it up. "Hey, I'm sorry."

Jonathan looked over at his friend and smiled a flat smile. "Too much bad history in this place, isn't there?"

George nodded in agreement without answering.

"You need to talk to the girl, George, the Harris girl."

"Yeah, I know. The sheriff is setting it up for Monday."

"So, meanwhile Sammy's sitting down there in the jail?"

"No, I got him out this morning. The judge up in Petoskey set bail and I got him out," said George. "He's back home with his mother. I told him to stay there."

They turned to watch as the ship's crew came forward to prepare to anchor the *EmmaLee*. Emily and Elizabeth came up on deck in their swimming suits. The two men watched as their wives approached, towels over their shoulders.

"Hey George, look at these two," said Jonathan. "Think they'd go for a pair of old worn-out locals?"

The women smiled and whispered something to each other as they came closer.

"What was that about?" asked George.

"I was just telling my friend Elizabeth here that we must have made a wrong turn to end up out here with the likes of you two," Emily said and laughed as she threw her towel at Jonathan.

"Come over here," he answered, holding out his arms. Emily came to him and they leaned against the rail and then kissed each other.

"Alright, break it up you two," said George. "Looks like we're going for a swim, McKendry."

The ship slowed to a stop and the anchor was dropped. The captain reversed the engines and backed off the anchor chain, securing it in the deep bottom of the bay. The water was glassy calm and the deep green of the cedars along the creek mouth reflected beautifully back across the bay.

They all noticed Emily's father coming out on deck with a fishing pole in one hand and a drink in the other. He walked somewhat unsteadily over to the side of the ship and set the glass down on the top of the rail. He started to fiddle with the rod and reel trying to free the bait hook. He moved over to an opening in the rail and prepared to cast.

"Daddy, catch some supper for us!" Emily yelled. She was about to walk over and help him when she noticed that he had dropped the fishing pole and stumbled slightly. "Daddy?"

Stewart Compton tried to reach for the railing to support himself, but then clutched at his chest and fell to his knees, a look of excruciating pain on his face. Emily stood frozen for a moment in shock as Jonathan ran by her to help his father-in-law. Before he could get there the older man cried out in a low moan and then fell over on his side.

Jonathan ran faster. "Stewart!"

"Oh Daddy!" Emily screamed.

Just before Jonathan reached him, the older man collapsed completely and then fell over the side of boat. They all heard the splash on the water as Stewart Compton fell helplessly into the bay.

Jonathan heard Emily scream again as he jumped through the railing, arms flying to steady himself as he fell towards the lake's surface. He could see the splash where Stewart had hit the water. He hadn't resurfaced. Jonathan splashed down into the water and then turned to swim back to where his father-in-law had gone in. He heard Emily yelling at him hysterically from above as he dove below the surface. Giving no thought to the cool chill of the water, he dove deep with his eyes wide open. He spotted him floating lifelessly with his arms and legs splayed out in the green darkness of the water. When he reached him he grabbed him by the shirt behind his neck and began kicking and paddling with his free hand back towards the surface, struggling with the heavy weight of the big man. He broke through and took a deep breath, pulling Emily's father up with him, trying to get his face up above the surface of the water. He could see that his eyes were closed and he seemed to be unconscious. Water spilled out from his mouth. He heard the crew shouting above him.

"Get the stairs over the side!" someone yelled.

A life buoy fell beside him and Jonathan reached out with his free hand for the support of the float. Then someone else splashed down beside him and he saw Emily come up next to him, panic on her face.

"Honey, hold onto the float here and try to help keep his head up!" Jonathan instructed.

"Daddy, are you okay!" she screamed.

Her father remained motionless and unresponsive in their arms.

The stairs were lowered down and George and a crewman ran down. George threw a line out to them and Jonathan held it tightly as they were pulled back the short distance to the ship. The men managed to get the lifeless form of Stewart Compton up onto the stair platform. His great mass lay there, his head to one side. Emily came up on the platform and pushed everyone away. She pulled open his shirt and put her ear to his chest. Jonathan watched as his wife became a doctor, trying to save her own father. She rose up and put two fingers against his neck trying to feel for a pulse. She looked up at Jonathan helplessly. She reached for his wrist and felt again for a pulse. She started crying as her mother came up and looked down at the platform.

"What in God's name?" her mother yelled.

Jonathan put his arm around his wife's shoulders as she started weeping uncontrollably. She looked at him and tried to catch her breath. She looked back at her father. "Jonathan, he's gone."

Chapter Seven

The midday summer rush of Charlevoix in season was in a full state of chaos and commotion. Cars moved slowly down the main street through town, backed up as far as one could see in both directions. More cars lined up on the side streets trying to inch their way out onto Bridge Street. The sidewalks were packed with shoppers strolling by the stores looking for something special in the window displays that they just had to have and boats of all sizes and shapes jammed the small harbor of Round Lake.

Sally Clark walked down the sidewalk through the crowds, occasionally saying "hello" to someone that she knew. The sign hanging above the door to her old art gallery loomed just ahead. The memories of her years running the business with her old partner, Gwen Roberts, came rushing back to her. She felt a sadness come over her and she often missed the business and her time with Gwen. She was still painting and Alex had built a wonderful studio for her back East. He had even helped to get her a showing at one of the more prestigious galleries in New York. The work had been both a critical and commercial success. She realized that she hadn't spoken to Gwen since George's funeral the other day.

Gwen had a new partner in business and in life. Sally had met her the previous summer. Her name was Tara Peterson. She was a painter that Gwen and Sally had shown in the gallery back when Sally still owned half of the business.

Sally slowed in front of the shop and took in the beautiful pieces that Gwen and Tara had displayed. She noticed one of her own paintings on an easel, a piece she had done out on the shores of Beaver Island. She hesitated for a moment, thinking about whether she should go inside. She was startled when she felt a hand on her shoulder. She turned to see Gwen Roberts smiling at her.

"Hello stranger," she said and then reached out to give Sally a hug. The two women stood there together for a few moments just holding each other. "Sal, I'm still so sad about George. How are you doing?"

Sally stood back and held on to Gwen's hands with her own. Taking a deep sigh she said, "I'm not sure I'll ever get over not having him around here. How can he possibly be gone?"

"Have you seen Elizabeth since the service? How is she holding up?" Gwen asked.

"I called her last night. She's going out to Montana for a few weeks to stay with her sister. She lives near Dillon up in the mountains and she's got a house full of grandkids for the summer that Liz can help mother."

"That should be good for her."

Sally turned to look again at the gallery's window. "The shop looks beautiful. You and Tara are doing a wonderful job. How's business?"

"We're off to a great start this summer. Mary Alice and her mother are in every other day to find another piece for the redecorating they're doing out there."

"Yes, I saw her Highness, Ms. Gregory, earlier this morning. Charming as usual," Sally said.

Gwen just shook her head. "She still gets to you, doesn't she?"

"Let's change the subject."

Gwen laughed and took her by the arm. "Come on in. Let me show you some of the new work we've brought in and I want you to say hello to Tara."

***

Rebecca Holmes was waiting on the foredeck of the *EmmaLee* when Will and Megan came back into Round Lake. Megan saw her leaning on the rail. "Oh good," she said. "I want you to meet my friend Becca. We've been pals up here for years."

"Is that her?" Will asked, pointing out ahead to the ship.

61

Megan watched as someone else walked up next to her friend on the deck of the *EmmaLee*. She could tell right away that it was her summer boyfriend, Rick Brandtley. She felt a nervous flutter surge through her body and then quickly, in her typical confident way, she thought to herself...*Well, they had to meet sooner, or later*. She watched as Rebecca waived. Will's small fishing boat cruised slowly up along the bow of the big ship.

Rebecca yelled down, "Rick and I came out to get you to take you to lunch." She didn't acknowledge Will sitting in the back of the boat at all.

Megan just waived back. She turned to look at Will. "Rick is another friend of mine."

"Is he your boyfriend?" Will asked calmly.

She was surprised by his directness. "Well," she said and hesitated. "Yeah, that's probably a good way to describe it." She felt her face flush and she didn't want to hurt Will's feelings.

"Do you love him?"

"Will!"

"Can he fish?" Will couldn't hide his smile.

"Will Truegood, you're an evil boy," she said sternly and then she started laughing, too.

Will pulled the small boat up to the platform as Rebecca and Rick came down the stairs.

"Hi guys," Megan said. "This is my friend Will. Will, this is Rick and Becca."

Rick reached out and caught the boat as it came alongside. "Good morning beautiful," he said.

"I thought you weren't going to be up until the fourth?" Megan answered.

"You don't seem very happy to see me."

"Of course I am." Megan jumped out of the boat and gave him a hug. She turned her face as he tried to kiss her and he got her on the cheek.

"I've missed you, kid," he said.

"I've missed you, too," Megan said, stepping back and feeling very awkward with the whole situation.

Will interrupted the welcome scene by saying, "Hey Megan, I really need to get going. I've got some chores I need to take care of this afternoon."

She turned and knelt by the side of the boat. "Guys, you should have seen the fish I caught this morning. Will took me out and I hooked this awesome steelhead right in the channel and we chased it way out into the big lake."

"It was a beauty," Will said.

"You must be quite the fisherman," Rick said to Will with a not so subtle edge.

"Yeah, we'll have to get out some time. Do you like to fly fish?"

"I don't think I'll have much time this summer. Megan and I usually keep pretty busy."

Will seemed to ignore his rudeness. "Megan, I'll see you. Thanks for coming out with me this morning."

"Will, that was the greatest time!" she said. "You'll have to take me again."

He reached back to pull the lever on the side of the motor into gear. "I'll see you. Nice to meet you all," he said as he steered the boat away from the *EmmaLee* and then out toward the channel into Lake Charlevoix.

Megan stood up and turned to face her friends, still feeling awkward and uncomfortable about all of this and at the same time, hating herself for feeling that way. "Well..." was all she could think to say.

"So who's this Will guy?" Rick asked. "What is he, an Indian, or what?"

"His family has been friends with Sally's for years up here. We met him up in the park after George Hansen's funeral the other day."

Rick must have decided to put the whole incident aside because he came over and gave Megan another long hug. "Hey beautiful, I really missed you."

"I missed you too, Brandtley," she said, reaching up and scruffing his hair.

Becca grabbed them both by the arm. "Come on, I'm starving. Let's go find some lunch."

As they walked up the stairs, Megan looked back and saw the small boat carrying Will Truegood disappear beyond the channel.

***

Louis Kramer saw his wife pull into the drive at the back of her parent's summer home. Her white Mercedes convertible came to an abrupt stop. Mary Alice Gregory quickly got out of the car and grabbed several bags from the passenger seat. He knew that look on her face and also knew that it meant nothing but trouble. Moving quickly to the front of the house, he was surrounded by large windows framing the view of Lake Charlevoix. A long dock stretched out into the lake in sharp white contrast to the deep green of the water. Several boat hoists held jet skis and a ski boat. A larger cruising yacht was tied up at permanent pilings at the end of the dock.

He heard the door slam closed and walked over to a bar against the far wall and poured a glass of red wine. *Hell, what do they say? It's 5:00 somewhere.*

"Louis Kramer, where are you?" yelled Mary Alice as she came through the house.

He sipped his wine and looked out at the lake, thinking about how he could escape the inevitable confrontation that awaited him. *What have I done this time?* He heard his wife come into the room and turned. "Hi dear, how is your morning going?"

She threw the bags down on a chair and came over to him, a look of intolerance and malice on her face.

"Care for a drink, dear?"

Mary Alice took a deep breath, trying to calm herself before starting. "Can you tell me what in hell is going on with Alex Clark?"

Stepping back in surprise, Louis placed his glass down on a table by the window. He could feel the familiar ache starting to build in his gut. "With Alex?" he said, trying to vie for time to react.

"Yes, with Alex! I just ran into Sally down in Charlevoix and she told me that you stopped by to see her last night."

"Honey…"

Not letting him finish, she moved closer. "Don't you think you might have told me about this little visit? Don't you think you might want to

64

let me in on what the hell this is all about?" Mary Alice reached for his wine glass and took a drink, staring directly into her husband's eyes. "I've never been so embarrassed!"

Louis decided on the spot that he had better go on the offensive. "Mary Alice, you've never given two shits for what goes on in my business! As long as the checks keep arriving and your credit card bills are paid, you seem to get by just fine. Why should I start sharing now?" As soon as the words were out he knew that this conversation was quickly going in the wrong direction.

The veins on Mary Alice's neck began to bulge out and her face turned red as her rage continued to grow. "Louis Kramer, you are going to sit down right now and tell me what the hell is going on!"

"Alright, honey, please settle down," he said, his Texas accent becoming more pronounced as he softened his tone. He reached over and took her by the arm, leading her to a couch where they both sat down. Leaning over, he stroked a few stray hairs out of her eyes.

She looked back without the least bit of patience or understanding in her stern expression. "You better be straight with me, Louie."

He repositioned himself on the coach and then took another drink from his glass of wine. "Alex and I have run into a little trouble down at the office…"

"Sally said that you're responsible for whatever the hell is going on here," she interrupted.

"Of course she would, honey. She just can't believe her perfect Alex could mess up."

"Just tell me what's going on!"

"Well, we were audited a few months ago and a couple of things turned up that the Feds are getting all excited about."

She reached for his glass and finished the rest of the wine in one long swallow.

Louis watched her and felt the nervous apprehension continue to flush through his veins. He had been able to stand up to and hold his own with some of the toughest business people in the world, but Mary Alice Gregory was in a whole different league when she was crossed.

"The Feds? What, like the IRS, or what?"

He hesitated for a moment. "Like the Securities and Exchange Commission and the Attorney General of the State of New York."

"Holy shit!" she screamed, jumping up off the couch.

"Dear, really now, it's just a little misunderstanding. Our damned financial guy makes a couple of mistakes and everyone gets all jumpy."

"Did Alex Clark know what was going on?" she asked.

He looked her in the eye and knew there was no escaping the truth. "No, he really didn't know exactly what had happened until the subpoenas came down."

"You've been subpoenaed?"

"Yeah…" he paused, gathering his thoughts. "We'll have to talk to a Grand Jury in…"

"A Grand Jury!" Mary Alice went over to the bar and poured more wine. "So what did you expect to accomplish with Sally last night?"

"Alex won't work with us on this. He's got his own lawyers."

"Sounds like he's being pretty damn smart distancing himself from the rest of you."

Louis felt his anger rising and he tried to stay calm. "Who the hell's side are you on, anyway?"

"I just don't appreciate having *Ms. High and Mighty* catching me downtown and knowing more about my husband's damn business than I do and finding out you've been dragging your ass over to her house trying to beg for fucking mercy!"

He tried his best to keep his temper under control. Walking over to the door out to the lake he turned and said, "I'm going to need you on my side, Mary Alice."

She didn't answer.

***

The diver stood dripping on the deck of the boat, reaching into a bag attached to a belt at his waist. The wind through the trees up along the hill had calmed in the later afternoon. Shadows played down across the quiet bay behind Holy Island. Sheriff Elam Stone sat watching, chewing on a big wad of gum, as the diver pulled something out of the bag. The sun caught the flat shiny surface of a large hunting knife and the reflection flashed brightly in his eyes.

"Holy crap!" the old sheriff said. "That's a big damn pig sticker."

The diver handled the knife carefully. His partner held out a big plastic bag and the diver dropped it in. "Found it down there in about twenty feet of water, lying out nice as day on the bottom. Couldn't have been there for more than a few days, or the sand would have silted over it."

"You pretty sure this is where Hansen's boat was?" Porter asked.

"Yeah, we matched up the GPS coordinates we took the other day when we found the old guy in the boat."

"He didn't have any knife wounds," the sheriff said.

"No," the diver responded, "I'm guessing the *friends* that came out to see him that day used this big knife to persuade the old guy to go overboard, and then they held him under until he drowned."

"Been thinking about this a lot," said the sheriff. "Can't figure why they'd pull him back into the boat after drowning him like that. Why not just leave him on the bottom and make it look like he fell out of the boat and drowned?"

The diver just shook his head. "Not very professional, leaving a weapon behind and all."

"Let me get that knife over to the lab in Traverse City, see what we can get off it," said Sheriff Stone.

***

The Falcon corporate jet lifted off the runway at LaGuardia and banked steeply to the west. Alex watched as the skyline of Manhattan spread out across the horizon, the late evening sun shining brightly behind the Chrysler Building. He turned away from the small round window and watched his attorney, Anna Bataglia, across the narrow aisle, searching for something in her tan leather shoulder bag. He couldn't help but notice the skirt from her gray suit was pushed up and she had crossed her long bare legs out in front of her. She turned and saw Alex looking at her and he looked away quickly.

Damn. When he glanced back over, he saw that she was smiling. *Sally is just going to love this house guest.*

"I'm glad you agreed to let me come along, Alex. We need to spend a lot more time getting ready for this hearing and I don't want to be a thousand miles away trying to get this taken care of by phone, or email."

"I know, you're right," he answered. "I just need to get up to Charlevoix to spend some time with Sally. She's really taking the loss of her old friend, George, awfully hard."

"I'm really sorry about your friend, Alex."

"Yeah, thanks. He was a fine old gentleman. We got to be close friends over the past few years."

"How much does Sally know about the business and the investigation?"

"She knows we're having some issues, but none of the details."

The plane continued to climb steeply and Alex looked out the window again, watching the big city begin to slip away behind them.

"For her own sake, keep her as far away from this as possible," Anna said.

Alex just nodded. "No luck on finding our friend, Littlefair?"

"No, the bastard has really slipped into a hole somewhere. But he'll turn up. The Feds aren't going to rest on you guys and your CFO is prime meat in all of this. The fact that he's running certainly won't help his cause, but you need to be able to distance yourself completely from that asshole."

"Guess I'm not surprised that our accountants are covering their asses, big time."

"Yeah," she answered, "they're damn good at making sure nothing sticks."

"As far as I know, Louis is still up in Charlevoix."

Anna placed her bag on the seat facing her and then adjusted her skirt, pulling it down with little effect. "I think it's time we had a very private discussion with your friend and soon to be former partner, Louis Kramer."

Chapter Eight

I think back about the Truegoods and remember a family that loved each other so much. They passed the traditions of their people down with each generation and for the most part, brought honor and respect to their family. Of all of them over the years, little Sammy was always my favorite. He had a sense of purpose and character that you don't often see in young men.

***

Sammy Truegood had been released from jail when George Hansen helped his mother post bail. Warned by the sheriff not to leave town, he had stayed at home with his mother the first night, but left the house early the next morning. In the early light he rode his bike out of town towards Petoskey, turning at the Boyne City road to head out along Lake Charlevoix. The bright sun cut through the trees ahead and he pedaled hard up the big hills and then enjoyed the feel of the wind in his face as he coasted down the other side. It felt good to be free out in the fresh summer air again. He tried hard to push away thoughts of Jennifer Harris and his arrest.

A couple of miles out of town he came to a narrow dirt road leading up into the trees away from the lake. He got off his bike and walked with it up the hill. Two small fawns came out of the woods ahead of him and bent their heads to feed on wild flowers growing along the road. Sammy was close enough to make out the white spots on their back and he stood quietly, hoping not to spook them away. He heard rustling in the brush and the mother doe came out, immediately seeing Sammy holding his bike. She stopped quickly and her ears twitched back and forth and he could see her nostrils flaring as she tried to gauge the threat. The twins turned to see their mother come out onto the road. They saw Sammy standing there, but apparently didn't feel threatened because they returned to their feeding. The mother finally had seen enough of the intruder and snorted at the young deer, and immediately looked up again. She turned and walked back into the woods, her two babies following obediently behind. Sammy watched them disappear into the heavy brush and was thankful for even the brief encounter with the deer.

Pushing his bike on up the road, he eventually came around a bend and could see an opening in the trees and brush up ahead. In a large clearing in the woods, the rough cabin of the Greensky Mission Church sat in the high grass. Missionaries in the early 1800's had come to the area, converting the Native Americans to Christianity. One of the local members of the Odawa, Peter Greensky, had become an interpreter for one of the early missionaries and had stayed to help start the first church.

Off across a field from the mission, a circle of maple trees had been planted years ago to form a ring around a gathering place with low wood benches. The legends of his people had said that this clearing had been used as a meeting place for the tribes of the Odawa. During one of these meetings, the chief from each of the tribes had agreed to plant a tree to symbolize the unity of the tribes. They swore an oath that as long as the coming of spring brought new leaves on the trees, the tribes would remain at peace. To help prevent the trees from being taken for lumber, each was bent and tied to grow at an angle. They became known as the Bent Council Trees. Many of the trees still survived and the place was used to this day for ceremonial gatherings of his people.

Sammy Truegood had come to the mission and the Bent Council Trees many times with his family. He always felt a special bond with his ancestors when he sat among the bent maple trees. The wind through the trees sounded like whispers from the past. He laid his bike down in the grass and walked out into the center of the circle of trees. Looking up into the sky through the trees, he turned slowly, listening to the wind.

***

Emily Compton sat down on the soft cushion of the white wicker chair on the porch of her parent's house. The big Victorian summer home looked out over a large green lawn and down the way to the lake. She closed her eyes and let out a long sigh, feeling the weight and grief of the past hours try to escape from her body. The family had buried her father earlier in the day up at the Charlevoix cemetery. The service had been attended by family, friends and a large number of her father's business associates from down in Detroit. Many of the attendees were now inside the house giving their respects to the Compton family. Emily had cried out so much of her grief and emotions over the past two days leading up to the funeral that she felt drained of any more energy to mourn. The realization that her father was gone, however, was still incredibly painful for her.

She heard someone come out onto the porch and sit down next to her. She felt the comfort of a warm hand reach for hers and then heard the reassuring voice of her husband, Jonathan.

"Emily, I wish there was something more that I could do for you. I know how badly this hurts. My father's passing was just so hard."

She squeezed his hand in response. A single tear ran down her cheek falling on her dark blue dress and spreading out slowly into the fabric.

"Really, is there anything I can get for you?"

She opened her eyes and turned to look at Jonathan McKendry. It struck her as such a blessing that now, after so many years of caring for her husband through the challenges and tragedies that he and his family had faced, he was here for her in the same way. She sat up and leaned over close to his face, looking into his eyes. She kissed him on the cheek and then on the mouth. When she pulled back she saw that his eyes were closed. "You're doing more than enough just being here with me. I love you, Jonathan McKendry."

He opened his eyes and smiled. "I love you, too," he said. Reaching over and taking her hands in his own, he kissed her gently on the forehead and said, "I do have something that I thought might cheer you up, maybe a little." A sly smile spread across his face.

"What have you done, Jonathan?" she said, forcing a smile to finally break through. She watched as her husband reached into the pocket of his jacket. He pulled his hand out with a closed fist and held it out in front of her. "Come on, Jonathan, I'm in no mood for suspense." As he slowly opened the fingers of his hand, she leaned forward to see a key resting in his palm. Emily looked up at him with a confused grin. "What have you done?"

"Do you remember that little house up on Michigan…?"

Before he could finish, she jumped up and sat down on his lap, threw her arms around his neck and kissed him. "Oh Jonathan, you wouldn't tease me about this, would you?"

Shaking his head *no* and kissing her again, he said, "No, and I can't wait to carry you across the threshold, Mrs. McKendry "

***

George Hansen parked his car in front of his office. As he walked up on the sidewalk, Connor Harris came around the corner. The two men saw each other and Connor quickened his pace. George stood and watched the man come toward him, noticing that he still moved with a slight limp from the fight with Jonathan's brother, Luke, back before the War.

"Hansen, wait up there!" Harris yelled. "I need to speak with you."

George put his keys in his pocket and crossed his arms, trying to remain calm. "Listen Harris, I have nothing to say to you without your family's attorney here."

Connor stopped in front of him, uncomfortably close, a furious look distorting his face. "Damn't, Hansen, then I'll talk and you listen. This damn Indian punk has got to pay for what he's done to my sister and I better not find you pulling any legal bullshit to get him off."

George laughed, in spite of his growing anger. "What if we try to get to the truth, Harris?"

"The truth?" Connor said. "The truth is that we know he was down there and he got those girls drunk and he raped my sister, Jennifer!"

"Let's have this out in the courtroom, Connor." George turned to go into his office. Harris grabbed him by the sleeve and pushed him up against the building. "By God, Hansen…"

Before he could finish, George came up quickly with both hands and pushed him away. Connor tripped backwards on his bad leg and fell to the pavement. George walked over and leaned down over him. "If you ever touch me again, Harris, I swear I'll kick your ass and sweep the street with you." He turned and went into his office and watched through the window as Connor Harris picked himself up and limped away down the sidewalk.

***

Jennifer Harris looked at the sailboats jockeying for position in the race offshore. The crisp white sails stood out brightly against the clear blue of the sky. She sat with her friend Elaine in wooden beach chairs and had a towel draped over her legs to protect a sunburn from the previous day. Through the boats, she could see all the way down Lake Charlevoix towards Boyne City.

"Hey, girls!"

Jennifer turned to see Andy Welton coming across the beach. Her heart sank as she felt the embarrassment again of what had happened with Sammy Truegood out at Fisherman's Island. She had held a school girl crush for Andy as long as she could remember and last summer he had finally noticed her. By the end of the summer they were an *item*, and through the long school year they had stayed in touch by letters, looking forward to the coming summer. She knew that he and his friends had found her out at the beach that night and she shuddered to think of them coming up and finding her passed out drunk and naked in the dunes.

"Oh great, it's Andy," she said to her friend. She wished that she could run and hide.

"Jenny, don't worry. It will be alright."

The boy came around and sat in front of them on the sand. He had his bathing suit on and old gray sweatshirt with *Charlevoix* on it. His brown hair was a mess of random curls pushed in odd angles from an earlier dip in the lake. He reached under the towel and rubbed one of her feet affectionately. "Hey Jenny, how are you doing?"

His touch startled her and she pulled back without thinking. Sitting forward, she wrapped her arms around her knees and looked down at the sand. "Andy, I really don't know what to say. I am so embarrassed about what happened."

"You don't need to apologize," he said, a look of anger washing over his face. "That sonofabitch is gonna pay for what's he's done."

Elaine jumped into the conversation, "Andy, you and the boys, well…it's just a good thing that you were out there that night."

Jennifer thought back again, trying to piece together the memories of that day. "I'm just so embarrassed how you found me, and I was so drunk."

"Didn't Elaine tell you that she found you first and she had you dressed and everything when we came to help take you back."

For a moment, this made her feel a bit better, but then it seemed odd that her friend hadn't told her about this earlier. She looked over at Elaine with a puzzled expression.

"Oh yeah, Jenn, I got you as cleaned up as I could before the boys came down. You were so drunk, I was afraid you were dead at first," said Elaine.

"The doctors said that I was darn close. If I ever smell a glass of whiskey again, I think I'll pass out and die."

"You know, the sheriff's been talking to us and we told him everything we know and what we saw," said Andy. "Have you seen him anymore? Is he still getting his case together against that damn Indian kid?"

"We haven't seen the sheriff for a couple of days," answered Elaine. "You haven't seen him again, have you, Jenn?"

"Actually, he called the house again last night and stopped over. He seemed confused about some of the details of what we've all been telling him." Jennifer watched as Andy and Elaine looked at each other with a curious expression.

"So, what was he asking about?" Andy asked.

"It didn't matter, I don't remember any of it."

Andy just nodded his head, staring at her, and then over at Elaine. "Well, the reason I was looking for you two, is we're having a bonfire down at the beach by North Point tonight. You guys want to come along? The whole gang's gonna be there."

Jennifer twisted uncomfortably in her seat. "You know, I'm not feeling much in the party mood, and I'm not sure my family will even let me out of the house."

"No, no… it's not like that. No booze, I promise," Andy said quickly. "You need to get back in the swing of things. Come on, why don't you come, and you too, Elaine."

Elaine answered first, "I'll get her there. She needs to stop moping around."

He stood up and brushed the sand from his legs and bathing suit. "Great, we'll get the fire going and meet you out there around 8:00." He leaned over and kissed Jennifer on the cheek.

She tried to smile. She knew that Elaine was right. She needed to get on with things and not let the whole summer slip away like this. "Thanks, Andy. We'll see you out there tonight."

The girls watched as he walked away across the beach.

Elaine stood up and reached for Jennifer's hand. "Come on, we need to cool off. I'll race you to the raft." She took off running, pulling her friend behind her. The two of them splashed out into the cold water and ran as far as they could before diving under the surface and swimming together out to the dive platform.

Chapter Nine

Sally stood at the center island in her kitchen preparing a salad. Lettuce and tomatoes and other assorted healthy things lay spread across the countertop. She was working on slicing a green pepper with a large knife. The smell of the pepper was strong and she began slicing more rapidly, thinking about how hungry she was. The late evening sun splashed through the tall window over the sink and cast a soft red glow across the room. The cell phone rang in her purse sitting behind her on the counter. She wiped her hands on a towel and walked over to answer it.

She could see on the display that it was Alex. She flipped open the phone. "Hi Dear."

Alex's voice sounded loud as he tried to speak over the sound of the plane's engines. "Hi honey. We're in the air, about a half hour out of LaGuardia. Should be landing in Charlevoix in another forty-five minutes."

"Who is *we?*"

"Anna's come along. We have to keep working on the case. I'm sorry, but there's just no time to waste."

"Off course, whatever you think," she answered, trying to hold back her true feelings about the intrusion of the *she-lawyer*, as Sally not so affectionately called her.

"Would you mind driving over to pick us up?" Alex asked.

"Megan and I left the Jeep out there for when you came in."

"Oh, that's right, thanks. Are you at the house?"

Sally tucked the phone between her shoulder and ear, and returned to her cutting board. "Yes, I'll be here. Have you eaten? I'm making up a salad."

"The pilots had some food for us. We'll be fine."

Sally chopped harder at the green pepper. *Oh, I'm sure everything is just fine!*

"Sally, are you still there?"

She threw the knife down and grabbed the phone again, walking over to the window to look out at the lake. "I'm here."

"How's my beautiful daughter?"

"She's doing fine." Sally's spirits brightened, thinking about her stepdaughter. "Her old boyfriend, Rick, is back for the summer, but he may have a little competition. You remember Will Truegood? His family has been friends of ours for years."

"Sure, I remember Will. How did that little affair come together?"

"We ran into him downtown the other day after the service for George." Sally watched out the window as a large sailboat turned to head into the channel to Round Lake.

"Well you tell her I miss her and I'm looking forward to giving you both a big hug when I get up there."

His words made her realize how much she missed him, too. "Be safe darling and I'll see you soon."

Alex said goodbye and Sally flipped the phone closed and walked over to put it back in her purse. She knew she was being unreasonable about Anna Bataglia. She was just so damned arrogant and spending way too much time with Alex. Sally didn't really have anything specific to be jealous about, but memories of infidelity in her first marriage years ago still left her overly sensitive. Alex had never given her any reason to doubt his feelings for her, or his faithfulness to their marriage.

She reached again for the knife and rolled a tomato onto the cutting board. With a hard whack, she sliced the tomato down the middle and the sound echoed out through the empty house.

***

Sheriff Elam Stone sat in his small office, looking at the stacks of unattended paperwork that were continuing to pile up. Wrappers and an empty paper cup were all that was left of his dinner. He thought about just throwing a match on the entire mess to make it go away. Most everyone had gone home for the evening. The night shift, even in the summer, was pretty sparse after all the recent budget cuts. His phone rang, breaking the silence and it startled him. He reached for the receiver. It was Jacob Henry, the County Coroner.

"Hey Elam, glad I caught you. Just got a call from the lab down in TC. They've been looking over that knife pretty close. It had been underwater quite awhile, but they were able to get some partial prints and trace DNA off the handle and blade. They're running it through the system, getting some help from the folks down in Lansing."

"You think there's enough there to get an ID?" Watts asked.

"They're not sure."

"How long you think they'll need?"

He heard his old friend laugh on the other end of the phone. "Damn, seems like all the computer crap they use these days shouldn't take more than a few minutes, you know, like on CSI on TV."

Elam Stone laughed with his friend. "So why does it take a week to get anything around here?"

"Good question. I'll keep after them," Henry said.

"Alright, talk to you," Stone said as he hung up the phone. He reached for the paper cup and saw that there was only ice left from his drink. He poured a couple of cubes into his mouth and swirled them around with his tongue, thinking about the investigation of George Hansen's death. A thought came to him and he reached for a phone book on his credenza. Finding the number, he picked up the phone again. The phone rang three times at the other end before he heard an answer.

"Hello?"

"Sally, this is Elam Stone down at the Sheriff's office. How are you tonight?"

He listened to Sally's puzzled answer on the other end of the line. "Well hello Sheriff, what's happened?"

"I'm not sure Sally, but I'd like to talk to you about George Hansen."

"About George?"

"Yeah, and you know, if it's not too much trouble, would you mind if I stopped over for a few minutes? I've got just a couple of questions you might be able to help me with."

"No, it's no trouble," Sally answered, concern still clear in her response. "But what's happened?"

"Why don't I just stop over. You're sure it's not a bad time?"

"No, please come right over. I'm just having a bite to eat and Alex will be getting into town a bit later."

"Thanks, Sally," he said. "I'll be right there. Shouldn't take more than a few minutes." He put the receiver back in its cradle and looked for his keys under the food wrappers and files on his desk.

Five minutes later he pulled into the driveway of Sally's house on Michigan Avenue. The flowers and shrubs all around the house were breaking out in early summer bloom and shadows from the tall oaks lay across the well kept lawn. He parked his patrol cruiser and went up to the front porch. He knocked on the sidelight window pane, looking inside. He saw Sally walk around a corner to come to the door. As she opened it, he thought back to her mother, Emily. Elam had known Jonathan and Emily back before their accident. Sally's mother had worked on a few medical issues for the Sheriff's Department over the years. He thought about what a damn shame it was that they were gone, and Sally's daughter, too. He also had heard about the trouble that Jonathan and his brother had with the legal system back in the 40's, but that had been before his time. He knew that Jonathan had been cleared of the charges in the murder of George's sister. It had been the older brother, Luke McKendry, apparently in a drunken rage who had taken the life of Catherine Hansen.

"Hello Elam, come in," Sally said, holding the door open for him. She led him out to the sun porch and offered him a seat. "Can I get you anything to drink?"

"No, really I'm fine, thanks." He settled himself in and watched as Sally sat across the small coffee table from him. Reaching for a pad of paper and pen in his shirt pocket, he said, "You sure have a beautiful view up here on the bluff."

"Yes, it's wonderful, a little blustery in the winter, though."

He looked through his random notes on the pad and then up at Sally. "Now I don't want you to get too upset at this point. I know how close you were to George."

Sally leaned forward, "What in the world's happened?"

"I would appreciate it if you would keep this confidential for the time being," he said.

"Of course."

"Well, here's the thing," he started. "We have more than a little reason to believe that George's death may not have been accidental."

Sally had a confused look spread across her face. "Not accidental?"

"Yeah, you see the coroner's report shows that he didn't die of natural causes. His lungs were full of lake water."

"Full of water? But…"

"Sally, George Hansen drowned that day out at the lake. The coroner's sure of it."

"But he was found in his fishing boat."

"We think he may have been pulled back into the boat," Watts said.

"You mean someone found him and just left him in his boat?" Sally had a glass of iced tea in her hands and placed it down on the table.

The sheriff squirmed a bit in his seat to get more comfortable. "Well, we think …"

"You mean you think somebody *killed* him?" she said.

Stone looked at Sally for a moment and then nodded. "Yes, that's exactly what it looks like." He saw her sit back in her chair, shaking her head. She looked out the window at the lake.

"How can that be? Not George… who would do this?"

"Well, that's what I thought you might be able to help me with. Do you have any idea who George might have been having some issues with?"

Sally let out an exasperated sigh. "God, I can't imagine. I swear the man was a saint."

"I know you haven't been up here as much in the past few years, but can you think of anyone that would have cause to want George, well…?"

"Sheriff, I'm just so shocked by this whole thing," she said. "I can't imagine who would want to hurt George. Have you talked to Elizabeth?"

"I've been trying to reach her. I guess she's on her way out to Montana."

"Yeah, she should be there by now."

"We'll get in touch with her, but I know you and George were real close and I just thought something might come to mind."

They both turned as they heard the garage door going up.

***

Alex pulled into the driveway with Anna sitting beside him in the Jeep.

He saw the sheriff's cruiser parked in front of the house. "What in hell is the sheriff doing here?" he said with alarm in his voice.

"God, I can't imagine they're trying to serve another warrant for you up here," the lawyer said.

"A warrant? No, I just wonder if everything's okay with Sally and Megan." He touched the garage door opener and pulled in quickly. He left Anna behind and went through the door into the house. "Sally?"

"We're on the porch, Alex," he heard her call from the back of the house. He kept on down the hallway and saw Sally sitting across the table from an older man in a sheriff's uniform. They both stood up.

"Honey, is everything alright?" Alex asked.

They came together and Alex hugged her tight, smelling the fresh scent of shampoo in her hair. She looked up and kissed him. "I'm so glad you're here," she said.

"What's going on?"

"Alex, this is Sheriff Stone."

The sheriff came over and shook Alex's hand and then looked past him as Anna Bataglia came into the room.

Alex turned, "Oh, Anna, you know Sally."

"Hello Sally, it's nice to see you again," she said, coming over to shake her hand.

Sally returned the greeting. "Anna, this is Sheriff Stone from our County Sheriff's office here in Charlevoix. He has some very troubling news about our friend, George Hansen, who passed away a few days ago."

"What's going on?" Alex asked.

"Elam was just explaining that they have evidence that George may have been murdered," Sally said with sadness in her voice.

"What?" said Alex.

"Why don't we all sit down," the sheriff suggested and they all pulled up chairs around the table. He explained the evidence that they were gathering and again asked if they had any idea who may have wanted George Hansen dead.

"I just can't believe this," said Alex. He reached over and took Sally's hand. He looked at his wife and saw the tears welling up in her eyes.

"We're checking with his law office to see what cases he's been working on," the sheriff said. "They've told us that he was pretty much full-time retired and just stopped by the office a few hours each week to check in with his partners. They're looking through his files to see if there's anything that would seem suspicious."

"I hadn't spoken with George in weeks, actually," said Sally. "It was such a surprise when Elizabeth called us in New York last week to let us know that George was gone."

Sally leaned her head over on Alex's shoulder and he put his arm around her.

"Sheriff Stone," Anna said in a stern lawyer-like tone, "I think maybe you should give Alex and Sally a little time to think about this. I'm sure they'll call if they have any ideas that might help you."

Everyone looked over at her in surprise and there was a stunned silence for a moment.

Alex scratched his forehead, trying to think through what could have possibly happened. "Yes, Sheriff, we will certainly think about any possible circumstances, but we haven't been in that close contact with George in the past months. You're surely checking with others around town?"

"Of course," he answered. "Let me ask one more thing, if you don't mind. Do either of you recall anything George may have said in a

82

conversation when you saw him last, or on the phone about anything that he was working on, or that was bothering him?"

Alex looked over at Sally again. She just shook her head no.

***

Megan walked down the beach below Park Street with her old summer flame Rick Brandtley. They were holding hands and their bare feet splashed in the waves breaking along the shoreline. The wind had calmed through the early evening and Lake Michigan lay flat and a shiny gray in the glare from the sun out towards the horizon. Loose stones were pushed up by the waves along the beach, washed in a thousand soft shining colors near the water, the rest a dull dusty gray up higher on the beach. A small fishing boat trolled slowly out towards the far point. Several people up ahead were letting their dogs run, leashes hanging limp in their hands.

Megan was thinking about how happy she should be that summer was finally here. School was over and she was in Charlevoix, back on the *EmmaLee*, and back with the boy she had been dreaming about all winter. She looked up at Rick walking beside her, sizing up the lines of his face and the style of his hair, feeling the warmth of his hand in hers. She remembered cold nights back in February where moments like this were all she could think about.

So why wasn't she floating above the sand, blissfully enjoying every moment of this long anticipated reunion? She felt Rick reach his arm around her waist to pull her closer and they continued walking along the water's edge. Memories of last summer started coming back to her. Their first kiss out on the beach at a bonfire; the first time he had asked her out on a date, just the two of them. It had been a wonderful night exploring the quaint streets of Harbor Springs up along the north shore of Little Traverse Bay. By the end of the summer they had become practically inseparable. Her father and Sally had been tolerant, but clearly concerned about how much time she had been spending with just one boy. They both seemed to get along well with Rick and he was always on his best behavior around them.

It seemed that she was always thinking about him that first summer; always having him somewhere in the back of her mind through the long school year; longing to see him over the Christmas holidays. And now, here they were together again, and all she could seem to think about was why didn't it feel as special as it did last year? Had they really changed all that much over the past months? If anything, Rick had grown more attractive, his body filling out and his face already tan and maturing with a soft brown stubble.

He stopped and turned to face her, pulling her into his arms and looking down into her eyes. She fell into him, laying her face on his shoulder, trying to search for the old familiar comfort and thrill from past memories of their time together. Lost in her thoughts, she felt his hand pull her chin up to his face and she looked into his eyes and smiled an uneven smile.

"Why so sad?" he asked.

She looked away out across the lake, a dozen thoughts racing through her mind.

"Megan?"

She shook her head, looking back at him. "Rick, I don't know, it's just been so long and now we're finally back here together and for some reason it just doesn't seem real yet. Why don't you pinch me," she said and laughed.

He took her up on the offer and pinched her gently on her bottom. She laughed and pushed him away. "Alright, so we're really here," she said.

Rick reached for her hand again and they continued on down along the shoreline. The sun was just touching the horizon and glowed a soft red and orange against the sky.

"This is going to be a great summer, Megan. School's over, all our friends are back up here. My dad bought a new wakeboard boat last week up at the marina that is so hot. We'll have to go for a ride tomorrow."

Megan heard what he was saying, but found that she wasn't really listening. Her mind was wandering off to nothing in particular, just a general sense of *why do I want to be any place but here right now?*

"Megan?" he asked again. "What in hell's the matter with you tonight?"

The hardened edge in his voice was clear and she looked at him again. "Really Rick, I'm sorry. I'll be alright."

"Don't tell me it's that damn Indian kid today? What was his name?"

She was caught off guard by his question and the sudden switch in the tone of the conversation. She tried to laugh it off. "You mean Will?"

"Yeah, Will Running Beaver, or whatever his name was."

Megan felt a cold chill run up into her brain and anger swell within her. "His name's Will Truegood and you have no reason to make fun of him, or his people, or anything about him. You don't even know him!"

He reached over and placed his hands on her shoulders. "Hey, I'm sorry. Really, I'm sorry. I'm sure he's a nice enough guy, but… but what's it going to look like for everyone to see you running around with another guy like that this summer?"

She tried her best to maintain some sense of calm. "A guy like what?"

"Oh, come on, Megan. You know what I mean. He's a damn local kid and…"

"And what!" she demanded.

"Hey, really… just calm down a bit," he said rubbing her shoulders, but she backed away from him and started to walk back toward the path up to town. He ran up next to her and tried to take her arm, but she pulled away.

"Rick, I'm going to go home," she said, walking with purpose back up the beach. He stopped and watched her walking away, a look of bewilderment on his face.

She looked back and saw him standing there.

"I'll call you tomorrow," he yelled.

She stopped for a moment and then nodded before heading back up the beach to town.

***

Alex Clark stood at the island in the kitchen with his wife and lawyer, an interesting combination of female forces, he thought to himself. Elam Stone had left some time ago and Alex had just opened a bottle of Cabernet. He unscrewed the cork from the corkscrew and sniffed it before placing it down on the granite countertop. The musty and fruity smell hung in his

85

nostrils. Sally had placed three glasses down in front of him and he poured the red wine into each glass. The deep red color of the wine splashed out into the clear glasses. Alex handed one to both Sally and Anna.

"To our great friend, George Hansen." He lifted his glass. "May he be at peace with his Maker." They all touched their glasses together and took a drink. He looked at Sally. "Again, I'm so sorry I couldn't be here for the service. It's just that…"

"I know," Sally interrupted, "you don't have to explain again."

Anna cleared her throat and placed her wine glass down on the counter. "I really am sorry that I've kept Alex away, but there are some very serious issues with this possible indictment that we need to be aggressively preparing for."

"With both of you here," Sally said, "it's probably a good time for me to get completely up to date on what's happening. I've heard Louis Kramer's side of the story."

Alex sighed deeply, shaking his head. "Louis and his financial guy that he insisted on bringing into the business have got us in a very tough spot."

"You know he says that you won't talk to him," Sally said.

"That's at my urging," Anna said. "We needed to get a better understanding of the situation and the details of the indictment before we started comparing information with Louis. It's very important that we distance ourselves from him as much as we can."

"But we are going to sit down with him privately while we're here this week," Alex said.

Sally sipped from her wine glass. "Without getting into all of the details, what are we looking at here?"

Anna walked around the island and then lifted herself up to sit on the counter against the wall. She crossed her long legs out in front of her. Sally couldn't help but look over at Alex to see if he was watching, but saw that he was filling their wine glasses again.

It's a very complex case with several interrelated issues," Anna began, "but fundamentally we're looking at SEC filings that were falsified to inflate earnings, and stock option contracts that were backdated to provide for more favorable returns to the option holders, which just happen to be Louis and his financial guy, Littlefair."

"But also Alex, right?" Sally asked.

"Yes, your husband would have benefited substantially from these fraudulent manipulations."

"Sally, I've told you that I had no knowledge of this. I trusted Louis and I had every reason to do so. We've never had issues like this in all of the years we've been in business together."

"So, why now?"

"There are indications that Louis has gotten in quite a bit over his head on some other business investments that haven't done well. We think he's trying to bail himself out by artificially inflating the value of the stock in this business," Anna said.

"And now we have a major shareholder who has filed an options-related lawsuit against us and is mounting a proxy fight demanding substantial changes in the board and our governance policies," Alex continued.

"Basically, it's a damn mess," Anna said.

"And what is the worst case scenario?" Sally asked.

Alex looked over at Anna. He had asked her to not frighten his wife with potentially how bad this could be, both legally and financially. Anna didn't respond and took a drink from her wine. "Honey, I don't want you to get overly concerned here, but there certainly are risks of significant financial penalties," he said.

"And what about jail?"

Alex looked down at his drink for a moment.

Anna answered the question cautiously on his behalf. "There are definitely civil and criminal charges on the table here. Louis and his team are at much higher risk in each of those cases. I feel that we are pulling together a strong defense for Alex. The fact that he has never exercised any of his stock options in this business, sold any of his stock, or benefited financially in any way to date from these manipulations, speaks very strongly in his favor."

Sally walked over and put her arm around her husband's shoulders and kissed him on the cheek. "I'm so sorry about all of this."

Anna jumped down from the counter. "We should set up a private breakfast meeting with Louis for the morning," she said. "Nowhere in public; maybe out at his place."

Sally squirmed and stepped back to lean against the sink. "If you want to keep this confidential, I wouldn't go anywhere near his wife's house. Mary Alice Gregory-Kramer is the last person you would want to trust for her discretion. Why don't you have him over here, or even out on the *EmmaLee?*"

"I'll go call his cell," Anna said. "And then I need to get down into town to get a hotel room."

Alex looked over at Sally. She caught his silent suggestion and offered, "You will certainly stay here with us. The guest room is all made up and we have lots of room for you and Alex to work. Or, if you'd like a little more privacy, you can stay out on the boat."

"Thank you, Sally. That's very nice of you. If it's not too much trouble, maybe I should stay out at the boat; give you two some time to yourselves as well."

Alex reached for his cell phone on the clip on his belt. "Let me call the crew and have someone meet us down at the docks with the launch. We can take you down in a few minutes." He made the call.

Anna came around the counter and stood next to Sally. "Really, I don't want you to think that we're not doing everything possible here to protect Alex. He really is innocent of any wrongdoing, although as president of the company, his oversight and controls will certainly be challenged."

"Anna, I know you and your firm are the best. Alex speaks very highly of you."

"Well, he's a good client. He lets us do our jobs," Anna replied.

Sally studied her face for any deeper meaning or innuendo, but detected nothing more. "Yes, I'm sure," she said, "and thank you for everything you're doing."

Alex finished his call down to the *EmmaLee's* crew. "They'll meet us down there in a few minutes at the docks. Sally, what do you make of all this with the sheriff and George?"

"I'm just in shock about the whole thing," she answered. "I can't imagine who would want to hurt George Hansen. I'm going to try to reach his wife Liz out in Montana later tonight."

Ten minutes later, Sally and Alex were down at the city docks in Charlevoix, waiting for the launch with Anna Bataglia. The *EmmaLee* rested at anchor out in the middle of Round Lake surrounded by dozens of smaller sailboats and cruisers.

"God, she's beautiful," Alex said.

"Well thank you, dear," Sally said and then laughed, knowing he was talking about his boat. "Sometimes I have to wonder who you love more."

"I can tell you," Anna said, "he talks about you a lot more than he does about that old ship."

"Well, that's certainly comforting," Sally replied.

Alex pulled Sally into a big bear hug and kissed her. "*EmmaLee* is the one who should be jealous. You won my heart all those years ago here in this sleepy little town, and it's never been the same between me and the boat," he said laughing.

"You're a lucky woman, Sally," Anna said. "When he first found this old boat, it's all he could talk about. I couldn't get him to focus on anything else."

"I didn't know you two had known each other for so long," Sally said.

"I've worked with Anna and her firm for years. I told you, they're the best."

"Thank you, Alex," Anna said, "we appreciate your business."

The launch pulled up beside the dock with one of the *EmmaLee's* deckhands at the controls. "Good evening ladies, Mr. Clark," he said as he helped them down into the long wooden launch, painted white to match the ship. They sat down on seats in the bow of the boat and the crewman steered them back out to the *EmmaLee*. "Beautiful night, isn't it?" he said.

"Yes, it's good to be back up here," Alex answered. He looked out across the quaint beauty of Round Lake; the incredible boats tied up along the city docks or moored out in the small inland harbor; the town of Charlevoix spread out up on the hill and the magnificent homes that had been built over the years all around the lake. He remembered the first day he had brought the *EmmaLee* back to Charlevoix. He had met Sally soon after they had tied up at the docks and had been so taken with her right from the start. It had been an interesting couple of weeks, getting acquainted and working through issues of their pasts and what the future together might hold. He felt so blessed that they had come together. She was the one true sanctuary that he could come back to, particularly at times like these when so many other things in his life were falling apart.

"Daddy!"

Alex turned to see his daughter come out of the side cabin door from the bridge. She ran up and jumped into his arms, giving him a big kiss. "Hi sweetie, I missed you."

"I missed you, too," Megan answered. "I have so much to tell you."

"Sally said that you were out with Rick tonight."

"I was, but well… I decided to get home early tonight. I just got off the phone with Becca and she's coming out to spend the night."

"That's great, honey," Alex said. "You know Anna."

Megan walked over and gave her a hug. "Hi Anna, welcome to Charlevoix. Have you been up here before?"

"Hi Megan, no this is my first trip. It's a beautiful place."

"We'll have to go for a cruise tomorrow, maybe out to Beaver Island if the winds don't come up too much. Daddy, can we?"

"We'll see, honey, we have a lot of work to do."

"You have an office here on the boat. You can work there and take some breaks to swim and fish. Wait 'til you hear about this fish I caught."

"We'll see. Sally and I are going to head back to the house. Megan, can you show Anna to one of the berths down below and get her comfortable. Show her where the galley is and who to call if she needs anything."

"Sure, we'll take real good care of her."

"Alex, I'll try to reach Louis tonight. What time do you want to meet out here for breakfast in the morning?" Anna asked.

"Let's roust him early. He hates that. How about 7:00?"

"I'll get it set up. If you don't hear from me, we're on for 7."

Alex and Sally both hugged Megan again and said goodnight.

"Goodnight Alex and thank you Sally for your hospitality and understanding in all this mess."

"Of course."

As Alex and Sally rode back to the docks in the launch, she looked up at her husband. "Is this all going to be okay?"

"What, the business?" he answered. "What's the worst that can happen? They take away one of my companies, I pay some fines and I watch Louis go to jail, the sonofabitch." He managed a strained smile.

"Are you telling me everything?" she asked again, looking into his eyes for any sign of hesitation.

"Trust me, if anyone can make this come out right, it's Anna."

Sally felt less than comforted by the stakes that were being placed in the hands of Anna Bataglia.

Chapter Ten

Emily McKendry was one of the strongest women I've ever known. She brought Jonathan back from the brink when so many others had given up on him. When we found out that my sister was gone, Emily was there for me, too. But, deep down, Emily was like most of us, she had her weaknesses and her fears and she felt real pain like we all do. Her father's passing that day on the big boat down in the bay hit her real hard, but it was the frailty and helplessness of a little girl that got to that place way down deep inside her.

***

Dr. Emily McKendry felt she needed to get back to work the next morning. She had relied on her partner, Dr. Julian Rose, to cover with her patients for the past couple of days and she had to catch up and give the poor man a break. Dr. Rose was 60 years old and had brought her into his practice two years ago with the thought that she would take over when he retired. She got down to the small physician's office they shared on Clinton and let herself in an hour before office appointments would begin. Emily was proud of the practice that she and Julian served and she loved the patients in this quiet little town. So many of them felt almost like family to her. She turned the light on in her office in the back and sat down to sort through phone messages and paperwork.

The office was decorated simply, mostly with pictures of her family and of Jonathan, and of course the family's boat, the *EmmaLee*. Her father had commissioned a model builder to create replicas of the ship for each of his three children. Emily's model of the boat, nearly three feet long, rested on a shelf on the far wall. Looking at it, she found herself reliving that terrible day of her father's heart attack out on the boat at Horton Bay. She put her head down in her hands and tried to hold back the emotions. Tears formed at the corners of her eyes and two drops fell on the papers beneath her. She reached for a handkerchief in her pocket and dried her face.

She heard a knock on the front door. Looking at the clock on the wall she saw that it was still 30 minutes until they would be open for appointments. There was another knock. She got up and walked down the hall to the reception area. Through the glass door she could see a woman standing beside a young girl. The little girl looked to be around eight years old, small and stooped, her head down, as if she was trying to disappear into herself. She had on a worn green print dress and dirty shoes. As Emily came closer she saw that the girl had spots of blood on her dress, apparently from a cut near her mouth, and she was holding her left arm still.

She didn't recognize the woman. Her face was mostly covered by an old wide-brimmed straw hat. What she could see of her face was plain with no hint of makeup. Her clothes were worn and faded, a dirty black skirt and rumpled gray blouse. Her old boots were even dirtier than the little girl's. She reached up to knock again as Emily unlocked and opened the door.

Emily knelt down in front of the young girl. "Are you okay, honey? Let me look at you." She lifted the girl's chin and watched as she grimaced and started to cry softly. She could see an angry bruise spreading out from a cut at the corner of her mouth. The blood was still flowing fresh and several drops had fallen on her dress.

"Can you help us, doctor?" she heard the woman ask.

Emily stood up and held the door for them. "Certainly, come in." She led them back to one of the examination rooms. The little girl moved slowly, walking with a slight limp and still holding on to her arm. In the room, Emily carefully lifted the little girl up on the exam table. "What is your name, honey?"

The little girl continued to look down at the floor, still trying to hold back tears. The woman answered. "This is my daughter Sara, Sara Slayton. I'm her mother."

"What's happened here, Mrs. Slayton?

"Can you please just help her?"

"Of course I can, but you need to tell me what's happened to your daughter."

Emily went to the sink and washed her hands and came back with some wet cloths to wash the wounds on the little girl's face. She looked over at the mother again.

"Just help her, please," the woman said, tears now forming in her eyes, too.

Emily gently touched at the cut on her face, dabbing away the blood.

The little girl flinched, but didn't cry out.

"Sara, can you tell me how you got hurt?"

She didn't look up or try to speak.

Emily noticed that she was still holding her arm. "What's happened to your arm, Sara? Where does it hurt?"

The blood flow on her mouth seemed to have stopped and Emily reached over to examine her arm. Pulling away her other hand, she gently tried to lift the little girl's left arm. She immediately cried out loud in pain and pulled back, grabbing it again.

"I'm sorry, sweetie, but we need to look at it. I won't move it again. Where does it hurt?"

The girl hesitated and then pointed to her elbow. Emily could see that it was hanging limp and at an odd angle and she had a strong sense that it was dislocated. "Here, let's get your face cleaned up. It doesn't look like you're going to need any stitches." She saw the little girl flinch again and look over at her mother with a frightened face. "Are you hurt anywhere else?"

Sara Slayton slowly shook her head no. "Mrs. Slayton, I think we need to take Sara down to the hospital to have an x-ray taken of this arm. I'm afraid it may be dislocated, if not broken." She looked at the woman for a response and saw the same frightened face that her little daughter had.

"I can't pay for a hospital. Can't you take care of her here?"

"Sara needs an x-ray. Don't worry about the cost. We can work something out, but you need to tell me now what's happened!"

Mrs. Slayton started to cry. "I really don't know. She was out in the barn helping her pa this morning with some chores and then she come running into the house all tore up."

"Did you ask your husband what happened?"

"No," she paused, "no, I didn't talk to Harold. I don't know what happened. I just wanted to get Sara into town to get help."

"Do you know if she's hurt anywhere else?"

"I don't know," the mother said, crying. "I really don't know!"

"Where do you live?" Emily asked.

"We have a farm down south of town, headed down t'wards Elk Rapids."

Emily reached for a clipboard on the counter. "What's your full name, Mrs. Slayton?"

"Agnes, Agnes Slayton. This is my daughter, Sara." Tears continued to stream down her face and her eyes were flushed red and swollen.

Emily noticed a bruise on Sara's neck and then on one of her arms. "I'll drive us down to the hospital."

An hour later the emergency room physician, Dr. Ellard, brought the x-ray slides into the exam room at the small Charlevoix hospital and hung them up on the light board for him and Emily to take a look at. They both could see the ugly break in her bone just above the elbow.

Dr. Ellard shook his head and spoke softly. Sara Slayton and her mother were behind them at the exam table. "Damn," he said, "this little girl took a pretty good fall for a break this bad."

Emily just nodded, a sad sick feeling coming over her. She turned to look at little Sara, and her heart ached at the expression on the girl's face. No one so little should be so frightened, she thought. Trying to force a smile across her own face, Emily said, "Sara, looks like you've got a pretty bad break in your arm there, but we're going to get you fixed up and get a cast on it, and I'll be the first to sign it for you, if you'll let me."

Sara looked up and then finally nodded before she looked up at her mother for confirmation. Agnes Slayton spoke softly. "Please do what you have to do and thank you."

Emily walked over and took Sara's other hand in hers. "Sara, I'm going to leave you here with Dr. Ellard. He's a really good doctor and he's going to make you feel much better. I need to get back to my office to take care of my other patients, but I want you to come back to see me the day after tomorrow to make sure you're doing alright, okay?"

The little girl nodded again without speaking.

"Mrs. Slayton, I need to speak with you for a moment out in the hall." The woman followed her out slowly

"Mrs. Slayton, I'm going to have to speak firmly with you."

The woman looked down at the floor, apparently totally overwhelmed by all that had happened.

"If you can't help me understand what's caused these wounds with your daughter, I'm going to be forced to call the sheriff and have him come out and talk to you and your husband." Emily reached over and took the woman's hands in her own. "Agnes, from the bruises I've seen on other parts of Sara's body, it looks like she's been falling a lot."

"No, it's not like that, really, she'll be okay," she said, a tired resignation in her voice.

"I want you to bring Sara back to see me on Wednesday morning and I want you to bring your husband. If you don't come, I'll be out to see you with the sheriff. Do you understand?"

"I'll bring her back."

***

Jennifer Harris stood with her friend Elaine in the sand that was cooling now as the sun just dropped below the far horizon of Lake Michigan. The beach bonfire roared as more wood was thrown on the pile. The fire crackled and spit and red coals glowed blazing hot in the darkening evening. A southern wind blew the smoke down the beach and off over the water of Little Traverse Bay.

Jennifer had a coke in her hand that she had pulled from an ice-filled cooler. The fire was surrounded by ten other kids, all that she knew as part of their summer crowd. Andy Welton hadn't arrived yet and she looked up the path into the woods again to see if he was coming.

"He'll be here, Jenn," Elaine said. "Don't act so desperate."

"I'm not desperate, but he said he would be here and I had to do some serious talking to get my mother to let me come out here," Jennifer said. "It's a good thing my father went back to Chicago for a few days this morning, or I'd be stuck in the house for the rest of the summer."

"Here comes your *sweetie*," Elaine sad in a mocking tone.

Jennifer watched as Andy Welton walked down the narrow path through the beach grass. He was with a couple of his friends and she could see that they were all having a little trouble walking in the loose sand. As they came closer she heard their loud joking and laughter. The boy behind Andy handed him a bottle and he took a long drink before handing it back. As he turned to continue on he tripped and fell. His friends laughed even more and he lifted himself up wiping sand from his face and clothes.

"Shut up you assholes!" he yelled.

The other boys just laughed harder as they passed the bottle around.

"I thought there was no booze out here tonight," Jennifer said to her friend.

Elaine just laughed. "They're just blowing off a little steam. You don't have to drink with them."

"I think I'm going to puke just thinking about it," Jennifer said.

Andy saw the two girls and staggered around the bonfire to get to them. With a heavy slur he said, "Jennifer Harris… the fairest of maidens." He tried to put his arms around her, but Jennifer pushed him away. The smell of whiskey on his breath was more than she could handle.

"God, Welton, you're tanked," Elaine said, laughing.

"I'm no such thing, just a couple of pops before we got here. You look great, Jenn."

She could see that he was having a hard time keeping his head steady and his eyes focused on her. "Andy, I just can't do this tonight."

"But I thought maybe you and me could have a little private time up in the dunes tonight."

Elaine giggled, but Jennifer looked at him angrily and shook her head. "Andy Welton, you know how much trouble I'm already in from drinking, and then you show up like this."

"I'm okay, really." He reached out and took her arm and tried to lead her away from the fire. She pulled away.

"No, Andy. I need to get home."

"How 'bout just a kiss…" He lunged for her and lost his balance again, nearly falling at her feet.

"Elaine, are you going to drive me home, or do I have to walk?"

Her friend just looked at her for a moment.

"I can't believe you're even thinking about this. I need you to take me home!"

"Jennifer, I'm sorry if I…" Andy mumbled.

"Yeah, I'm sorry, too."

***

Sammy Truegood was riding his bike into town to meet with his lawyer, George Hansen. It was late morning and the air was still cool in the shade of the tall oaks along the road. He watched the beautiful homes passing by that had been built along the crest of the dunes on Lake Michigan. The lawns and gardens were immaculately kept and large cars, spotlessly clean and shining, sat in the driveways. He looked up and marveled at the sight of the tree canopy racing by overhead, bits of blue sky and the light of the morning sun shining through the patterns of leaves.

He came up to the stop sign at the main street into the town of Charlevoix. He could see down the big hill to the bridge across the channel into Round Lake and on past into the commercial district of shops and restaurants. Looking to his left for traffic, he pedaled his bike out onto the road and started down the hill. It was steep and his bike picked up speed. He braked as he approached the bridge where the road narrowed. He sensed something over his left shoulder and turned to see a dark green sedan moving at the same speed, keeping a constant distance just behind his rear wheel. The sun left a bright glare on the windshield and he couldn't see who was inside. He slowed even more as he came to the drawbridge and the car slowed with him.

As he glided across the bridge as close to the curb as he could stay, the green car slowly came alongside and someone rolled down the window in the front passenger seat. Sammy could hear loud voices and laughter come from inside and then he saw one of the boys from out on the beach trail, the day he had been with Jennifer and Elaine. He didn't know the boy's name.

"Hey chief," the boy yelled, leaning out of the window of the car. "Nice ride you have there. What kind of mileage does it get?" More laughter echoed out from inside the car. While he didn't know his name, he could see Andy Welton behind the wheel of the car.

Sammy was thinking that he was in no mood to take any aggravation from these summer punks. Then, suddenly the car veered to the right directly into Sammy and his bike. There was nowhere to go except into the back of a black pickup truck that was parked in front of the stores on Bridge Street. As his bike hit the back of the truck hard, Sammy braced and tried to push up with his legs. He was thrown out over the handlebars as he heard the screeching metallic sounds of the bike crashing against the steel bumper. Immediately he crashed down into the cargo bed of the truck and then slammed into the back wall of the truck's cab, pain shooting through his hip and back. It had all happened in a split second and he paused for a moment to see where any more pain would be coming from. He managed to lift himself up and look through the back window at his attackers driving away. A hand was stretched out of the passenger's window, leaving him a not so gracious gesture.

Several people came over to help him, but he waved them away. He rolled over on his back and looked up at the sky. His body was shaking and he tried to control a rage that was pounding in his head. The words of his lawyer, George Hansen, came back to him. *You need to stay out of trouble and whatever you do, stay away from anybody who was near that beach that day.*

Chapter Eleven

Megan Clark looked at the lights illuminating Bridge Street and the city docks along the Round Lake waterfront. She and Rebecca Holmes sat in lounge chairs on the foredeck of the *EmmaLee*. A large bowl of popcorn rested on a table between them along with glasses filled with iced soft drinks. The ship's intercom system played a song from a Mary Chapin Carpenter CD. The lyrics from *Don't be late for your Life* carried softly across the deck of the boat, only somewhat diminished by the noise from other nearby boats.

Above them she could see that the sky was clear and the shapes of constellations were just coming into focus as the night darkened. A thin slice of moon made its first appearance over the tree line. Both of the girls had brought blankets out as the evening cooled and they had curled up in them in the chairs, comfortable and warm.

"So who's this *Anna* chick?" Rebecca asked.

Megan had been preoccupied with the sights and sounds of the little harbor and she didn't hear the question. "I'm sorry…"

"Anna, who's this Anna person we met?"

"My father's attorney. She's helping him with some legal issues."

"Man, she's some hot number. What's Sally think about all this?"

Megan laughed and reached for her drink and a handful of popcorn. "My dad's so straight, I'm sure Sally has nothing to worry about. They're all having a big meeting out here on the boat in the morning. *Uncle Louis* will be here. You've met him haven't you? My dad's partner?"

Rebecca nodded and said, "Yeah, the crazy man who married Mary Alice. What was he thinking?"

"Yeah, I can't believe it's lasted this long," Megan said.

"So tell me what happened with Rick tonight? I need all the details, come on."

Megan didn't answer right away. She sighed and shook her head. "You know, this is the strangest thing. I've been looking forward to this summer for months now and getting back up here to see Rick and now we're here and suddenly I just don't seem to feel the same attraction."

"What did he do?"

"You know, he didn't do anything. He couldn't be nicer," Megan explained. "He seems a little miffed about seeing Will Truegood here, but I've told him that Will is just a friend. I can't believe he's really jealous."

"Are you crazy? Men are stupid about stuff like this. They get jealous if we leave too big of a tip with a waiter. And Will, he's this good looking *outdoors* type with long black hair and you're spending time with him. What do you expect?"

"I don't know and I'm beginning to think I don't really care."

***

Louis Kramer hit the speed dial on his cell phone and waited as the numbers were dialed. He was sitting out on the dock at his in-laws summer beach house, a cold frosted beer mug in his hand, now half empty. He had turned the lights out on the dock and he sat in the darkness with only the glow from the end of his cigar illuminating the space around him. The waves were coming in from the southwest and they broke repeatedly behind him on the shore.

"Hey Louis," the voice on the receiver said. It was Bob Littlefair, the soon to be former CFO of Alex and Louis' newest subsidiary. "I thought I said not to call me unless it's absolutely necessary."

"I know," Louis said, "and it is. Where are you anyway?"

"You're better off not knowing for now, but I have to tell you, I've got to come in. My lawyer's telling me the Feds are spitting mad. Me disappearing is only making it worse and I'm not going to run from this damned thing for the rest of my life!"

101

"Please just wait another day or so. I'm meeting with Alex in the morning. He and his bitch lawyer have finally agreed to sit down and get our stories straight on all this."

"Don't trust them for a minute, Lou!" Littlefair said. "They've got one thing in mind and that's saving his ass."

"I know that and I plan to show both of them that Alex is a lot more wrapped up in this shit than he seems to think."

***

Sally and Alex had stopped in at the Weathervane along the channel on their way back home to have a drink. They sat at the small bar on tall stools, two glasses of wine in front of them. There was the normal busy summer crowd dining and drinking, enjoying the beautiful evening in Charlevoix. The place was darkly lit with candles helping to set the mood. The bartender stood nearby drying glasses, holding them up to the dim light to check for spots. The sounds of an acoustic guitar could just be heard above the crowd.

Alex rested his hand on Sally's on top of the bar. "It is so nice to finally get up here and away from the city," he said, "and to be with you."

"I was hoping you'd remember that last part," Sally said. She leaned over and kissed him on the cheek. "I've really missed you."

Alex pulled her closer and held her chin gently to kiss her on the mouth. "I've really missed this," he said and kissed her again.

She smiled and looked back at this man who had come into her life so suddenly those few summers ago here in Charlevoix. The past five years had gone by so quickly as time often does, she thought, but what a blessing to have Alex and Megan, to be part of a family again. To have two people that loved her and shared their lives with her. For so many years after the boat accident that had taken her parents, Jonathan and Emily McKendry, and her only daughter Ellen, she had been drifting aimlessly. Her friends, Gwen Roberts and George Hansen, had helped to keep her from going completely over the deep end after the tragedy. And then Alex Clark had come to town and given her life back.

She rubbed the back of Alex's hand. "Are you getting better looking with age, or is it just the low lights in here?" she said and then smiled.

Alex just shook his head and took a drink from his glass of wine. "That's quite a pick-up line. You think I'm that easy?"

"Oh, I *know* how easy you are."

"So how's the water in the hot tub?"

"About perfect."

Alex waived to get the attention of the bartender to get the check. The man nodded and went over to the cash register to ring up the bill. "I keep thinking about George and the sheriff's visit. Would you have ever thought that anyone would be out to hurt George?"

Sally finished the wine that was left in her glass. "No, there has to be another explanation, unless he was having a problem with something in his legal practice. He occasionally dealt with some tough customers. I didn't think he was really working that much anymore."

They walked out of the restaurant and headed up the hill toward the house. Sally felt Alex's warm hand in hers. They walked slowly, enjoying the night. "By the way, I've been meaning to ask, of all the lawyers in New York, you had to find one that looks like Eva Longoria."

Alex laughed. "She is pretty damned attractive isn't she," Alex said.

Sally pulled her hand away and punched him playfully in the arm. "Alex Clark, she better be the *best* damned lawyer in New York, or…"

"Or what?" Alex interrupted.

"Or you'll be in that hot tub all by yourself for a very long time."

***

Connor Harris walked out onto the porch of the family's summer home in Charlevoix. He moved slowly and with measured steps. At just over 84 years of age, a long series of health issues continued to slow him down. What little hair was left on his head was a dull white and deep circles sagged beneath his eyes. Brown age spots stood out on his pale skin.

Having been released from prison just five years ago after being convicted of numerous charges related to bribery, extortion and tax evasion involving large real estate deals in downtown Chicago, he had spent the past few years in semi-retirement working behind the scenes to help his son's business. Dylan Harris was forty-six years old, lived in Chicago and had taken over what was left of his father's crumbling real estate business when he had gone to prison in 1987.

Connor sat in a chair and looked out across the lake. While the body continued to fade, his mind remained sharp and focused. Memories of past summers always came back to him when he sat out on this old porch.

Chapter Twelve

That Slayton family that lived out south of town, they were a bad lot, the most of them. How Harold Slayton ever had a wife and daughter as sweet as Agnes and little Sara, I'll never pretend to understand. His two brothers were darn near as bad; too much whiskey and too much anger. They'd been beaten by their daddy and the whole cycle just seemed to carry on.

***

Emily looked at the clock on the wall of her office and was surprised to see it was after 7:00. Office hours had ended at 5, but she had kept on, trying to catch up on paperwork. Her desk was still covered with random piles of reports and other assorted medical forms. Behind the desk, a large bookshelf held volumes of medical texts and a few pictures of her family and Jonathan. She rubbed her temples and pushed thick curls of wavy brown hair back out of her eyes. There was a small window on the wall to her left and she could see the row of low buildings across Clinton Street. A few people walked by on the sidewalk including a young mother pushing a small child in a stroller. She remembered Sara Slayton from earlier in the morning. Her heart still ached for the little girl. Dr. Ellard from down at the hospital had called just before noon to tell her that he set the broken bone in Sara's arm. He was very concerned that there were other signs of past injuries and assorted bruises. *How could any human being hurt a child like that?*

Emily stood and took her white jacket off with the name tag, *Dr. McKendry* above the chest pocket and hung it on a coat rack sitting in the corner of the office. She thought about calling Jonathan, but she knew he was up at the new house doing some painting before they moved in. *I'll see him in a few minutes.*

Out on the sidewalk, she turned and locked the door to the office. She was tired, but it had been a good day to immerse herself in her work and try to start putting the loss of her father behind her. Her car was parked back behind the building. As she walked around the corner to the parking area, a man was standing right in front of her, leaning against the building. He was only a few feet away and Emily could smell the liquor on the man mixed with stale sweat. He wore old faded dungarees over a green plaid shirt that was frayed at the sleeves and an old brown felt hat on his head that was sweat-stained and dirty. His face was weather worn and creased, and a stubble of gray beard stood out on his reddish face.

The man pushed himself away from the wall and stood right in front of her, grabbing her arm. Emily stood frozen; too shocked to understand what was happening, or what to do. He just looked at her for a few moments through eyes that seemed clouded and distant. When he spoke his breath made her wince and pull back.

"You the doc who seen my little girl, Sara, this mornin'?"

Emily was too frightened to answer and looked around quickly to see if she should yell for someone to help her. There was no one else in the parking lot or coming down the sidewalk.

He grabbed her arm more urgently and pulled her close to his face. "You answer me, godammit!"

Emily turned her face and tried to keep her fear under control. "Please, just let me go home," she pleaded.

He pulled her along until they were over behind a large, dirty green truck. "I'm gonna ask you one more time if you's the one saw Sara today?"

Emily gathered herself and looked directly into his eyes, anger beginning to replace her initial fear. "Yes, I saw your daughter, Sara," Emily said, trying to keep her voice from breaking. "She was hurt very badly."

"Well hell, she just fell down in the barn. Didn't think she even needed to see no doctor."

"Her arm was broken very badly and she was covered with bruises." Emily's anger continued to surge. "If you hurt that little girl again, I swear I'll have the sheriff out there!"

Harold Slayton sneered and pulled her closer. "I'm tellin' you right now, lady, if you talk to anybody 'bout this, I'll be back to see you again and we'll be doing a lot more than just talkin'! You understand?"

Emily just stared at him, trying as hard as she could not to shake and show her fear. She wouldn't give him that satisfaction.

He shook her by both arms and said, "Do you hear what I'm sayin'?"

Emily nodded slowly. She felt his grip let go and he backed away. She watched as he opened the door to the green truck and climbed in, never taking his eyes away from her. She knew right then that she would never forget the look of hatred and evil in those eyes. He pulled out of the parking lot and drove away.

***

Elizabeth Hansen brought a tray of iced tea into the living room of their house. Mary and Sammy Truegood sat on the couch together facing her husband, George. She set the tray on the coffee table and handed the glasses to everyone. The window behind the couch looked across to the woods on Park Street above the beach on Lake Michigan. Through the tall pines, glimpses of the lake could be seen, the water glittering a bright silver color in the late evening light.

Sammy Truegood had a bandage on his forehead with a small trace of blood showing through. His mother dabbed at her eyes with a handkerchief trying to stem the tears that were gathering in small pools. George Hansen sat forward in his chair, his hands clenched in front of him. "Are you sure you got the license number correctly, Sammy?"

The boy nodded.

"I'm going to go call the sheriff. You think there were three boys in the car?"

"Yes, Mr. Hansen. It was the boys that were down at the beach that night… when Jennifer got hurt," Sammy said.

"Did you do *anything* to provoke them?" George asked.

107

"No, I told you, I was just riding down the hill and they pulled up next to me and then they ran me off the road."

"We're lucky they didn't kill you," Elizabeth said.

"Are you sure you're not hurt anywhere else? I can have Dr. McKendry come over," George offered.

"No, thanks, I'm really okay, just a couple of scrapes."

George stood up and walked toward the kitchen. "I'll be back in a minute. Let me see if I can reach the sheriff or someone down at their office.

An hour later, Sheriff Willy Potts rang the doorbell. Elizabeth let him in and he joined George and the Truegoods in the living room. Sammy explained what had happened earlier on his bike, describing the car and its occupants and giving the sheriff the license number.

Potts sat there shaking his head and taking notes on a small pad as he listened to the story. "Well, it sure sounds like Andy Welton and his two buddies. I'll head over there tonight and have a little talk with him and his parents."

"Would you like some tea, Sheriff?" Elizabeth offered.

"No thanks, Liz. I'm going to get on over there before it gets any later."

"Willy, I think we should press charges here," George said. "This is completely unacceptable. They could have killed the boy."

Potts reached for his hat on the table. "I'll be happy to take a complaint on those damn fools, George," he said. "You know I've been talking some more to the Harris girl and her little friend, Elaine, and also these boys. The more they talk, the more the stories start heading in different directions, about that night out at the beach I mean."

"Different directions?" George asked.

"Well, Jennifer Harris doesn't remember a thing because she was so darned drunk. Her friend Elaine was almost as bad when they brought her in, but all of sudden she's got this clear recollection of all the night's events."

"Like what?" Sammy asked.

"Well that first day, she said that she didn't see you with Jennifer. I mean she didn't see you actually...well, actually attack her."

"That's because I didn't touch Jennifer!" Sammy shouted.

"I know, son. But, her story's changed. She's claiming now that she found Jennifer Harris in the dunes passed out drunk and mostly naked and that she was able to wake her up for a bit. She says that she was asking about you, Sammy, about where you'd gone."

"That's a damned lie, sheriff!" Sammy said, jumping up and walking around the table.

"Son, just settle down. She's also claiming that Welton and his two friends were down at the beach at the fire the entire time."

"I told you I saw them on the path in the woods. They tried to start a fight with me."

George walked over and put his hand on Sammy's shoulder. "So now you're telling us you've got a witness that will testify against Sammy?" he asked.

"I'm afraid so."

"Mary, I'm sorry to ask about these details in front of you like this," George said, "but Willy, what is she claiming that she actually saw? Did she say she saw Sammy actually raping Jennifer Harris?"

Mary Truegood let out a low moan and covered her face in her hands.

"No, no she's not saying that, but she is saying that Jennifer was lying in the sand naked asking about young Truegood here."

Sammy rushed over to stand in front of the sheriff. "I swear to you that nothing happened."

"I don't know, son," the old sheriff answered. "Let me get over to the Welton's and have another chat. Sammy, if you want to sign a complaint I can bring them all in."

"What good will it do?" Sammy asked.

"Honestly, not a lot. I'm sure they'll deny the whole thing. Doesn't sound like anyone that helped you down there this afternoon really saw what happened."

"No, we've already covered that," said George.

"I've had trouble with these boys before. Let me get after 'em again on this," Potts said.

"I have the whole lot of them scheduled for depositions the day after tomorrow," George said. "They better damn well have their stories straight by then!"

***

Emily McKendry's hands continued to shake holding the steering wheel of her car as she pulled into the drive of the house. Jonathan's old truck was parked in the garage, the lift gate down with several cans of paint and tools lying in the truck bed. She went through the garage and the back door into the house. Her heart was beating hard in her chest and beads of sweat glistened on her forehead. She couldn't get the thought of Slayton's words out of her mind. *I'll be back to see you again...*

She could hear Jonathan banging around out in the back of the house. She walked into the big living room and saw him working on the back sun porch. He looked up when he heard her come into the room.

"Hey beautiful..." Then he saw the look on her face. "Emily, what's going on?"

She walked quickly to him and reached her arms around him, burying her face in his chest.

"Emily?"

She pulled back and took him by the arm to sit on an old couch along the wall. "We have a problem," she said as they sat down. After she retold the story of little Sara Slayton and her injuries, and then her father's visit and threats just a few minutes earlier, Jonathan sat forward on the couch, his hands clenching his knees.

"Where does this sonofabitch live?" he said, his face flushing red and veins along his neck pulsing.

Emily pushed the hair back out her eyes and leaned back on the couch, looking at the ceiling. She took a deep breath to try to calm her reaction. "They live on a farm south of town, but don't we need to get the sheriff's office involved in this?"

"Honey, there's no way I'm going to let this guy threaten you like this. We're going out there now!"

110

She reached over and placed her hand on his. "We need to think about the little girl. What's he going to do to her when we leave if we show up out there and confront him."

Jonathan considered her words for a few moments. "Okay, we'll get Potts to go with us, but we need to do it now, and maybe we need to get that little girl and her mother out of there."

"I'm so afraid for her. You can't imagine how frightened she was. It would just break your heart."

Jonathan got up. "Let me see if the phone's turned on in the kitchen.

Forty minutes later they followed Sheriff Potts cruiser as he turned into a dusty dirt drive. An old mailbox had *Slayton* hand painted in crude style. Through the dust from the car in front of them, Jonathan could see a dilapidated farm house just ahead, the white paint faded and peeling. The front porch sagged and a screen door hung half open. Chickens scattered from the drive as they pulled up and stopped. They all got out and gathered in front of the house. There seemed to be no movement or noise coming from inside, but the wind rushed through the leaves of a big oak tree above them and a rusty windmill spun with assorted creaks and moans on a tower over by a worn red barn.

Sheriff Potts stepped up to the porch. "Mr. Slayton, this is Sheriff Willy Potts. Will you come out here please? I need to have a word with you."

There was no response.

The sheriff stepped up onto the porch and knocked on the door. "Mr. or Mrs. Slayton, are you home?"

Agnes Slayton came to the door. Emily gasped when she saw that her face was badly bruised around her right eye.

"Mrs. Slayton?" the sheriff asked.

She nodded, her hands clutching her dress in a clump at her waist.

"Mrs. Slayton, I'm Sheriff Potts. Are you okay? What's happened here?"

The woman looked out and saw Emily and they made eye contact. Emily felt her heart breaking again and she saw the hopelessness in Agnes Slayton's eyes.

"You all need to go away. We'll be alright."

"Where's your husband?" Jonathan asked, walking up onto the porch next to the sheriff. "I'm Dr. McKendry's husband. Your husband came to town today and threatened her about all this."

Sheriff Potts held a hand out in from of him.

"Jonathan, hold on just a minute. Mam, you need to tell me where your husband is."

"He's not here," the woman said, reaching up and touching the bruise on her face, flinching as her hand made contact.

"Is Sara okay?" Emily asked from behind the men.

"Sara's fine. Thank you, Doctor, for what you did today. But, you all need to leave. This won't get no better with you bein' here."

"Where'd your husband go, Mrs. Slayton," the sheriff asked again.

"I don't know. Into town I guess."

Then Sara Slayton walked slowly and cautiously up behind her mother. Emily could see the cast on the little girl's arm and she walked up on the porch past the men and knelt down next to her. "Sara, let me see your new cast. It looks like Dr. Ellard did a really nice job. Does it feel okay?"

The little girl nodded and looked down at her feet.

Emily reached out and smoothed the hair on the top of Sara's head, then she looked back at her husband and the sheriff. "You know we can't leave them here."

"Emily, we have no right to take them, and they may not want to go," Potts said, looking back at Agnes Slayton.

The woman's face looked tired and defeated. "You all will just make this worse, please go."

Chapter Thirteen

Will Truegood threw the covers back from his face and blinked at the bright sunlight coming in through his window. He held his arm over his face for a moment and tried to clear those early morning cobwebs that keep you stuck between deep sleep and the consciousness of another day. The old cabin he lived in sat back in the woods surrounded by heavy cedar swamp. His family had built it years ago and it had always been his favorite place as a young boy. The beautiful Horton Creek was just over a low rise behind the cabin and he could hear the soft whisper of the water through his open windows. When he got older his father, Jonas Truegood, gave him the cabin and they still came here together often to fish, his father mostly sitting on the bank out of the flow while Will cast to the trout lying in behind the rocks and cedar stumps.

Will sat up in bed and thought back on the memories he had with his father; the fish they had caught, the stories he had passed on. He got up and walked to the small kitchen and got a bottle of juice out of the refrigerator. The clock on the stove said that it was just past ten. He yawned and walked out the front door to the big porch that ran all across the cabin. Something immediately seemed out of place and then he saw a red Porsche convertible sitting in the dirt driveway behind his truck. *What the hell?*

Setting the juice down on the rail of the porch, he walked out to the car. The convertible top was down and a set of keys was lying on the tan leather seat. He reached down and grabbed the key ring, seeing that there were three other keys besides the one for the car and then he looked around trying to sort out *how* and *what* and *why* in his head.

The sound of a car coming through the woods on his road caused him to look up. He saw a blue and white police car come around the last stand of trees. *Boyne City Police* was lettered on the side door and two officers were sitting in the front seat. The car came to a stop behind the red convertible and both officers got out.

"Mornin' Will," said the officer that had been driving the patrol car.

"Mornin' to you, Freddie," answered Will Truegood. He had been friends with Fred Grant since they were boys

"Nice ride, Will," Officer Grant said, walking around the Porsche. "When'd you get it?"

"You know I don't have a car like this, Freddie. I just came out this morning and the damned thing's sitting in my road."

"You got company?"

"Not so I can see," Will said, looking around.

Officer Fred Grant stood looking at him for a few moments and then over at his partner who was standing on the other side of the convertible. "Well, here's what seems to be coming down, Will. We got a call early this morning, about two, that some *Indian boy* they said, was joy ridin' around in this fancy red convertible and it just didn't look right. Then about two hours ago we get this call that a red Porsche was missing this morning."

Will felt a chill run through him and he swallowed hard. "Now Freddie, that's damn nonsense. You know me, I'm no car thief. Who the hell called you?"

"Last night, don't know… anonymous call. This morning, a young Ms. Wainwright from Charlevoix called and said her car was gone when she woke up today. We just been driving around this morning checking out a few people we know who fit the *description*."

The fear that was building from deep within him turned suddenly to anger. "There's no damn way you think I stole this car, Freddie!"

"What am I supposed to think? We pull up, here's the car. You got the keys in your hand."

***

Sheriff Elam Stone was a man of routines. Every morning he got his coffee from the shop down on Bridge Street. He always offered to pay; they never took his money, but he never stopped offering. He always got a paper out of the machine in front of the book store. *Damn, when did papers start costing 75 cents!* He sat down on one of the tables in front of the coffee shop and took a sip from the coffee. He hadn't put the lid down snug and the hot liquid spilled out on his chin and down the front of his shirt. "Damn!"

The cell phone on his belt started ringing and he grabbed some napkins from a dispenser on the table and tried to dry himself off. He flipped the phone open. "This is Stone."

It was Jacob Henry from down at the coroner's office. "Morning, Elam, it's Henry.

The sheriff was still blotting at the coffee stains on his shirt. "Whatta you got?"

"Took a while for the boys down in Lansing, all that fancy lab crap they've got down there, but they got some DNA off that knife in the Hansen case."

"You're shittin' me, that thing's sitting on the bottom of the lake for how long? There's still DNA?"

"Yeah, they got a match, too.

Sheriff Stone forgot his coffee and paper and started walking fast to his car, the coroner's voice going on in his ear.

***

Alex and Anna sat at a table up on the rear deck of the *EmmaLee*. Three places were set for breakfast. The third seat was empty and the plate was covered with a silver lid. It was early morning on Round Lake and the gulls were just getting about their business, flying up high and looking down for dead bait fish or other possible snacks dropped overboard the night before. A light breeze came over the side of the ship, but the sun up over the trees was warm at their backs.

"Just like Louis Kramer to be late for a damn meeting," Alex said. "I'm not sure I ever remember him showing up on time."

"How in the world did you ever get into business with this guy, Alex?" Anna asked and then filled her mouth with cheese omelet.

"We met back in school, fraternity brothers, the whole fraternal bond crap," Alex said. "The guy's as smart as a whip and I don't know, we just started working on some ideas after we got out of business school and one thing led to another."

"Well, here comes the *man of the hour* now," Anna said. Alex looked over and saw the launch coming out from the docks towards the *EmmaLee*. Louis Kramer was sitting up in the front seat with a brown leather briefcase on his lap. The crewman stood in the back of the boat, hands on the wheel. Alex and Louis made eye contact across the water, but neither of them changed expression.

A few minutes later, when Louis walked across the deck toward the table, Alex and Anna both remained seated and offered no welcome. He sat at the empty chair and placed his briefcase on the deck beside him and then glanced at both Anna and Alex before finally speaking.

"I believe this meeting is officially called to order," he announced with a smirk.

"Cut the comedy, Louis," Alex said. "Let's start with you explaining what in hell you were thinking!"

"Oh, so we're going to postpone the niceties." Louis said.

"Lou, I'm serious. I want straight answers now. No bullshit, no more lies. If I get even the slightest hint of a fucking smokescreen here, this meeting is over and from now on, my lawyer will talk to your lawyer, period."

"Message received," Louis said solemnly. "So let me cut to the chase. For the past weeks all I'm hearing from you and your attorney here is... *What have you done, Louis? What were you thinking, Louis?*" He paused again looking for a moment at both of them. "What you're failing to remember Alex, and frankly it blows my mind that your memory is this selective; what you're failing to remember are the dozen meetings that we both sat together in discussing all of these accounting issues with full disclosure from our chief financial officer. What you're also choosing to forget is your signature on all of the documentation related to these transactions."

"Alex, what in hell is he talking about?" Anna asked.

116

Alex sat silent for a moment, looking at his partner. "Louis, let me be very clear," Alex began, "at no time did I observe, condone or approve any of the crap that you and Littlefair have pulled here."

Louis Kramer shook his head and smiled. There was a coffee pot on the table and he reached out and poured a cup. After he took a sip he said, "Clark, you are really good. You are really fucking good. I just can't figure if you are really this naïve and stupid, or the best damn liar I've ever seen."

"Kramer, you better start throwing some proof down on the table around these allegations, or this meeting *is* truly over," Anna said.

He lifted the covered breakfast plate in front of him and set it down across the table, then reached for his bag and began pulling folders out. From one of the folders he pulled a stack of papers that he placed in front of him. "Okay, this first stack of documents are the official meeting notes from fourteen different meetings attended by our friend, Alex Clark. You will see that during these meetings we openly discussed every damn issue the SEC is trying to nail our ass on. Alex, you were an active participant in those discussions and approved the decisions that were made."

Alex stood up and pushed his chair back. "You are so full of shit, Kramer! I don't know where these so-called *documents* came from, but clearly they're fabricated."

Anna reached over to look through the papers.

"Of course, Alex, I didn't expect you to just sit here and confess everything here in front of Ms. Bataglia," Louis said.

"There's nothing to confess, goddamit!" Alex yelled.

"Louis, there are no other people listed as attendees in these meetings. Are you trying to tell me during this entire span of time that no one from your company ever sat in on any of these meetings with you, Littlefair and Alex?" Anna asked.

"Ah, counselor, these are fairly sensitive issues. We didn't call a fucking annual meeting to discuss this shit!"

"Let me see this stuff," Alex asked, reaching for the papers from Anna.

"While you're glancing at all this, let me also present the second file that includes your signature on a dozen documents that authorize the transactions that we're getting raked over the coals on."

"This is bullshit!" Alex said, kicking his chair back and sending it toppling across the deck.

"Alex, just sit down," Anna said. "Let's hear him out. I assume these are duplicates that we can keep and review," she said, referring to the files.

"Absolutely, and before you start claiming fraud and that this is all fabricated, let me also remind you, Alex, that not six months ago, we were together for lunch at the Drake Hotel in Chicago after a meeting with some of our investors. We both agreed that the delays in technical engineering were going to spook the market and our stock was going to tank. We also agreed with our CFO's recommendation to do some *creative accounting* with the financial reporting to the street. Don't tell me you slept through that discussion, too."

Anna looked over at Alex. He sat there for a moment looking through the papers in front of him without speaking. Then he looked up at Louis Kramer. "This is the biggest pile of crap I've ever seen Kramer and I don't know how long it took you to pull all this shit together, and who you got to forge these signatures, but no judge is going to believe you."

"Of course they'll believe it! And when they check your calendar over all these months they'll see you attended each of these meetings."

"What in hell are you trying to pull here, Kramer?" Anna asked.

"Obviously we need a united front against the Feds. If we're not together on this, everybody's going down. Together, without access to any of the paperwork on this table of course, they don't have a prayer in making anything stick."

"So if I'm getting this right," Anna began, "now you're blackmailing your partner with fabricated documents to back up your lies and fraudulent activities."

"You use such harsh language, counselor. I think it would be more appropriate to describe all of this as *insurance.*"

118

"Insurance that I won't throw your fucking ass under the bus!" Alex said. "Get the hell off my boat and out of my sight before I throw your fat ass overboard!" He started around the table towards Kramer.

Louis stood up quickly and put his hands up to block Alex's advance. "Just settle down now, *partner.*"

"Partner!" Alex scoffed. "I knew you were getting in over your head on some other deals, but I never thought you'd betray our trust after all these years."

"It's a cold world out there, partner," Louis said.

Alex came around the table and grabbed Louis' shirt under the neck. Anna jumped up and tried to squeeze between the two of them.

"Alex, let him go. This won't help," she said.

Alex released his grip and watched as Louis picked up his bag. As he turned to leave he stopped and looked at Anna. "See you in court, counselor."

***

"Vince Slayton?"

"Yeah, you heard of him?" the coroner, Jacob Henry asked.

Sheriff Elam Stone sat across the small table in his office. "I know Slayton, and his brothers. They're all bad news, been in and out of jail for generations."

"So he's local?"

"Uh huh, they all live near each other out south of town." Stone kept looking down at the evidence report on the table in front of him. "So what do you think went down here? This creep, Slayton, encourages old man Hansen out of his boat with this big pig sticker of a knife. Then he drowns him, probably just holds his head underwater 'til he stops kicking, and then drags him back into the boat."

"And he drops the knife while he's struggling with the old man," the coroner adds.

"So what's Slayton got against George Hansen?"

"That would be your job to find out, Sheriff."

***

119

Sally called ahead to get the launch to take her out to the *EmmaLee*. On the ride out to the boat she saw Alex and Anna Bataglia sitting at a table on the deck of the boat and there was no sign of Louis Kramer. As she came onboard, Megan came up from below and ran into her with her friend Rebecca.

"Hey, good morning, Sally."

"Hi girls, how did you sleep out here?"

"Like a baby," Rebecca said.

"Good, I just came out to check on your father. Can't have him working all day here in God's Country," Sally said.

"They're around back," Megan said, pointing to the rear of the ship. "Becca and I are going to go up to Petoskey for the day, do a little shopping, eat a little good food."

"Sounds great, why don't you take the Jeep that's up at the house."

"Thanks Sally, we'll be back for dinner, what... around six?" she asked her friend.

"Yeah, six."

Sally gave her a hug and kiss on the cheek. "You drive safe."

The girls headed down the stairs to the launch and Sally continued to walk back to find Alex. When she came around the aft cabin she saw Alex and Anna deep in conversation. They were leaning in close across the table and Anna had her hand over Alex's. She pulled it quickly away when she noticed Sally standing there. Sally felt little prickles of anger up the back of her neck, but tried to remain calm.

Alex turned when he saw Anna look up. "Hey, honey, join us." He motioned to the seat next to him.

Sally sat down and put her large shoulder bag on the deck. "You two seem busy, maybe I should come back."

"No, we're just going back over our friend, Louie Kramer and the A-bombs he dropped on us this morning," Anna said.

"Bad meeting?" Sally asked.

"The sonofabitch has fabricated an entire scenario that implicates me in his fraud, and he's blackmailing me to cooperate with him in the defense." Alex pressed a buzzer sitting on the table.

"It's a slick move, Alex," Anna said. "I need some time to look through these documents that he left with us, but it looks pretty damned incriminating."

A young woman wearing a crew uniform came up to the table. "Yes, Mr. Clark?"

"Sally, do you want any breakfast, something to drink?" he asked.

"Just some coffee please."

The girl nodded and walked away. Sally looked across the table at Anna Bataglia. As usual, she was immaculately dressed in a white silk dress, open generously at the neck. A diamond pendant hung in the tanned cleavage of her breasts. There were more diamonds adorning her wrists and two other fingers, although no wedding ring. Sally knew that Anna had left her husband over a year ago.

Anna pushed her chair back and said, "Why don't I leave you two to enjoy a little time together. I'm going to go below and look over these papers and make a few calls back to New York." She smiled down at Sally with what seemed to be a sincere effort.

"Thanks Anna," Alex said. "You need to give me a point of view on this Kramer bullshit, fast! We can't let this go any further."

"Give me a couple hours." She picked up her stack of papers and bag and walked around the corner.

Sally looked at her husband seeing the lines of worry and stress around his eyes, the uncharacteristic clench of his jaw, the nervous tapping of fingers. She reached over and took one of his hands. "I love you, Alex Matthew Clark."

He had been looking down in his coffee cup. When he looked up his face brightened and he smiled at her. "Let's get out of here for a while."

Thirty minutes later a crew member pulled the little Chris Craft, *EmmaLee II*, up along side the big ship. Alex and Sally climbed in as the crewman held the boat for them and then pushed them away.

"You drive," Alex said as he helped Sally up into the front seats.

"How much time do we have?" Sally asked.

"As much as we need."

Sally pressed the throttle down to a low speed, keeping the wake low. The familiar feel of the boat came back to her and as always, she marveled at the classic beauty of the old boat and the memories shared with her family rushed through her mind. She steered the boat slowly out toward the channel to Lake Charlevoix, selecting a course along the south shore of Round Lake, along the spectacular new homes that had been built in recent years and older boathouses that had been restored. The *EmmaLee's* original boathouse from back in the 30's when her grandfather had owned the ship had been converted to condominiums and stood elegantly against the hill, the docks full of large sailboats and motor yachts.

She thought back to pictures of the big ship tied up there and her mother, Emily, on the deck of the *EmmaLee*. Her father, Jonathan McKendry, had restored this old Chris Craft for her as a present from her father. She remembered a story her father had told her about cruising by the big ship right where they were now and first falling in love with her mother. As always, when memories of her parents came back to her she subconsciously threw up a wall in her mind to block the pain from when they were both lost out on the big lake with her daughter, Ellen, those many years ago. She looked back over at her husband, Alex.

"Why the tears?" he asked, reaching out to put his arm around her shoulder.

"Nothing, I just love being out here with you again. Where should we go?"

"You're the captain."

When they finally cleared the channel into the lake she looked for boat traffic in both directions and then powered the *EmmaLee II* up into the broad expanse of blue water out ahead. A fleet of small sailboats from a sailing class moved in random directions off to their left in front of Depot Beach and the old train station. Two jet skis loudly flew across the water a few hundred yards in front of them throwing off giant rooster tail wakes behind them. Sally sat up on the back of the seat so she could feel the wind in her face and hair. Alex joined her and she held on to his knee with one hand as she steered with the other.

ON PAST HORTON CREEK

They cruised along the north shore of Lake Charlevoix pointing at new homes that had been built, familiar places they had seen or visited before. As they went by the inlet into Oyster Bay they could see dozen of boats of all sizes and descriptions already gathering for a day of partying in the calm bay. A gray haired couple paddled slowly along the shore in long white kayaks, their paddles moving in a synchronized rhythm.

Sally pressed the throttle down until the engine rumbled behind them at nearly full speed. Before long she turned the boat slowly around the point into Horton Bay. The gentle calm of the bay greeted them as they cleared the point and Sally throttled back and the big wake from behind caught up with them and the swell pushed the little Chris Craft up and forward and then it settled on the flat surface. A large sailboat was at anchor in the middle of the bay and two people worked along the deck, preparing for the day's coming sail. All else was quiet on this morning and images of the deep green woods reflected back at them across the water. She turned the engine off and they floated now in silence. Neither spoke for a while, enjoying the quiet tranquility of the place and just being together. The couple on the sailboat waived from a distance when they saw the little boat drifting into the bay.

"Every time I come down here," Sally said softly, as if she might break the serenity of the scene, "I feel like this is a magical place that only exists in my memories and I have to wonder if it's all real, and is it here when I'm gone?"

Alex slid over closer to her and held her close to him. "I know how much this place has meant to you and your family over the years. I wish that I could have known your parents and spent time with them when they were here."

Sally smiled and turned to kiss him on the cheek. "Old Horton Creek over there, Daddy used to fish with George and I always laughed at the stories and lies they would tell about the fish they caught." She laughed, thinking back on her father with *Uncle George*. "We've come a long way past those old days on Horton Creek. How can time pass so quickly?"

"You know," Alex said, "every day up here *is* magic and a special gift. It can take away all the other crazy worries we have in this world."

123

Sally turned and kissed him, this time on the mouth and they sat there together holding each other, listening to the birds in the trees, feeling the soft breeze coming now from over the hills to the west, letting the moment just hold them and comfort them.

Chapter Fourteen

I can remember Dr. Emily McKendry having no second thoughts about reaching out to help Agnes Slayton and her daughter, Sara. Those days, that summer in 1952, were tough for many of us, but Emily really stirred up a hornet's nest.

***

Emily stood at the sink in the kitchen as she finished filling the coffee pot and plugged it in on the counter against the outside wall. Boxes were stacked all around her as they were beginning to pack for the move up to the new house on Michigan Avenue. Agnes and Sara Slayton sat at a small table in the corner, plates of eggs and toast in front of them. The little girl wore the same faded dress that she had on from the previous day when Emily had insisted with Jonathan and Sheriff Potts that they get them away from the Slayton farm and any more abuse at the hands of Harold Slayton. There had been no time to gather clothes or other belongings.

"I'm going to take you both shopping downtown when we finish breakfast, get you some new clothes and a few things at the drug store so you can get freshened up," Emily said.

Agnes Slayton finished swallowing her orange juice and placed the glass back on the table. "Dr. McKendry, you really don't need to do that." Her face showed a weariness that caused all the curves in her face to sag and there was a deep sadness in her eyes. The bruise on her cheek had faded some, but still left a grim reminder of the previous day. "We can't thank you enough…"

"Agnes, I really want to do this for you and Sara. You deserve so much more," Emily said.

125

Jonathan walked into the kitchen dressed for work down at his boatyard, heavy denim jeans and a well-worn canvas shirt. On his head was a *Detroit Tigers* ball cap that had seen more than a few seasons. "Good morning to all," he said, checking out the coffee pot that was just beginning to perk. "Emily, can I speak with you for a minute," he said, gesturing that they should go out the side door. He closed the door behind them and walked out along the narrow drive. Large oaks framed the sky above them and the flowers that Emily had planted along the house were filled with bees making their way among the blossoms. Jonathan's truck was parked on the street in front of the house.

"Honey, I'm not sure I want to leave you alone today. This Slayton guy isn't just going to go away. He's gonna come looking for his wife and daughter."

"I know," Emily answered, wiping her hands on a white apron tied around her waist. "I already talked to the sheriff on the phone this morning. He's going to have one of his men keep an eye on us today."

"I'm so damned tempted to go back out to that farm and *talk* some sense into that worthless piece of trash."

"Jonathan, you stay away from him! Let the sheriff take care of this."

"If you see him even peek around a corner today, I want you to call me, you understand?"

"We'll be fine."

He took her in his arms and held her close and she felt the warm comfort of him around her and the smell of boats and varnish in his clothes. "I love you," she said softly.

"I love you too, sweetheart," he said and then he kissed her as his eyes lingered on hers. "You've always been the one to take in the lost puppy, haven't you?"

"Kind of like you a few years back," she teased.

***

Jennifer Harris sat on the front porch of their summer house, a big cotton robe pulled up tightly around her neck. On her lap was a new copy of *The Diary of Anne Frank* that had just come out earlier in the year. She

126

reached for a mug of coffee on a small table next to her. When she looked up she saw Sammy Truegood coming up the front walk. She felt a hollowness in her stomach and she looked around quickly to see if anyone else was nearby. Putting the coffee back down she stood up and started to walk to the door.

"Jennifer, wait," Sammy said.

She stopped and looked over her shoulder. Not sure if she was feeling fear, anger or both, she did know that she didn't want to talk to him. "You need to leave, now!"

"I just want to talk to you for a minute."

"I can't believe you came here!" she said.

"Jennifer, just give me a minute, please."

She stood staring at him, wondering to herself if she should run inside. Her brother would be furious if he found them here. Her father was still back in Chicago. "Sammy..."

"I just need you to know that I didn't do any of those things your *friends* are saying," he said. "I would never treat you that way. I would never hurt you."

Jennifer shook her head slowly and looked at the wood planks on the porch at her bare feet. "I don't know what happened, Sammy."

The door behind her opened and she turned to see her brother Connor coming out onto the porch. He had a furious look on his face. "Connor, it's okay, Sammy just came by..."

Connor pushed her aside and almost ran down the porch steps. "You sonofabitch, I ought to kick your ass."

Sammy held his ground and Connor reached out and grabbed his shirt near both shoulders, pushing him back. Sammy could see the hate in his eyes and he knew there would be no reasoning with the man. He slapped his arms away and braced for a fight. Connor came at him again, this time swinging wildly, a punch that Sammy easily ducked under.

"I don't want to fight with you, Mr. Harris," Sammy said. "I came to tell Jennifer and your family that I didn't do these things they're saying. You have to believe me."

Connor rushed at him again and grabbed him by both arms and tried to throw him to the ground. Sammy pulled his right arm free and swung out hard to defend himself, catching Connor on the cheek. He could feel bones in his fist breaking as the punch landed with a loud smack on Harris' cheekbone. The blow landed solidly and caught Connor off balance. He staggered and then fell into the grass. His eyes glassed over and he looked up with a dazed expression.

"Sammy, stop!" Jennifer screamed, running down from the porch. She came up next to him and looked down at her brother lying on the lawn and then back at Sammy Truegood. "Haven't you done enough?" she yelled. "You need to leave now!"

Sammy started backing down the walk. "You just need to believe me that I never touched you. I never hurt you."

***

The bright light of the sun came through the small smudged window of a room at the Sheriff's Department. It was shining directly in the eyes of George Hansen and he got up from the table and went over to close a dusty old blind. The room smelled of stale coffee and cigarette smoke. He sat back down and looked across the table at Andy Welton. The boy was well-dressed in the current styles of the summer kids, his sandy hair neatly combed. Sheriff Willy Potts sat at the end of table listening to George take his deposition from the young man.

"Now let me make sure I have all of this correct, Mr. Welton," George said, you and your friends were down at the beach that night with Jennifer Harris and you were the one who brought the liquor?"

"Yes sir," Andy said, his hands folded in front of him on the table.

"And you shared that liquor with Jennifer and her friend Elaine that evening?"

"Yes we did, sir, and to the other kids who were down there."

"And that included Mr. Truegood?"

"No, I don't remember that he was drinking."

"And as the evening went on, you noticed that Jennifer Harris had disappeared from the campfire and you sent Elaine looking for her?"

"Yes, well…she had been sitting in this old rusted red chair somebody had left down at the beach and then she was gone," Andy said, his hands beginning to fidget.

"Why didn't you go looking yourself," Sheriff Potts asked.

Andy looked over at the sheriff and considered his question for a moment. "I don't know, I just asked Elaine if she had seen where Jennifer went off to, and then she got up and went to look for her."

"And where was Sam Truegood when all this happened?" asked George.

"He was gone, too."

"But he wasn't gone because you ran in to him and tried to start a fight with him?"

"No, I told you, that was later when we saw him coming back over the dunes and we didn't try to start anything. We were just goofing around."

"So you saw him later, after Elaine had found Jennifer?" the sheriff asked.

"That's right."

"But, you didn't see him with Jennifer?"

"No, just when we first got down to the beach and they had all been swimming."

"So, tell me again why you think Sammy was with her when she was… when she had intercourse," George asked, looking down at his notes and jotting some additional entries.

"I don't think anything, Mr. Hansen. We all saw Sammy coming back over the dunes from that direction and then Elaine went up there and found her passed out and… well you know, she had been attacked."

"Tell me what time again you think this all occurred, when you saw Sammy coming back and Elaine went to find Jennifer Harris," asked George.

"I told you, I think it was around 10:30, at least it was pretty dark by then."

"Sammy says he was back in town by 10 and heard about Jennifer being at the hospital later from one of the other kids that had been down at the beach," said Potts.

Andy scratched his head. "Well, again, I'm not exactly sure on the times."

"You don't seem to be exactly clear on many of the facts about that night, Mr. Welton," George said, looking him directly in the eyes.

"Look, we'd been drinking a little too, and well, you can't expect me to remember everything."

George slammed his fist down on the table and Andy Welton jolted back in his chair. "I expect you to tell the truth!" he yelled. "And you better damn well be ready to tell the truth when I get you on the stand in court!"

Andy recovered some sense of composure and returned George's intense stare. "You can try to twist this any way you want, sir, but I'm telling you and my friends will tell you, that damn Indian had his way with Jennifer and you better not let him off the hook with any damn legal crap!"

George closed his folder and put the pen in his coat pocket. "I think we're done here, Sheriff."

***

Emily McKendry walked into the waiting room of her clinic with one of her patients that she had just finished with. It was an older woman with bent posture and a slow plodding gait and Emily walked with her, holding her arm.

"Thank you, Mrs. Prescott," Emily said, stopping to let the woman talk with the receptionist. "You get that prescription filled and you should be feeling much better by tomorrow morning.

The old woman nodded and started reaching in her purse to pay the young girl behind the desk.

Emily looked over and saw Agnes Slayton sitting on the floor in the corner playing a game of checkers with her daughter, Sara. They had gone shopping earlier in the morning and both had new dresses on and new pairs of shoes. The sheriff's deputy sat in a chair along the far wall reading a magazine. Emily walked over to Sara and her mother. "Who's winning?"

Sara looked up with a big grin and said, "I won three games already, Dr. McKendry!"

The girl's mother looked up and smiled, too and Emily felt some sense of relief in seeing them with happy expressions in spite of the bruises on their faces and bodies.

"Are you two getting hungry? It's close to lunch time and I thought I would run out and pick up some sandwiches from down the street," Emily offered.

"I really like peanut butter and jelly," Sara said quietly.

"That would be real nice," Agnes said, "whatever you can get will be just fine. And thank you again so much for helping us." She looked down at her new dress. "I'm just worried about Harold and…"

"I told you not to worry about him anymore. We'll let the sheriff take care of that."

"But what if they arrest him? Who's going to take care of the farm and everything?" Agnes said, panic spreading across her face.

"The first thing is to make sure that you and Sara are safe. Do you understand me?"

Agnes Slayton nodded slowly, but doubt was clear in her expression.

"You wait here, I'll run down the street and then after lunch I have a break in appointments and I can take you back up to the house for the rest of the afternoon," Emily said.

She went out into the bright noon sun and walked down to Bridge Street. The heat of the day was building and she felt a sweat breaking out across her forehead. She saw him coming before Harold Slayton noticed her on the sidewalk in front of him. Emily stopped, feeling the prickles of fear rush through her. She looked around quickly to see if she could call anyone for help. When she looked back, Slayton had seen her and was coming quickly her way.

"Lady, you hold up there, dammit!" he yelled.

Emily knew it was pointless to run and she stood there watching him come up in front of her. She could smell the whiskey on his breath again. His old tired face was unshaven and puffy and his eyes were clouded gray and wet.

"You seen my damn wife and kid?" he asked, his words slurred and thick.

"Mr. Slayton…"

He reached out and grabbed the front of her blouse and jerked her violently towards him. "You gonna stop messin' in other people's business, lady. I don't care if you are some fancy doctor."

Emily struggled to pull his arm loose. "Let go of me!"

Before she could react he lashed out and slapped her across the cheek with the back of his other hand. Emily's head flew back and her blouse ripped free of his grasp as she fell to the pavement. The pain of the blow flashed through her brain and she closed her eyes as she fell until the back of her head crashed into the brick wall of the storefront. She felt a new wave of pain and then a dull fogginess and her vision blurred as she tried to look up at Slayton. She could see him leaning down for her when someone came up behind him and grabbed him and then threw him up against the wall.

Emily could see what was happening but it all seemed to be in slow motion and then she felt her consciousness fading. As the last vision of Harold Slayton faded, she sensed a darkness coming over her and the last thing she remembered was his angry voice yelling at her.

Chapter Fifteen

Megan Clark and Rebecca were driving back into town from Petoskey late in the afternoon, just coming down the hill to the drawbridge when the cell phone in her purse rang. She reached down and found it.

"Hello, this is Megan."

"Hey, Megan, this is Will, Will Truegood."

"Will, how are you? How did you get this number?"

"Your mom, I mean Sally gave it to me."

"Well hi!" she said, looking over at her friend Becca with a surprised look. Becca gave her a disapproving scowl in return. "So, what's up?"

There was silence for a few moments on the other end of the phone and then Will answered quietly, "Megan, I need some help."

"Well sure, what kind of help?"

"Can I come over to see you?" he asked.

"Sure, we're just getting back into town. Where are you?"

"Well, I'm at the sheriff's office here in Charlevoix."

"The sheriff?" Megan asked.

"The sheriff!" Becca echoed.

"It's a long story, but I need to talk to you."

"Can you meet us down in the park? We'll be there in just a minute," she offered.

She listened to Will say, "Okay," on the other end of the line and then the phone clicked dead.

Megan found a parking space along Bridge Street and the two girls managed to cross in the heavy traffic. They found an empty bench along the

133

sidewalk at the park and sat down looking for Will Truegood to come through the crowds.

"What in the world do you think that boy got himself into?" Rebecca asked.

Megan just shook her head and didn't answer.

"Megan, you really don't need these complications. What's Rick going to say?"

She looked over at her friend. "Sometimes I have to ask myself what you could possibly be thinking," Megan said. "Will is a friend and it sounds like he needs help."

"What if it's drugs or something?"

"Let's just see what he has to say, and forget about what Rick might say, alright?" She looked over to her left and saw Will coming down the sidewalk. They made eye contact and Megan waved. She could see a tired and confused expression in his face.

He sat down next to her and leaned forward with his hands on his knees, looking at the ground. "Thanks for coming down," he said slowly.

Even his voice sounded different Emily thought, no longer confident and playful, but almost defeated. She put her hand on his shoulder. "What's happened?" she asked.

He looked up at her. "I got arrested this morning for stealing a car."

"Ohmigod!" Rebecca said.

Megan turned to her friend and gave her a look that said, *Calm down or leave!* She looked back at Will Truegood. "You were arrested?"

He told the girls about the whole story, waking up that morning, the red convertible, the police.

"How can a car like that just show up in your driveway," Megan asked. "Wouldn't you have heard someone driving it up to your house?"

Will stood up and started pacing in front of the girls. "I've been thinking about that all day and all I can think is that whoever left it there pushed it down my road with the engine off."

"Why would anyone want to do something so stupid," asked Rebecca.

"Good question," Will said and then sat back down next to Megan. A police car cruised slowly past and an officer in the passenger seat watched Will as they went by. He jumped up again, obviously nervous and concerned. The patrol car kept moving on down the road.

"And who's car was it," Megan asked.

"Some lady named Wainwright, here in Charlevoix."

"I bet it's Melissa Wainwright," Rebecca said. "She's got a little red sports car."

"You know her?" Will asked.

Megan got up and walked over to lean against a tree trunk next to the sidewalk. "She's one of the kids that run with our group up here in the summers," Megan said. "She's from Chicago."

"She must be really pissed about all this," Rebecca said.

Megan looked at Will and was thinking about the series of events that he had described and the revelation that it was Melissa Wainwright's car.

***

Louis Kramer was sitting in one of his wife's family boats moored at the dock. He had a glass of beer in one hand and a cell phone to his ear with the other. He finished the call to his assistant back in New York. The boat rocked and he looked behind him to see two men coming over the transom. He jumped up, dropping his beer, the glass breaking on the deck of the boat.

"Hey Louis, glad we finally found you. Don't answer your phone very regularly, do you? Very rude, very rude," the first man said, a big man dressed in a crisp blue blazer with a pink and blue striped shirt open at the neck. His hair was dark but graying and cut short, the ends standing straight up on top. His face was puffy and flushed and he spoke with an accent that had clear ties to New York. The second man, even bigger, stood behind him and just stared at Louis with a practiced glare.

"Hey Alberto," Louis said nervously. "I've been trying to call you back."

"Yeah right, Kramer," the man named Alberto replied. "Just relax and sit down. We need to have a little talk."

"Alberto, listen man, this whole thing will work itself out."

135

"Louie, just shut up for a minute." The two men pulled chairs over to sit in front of Louis Kramer. "You know that we have a sizable investment in your little venture here, a legitimate investment in the stock of this damn business that you and Alex Clark have managed to totally fuck up with the Feds."

"I've told you…"

"I said shut up!" Alberto said loudly and then leaned forward close to Louis' face. "When I bought the block of stock and invested in your new company, I told you that I trusted you to run the business in a manner consistent with your other successes with Clark. I thought we had an agreement about that."

Louis just nodded.

"I'm sure you know how the value of those shares has fallen in the last weeks and now they've suspended trading. Do you have any fucking idea how much money I have at stake here?"

Louis swallowed hard and just shook his head again.

"I'm just here to tell you that we expect you to make this right, one way or the other. Do you understand what I'm saying?"

"Alberto, we've known each other a long time and you *know* I will make this right."

"Let me be very clear with you, I don't care if your ass rots in jail for 25 years, you're going to make this right for me one way or the other."

"You know the legal system better than I do," Louis said, trying to smile. "This could take a while to work itself out, but…"

Alberto stood suddenly and the chair flew across the deck of the boat behind him. "I'm not a patient man, and I have no intention of waiting for you to get your ass run through the mill by these guys."

"If you're saying you want to get cashed out, hell that's close to twenty million bucks! I can't get that kind of cash."

The big man next to Alberto stood up and towered over Louis, his expression never changing.

"Oh, I think you can do amazing things when you put your mind to it, Louie."

The sound of footsteps on the dock caused all three men to turn. Mary Alice walked up to the side of the boat. She was wearing a black swim suit cut low in front with a flowered wrap around her waist. "Louis, would you like to introduce me to your friends," she said.

Alberto answered first, "We were just leaving, mam." He reached out his hand to shake hers. "I'm Alberto Manta and this is my friend, Raul."

"Nice to meet you," Mary Alice said unevenly.

"We're old friends of Louis and we were in town, so we just wanted to stop by quickly and say hello."

Mary Alice looked over at Louis and could see the uneasy look on his face. "Honey, have you asked your friends to stay for a drink?"

"No…" Louis started to say.

"No thank you, Mrs. Kramer. We really were just leaving and have to get back to the airport."

The two men climbed out of the boat and Mary Alice moved aside to allow them to pass. Alberto turned and said, "Nice seeing you again, Louie. Nice to meet you, Mrs. Kramer. Call me tomorrow when I'm back in New York, Louie and we can work through the details."

"Sure," Louis barely managed to say without choking. He watched as Alberto Manta slowly walked away down the dock, followed by Raul.

"You really need to give me more warning when you have friends coming over," Mary Alice said.

Louis didn't answer; he just kept watching the two men walk up the lawn and around the house. Under his breath he whispered, "Shit."

***

The sun was nearly down over the far tree line across the field of low corn. Sheriff Elam Stone drove slowly up the drive of the old farmhouse of Vince Slayton. He had a deputy sitting beside him and another patrol car with two officers behind them. The dust blew up around the cars and made it difficult to see the house as they came to a stop. A big German shepherd dog came running around the house barking and showing a lot of big teeth.

"Crap!" the sheriff said. Looking over at his deputy he said, "Billy, can you reach that tranquilizer gun in the back. We need to drop that damn dog!"

Through the dust Elam could see a man walk out onto the porch of the house that hadn't seen fresh paint for decades. The roof sagged over his head and looked like it could crash down on him at any minute. The man whistled and the dog came running back up on to the porch and he tied a rope that was lying by his feet to the dog's collar.

"Let's go, Billy," the sheriff said, releasing the snap over the .45 automatic in the holster at his waist and opening the car door. The three deputies spread out in a formation behind him and they all walked slowly up to the porch.

"You Vince Slayton?" the sheriff asked.

"What d'ya want?" the man on the porch said. His face seemed to have a permanent scowl carved across it and his right hand twitched like he was trying to chase a fly away from his leg. He was wearing faded Army surplus camo pants and a white t-shirt cut off at the shoulders with a picture of Kid Rock on the front. His hair was a dirty brown color and tied in a long pony tail down to the middle of his back.

"I asked you a question, son," the sheriff said. "You Vince Slayton?"

"Yeah, I'm Slayton, what the hell you want?"

"We're gonna need you to come with us to town to answer a few questions."

"We can talk just fine right here." The big dog stood by his side and growled, his lips curling up to reveal those teeth again.

"No, actually we can't talk here," Stone said, "and you're going to town with us now!"

Slayton stood staring at them for a few moments, his expression never changing.

"Are you going to make this more difficult than it needs to be, Mr. Slayton?" Elam Stone said, wiping away the perspiration that was starting to form along his brow.

Another man walked through the door and stood behind Slayton, a younger looking version about twenty pounds lighter. "What the hell's all this?" the man said.

"The boys here need to talk to me."

"Bout what?"

"Yeah Sheriff, bout what?" Vince Slayton said.

Stone could feel his patience running to a low ebb and said, "Let's just go into town."

"You got a fucking warrant?"

"Well, as a matter of fact we do, and a couple of my men here are going to stay behind and look around a little."

"What the hell's this about!" the other man shouted.

"Who is this?" Stone asked.

"My little brother," Slayton answered.

"Tell your brother to shut his damn mouth and you get your ass down here now, or we'll haul it outta here, you hear me!" the sheriff said.

Vince Slayton turned and whispered something to his brother and then started slowly down the rickety old steps of the porch.

Sheriff Stone nodded to one of his deputies and the young man came up and met Slayton and patted him down for weapons.

"I ain't got no lawyer," Slayton said.

"You think you need one?" the sheriff said.

***

Sally and Alex pulled the *EmmaLee II* into the small boathouse along the south shore of Round Lake. Alex secured the lines and Sally went over to pull the switch to let the big door down.

"I'll never forget the first day you brought me down here," Alex said.

"Down to the boathouse?"

"Yeah, you know, that first summer."

Sally smiled and came over to him and put her arms around his waist. "I remember." She lifted up on her toes to kiss him. "I think little *Emma* here stole your heart more than I did."

Alex laughed. "I have to admit that I had an immediate attraction for this little lady when I saw her floating here that day. But there was this tall blonde that really got my attention." He kissed her again. "What's that story you tell about your suspicions that your parents lost their virginity down there on those soft leather seats?"

"We'll never know for sure," Sally said, squeezing him closer to him.

"I wonder how they did it?"

"Alex!"

"No, I mean those seats aren't very big and…well you know what I mean?"

"I'm not sure I do, Mr. Clark."

He took her by the hand and stepped back down into the *EmmaLee II* and then helped Sally down, too.

"I think these back seats probably had the most room to… maneuver, don't you think," Alex said.

Sally just smiled back at him. They sat down together on the back seat of the little runabout. He had his arm around her and he pulled her closer to him and kissed her on the forehead and then on each cheek. When he pulled back he looked into her eyes and they still shined even in the dark shadows of the closed-up old boathouse.

"I think we both have far too many clothes on to really know if this is going to work," she said, trying to keep a serious expression.

He reached for the buttons on her blouse. "I think I can help with that."

Chapter Sixteen

The Slayton family was always a sad story. Years of poverty and alcoholism and abuse piled up year after year, the next generation always the unfortunate victims of the last.

***

The first sensation of consciousness was the warm touch of someone holding her hand. Emily opened her eyes and was immediately blinded by the bright overhead light. She squinted to look around and then realized that she was in one of the examination rooms in her office. The voice of her husband caused her to turn and Jonathan stood there holding her hand, talking to her partner, Julian Rose. The doctor was dabbing gently with a wet cloth at a cut on her cheek and she could see the bright redness of her blood on it.

"Is she going to need stitches?" she heard Jonathan ask.

"Not here on her face, but that cut on the back of her head is going to take a few. Let's keep that ice bag on it a while longer," Dr. Rose said.

Emily then felt the icy cold under the back of her head and the sharp pain of the cut on her cheek. The right side of her face felt swollen and heavy.

Jonathan noticed that she was looking at him. "Emily…?"

She tried to smile, but it hurt to move her face. "What's all the fuss?" she said.

"Thank God you're back with us," Jonathan said and then squeezed her hand softly.

"Emily, just lie still for me a little longer. I want to get this cheek cleaned up and dressed and then we'll see about the back of your head," Dr. Rose said.

The memory of Harold Slayton in front of her on the sidewalk came back to her. She closed her eyes and couldn't help but shiver from the images. The cold fear that she had felt was frightening and the furious, hateful look in the man's eyes would haunt her forever, she knew.

"Are Sara and Agnes okay?" she asked slowly, finding it difficult to put the words together.

"They're fine," Jonathan said. "The sheriff took them over to his office and they're going to find another home for them to stay for a while."

"Where's Slayton?" she asked weakly.

She watched an angry expression flare on Jonathan's face, "The bastard ran away and by the time someone called the sheriff, he was nowhere to be found."

Emily felt the fear rush through her again, knowing that the man was still out there. She tried to sit up on the exam table, but Dr. Rose held her shoulder gently. "You need to stay still. That head wound is ugly and you probably have a concussion."

***

Sammy Truegood watched the doctor wrapping his hand as he sat on a table in the emergency room of the small hospital in Charlevoix. He had called his mother and George Hansen had brought her down. They both stood watching the doctor working on him.

"X-rays show a couple of broken bones behind the outside knuckles. Nothing serious, but he'll have to keep it bandaged up and immobile for a few weeks," the doctor said. "I'll be back in a couple minutes." He walked out of the room and closed the door behind him.

Sammy saw his lawyer, Mr. Hansen, shaking his head. "Sammy, I told you to stay away from those people. Son, what were you thinking?" George asked.

"I had to try to explain what happened. I just can't have them thinking that I did these things."

His mother came up and put her arms around him and he could feel her tears against his cheek. "Momma, I'm sorry. I'm sorry about all this."

The doctor came back into the room. "Sheriff Potts just called. He's been looking for Sammy and thought he'd try down here. · He wants you to bring him down to his office."

George nodded without answering. He turned to Sammy and said, "Now you're sure that Connor Harris started this and took a swing at you?"

"He came after me and I tried to explain that I just wanted to talk and tell them that I didn't do this, but he just kept coming after me," Sammy said. "Then he tried to hit me and throw me down and I had to stop him."

"I'm sure our friend, Connor Harris, will be waiting for us at the sheriff's office with his own version of the story. Sammy, I've got to tell you that this isn't going to help our case at all. They're going to say now that you attacked Jennifer's brother, just further proof that you're dangerous."

Mary Truegood stepped back and looked at her son. Sammy felt terribly sad to see the look of desperation on her face. "Momma, I'm..."

"Sammy, you need to listen to Mr. Hansen. You're not helping yourself. You're making this all so much worse."

The pain in his hand throbbed and the look of Jennifer Harris' frightened expression remained clear and haunting in his mind.

An hour later they all sat around a small table in Sheriff Potts' office. The sheriff was on the phone talking, making notes on a pad in front of him. "Okay, okay, I'll take care of that," he said, shaking his head as if the caller could see his expression. He hung up the phone and then stood to walk around his desk. He pulled the heavy gun belt and his pants up higher around his round belly. "Sammy, damn if you don't know when you've had enough."

Sammy looked down at the table and the glass of water in front of him.

"That was Harris. He's on his way down to file a complaint." The sheriff took one of the seats across from Sammy. "Now, I've heard your side of this story. You sure you've got nothing else you want to tell me?"

Sammy shook his head *no*.

"Let me ask you something else, son, if you don't mind, George?"

143

"No, go ahead."

"That night, down at the beach, you remember Jennifer Harris leaving the fire to go up into the dunes?"

Sammy sat for a few moments without answering, then he shook his head, "No, I really don't remember. She was sitting near me and Elaine and some of the other kids and they kept passing bottles around and she was taking some awful long drinks."

"So why'd you get up and leave then?" the sheriff asked.

"I knew I had to get back into town and that crowd was getting pretty out of control. I just didn't want to be part of it."

"And that's when Welton and his buddies tried to jump you?"

"Yeah, they stopped me on the trail."

"Did you say goodbye to Jennifer, or any of the others?"

"I guess I did, I don't know. They wouldn't remember anyway."

"Sammy," George said, "it's real important that we have this sequence of events clear. Last time you saw Jennifer Harris, she was sitting at the fire with the other kids?"

Sammy looked at his lawyer, the memories of that evening swirling in his head. Then a helpless feeling came over him and he realized he wasn't sure.

***

Jennifer Harris walked up the sidewalk to the sheriff's office with her brother, Connor. She was having a hard time keeping up with him. He hadn't said a word to her since the fight with Sam Truegood, other than to insist that she come with him down to see Sheriff Potts. As they walked up to the door it swung open and George Hansen came out followed by Sammy and his mother. She watched as her brother tensed and then stopped abruptly.

George saw them and stopped, too, putting his arm out to hold back the others. "Harris, we don't want anymore trouble with you," he said.

Connor stared straight at Sammy with a hateful glare. "This boy here has got to be put away. First he attacks my sister and then he has the nerve to come to our house. Then he comes after me. I'll have your ass thrown in jail where you can't hurt anybody else!"

"Mr. Harris…," Sammy started.

George held up his hand to silence him. "Let's just get out of here."

Jennifer met Sammy's gaze and she had a helpless feeling that all of this was spiraling so far out of control.

George herded Sammy and his mother around them on the sidewalk. Connor grabbed Sammy's arm as they tried to pass. "I'm warning you, don't ever come near my house or my family again, ever!"

George came between the two of them and pushed Connor's hand away. The two men stood face to face. "You and I aren't through either, Hansen."

***

Harold Slayton sat in his truck parked along an old dirt two-track road leading down to the lake near Ironton. He reached for the pint bottle of whiskey on the seat next to him and took another drink. It was early evening and the sun had gone down behind the trees up on the hill and the shadows spilled out onto the waves coming up onto the deserted beach. One boat cruised slowly, far offshore and a flock of ducks flew into the marshes across at the far point of the bay into the South Arm of Lake Charlevoix. His mind was muddled with random thoughts, dulled by the whiskey. He rubbed at his forehead, the familiar ache in his brain from too much to drink.

A cold anger swept through him again. *That doctor needs to keep herself out of our business.* He remembered the satisfaction he felt in slapping her and watching her fall to the ground. *Hope that knocked some damn sense into her.* He thought about his wife and could only feel disgust and anger for them taking his little girl away. He just wanted this all to be over and have his family back at the farm.

He took another drink, a long one this time and he drained the bottle and the whiskey hammered at his brain. The bottle dropped from his hand to the floor of the truck. He leaned his head back against the cold hardness of the rear window of the truck. He closed his eyes and felt the comfort of darkness and sleep wash over him.

***

George Hansen sat in the kitchen of Jonathan and Emily's house, a cup of coffee warm in his hand. Jonathan was cleaning up some dishes in the

145

sink and then came over and sat across the table from his friend, turning on a light switch on the wall as the late evening light faded outside.

"She's been sleeping for a couple of hours since we brought her home," Jonathan said. "Damn George, that sonofabitch Slayton…"

"No sign of him, yet?"

"No, I talked to Potts about an hour ago and his men were still out looking for him. He asked if I wanted someone to watch the house tonight."

"Probably a good idea," George said, then taking another sip from his coffee.

"No, we'll be alright. I hope the asshole *does* come by here. If he ever gets near Emily again, I'm afraid of what I might do to him."

"You need to let Potts take care of this."

Jonathan nodded. "I know, I know. It's just that it scares me. He could have killed her today."

George looked at his friend and could see the strain of all this in the deep creases in his forehead. "The doc say she's gonna be alright?"

"She fell pretty hard and hit her head on that brick wall. He wants her to stay down for a couple days," he answered. "And her face," he paused, trying to hold back the wetness building in his eyes. "She looked so afraid and she's got this terrible bruise on her cheek."

"Jonathan, they'll find this guy and put him away and you won't have to worry about this," George said, trying to reassure his friend. "It's been quite a day. You haven't heard about Sammy, have you?"

"No, what now?"

George shared the story about Sammy's visit to the Harris house and the confrontation at the sheriff's office.

"It's about time someone took a shot at Connor Harris. Good for Sammy!"

"*Not* good for Sammy. He's got enough trouble and now an assault charge against the brother of the girl he's accused of raping."

"I know, I'm sorry," Jonathan said.

"I was feeling better about this case and the boy's chances. No one's come forward that actually saw Sammy with the Harris girl. It really could have been any of those boys out there that night."

146

"So, why Sammy?"

"All of Jennifer Harris' friends have convinced her it was him," George said. "I'm beginning to think that Sammy wasn't even down there at the beach when she was attacked. Hell, I don't even know if she was attacked. She was so drunk; she could have just had sex with someone out there in the dunes, passed out and never remembered what happened."

"You think so?"

George scratched his head and looked out the window. "I don't know. One thing I do know is Sammy didn't do this."

"He's not a bad kid. All kids make mistakes, but I don't see Sammy doing this."

"Well, I felt better about the judge having the same point of view until Sammy broke his hand on Conner Harris' face this afternoon." He finished his coffee and stood up. "Look, I need to get home to see Elizabeth before the rest of this day slips away. You tell Emily not to worry; we'll get this Harold Slayton guy put away."

***

Sammy Truegood walked through the woods along the dunes at North Point. It was dark and the moon was only the slightest sliver, but he knew the trail and made his way easily. He came out onto the flat beach and the sand gave way beneath his feet as he walked down to the shore. The water was calm and black against the night sky and he could see the reflections of lights on a tanker far offshore. Mosquitoes buzzed around his head but didn't seem to want to land.

His hand throbbed under the wrapped dressing. He gently squeezed a soft fist with it and the pain shot up his arm. Connor Harris and his threats continued to shake him and he struggled to think that he had made the situation even worse today. He knew he would have to continue to defend himself, but he also knew that he had to let his lawyer do his job and not make the job any harder.

He thought about the words of his grandfather and the precepts of his people. *Look up to the skies often, by day and by night, and see the sun, moon and stars which shine in the firmament, and think that the Great Spirit is always looking down upon you.*

Chapter Seventeen

Anna Bataglia stood on the docking platform alongside the massive white hull of the *EmmaLee*, the big ship floating motionlessly in the calm water of Round Lake. She dipped a few toes in the water and pulled back quickly, feeling the early summer chill of the water. She was dressed in a simple black tank suit that she had brought along, the one that she wore when she swam to workout back in the city. She had been on the phone most of the day checking in with her office and following up on the many surprises that Louis Kramer had laid on them earlier. She had decided a swim would help to clear the cobwebs.

Boat traffic was heavy on the little inland harbor. A brightly colored ski boat with wake boards hanging on the sides of a chrome tower cruised slowly by with four teenage boys. They noticed Anna and turned the boat to come closer.

"Hey lady, go for it!" one of them yelled. "The water's fine."

Anna tried to ignore them, but they wouldn't let up.

"Want to borrow a wetsuit?"

She just smiled back and finally they lost interest and moved off, certainly looking for females closer to their own age to harass. She took a big deep breath, gathering her courage and then two quick steps toward the water and launched out into the air, knifing down into the water like she used to do as a young girl racing for her college swim team. The icy shock almost took her breath away and she came quickly to the surface and let out a yell, "Yeeow!"

She knew she needed to keep moving to allow her body to adapt to the cold chill of the lake and she started swimming a slow practiced stroke across the surface. She headed toward a long white boathouse on the north shore, passing navigation buoys and boats tied up at anchor buoys along the way. When she reached the boathouse she stopped and looked up at the magnificent homes on the hill overlooking the harbor. The gardens were coming into bloom and the colors blended together in a soft canvas of brilliant hues.

She started back towards the *EmmaLee*, her body now accustomed to the cold and feeling renewed and energized from the swim. She could see the *EmmaLee's* long expansive hull and elegant lines up ahead and she stopped in wonder, just to look at the big ship. Treading water in the middle of the lake, she thought about her client, Alex Clark, and the incredible good fortune that he had enjoyed in his business, now threatened by the betrayal and ineptitude of his friend, Louis Kramer. She often found herself struggling to put more personal thoughts about Alex from her mind. She had felt a strong physical and emotional attraction from the first time she had met him years ago in their first business meeting. Working as closely as she had with him over the years, they had come to know each other very well, but neither of them had ever tried to cross the precarious barrier that leads to intimacy.

A feeling had been nagging at her ever since they had arrived in Charlevoix. There were, of course, all of the emotions and stress of the legal case that she was attempting to defend for Alex, but there was also something deeper. She realized now, floating in the cold water of Round Lake with the spectacular scenery of the quaint little town of Charlevoix all around her and the incredible beauty of the *EmmaLee* floating there in front of her, that the feeling that was gnawing at her was the harsh reality of jealousy.

***

Alex and Sally sat together on the small launch as it made its way out to the *EmmaLee*. She held his hand in her lap and the memories of their lovemaking, just a short time before in the old boathouse, still sent a warm glow through her body. She looked over at the face of the man that she had come to love so deeply and watched the wind blow his hair in random

149

directions and the sunburn coming out on his cheeks from their earlier ride down to Horton Bay.

He looked at her and smiled and he leaned over and kissed her. She felt the familiar wetness of his lips and she reached up and held his face close to let the kiss linger.

"You are beautiful, Sally McKendry Clark."

She felt a flush across her face. "Thank you, dear, and I'm also very fortunate."

"And in what way would that be, Mrs. Clark?"

"Fortunate to have found you."

He kissed her again and then the crewman slowed the launch as it approached the docking platform. Alex helped Sally out of the boat and as the launch pulled away, he noticed the swimmer coming towards them. "Who could that be?"

"I think Megan's probably still out with Becca," said Sally. "It looks like Anna."

They both watched as Anna swam up to the platform and then stopping to look up, noticed Alex and Sally standing there.

"Well, hello to you both," she said.

"Anna, a little cold swim to get the juices flowing?" Alex asked.

"I think those juices may be frozen, but I'm certainly awake," she said, treading water in the lake, sparkling drops of water hanging on her eyelashes and the ends of her ears, her hair swept straight back and shining.

"Here, let me give you a hand," he offered, reaching down and taking her hand to lift her out of the water. Sally stood back out of the way and Alex lifted her easily up out of the water. There was a towel on a small stool and Sally reached for it. She looked back and saw Anna standing there dripping and shivering, the wetness of her suit clinging tightly and almost transparently to every curve of her body. She threw the towel for her and then looked at Alex who she saw was doing his best not to stare at the form of Anna Bataglia. She wasn't sure she could blame him. What man wouldn't be tempted to steal at least a quick glance.

"Anna, we thought you might like to join us onboard for a little dinner cruise tonight," Sally offered.

"Of course, that would be fabulous. Thank you," she answered. "I'll need to change and get showered, but it shouldn't take long."

"Take your time," Alex said. "We won't pull anchor for another hour or so, anyway."

Later as the sun was setting over the hills of Charlevoix, Alex stood at the rail of the *EmmaLee* as it cruised slowly along the shores of the Belvedere Club. The classic summer homes were set against the trees along the bluff, the beach cabanas in a dozen pastel colors along the shore and the old pea soup green Casino sitting down near the channel.

He had just ordered a vodka martini, Grey Goose, very dry with three olives. A server from the galley brought the drink to him and the glass was frosted cold and filled nearly to the top. He thanked the young woman, Mandy, and she left to go below. Anna and Sally were still getting dressed for dinner. He sipped the drink and swirled the cold smooth liquor around his tongue, enjoying the flavor and the aroma of the vodka. He thought back on the past few summers that he had spent here with Sally and about what a blessing it had been in his life to find this woman. At times, the dark reminders of the death of his first wife would come back to him, the time with the cancer and the failing and the loss; the grief that he and Megan had worked through and still had to work through on occasion. Sally had helped them both to fill some of that loss. She had experienced the pain of losing those that were close to her, even her young daughter in the boating accident with her parents. It was common ground for them, a place to share a sense of understanding and support.

The meeting with Louis Kramer earlier in the day rushed back into his thoughts. His anger returned at the thought that his former friend that he had placed so much trust in had betrayed him so ruthlessly and now was using even more treachery. It hurt him deep in his gut that someone who had been that close to him for so many years, who had shared so much success, could have betrayed him so heartlessly.

He thought though that it was strange that he didn't feel more worried about the outcome of the investigation. He knew he had a good defense with Anna and her team, but it wasn't just that. He didn't feel threatened about losing money or a business, or even his reputation. Maybe he was being naïve about all this, but he knew that he had done nothing wrong and he felt confident in knowing inside that he had always done the right thing when choices presented themselves. That had to count for something.

He heard footsteps on the deck behind him and he turned to see Anna coming toward him. She was dressed in a flowing white dress cut just above the knees, thin straps revealing bare shoulders and white high-heeled sandals on her feet.

"My, you look ready for summer," he said. "That's a beautiful dress."

"Thank you, only fitting for a cruise on the *EmmaLee*."

"Would you like a drink?"

She nodded, asking for a glass of red wine. He went over to an intercom box and ordered two glasses of a favorite cabernet. Coming back to her he said, "Thank you for all the hard work on this defense."

"Yeah, this is tough duty," she said, looking up at the beauty of the lakeshore, lights now coming on in the houses and along the streets. "How do you ever come back to the city?"

He laughed and took another sip from his drink. "It's very hard, trust me, it's very hard."

A member of the crew brought the wine up on a tray and served one glass to Anna. "Thank you." Alex took the other and placed it on a small table by the cabin wall.

Sally walked up at the same time. Alex looked over and watched her come across the deck, her slow graceful movements, the beauty of her hair blowing back in the light wind. She had on a blue dress that she had worn that first summer they had met.

"Hello beautiful," he said. He reached out for her and hugged her and then kissed her on the cheek.

Anna backed up a few steps along the rail. "Hi Sally, you do look beautiful tonight."

Sally looked over at Anna and smiled, "Thank you Anna, just some old thing I pulled out of the closet. Your dress is magnificent."

Anna looked down assessing herself, "Just some old thing…" and then she laughed.

Alex stood there looking at these two beautiful women that he would share food and drink with tonight and the one special woman that he would share his bed with later in the night and all thoughts of lawsuits and investigations seemed a distant concern.

***

Megan Clark walked up to the big white house on Dixon Street that sat on the hill overlooking Round Lake. A circle driveway in the front was filled with a black Range Rover and a much smaller red Porsche convertible. She walked by the cars and up on the front porch. Pushing the button on the wall, she heard the chimes ring and quickly saw a woman coming down the front hallway through the sidelight window of the door.

The door opened and a woman who appeared to be in her sixties, dressed immaculately in a black evening dress, greeted her. "Well hello, Megan. How nice to see you. Please come in."

"Thank you Mrs. Wainwright. How have you been?"

"Fine dear, just fine. Are you up for the whole summer again?"

"For most of it I hope," said Megan. "Is Melissa home?"

"Why yes, of course, just a moment? How are your father and Sally?" the woman said as she walked down the hall.

"They're fine, out on the *EmmaLee* tonight, having some dinner."

"Yes, I saw the *EmmaLee* going out earlier tonight when we were having drinks on the back deck. What a beautiful ship. We're all so glad that your father brings her back now every summer."

"So am I, I love this place."

"Wait just a moment, I'll go find Melissa. Can I get you anything?"

"No thanks, I'll just wait out on the deck."

"Certainly, go ahead, everyone's already left for dinner. I have to meet them over at the Club."

Megan walked through a large sliding glass door and out onto the wide deck across the back of the Wainwright's house. As she reached the rail she looked down on the breathtaking scene of Round Lake and the boats and the lights coming on in the homes along the shore and up through town.

153

The *Beaver Islander* was just pulling into its berth along the pier by the channel and crowds of people were waiting along the fence to pick up friends and loved ones after their excursion over to the island twenty miles out on Lake Michigan.

She heard a door open behind her and turned to see Melissa Wainwright coming out. She still had a bikini top on from a day in the sun and cut-off blue jean shorts. Her red hair was tied up on top of her head in loose curls.

"Hey Megan, thanks for stopping over. I've been meaning to call you since we got up here last week." She came over and gave Megan a hug and kiss on the cheek.

"Hi Melissa, welcome back for another action-packed summer. How was school?" Melissa had just started at Princeton this past year.

"A bitch really. I'm studying my butt off."

"I'm sure you're doing fine, *Ms. Rocket Scientist.*"

"Hardly, so what's up? You want a drink or something?"

"No thanks, you're mom already offered. I just wanted to ask you about something."

"What's that?"

Megan jumped up and sat on the rail and then crossed her legs in front of her. "I heard that your car was stolen last night."

The bright look on Melissa's face faded quickly. "Where'd you hear?"

"A friend told me today. What happened?"

Melissa hesitated for a moment and looked out over the harbor. "Well, I'm such an idiot, I left the keys in it out on the driveway last night. I was inside for twenty minutes and I came out and it was gone. My parents are furious with me."

"But I see you got it back already."

"Yes, the police found it this morning, some Indian kid had it down the lake somewhere. Thank God he didn't wreck it. My dad would have killed me!"

"Melissa, I know this kid," Megan said, her tone serious.

"You know him?"

"Yes, his name is Will Truegood and I don't think he stole your car."

Melissa Wainwright hesitated again. "Well of course he did, they found it parked at his house this morning."

"Melissa, what's going on here?"

Melissa got an angry look on her face. "What do you mean, there's *nothing* going on other than some kid steals my car and now you're standing up for him. What in the hell is that all about?"

"I know Will Truegood and I know he didn't steal your car."

"That's ridiculous!"

"Melissa, did someone put you up to this?"

"Alright, that's enough!" Melissa yelled. "I think you better leave."

"Melissa…"

"I can't believe you're doing this to me, Megan."

"I'm not doing anything to you. I'm trying to help a friend."

"I thought *we* were your friends!"

***

Mary Alice Gregory sat at the corner table of the dimly lit restaurant looking out over the small lake at the Charlevoix Country Club. Her husband, Louis Kramer, seemed lost in the glass of bourbon in front of him. The restaurant was about half full and Mary Alice had just returned from walking among the tables and saying hello to all the people that she knew, which was just about everyone.

"Louis, you're making a scene with this morose, self-absorbed, *oh pity me* attitude tonight. Is it those two gorillas that came to see you this afternoon?"

Louis looked up and then took a long sip from his drink. "Gorillas?"

"Yeah, Harry and Larry from New York. God, they looked like a pair of hit men from the Bronx."

Louis blanched at the reference and took another drink.

"Would you please tell me who the hell these guys are," she demanded.

"Alberto is a large shareholder in our new company. He was here today checking on his investment."

"Couldn't he just call?"

155

"He said he was in the neighborhood."

***

Vince Slayton sat across from Sheriff Elam Stone in a small conference room. One of the deputies stood near the wall. The fluorescent lights in the ceiling cast a bright glare on everything in the otherwise dingy room. Slayton sat slumped over, his arms crossed in front of him on the table, a glass of water half gone by his side.

"We'll have a court appointed lawyer here for you by tomorrow morning, Mr. Slayton. You've been read your rights. You know you don't have to speak to us until your attorney arrives."

Slayton just grunted without looking up.

"It wouldn't hurt your cause, though to help us out with a couple of questions tonight," the sheriff said.

"Why don't you just go to hell!" he said, looking up at Stone. "What's this all about anyway?"

The sheriff pulled a plastic bag out of a satchel lying on the table. He placed it between them and a large knife was clearly visible. "You ever seen this knife, Mr. Slayton?"

He looked at it and didn't respond.

"Must have seen it one time or other," Stone said. "Got your DNA all over it."

Slayton looked up, surprised. "DNA?"

"That's right, Mr. Slayton, the lab down in Lansing confirmed it. Think you might remember now seeing it before?"

Again, he didn't answer.

"Any idea how this big old knife found its way to the bottom of the South Arm, right under the boat where we found old Mr. Hansen dead and apparently murdered?"

"Now hold on!"

"What, Mr. Slayton?"

"I didn't have nothin' to do with no murder!"

"So, I got your attention now. So how do you know George Hansen, or I guess I should ask, how *did* you know him?"

"Never heard of him."

Stone turned to his deputy. "Looks like we're not gonna get very far tonight. Put him back in his cell." He turned back to Slayton. "You know, we're talking murder here, Mr. Slayton. That's damn serious stuff. You can tell, I'm real damn serious about this. George Hansen was a good man and a good friend of mine and anyone who had anything to do with this is gonna get their ass fried! You hear me?"

Chapter Eighteen

You often hear people say that it's just 'human nature'. Is it possible that 'human nature' can harbor such evil in men at times, such treachery and willingness to hurt others who are too weak to defend themselves? What's human or even natural about any of that?

***

Sara and Agnes Slayton stood next to Emily's bed. The yellow walls and white lace curtains brightened the room even though dark clouds swept by overhead and a light rain was falling outside on a cool summer morning in Charlevoix. A clap of thunder sounded in the distance.

Agnes was holding Emily's hand in hers. Emily looked up at the woman whose face had aged far beyond her little time on this earth and then at little Sara who stood by her mom, a worn teddy bear under her arm.

"Dr. McKendry, I'm just so sorry about all this."

"Agnes, none of this is your fault and you've got to stop thinking this way."

"We shouldn't have come into your house. We shouldn't..."

"Agnes, please. I knew what I was doing and I still know that I did the right thing."

Agnes looked out the window and she blinked at a flash of lighting as another clap of thunder rumbled outside. "I'm taking Sara home today, Dr. McKendry."

Emily tried to sit up, but the pain in the back of her head seared through her brain and she eased back down into the soft pillow. "Agnes, no, you can't go back there until they find Harold."

"We'll be okay," she said sadly, "we've been through this before. We need to be in our own home."

, "You can't put your daughter in danger like this anymore."

"I won't let him hurt her. You believe me now, Dr. McKendry, that man won't hurt Sara again."

The little girl looked up at her mother and it broke Emily's heart to see the sad uncertainty in her face. "Agnes, you can't protect yourselves, can't you see that?"

"We'll be alright. The sheriff said he'd send some of his men by regular."

Emily squeezed her hand tightly, "Please don't do this. You know you're welcome to stay here."

"Thank you, but we need to be home."

***

Jonathan turned off Highway 31 on to the dirt road that led back to the Slayton's farmhouse. He drove his truck slowly over the big pot holes in the road, filled this morning with brown muddy water from the rain. He could see the old farmhouse up through the trees and slowed, looking for Slayton's truck. It wasn't in the drive next to the house and he didn't see anyone moving around. He stopped in front of the house and looked at the sad state of disrepair of the place and everything around. Rusted farm machines were left about in no particular order. Toys were scattered here and there and even a few dishes.

He sat in his truck, the engine running, his side-by-side 12 gauge shotgun sitting on the floor next to him propped up on the passenger's seat. There was a shell in the breach. He looked over at the gun and couldn't help but shiver at the thought of actually shooting a man. He had brought it for protection, having no idea what Slayton might do if he did find him.

Back in the War he had never had to shoot at a man. He had served on an aircraft carrier in the Pacific and had been shot at often enough. He thought about the men he had seen die during those years. Many were good friends and he wondered to himself how a low piece of trash like Harold Slayton could be allowed to live on this earth when so many good men had been taken away.

Jonathan opened the door and got out. He left the gun on the seat inside and started to walk around the side of the house. He could see a barn off behind the house, probably painted red at one time, but now a dingy and peeling grey and brown.

As he got to the back of the house he stopped suddenly and saw the rear tailgate of a rusted truck sticking out from behind the barn. He looked around, but still didn't see anyone. He started backing slowly up toward his own truck when he heard a door open. A chill rushed through him and he turned to see Harold Slayton coming out of the back door, a shotgun in his hand. The two men stood staring at each other for a moment.

"Who the hell are you?" Slayton yelled.

Jonathan watched as Slayton slid the safety off on the gun. He held it low pointing at the ground below the dilapidated old porch.

"You Harold Slayton?" Jonathan asked, trying to control his voice and keep his legs from shaking.

"Who wants to know?"

"My name's Jonathan McKendry."

"You that bitch's husband?"

Jonathan clinched his fists and had to breath deep to keep from rushing at the man. "I'm here to tell you Slayton that I don't want you coming near my wife again. I mean it."

Slayton laughed. "You talk pretty tough for a man that's got two barrels a 20 gauge aimed at his balls."

"Why don't you put that gun down and you and me get this taken care of right now," Jonathan said through clenched teeth.

"I think you better get the hell off my property. And don't go sending the law out here, cause I'll be gone again. Gone like the wind, ya hear?"

"Slayton, did you hear me about my wife?"

"Go fuck yourself, McKendry and get the hell out of here before I blow a good size hole in your gut."

"This isn't over, Slayton."

"Oh, I know it aint over. You two just keep your noses outta our family's business, ya hear?"

"It's my business now, Slayton. How could you hurt that little girl, let alone your own wife?"

"They only get what's comin' to em."

Jonathan started towards the porch and then stopped when Slayton raised the gun to his shoulder. "Alright Slayton, another time maybe."

"You don't get your ass outta here, they ain't gonna be no other time."

Jonathan backed away slowly. When he got to his truck he climbed inside and looked at his own shotgun lying against the seat. For a brief moment he was tempted to reach for it. He looked out through the windshield and saw Harold Slayton coming around the side of the house, the gun still resting in his hands. He put the gearshift in reverse and backed around. As he pulled out to leave he saw Slayton walking up onto the front porch of the house. Jonathan could see him staring back at him through his rearview mirror all the way out to the main road.

***

The nurse from Emily's office, who had been staying at the house through the day while Jonathan was away, came into Emily's room. "Dr. McKendry, you have another visitor."

Emily had been dozing off and she looked over at the nurse. "Who's here?"

"He says he's an old friend."

"Tell him to come in."

Emily tried to sit up as best she could and she adjusted her blankets around her. When she looked up at the door she couldn't have been any more surprised when she saw Connor Harris standing there. "Connor!"

"How long's it been, Emily?"

Back in their teens they had been close friends during the summers up in Charlevoix. Their parents had also been friends and for two summers just before the War they had even dated. That was before the summer of '41 when she had met Jonathan and Connor had his run-ins with both the McKendry boys.

"How are you?"

161

"I've been better," he said, touching the swollen bruise on his cheek and walking into the room and over to the side of the bed. His left eye was almost swollen shut and angry colors of blue and black spread out beneath it.

"I'm so sorry about Jennifer. Is she doing any better?"

"She'd be a lot better if it wasn't for that damned kid that had his way with her."

Emily could hear the old bitterness and anger in his voice that eventually alienated him from her all those years ago. "Connor, why are you here?"

"I heard about this Slayton mess and that you had been hurt. I just wanted to stop by to see how you were doing."

"I'll be alright, it's just going to take a day or so in bed to get this pain in my head to go away."

"You need to be careful around this Slayton fellow. All I'm hearing around town is how much trouble this guy is."

"I think it's a little bit late to worry about that now," she said, touching the bruise on her own cheek. She tried to smile, but it still hurt.

"Emily, it's good to see you. It's been far too long."

She just nodded.

"Do you ever think back to those summers we used to be together?"

"That was a long time ago."

"Yeah, I know. How are you and McKendry doing?"

"We're doing great. Jonathan's boat business is really doing well and we just bought a new house up on Michigan. We'll be moving up there in a couple of weeks."

"Yeah great," he said with little conviction.

"Connor, why'd you really come?"

"You're still friends with George Hansen, the lawyer?"

"He's probably our closest friend up here, why?"

Connor walked to the end of the bed and leaned on the brass railing. "I'm just worried that he's asking a lot of questions about that night out on the beach with Jennifer. I'm afraid he's going to get that Indian kid off."

"Did you ever think that he may just be innocent?" She watched as his face tightened and he looked away out the window. The rain was still falling in steady sheets now against the window pane.

"Emily, that damn kid attacked my sister and your friend Hansen is going to get him off as if nothing happened."

"And what do you expect me to do about it, as if I would anyway?"

"Emily, our families have been friends for a long time and you and I go back a long way. You know we used to have feelings for each other."

"Connor..."

"I'm just asking you to try to talk some sense into this Hansen guy, to at least get him to consider the evidence against this punk."

"From what I hear, there isn't any. Connor, George is just doing his job." She heard footsteps in the hall and then saw her husband walk through the bedroom door.

Jonathan stopped in surprise when he saw Connor Harris at the foot of their bed. "What the hell are you doing here?"

"McKendry, just settle down. I heard that Emily had been hurt and I just stopped by to see an old friend."

"Just get the hell out, now!"

"Jonathan!" Emily said.

"Emily, it's okay," Connor said and then he turned to look at Jonathan. "You know, I think back to that summer a lot, what was it, '41?"

Jonathan didn't respond.

"I never had a chance to say how badly I felt about Hansen's sister, what was her name...?"

"Catherine," Jonathan said, trying to keep control.

"It was a real shame, how it all came out."

"She'd be alive today if it wasn't for you, Harris."

Connor backed up as if Jonathan was going to come after him. "Look, I don't want any trouble, but it was your own damn brother that killed her!"

"Connor!" Emily screamed.

"Harris, you get out of my house now before I throw your ass out."

"Settle down, I'm leaving."

163

"I don't want to see you around here again," Jonathan said. "You stay away from Emily, do you hear me?"

Connor looked over at Emily and then stared hard back at Jonathan. Finally he turned and walked out of the room without saying another word.

***

George Hansen opened the door of the courthouse for Mary Truegood and her son Sammy. They had just come from the preliminary hearing that would finalize the charges against Sammy in the Jennifer Harris case. George stopped on the front steps and turned to face the Truegoods. "I'm so sorry that I wasn't able to head this off. It's just amazing to me that the Judge can hand down these charges with so little direct evidence."

"What did all of this mean, Mr. Hansen?"

"Sammy, you're being charged with first degree sexual assault," George said.

"I didn't do this! This is so unfair!"

"Sammy, as long as Jennifer Harris and her friends stick to their stories, which I have to say are extremely circumstantial, there is the possibility that the prosecutor can get a conviction."

"And how bad could that be?" Mary Truegood asked.

"I'm afraid that Sammy could be in jail for a very long time."

"What does *circumstantial* mean," Sammy asked.

"Well, it's a little confusing, but basically it means that there are a series of events or circumstances that lead to a conclusion that something happened," he explained. "The good news is that it's very difficult to get a conviction based entirely upon circumstantial evidence. So far, no one has come forward as a witness to actually seeing anything improper happening."

"That's because nothing did happen!" Sammy said.

"I know son. The biggest challenge we have is the testimony of Jennifer's friend, Elaine Howard, who says that she saw you coming back over the dunes just before she went back there and found Jennifer."

"I've told you, that's a lie!" Sammy protested.

"Doesn't she have to tell the truth in the court, Mr. Hansen?"

"She will take an oath and if she doesn't tell the truth, that's called perjury and she could be charged with a crime. Let's hope that is enough to convince her to do what's right."

"But why is she doing this?" Sammy asked. It was the hundredth time he had asked this very same question, both in his mind and with his lawyer, George Hansen.

George sighed and looked off across the lawn of the courthouse. "I don't know, Sammy. I really don't know."

Chapter Nineteen

Anna Bataglia sat across the big mahogany table in the dining cabin from Sally Clark. Alex sat at the head of the table and reached for the bell to have the server come back in with dessert. Behind him on the wall was a painting that Sally had done of the *EmmaLee* that first summer the ship had come back to Charlevoix. It was a scene from Round Lake with the ship at anchor and the homes along the hill on the north shore as a backdrop.

Anna watched Sally as she finished her meal and again the feelings of an aching jealously came back to her and she tried to push the thoughts away, but *damn*, here was this beautiful woman who had met one of the nicest and richest men in the country; homes in New York, Charlevoix, Palm Beach, the Bahamas, this incredible ship, the jets and on and on. She thought about her own failed marriage and how Richard had never come close to measuring up to Alex Clark. *Maybe this is just the wine.*

"Ladies, would you like a different wine with dessert?"

"Sure," answered Anna almost too quickly.

Sally looked up somewhat surprised at Anna's response. She had noticed that the lawyer that was supposed to be keeping her husband out of jail and financial ruin had been having no trouble emptying her wine glass all evening. Alex had been pouring rather heavily for everyone and she noticed that he was also a little over the edge of intoxication, but she realized that he probably needed to forget about his problems for a few hours. "Just decaf coffee for me now, honey," she said to Alex.

The server brought a dessert tray out that included several pies made fresh down in Traverse City, a chocolate cake and assorted pastries. They each made their selections and the server went back into the galley to prepare the plates.

Anna looked over at Alex and spoke slowly to avoid slurring her words. "This was a marvelous dinner, Alex. Thank you for including me."

"I'm glad you're enjoying it," Alex replied.

"Where are we cruising tonight, by the way?" she asked.

"Just a few miles down Lake Charlevoix and then back," Alex said.

"We really should have dessert brought up on deck." Sally said. "It's such a beautiful night."

"Great idea," said Alex and then he went back into the galley to give the instructions.

Anna couldn't stop herself with the short moment alone with Sally Clark. "Sally, do you know that you are one of the luckiest women in the world?"

Sally's defenses went up. The question seemed so out of place. "Luckiest?"

"You're practically living like a princess."

"A princess?"

"And then to have Alex Clark," she stopped, her brain finally pushing through the fog of the wine to realize what she was saying.

Sally was shocked by the outburst and didn't know what to say.

"Sally, I'm sorry, it's just that…"

"Just what…?"

Anna reached for her wine glass and finished the small amount left in the bottom. "Well…"

Alex walked back into the cabin. "Everyone ready?" He looked at the strange expression on both women's face. "Did I miss something interesting?"

Sally and Anna looked back from Alex. They both stared at each other for a moment and then Sally said, "Yes Anna, what were you saying?"

"I think I've said enough."

***

Dylan Harris walked along the waterline on the shore, the wet sand soft and leaving deep foot prints behind him. He had a cell phone to his ear with one hand and a cigar burning in the other. The last light of day was fading through the tall trees and the big bullfrogs in the marshes were the only sounds in the quiet bay. He had the strong facial features of his father, Connor in his youth; full sandy brown eyebrows and long straight brown hair edged in gray and brushed straight back.

"I need those revised site plans up here tomorrow. I don't care if you have to get on a plane yourself and bring them to my front door for breakfast, but I need them tomorrow!"

He continued to walk as he listened to the response on the other end of the line.

"I'm through listening to excuses, damn it! Get it done!"

He slapped the phone against his thigh to close it and then stuffed it into the inside pocket of his jacket.

***

Megan had agreed to meet Will Truegood at ten o'clock out on the south pier by the lighthouse. Will had suggested that it was probably better that they not be seen together in town any more than necessary until this car theft situation had been worked out. As Megan walked out along the broad expanse of the steel and concrete structure she passed fishermen sitting patiently on chairs watching their poles lean against the metal rail, lovers walking arm in arm and a few random teens on skateboards. The sun had dropped below the far horizon across the lake, but the sky was lit up in bright reds and blues against the scattered shapes of clouds.

The light on top of the lighthouse turned slowly covering all points on the compass, a beacon to travelers for countless years for safe passage into Round Lake and the little town of Charlevoix. Only when she came around the big white structure of the lighthouse could she see Will Truegood leaning against the rail at the end of the pier, watching the sunset sky fade into another night. He didn't seem to notice her come up next to him.

"Lost in thought?" she said.

He looked up, startled and smiled when he saw her. "I was just thinking of the words of my people that my father and grandfather shared with me as a kid."

"What was that?"

168

"It's about looking to the sun and the moon and the sky everyday and knowing the Creator is watching down on us."

Megan joined him in looking out at the spectacular fading sky display. "Only a God in heaven could create something so beautiful," she said. When she turned back he was staring at her. "What?" she asked quietly.

"Something so beautiful?" he said, looking directly into her eyes.

"The sky, Will."

A smile slowly came across his face, "Right, the sky."

Megan was a little flustered at his not so transparent flirting. "I had a conversation with my friend Melissa about her car last night."

Will seemed to come back to the moment and the smile faded. "Melissa... what did she have to say?"

"She claims that it was taken from her driveway when she left her keys in the ignition."

"Who leaves their keys in their car anymore?" he said.

"Exactly, and it's just too coincidental that a friend of mine would have her car stolen and end up in your driveway."

"What's going on here?"

"I'm really not sure, but I have someone else I need to talk to."

"Who's that?" Will asked.

Megan leaned her back against the rail and looked back down the channel to the big blue drawbridge. "Just a friend."

"Megan, thanks," he said. "I don't know what the hell is going on here, but the cops don't seem too interested in helping me find out."

Megan shook her head and sighed.

"What is it?" he asked.

"I don't know. I should probably make a couple of calls before it gets any later. Where are you staying tonight?"

"I should get back out to the cabin, but my truck is still out there."

"I can give you a ride," Megan offered. "I need to go up to the house to get the Jeep. I'll meet you downtown."

"How about the coffee shop? I'll get us something to drink."

They walked back down the pier together and when they got to the bridge, Megan headed up the hill to get her car. Will turned to go down to the coffee shop.

"I'll be back in a few minutes," she said and waved to him.

As she walked across the bridge she took the cell phone out of her purse and hit a speed dial number. The phone rang four times before the answering mailbox came on. She listened to the recorded message. "*Hello this is Rick, sorry I missed your call. Leave your number and I'll call you back.*" She waited for the beep and then answered, "Rick, it's Megan. I really need to talk to you tonight. Call me."

Looking up, she nearly ran into Gwen Roberts, Sally's old partner in the gallery down on Bridge Street.

"Megan, is that you?" Gwen asked.

"Hi Gwen, I'm sorry I didn't see you. How are you?" She gave Gwen a hug and then stepped back.

"I don't think you've met my new partner. Megan, this is Tara Peterson."

Tara stepped forward and held out her hand. "Hi Megan, it's really nice to meet you. I had a chance to see Sally the other day and Gwen has told me so much about your family and the *EmmaLee*."

"Hi Tara," Megan said, returning her greeting and hand shake.

"We're just coming back from dinner at the Weathervane," Gwen said. "We really need to get together with you and your folks, Megan."

"Oh I know Sally and Dad would love to. Maybe we can all take a little dinner trip on the *EmmaLee*. Let me check how long my dad is going to be up here. I'm not sure when he has to get back to New York, but Sally and I plan to be up for most of the summer."

"That's what Sally said the other day," Gwen responded. "That's great, just call when you have a chance to check with them. And stop down to the gallery when you get some time. We would love to show you some of the new work we have in this summer."

"Okay, great. I'll have Sally get back in touch and Tara, it was really nice to meet you."

They said they're good-byes and the two women passed on the bridge and continued on into town. Megan watched them go for a moment and thought back to the first summer she had met Gwen here in Charlevoix. She knew how close Sally and Gwen had been. It would be nice to get everyone together again, she thought.

***

The *EmmaLee* had dropped anchor back in the small harbor of Round Lake. Alex and Sally had decided to stay on the ship for the night. They both were sitting on lounge chairs on the rear deck of the boat. Anna had excused herself earlier after several cups of coffee to go to bed. She hadn't said anything else to Sally about her earlier comments on her relationship with Alex Clark.

Sally, however, had been unable to think of little else. She knew that Anna had certainly had too much to drink, but that really didn't excuse the emotions or intent behind her remarks.

"What a beautiful sky," Alex said, looking up at the stars above them.

Sally looked over at her husband, considering whether she should say anything about Anna, or not. *Doesn't he have enough to worry about?*

"Sally?"

"I'm sorry, honey, what did you say?"

"Look at this sky," he said again, reaching for her hand.

Sally looked up at the clear black sky and the brilliant display of a million shining stars and constellations. "It's gorgeous."

"We should get some blankets and just sleep out here under the stars tonight." Alex said.

Sally laughed and said, "I thought it was only Anna that had a few too many glasses of wine tonight. I'm not sleeping out here! It gets cold up here at night."

"I know, but still…"

"Alex…"

"I'm just kidding. Anna did get a little wasted tonight, didn't she?"

"A little?"

171

"That's really not like her. I don't know what was going on," Alex said.

"I know she's working hard for you and the whole situation is more than a little stressful, but I don't think getting drunk is going to help."

"It's really just not like her."

Sally couldn't help but be honest with him about what had happened earlier. "You've known Anna for a long time haven't you?" she asked.

Alex squeezed Sally's hand more tightly and turned in his chair to face her. "Just professionally, dear. Nothing more."

Sally sat there for a few moments looking at her husband. "You may already know this, but Anna Bataglia seems to have more than just a professional attachment to you."

Alex choked before he tried to speak. "What are you talking about?"

"When you stepped into the galley tonight, Anna started in on *how lucky I was to have you* and how *I'm so fortunate to live like a princess* and…"

"Oh Sally, come on. She just had a little too much to drink."

"Whatever, Alex, I'm just telling you that women have a sixth sense about these things and I can tell you that your lawyer has the hots for you."

***

Megan pulled into the dark wooded drive leading back to Will's cabin. He sat next to her in the dark giving directions.

"How did you ever find this place?" she asked.

"It's been passed down through the family. My grandfather built the original cabin years ago." The cabin came into sight up ahead in the car headlights.

"Will, this is so cool back in here."

"Yeah, Horton Creek is just out behind there."

She stopped the car and put the transmission in park. "Will, there's something I need to tell you."

"Sure."

"I'm not sure, but you remember meeting my friend, Rick, down at the boat."

"Yeah, the big friendly guy," he said sarcastically.

"You know who I mean," Megan said. "Well, he's not particularly happy about the time that you and I have been spending together."

"I guess that's his problem."

"No, you don't understand. He and I have been dating since last summer and well, the other night he got a little upset about you and me."

"What *you and me*? We just went fishing!"

"I know, but you have to know Rick."

"So why are you telling me this? You don't want to see me anymore?" he asked.

"No, it's not that. I tried to reach Rick earlier, but he hasn't called me back. This stolen car thing…"

"What about it?"

"I told you I went to see Melissa tonight and she was just so weird about the whole thing and when I confronted her on it she got all defensive and upset with me."

"Why would she get mad at you?"

"Well, I guess I implied that I didn't believe her story."

"So what do you think's going on here?" Will asked.

Megan turned in her seat to face him. "It's just so weird that her car would end up down here and then get reported stolen. I just can't help thinking that Rick was involved in this to get you in trouble."

"You're kidding?"

"He's good friends with Melissa, too and…"

"That sonofabitch!"

Megan put her hand on his arm. "Will, I really didn't want to say anything until I was sure, but…"

"We need to go back to town to find this guy," Will said, clearly irritated.

"No Will, let's wait until…" She stopped when she saw headlights pulling up behind her on the road. The vehicle came to a stop but the lights continued to shine brightly through the back window of the Jeep. Megan and Will both looked back, squinting, trying to see who it was.

"What the hell," Will said and turned to open his door. He got out and started to walk back around the Jeep. Megan jumped out, too and met him at the back of the car. They stopped when both doors on the vehicle in front of them opened. The lights still shined in their eyes and Megan couldn't see who it was at first until Rick Brandtley walked up into the light and stopped in front of them. His friend Jimmy Norton came around and joined him.

Megan was shocked to see the two of them. "Rick, what..."

"Megan, you need to leave. We'll talk later," Rick said in a low and threatening voice.

Megan was immediately irritated by his tone and said, "Rick, I just gave Will a ride home."

"Yeah, I know. I saw you pick him up in town. Jimmy and I were sitting over in the park."

Will stepped forward and stood between Megan and Rick. "Brandtley, how'd you find this place?"

Rick seemed surprised at the question and hesitated a minute before answering. "We followed your ass out here."

"Rick, you need to settle down," Megan said.

"Megan, you need to get in your car and go home. I'll call you later. Jimmy and I need to have a few words with your friend here."

Will started toward Rick until Megan grabbed his arm. "Will, don't! Rick, this is ridiculous. Nothing's happened here. Will and I are just friends."

"Yeah, I've noticed. Megan, you and I can talk about this later, but now you need to leave!"

"I'm not going anywhere!" she said, pushing Will back to get in Rick's face. "What do you know about Melissa's stolen car?"

"What are talking about?" Brandtley said.

"How convenient for Melissa to leave her keys in the car and then it ends up out here in Will's drive."

"Because he stole the damn thing!" Jimmy Norton said.

"Rick, if you had anything to do with this, I swear..."

"Megan, you don't know what you're talking about," Rick said.

"Brandtley, you need your friend here for this little *discussion* we need to have?" Will said, slowly pushing Megan aside. He got within inches of

Rick Brandtley's face and said, "Why don't you and I step around back and have this discussion alone."

Rick pushed out suddenly with both hands and knocked Will back into Megan.

"Rick, stop it!" she screamed. "Both of you stop it!" She couldn't help herself, but she started to cry. She wiped her tears away with both hands and then said, "Rick, you and Jimmy get out of here, now. I'll be back to town later and we can talk."

"No, we're going to..." Rick started.

"Rick! I'm serious, if you ever want to see me again you better leave now!" Megan said.

He hesitated for a moment, looking back at her and then over at Will Truegood. "Okay Jimmy, let's go." Then he pointed at Will. "You need to stay out here in the sticks where you belong. Stay away from Megan, you hear me?"

"I'll go wherever I want you asshole and get off my property!"

Rick started back towards him and Megan jumped between them holding him back. "Leave now!" she screamed again.

Rick reluctantly backed away and both he and his friend got back in the car. As he turned around he rolled down his window. "I don't know what's up with you this summer, Megan, but this shit has got to stop."

She didn't answer him. He looked at her for a few seconds and then jammed the transmission into drive and spun the wheels of his car as they left. Megan and Will stood together watching as the red tail lights sped out through the trees to the main road.

"Megan, you didn't have to stand up for me there."

She turned to look at him. "Are all men as stupid as you two?"

"What?"

"This is all ridiculous," she said, turning to walk back to the Jeep.

"Megan, I'm sorry, but I'm not going to take that kind of crap from that guy and if he had anything to do with this car theft, I'm going to have some *serious* words with him!"

"Well, we'll have to see about that," she said.

"What are you going to do?"

"I don't know!" she said, sniffing and wiping away more tears.

Will grabbed her by the arms and held her close. He just looked at her for a moment and then said, "Megan, thank you for what you're doing to help me."

"Yeah, a lot of good I'm doing."

"You really shouldn't be risking your friendships like this. I can take care of myself."

"What, by beating up Rick Brandley? That's going to do a lot of good."

"I don't know…" he responded.

Megan looked at this boy that she had known for such a short time. She couldn't deny that her feelings were growing for Will Truegood. *Great Megan, this is a going to a real fun summer!* She realized that he was holding her and she slid her hands down to take his. "Will, I don't want anybody to get hurt, particularly over me."

"I know."

They stood looking at each other. Megan felt his hands in hers and the warmth of his touch was soothing and reassuring.

"Megan Clark, you're a special girl," he said.

She just kept looking at him in the dim light shining around the side of the Jeep.

He leaned forward slowly and she knew that he was going to try to kiss her and in that split second she decided that things couldn't get any crazier, so why not. She closed her eyes and felt his lips touch hers. The cool wetness of it surprised her and she pulled back and looked at him and then kissed him this time. They stood together then and only the sounds of the motor running and a few crickets in the weeds broke the stillness of the night.

"I better go," she said.

Chapter Twenty

Jonathan McKendry and I had been through enough together that I should never be surprised by how he reacted to things. I guess he was about as headstrong as I am and when it came to Emily, he was never one to think too clearly.

***

Jonathan put the phone down in the kitchen and started back to the bedroom to check on his wife. He had just spoken to Sheriff Willy Potts to tell him that Harold Slayton was back at the farm. Potts had asked him how he knew where the man was. Jonathan told him what had happened when he went out to the farm and the old sheriff had yelled at him to stay away from Slayton and let him and his men take care of the situation.

Yeah right, Jonathan thought to himself as he walked back along the hallway. He remembered the look on Slayton's face when they had confronted each other and he also remembered the two barrels of the shotgun staring back at him. When he got to the bedroom, Emily was asleep. He was still furious that Connor Harris had come into their home. *I don't care what happened to his sister, that asshole needs another board across his head*, he thought, remembering the night his brother Luke had come to his defense and attacked Connor Harris. Jonathan had been pleased to hear that Sammy Truegood had landed at least one good shot on the sonofabitch.

The nurse was sitting next to the bed reading a book.

He turned to leave and whispered, "I'll be back in a bit."

He drove out to his boatyard on the road south of town to East Jordan. He pulled up and parked in front of the low building that held his office. A large boathouse and storage facility sat behind it, painted white with a sign over the big front door that read, *McKendry's Boatworks*. His employee's cars were parked over on the side, but there was one other car parked in front of the office. He went inside and his assistant and bookkeeper, Tracy, was at her desk. She nodded over to the right where he saw a customer sitting in his office, a Mr. Tom Fitzgibbons from Detroit. They were about done working on his new boat.

He walked into his office. "Tom, how are you?" Jonathan reached out to shake his hand.

Fitzgibbons stood and Jonathan could tell from the look on his face that something was wrong. "Morning, Jonathan." He was a big man, several inches taller than Jonathan and probably twice as big around. His white shirt was crisply starched, but not tucked in, probably because his belly stuck so far out over his belt. Jonathan noticed the big gold ring on his right hand with a fraternity sign of some kind etched on a blue stone.

"What's up, Tom? Your boat should be ready in a couple more days."

"Jonathan, I don't know if you're aware, but we are real close with the Harris family, Jennifer and Connor Harris' parents."

"No, I didn't know that. It's really too bad about Jennifer," Jonathan said.

"Yes, it really is and that's what I wanted to talk to you about."

Jonathan was immediately concerned. He walked around his desk and sat down. "What's the problem, Tom?"

"This boy, Sam Truegood, works for you doesn't he?"

"Yeah, for over a year. He's been doing a great job."

The man squirmed a bit in his chair. "You know what he's done, with Jennifer I mean?"

Jonathan sat forward and crossed his hands in front of him on the desk. "Now Tom, you know that hasn't been proven yet and from what I'm hearing from my friend George Hansen who is defending Sammy, there's little or no evidence that he even touched the girl." Jonathan could see that Tom Fitzgibbons was getting more and more irritated.

"That's the thing here, Jonathan, you and your friend Hansen are defending this boy and he should be rotting in jail for what he's done!"

"Now wait a minute, Tom…"

"No, you wait a minute. People in town are all talking about this and no one can believe that you're taking the side of this Indian kid."

"Tom, you need to stop right there," Jonathan said.

"No McKendry, you need to stop. You need to stop and think about what you're doing. Is that kid still working here?"

"He sure is. He's out on bail and he's welcome to work here as long he wants, or until a court of law says otherwise."

"That's a real bad decision, Jonathan. You've got a business to run here and if you want any more business from the people of this community you better think again about how you're protecting this boy."

Jonathan felt the anger burning inside him and he tried to keep calm with this man who was not only a very big customer, but also quite influential with the summer families that came up to Charlevoix each year. "Tom, listen to me on this. George Hansen and the sheriff have done a lot of work and the facts are just not adding up."

"The boy was charged with sexual assault against Jennifer Harris!" the big man bellowed, his face turning red.

"Charges are one thing, Tom, proof is another."

Tom Fitzgibbons stood and looked down at Jonathan. "You're making a real bad decision about this boy, McKendry. If you and your friend Hansen want to keep working in this town, you should really reconsider how you're handling all this."

Jonathan stood up quickly. "Tom, I appreciate your business and I'll have your boat for you in a couple of days and I hope to build another one for you someday, but I will *not* condemn a young kid who may very well be innocent!"

Fitzgibbons shook his head in disgust. "That's a real shortsighted decision, McKendry."

***

George Hansen walked in to the drugstore and up to the lunch counter. He ordered a cup of coffee and a donut to take back to his office. As he was walking out the door he ran into an older woman that he knew from some legal work he had done this past year. Her name was Howard and then it occurred to him that she was Elaine Howard's mother, Jennifer Harris' friend from the beach. *Oh great!*

"Good morning Mrs. Howard," he said, holding the door for her. She was a slight woman, barely coming up to his chest and rail thin. Her clothes were cut elegantly and the hat on her head had a small pheasant tail feather that brushed his chin as she walked by.

The woman looked up and recognized George and immediately got a sour look across her face. "George Hanson, I need to speak with you!"

He stepped back into the store with her. "How are you today, Mrs. Howard?"

"Do you have any idea what you're doing?" she said loudly.

George knew where she was going with all this. "What's that, Mrs. Howard?"

"How can you stand up for this Indian boy?"

"You mean Sam Truegood?"

"Yes, and you're defending this boy who attacked little Jennifer and could have just as well had his way with my Elaine!"

"Mrs. Howard…"

"Listen George, I just saw your wife Elizabeth down the street and I told her the same thing. You need to think twice about helping this boy. The whole town is not looking very favorably on your decision."

"The whole town," he repeated, trying to remain calm. "The whole town, or just you and the Harris family?"

"George…!"

"Mrs. Howard, please. I can understand how you feel, particularly with your daughter involved in all this, but this is what I do. This is my job. I'm a lawyer. I defend people."

"You don't have to defend anybody if you don't want to!" she said and then walked away quickly to the back of store.

He watched her leave and then turned to go out the door. He noticed that the young girl behind the counter was watching him. She wasn't smiling either.

***

Sheriff Potts drove Agnes and Sara Slayton out to their farm. They sat in the back and he looked at the little girl in his rearview mirror. She was reading a book and except for the nasty bruise across her cheek, she looked like any normal happy girl. He felt his anger boil as he thought about the way Slayton had been treating his family.

A deputy sat beside him. They had received Jonathan's call earlier in the morning that Slayton had been back at the farm. He doubted that he would still be there, but decided it was best to bring along some additional help.

"Sheriff, this is awful nice of you to bring us out here," Agnes Slayton said.

"Not a problem, Mrs. Slayton," he said, looking at her in the mirror. "I'm not sure this is such a good idea, but I'm going to leave Deputy Jurgenson here with you for a few hours to help you get settled in and to talk to your husband if he happens to stop back."

"You're going to arrest him, aren't you," she asked.

"Well, yes we are, mam. A man can't go around attacking people like he did with Dr. McKendry and we can't have him treating you this way either."

"Sheriff, I'm sorry about what happened to the doctor, but we can take care of ourselves out here."

"With all due respect, mam, it doesn't look like you're doing a very good job of it."

The *Slayton* mailbox was up ahead on the left and the sheriff slowed the patrol car to pull into the road back to the farmhouse. The rain had stopped, but big puddles of brown water and mud covered the old road. He turned to his deputy. "Keep a close eye now."

He drove slowly over the bumpy road and as the farmhouse came into view he scanned the area to see if there were any signs of Slayton. Jonathan had said that his truck had been parked out behind the barn, but he couldn't see back there yet. He pulled up to the side of the old white house and turned off the car. They all sat quietly for a bit, looking around to see if Slayton would come out. There seemed to be no sign of anyone around. He turned to the backseat and said, "Okay, let's get you going here."

Everyone got out of the car and Potts watched as his deputy walked with Agnes Slayton and little Sara into the house. He walked around to the back and he could see the old sagging barn, but as he came around to the backyard there didn't appear to be any truck parked back there. A few chickens came out from the other side of the house and he kept walking back to the barn, his boots sliding in the fresh mud from the rain storm. As he came up to the big door that was closed on the front of the barn he saw tire tracks around to his left. When he walked over it was clear in the mud that a truck had pulled in, then backed out and left. The tracks looked like they had been made fairly recently.

The sheriff unbuckled the holster for his gun and walked into the barn. Light from a side window let enough light in that he could see a rusted old tractor parked in the back. The smell of manure and rotting hay was overpowering and he covered his nose. He walked back out into the light and the fresh air. The Slayton house looked like it could fall over in the next big wind.

***

Sammy Truegood was working up in the big cruiser being built for the Fitzgibbons family. He was finishing up on some wiring for the electrical system. He was having a little trouble with the bandage on this right hand from hitting Connor Harris. This was his first day back at work since the incident at the beach and when he had arrived earlier in the morning his co-workers were cool at best. Most just turned and ignored him when he came in. His boss, Pete Borders, was the shop supervisor and had always been a big supporter for Sammy. He was an old grizzled local who had worked on boats his entire life. Jonathan had hired him away from a bigger company down in Cadillac a few years ago.

When he saw Sammy come in that morning, he walked over and pulled the boy aside. "I know Mr. McKendry wants you back at work, but I don't want no trouble from any of this getting' in the way of the work. You hear me?"

Sammy had just nodded and gone over to sign in on his time card and then climbed up into the Fitzgibbons boat to go to work. The other workers kept their distance. Occasionally Sammy could hear whispers and when he would look over they would turn away.

Later that morning, Sammy heard his named called. He went over to the side of the boat and saw Jonathan McKendry standing there. "Sammy, come on down. I need to speak with you."

The two walked together out through the big boathouse door and stood in the wet gravel, dark clouds still moving low over the buildings.

"Sammy, you doing okay?" Jonathan asked.

He looked up at the man that had been so kind to him these past couple of years, the man who had given him this opportunity in life. The McKendry's had become close friends with his family over the years and Dr. McKendry always dropped Christmas presents by their house, and occasionally a loaf of fresh bread that she had baked.

"Mr. McKendry, I'll tell you, I've definitely been better," he said.

"I know, son."

"I just keep asking myself why these people are doing this to me, making up these charges and all. You know I didn't do any of this, Mr. McKendry?"

"Yes, I know, but you're going to have to be real strong through all this. A lot of people have got their minds made up about what happened out there that night. You just need to keep faith that the truth will all come out."

"Thanks for having me back to work," Sammy said.

"The boys giving you any trouble in there?" Jonathan asked.

"No, I'll be alright. I better get back. Old Pete will come looking for me."

Jonathan laughed and said, "I'll take care of old Pete. You get back in there. We need to get this boat in the water by the end of the week."

"Thanks Mr. McKendry." He walked back into the boathouse and climbed the ladder up into the Fitzgibbons boat, the smell of fresh varnish and sawdust sweet in the air.

***

Jennifer Harris came out of a clothing store along Bridge Street with her friend Elaine. Both had bags with new purchases in their hands and Jennifer carried an umbrella although the rain had stopped over an hour ago.

The sidewalks were crowded in spite of the weather and the two girls moved out into the flow of the summer people shopping along the main commercial district of Charlevoix.

Jennifer looked up ahead and saw a family that she recognized, the Fitzgibbons; Mrs. Fitzgibbons and her three daughters, all in high school, but younger than Jennifer. The woman saw her and Jennifer watched as a strange look came across her face as she slowed and put her arms out as if she was trying to protect her daughters. Jennifer and Elaine continued to walk up to them. Jennifer felt the familiar emptiness inside coming back.

"Good morning, Mrs. Fitzgibbons," she said.

The woman just stared back at her for a moment and the three daughters all remained silent as well and Jennifer could see that they were startled and maybe even a little afraid. She nodded to the girls, Elaine stood quietly beside her.

"It's nice to see all of you," Jennifer continued.

Finally the woman spoke, but with a sharp edge she said, "Jennifer Harris, you should be ashamed of yourself!"

"Excuse me?" Jennifer said, the feeling of her heart sinking in her chest growing stronger.

"You've embarrassed your family and all of us summer people..."

"Mrs. Fitzgibbons!" Elaine said loudly, interrupting the woman. "You have no right to say that!"

Jennifer held up her hand to quiet her friend. "Elaine, it's alright." She looked back at the woman and her three daughters who had always been so pleasant and friendly with her. "I'm sorry you feel that way, Mrs. Fitzgibbons and I'm sorry for what's happened."

"Well I guess," the woman said and then she made a great flourish in herding her daughters around Jennifer and Elaine and then on down the sidewalk.

Jennifer turned to watch them walk away. Images from the night on the beach flashed back in her mind as they had been so often in the past few days; swimming with Sammy and Elaine, the big bonfire, the bottles of whiskey. The thought of the whiskey made her shiver and she tried again to force her mind to remember what had happened up in the dunes.

ON PAST HORTON CREEK

***

Sara Slayton sat in an old wicker chair on the porch of their house playing with her favorite doll, taking its worn dress off and then putting it on again, brushing at the doll's hair with her fingers. It was hard with the cast on her arm, but she was managing. She had been out there since the deputy had been picked up and left over an hour ago.

The clouds from the morning's rain were breaking apart and patches of blue were showing through the dark clouds. Rolling waves of sunshine moved slowly across the muddy front lawn and then the gray shadows would come again. The little girl looked up when she heard the sound of a car's engine. Her father's battered and rusted truck was coming up the front drive splashing brown water out of the puddles. She could just see the outline of her father through the glare of the windshield.

Chapter Twenty-one

Alex Clark sat on the deck of the *EmmaLee*, wrapped up in a heavy cotton robe, drinking his coffee as morning forced its way upon the quiet little harbor. His hair was going in all directions and a dull ache in his temple was a reminder of one too many bottles of wine from the previous night. He sat staring at the other boats anchored across Round Lake and the long white boathouse over towards the Chicago Club, but it was all in soft focus because he was thinking about the trouble he was facing with his business and the betrayal of his partner, Louis Kramer.

Then he remembered Sally's comments just before they turned in last night about his lawyer, Anna Bataglia, and her suspicions that Anna was holding some attraction for him. He sipped from his coffee mug and leaned his head back to let the warmth of it work its way down. Anna was a damn attractive woman, he thought and he couldn't deny that he found her attractive in some detached way; her intelligence and savvy; certainly her physical attributes. But he had never approached the issue with her over the many years they had worked together. She had been married most of that time, as had he until his wife had died a few years before he met Sally. He was not surprised to hear of Anna's supposed interest in him. There had always been something between the two of them, just below the surface; a place that neither of them had ever chosen to approach.

He looked up when Anna came up from below and walked over to him, taking a chair next to his. She was wearing a black jogging suit with white stripes down the outside of her legs and arms. Her hair was only slightly less disheveled than his, tied back with a black ribbon, loose ends going in all directions.

"Morning," he said.

"Good morning, Alex." She sat down slowly as if there were eggs on the cushion that might break.

"Late night, eh counselor?"

"Yes, much too late. Did someone just open up my mouth last night and pour a barrel of wine down my throat?"

Alex laughed and reached for the carafe on the small table between them. "Coffee?"

"How about some morphine for this headache. Yeah, I'll have some coffee." She reached for the other mug and held it up while he poured.

"Sally tells me that the two of you had an interesting conversation last night," he said.

Anna looked over at him with a puzzled expression. "What was that?"

Alex started to have second thoughts about even bringing it up, but *what the hell*, he thought. "Is there something between you and me that we need to talk about?" he asked.

"About the defense?"

"About you and me."

He could see Anna's mind working quickly to respond. He rarely saw her lose her composure like this. *Maybe it's the hangover.*

"Alex, there's no time for this now. We need to stay focused on the investigation."

"I didn't bring it up."

"Look, I'm sorry if I upset Sally last night. I had too much to drink and I got stupid. I'm sorry."

"Is that all it was?" he asked.

She didn't answer right away, but just looked back at him. They both turned when Sally came around the corner of the cabin wall.

"Hey, good morning to you," Alex said.

Sally came up and pulled another chair up forming a small circle of the three of them. She already had a cup of coffee in her hands. The air was still cool from the previous night and goose bumps stood out on her bare legs beneath the khaki shorts that she was wearing. "Morning, all."

"Good morning, Sally," Anna said. "I think I owe you an apology for last night."

"Anna…"

"No, really I'm sorry. I was just telling Alex that I get stupid when I have too much vino."

Sally looked back at her for a few moments trying to read any deeper meaning or intent in her words. "Let's just put it behind us, fair enough?"

"Fair enough," Anna replied.

Alex cleared his throat, not because he was trying to get anyone's attention, but because he was still feeling the effects of the wine. "Anna, what's the plan today?" he asked.

Anna took a deep breath to gather herself and clear her mind. "I'm waiting for a couple of callbacks this morning on the inquiries I made yesterday on some of our friend, Louis', little surprises. We should spend some time later this morning, or first thing this afternoon. Then, I really need to get back to New York tonight, or as early as possible in the morning. I have to cover a lot of ground tomorrow."

"If you don't need me, I'd like to stay a few more days," he said.

"That should be fine. We can talk by phone if necessary."

"Let me call the service and see when we can get the plane back here tonight," he offered.

"Thank you, that would be great."

"Honey, what have you got planned for the day?" he asked.

"We should try to spend some time with Megan, maybe take a picnic somewhere on the little *Emma*."

"That's a great idea. I haven't seen my daughter for more than five seconds since I got into town."

"I heard her come in a little late last night, so I'm sure she's still sleeping," Sally said.

Anna stood up. "If you two will excuse me, I need a shower and a bottle of aspirin. I'll call you a little later, Alex."

"Fine Anna, I'll have my cell with me."

She walked away and disappeared into a side cabin door. Alex watched her walk away and then noticed Sally watching him. "I tried to clear the air with her this morning, about last night."

"And what did she have to say?" Sally asked.

"She apologized for having too much to drink and said that we really need to keep focused on the investigation."

"But she didn't deny her feelings?"

Alex sat forward in his chair and reached for her hand. "Sally, whatever personal feelings she may have for me or anyone else are secondary right now and she knows it. She's a professional and will not do anything to jeopardize the defense we're preparing, or frankly, to jeopardize her biggest client's relationship with his wife that he loves very much."

"I saw you watching that tight little bottom of hers."

Alex squirmed and shook his head. "Guilty as charged. It's a *man* thing, we just can't help ourselves."

"Alex, I trust you and I love you. It's Anna Bataglia I'm worried about."

***

Louis Kramer waited while the phone was ringing, sitting on a deck chair on the front porch of his wife's lake house. A voice answered at the other end. It was their company's financial manager, Bobby Littlefair. His voice sounded groggy and distant. "Hey, it's Lou."

"This better be important, it's two o'clock in the morning here."

"Where are you?"

"I'd rather not say on an open line. What do you need?"

"Our *friend*, Alberto, came to visit yesterday."

"You still in Charlevoix?" Littlefair asked.

"Yeah, but I'm heading back to the city tomorrow."

"What did Manta want?"

"What do you think, he wants his money."

"The stock has been suspended on the exchange. He can't sell any shares."

"He doesn't want to sell shares, he wants us to cash him out and make him whole in the process."

189

There was silence on the other end of the line for a few moments. "What, he must be down ten million where the stock is now."

"In round numbers," Kramer said.

"Did you tell him to fuck off?"

"Yeah right, you don't talk to Alberto Manta like that if you want to stay on the right side of the dirt." Louis swallowed hard. "Can't we pull some money out of one of the other companies?"

Littlefair choked on the other end of the line. "Shit, we're looking at 25 to life for what's already gone down and you want to pull some more crap like that."

"You can make the paperwork come out right; you're a magician, Bobby."

"I'm not digging this hole any deeper, Lou."

"Look, Manta is serious. We need to cash him out of this."

"There is no fucking way, Kramer!" The Feds have everything locked down. We can't sniff near any of those accounts without sirens going off."

Louis felt his gut rumble. "Yeah, you're right."

"Look, I need to get some sleep," Littlefair said.

"You need to come home, Bobby."

"My lawyer's working on it."

***

Sheriff Elam Stone walked through the door to the law offices of Hansen and MacGregor. Bill MacGregor had been taking over the practice from George for the past ten years, but George had still kept working on a few cases that interested him. MacGregor met him in the lobby when he heard the bell over the door ring. They went back to a small conference room.

"Coffee, Elam?"

"No thanks, Bill. I've had my four cups already this morning."

They both sat down. "What can I help you with, Sheriff?"

"A couple more questions since we talked the other day. You ever heard of a man named Vince Slayton?"

MacGregor thought for a moment and then shook his head, "Don't believe I have."

"So you don't know if George had any dealings with the man?"

"He may have. I never knew everything that George was working on."

"Any way you can check?" the sheriff asked.

"I've been through the files and I don't recall anything about a Vince Slayton."

Stone put his hat down on the table and fidgeted with the brim. "Any chance I can take a look at those files, Bill?"

"You know that's privileged information between lawyer and client, Elam."

"Right. Again, like we talked about the other day, nothing in those files, or anything that George had been working on that would have him on the wrong side of the wrong people?"

"No, really, Elam, it was pretty ordinary stuff."

***

Connor Harris walked into the darkly lit den of their summer home. Richly stained mahogany paneled walls were framed with tall book shelves filled with novels and business books and family mementos. His son Dylan sat behind the big desk, a phone to his ear, papers spread out in front of him. Dylan was fifty-four years old now and Connor noticed that his age was beginning to show with lines along his face, sagging cheek lines and touches of gray in his hair. His mother had not aged particularly well either, he thought. They had divorced twenty years ago and he had rarely seen her since. The last he had heard she was living with a retired dentist in a little beachfront condo on Clearwater Beach. *Good riddance!* Dylan had been running the family's real estate development business since his father had been sent away to prison, but Connor had kept an active hand for the years since he had been released..

Dylan looked up when he saw his father walk into the room and he gestured for him to wait just a moment and grab one of the chairs on the other side of the desk. When he finished his conversation and put the phone back in the cradle, he took a long sip from his coffee. "Hey, Pop."

191

"The plans come in?" Connor asked.

"Yeah, I was just looking at them. Fed Ex came about an hour ago."

"What do you think?"

"The planning commission is still going to have issues with how this lays out on the property with this wetlands bullshit," he said, pointing to an area on the building site plans laid out in front of them. "If we don't use a good bit of this land area we can't put enough units into the project to make the numbers work."

"I know." Connor said. "How do we stand with the commission and how they'll come down on this?"

"It's too damn close, plus the resident association adjoining the property is still raising hell."

Connor got up and walked over to a window looking out on the side yard of the property. "You know we need to make this work," he said, looking back at his son.

Dylan Harris sighed deeply, returning his father's stare. "I know we're down to not many options."

"There are *no* fucking options!" he yelled.

Dylan was startled at the unexpected outburst and sat back in his chair. "Dad, I know. We'll make this work."

***

Megan woke later than she had planned, the sun coming through the small round window in her room on the *EmmaLee*. She pushed back the covers and looked over at the alarm clock to see that it was already 10:30. Thoughts of the past night's events with Will Truegood came back to her. She could still feel the kiss on her lips and the suddenness of the whole situation continued to surprise her. After a few moments of awkward silence she had gotten back into her car and left without even saying goodnight. And then she remembered the scene with Rick. His true nature seemed to be coming out over this *Will* situation and it wasn't pleasant. If he had anything to do with this car theft she knew that she would never be able to forgive him.

There was a knock at her door. "Come in."

Sally walked in and came over and sat on her bed. "Good morning, sleepy."

"Morning."

"Late night?" Sally asked.

"No, but an interesting one."

"What?"

"I'll tell you about it. Where's Dad?"

"He's in the shower. He feels badly that he's barely seen you since he got in. He wants to take us to lunch. We thought we might take little *Emma* down to the Landings and get a big juicy cheeseburger. How does that sound?"

Megan thought for a moment about Will and Rick and how she was going to deal with the whole mess. *I guess it can wait until this afternoon.* "Sounds great, let me get presentable."

Forty-five minutes later the launch dropped the three of them off at *EmmaLee II's* boathouse. The ride down to the South Arm of Lake Charlevoix was exhilarating but uneventful and the roar of the inboard engine of the little boat made it impossible to talk. They all sat back and enjoyed the wind in their faces and the beauty of another glorious summer day in the North.

They approached the little waterfront restaurant sitting next to the landing of the Ironton Ferry. The docks were nearly full with boats coming in for lunch and out on the deck most of the tables with their bright colored umbrellas were already filled with people. Alex found an empty slip and maneuvered the old Chris Craft into the dock. A mother and eight baby ducks scurried out of the way. Sally and Megan jumped out and secured the lines.

They were fortunate to get one of the few remaining tables outside on the deck and they all ordered cheeseburgers and fries with iced cold Coke's. As they waited for the food to arrive Alex turned to his daughter and asked, "Well stranger, how is your summer going so far?"

Megan shook her head and smiled. "I'm not sure where to begin."

"You've only been up here for a few days," he said.

"She has a new friend," Sally said.

The drinks were served and the waitress scurried away.

"Who's that?" Alex asked.

Megan looked over at Sally. "You mean Will?"

Sally nodded, taking a sip from her Coke.

"Who's Will?" her father asked.

"Will Truegood."

"Oh sure, how is he?" Alex asked.

"Not great, he's been arrested for stealing a car." Megan said and watched as Alex and Sally both set their glasses down with surprised looks.

"He didn't do it, Daddy," she said. "He's been set up, I'm sure of it."

"Set up?" Sally said. "Why would anyone do that?"

"What's going on, kid," Alex asked.

"I still can't believe this, but I think it may be some of my friends."

"What!" Sally said.

"It was Melissa Wainwright's car and it ended up out at Will's cabin the other morning. The police were tipped off and they came out and arrested him."

"Is he in jail?" Sally asked.

"No, he's been released and I've been trying to help him."

"I'm not sure you need to be getting tangled up in a car theft," Alex said.

"I'm not getting *tangled up*. I'm just trying to help."

"What friends are you talking about?" Sally asked.

Megan hesitated for a moment, regretting that she had even opened up this line of discussion.

"Megan?" her father asked.

"I think it might be Rick."

"Rick Brandtley?" Sally said quickly.

"Your boyfriend?" Alex asked.

Megan nodded and looked away across the narrow channel of the lake. The ferry was about half way across from the far shore with a full load of four cars and several people with bicycles standing along the rail. She looked back at her father. "I've been spending a little time with Will and Rick is pretty upset about it."

"So you think he set Will up with this stolen car?" Sally asked.

"That's a pretty serious allegation, Megan," her father said.

"I know, but it's the only thing that makes sense."

"Megan, I've known Will and his family for years and I really can't believe that he would do this, but are you sure?" Sally said.

"He didn't take that car, Sally."

"So what are you planning to do about all this?" Alex asked.

"I drove Will home last night and Rick followed us and there was almost a really ugly scene."

"Oh honey," Sally said.

"I confronted Rick about the car and he got really angry and he and Will almost got in a fight. It was awful!" She could feel tears building again, just remembering the events of the evening.

"You need to be really sure about this, honey," her father said.

The baskets of food came and the three of them waited while the waitress laid everything on the table and then left to go refill their drinks.

"Megan, I'm serious. You can't implicate innocent people in a crime like this, particularly your friends."

"I know, Daddy."

"If you're wrong about this…" he said.

"I know!"

Chapter Twenty-two

There are many memories of course that we've all shared over the years, mostly good and glorious memories, but also some that continue to haunt us and keep us awake at night. Jonathan's brother Luke found no other escape but the fiery inferno of a burning building to kill himself after taking my own sister's life in a drunken rage. Even years later, Jonathan would tell me that he'd sit straight up in bed at night and scream, trying to yell at his brother to get out of the old boathouse. He told me that the image of the roof coming down in flames on his brother's head was as real and vivid in his mind as the night it happened. We all tried to move on beyond those memories and the losses that we shared. Some memories never fade.

***

Emily McKendry came out of the shower with a towel wrapped around her, moving slowly over to the sink. She had been awake for just a short time. Jonathan had left earlier for work and the nurse would be coming to check on her any minute. She knew she couldn't spend another day in bed even though her partner, Dr. Rose, and Jonathan in particular, had insisted she continue to rest. She looked at the face staring back at her in the mirror. The bruise across her cheek was beginning to fade some. She could still feel the slightly dull ache in the back of her head where she had fallen after being struck by Harold Slayton. She was still worried about Agnes and Sara going back to the farm. She reminded herself to call Sheriff Potts to check on them.

After she was dressed she tried to fix her face and hair up as best she could and then went downstairs and made a quick breakfast of eggs and toast. She knew she didn't feel up to walking to her office, so she got the keys and drove into town in her car. She drove by her office and on down to the Sheriff's Department.

Sheriff Willy Potts was surprised when he saw her walk into his office. "Dr. McKendry! How are you feeling?"

"I'm fine, Willy."

"Forgive me, but you don't look totally fine, Doc."

She touched her bruised face and smiled. "Really, I'll be okay."

"I'm afraid we're having no luck finding Slayton."

"Willy, I'm so worried about Sara and Agnes being out there at the farm."

"I know, we tried to talk them out of it. I had a deputy stay out there for a few hours with them yesterday and of course, the bastard didn't show up."

Emily sat down in one of the chairs by his desk. "Do you think you could run out there quickly with me this morning? I just want to make sure they're okay."

Potts scratched his head and thought about her request for a moment. "I suppose it couldn't hurt. We need to go now, though. I need to be back by eleven."

Emily sat in the patrol car next to the sheriff as they approached the road to the Slayton farm. She could see the old house off in the distance through the trees. They turned onto the road and as they slowly bumped along, Emily got a sick feeling in her stomach. They pulled up to the house and she couldn't see anyone around. The front door had been left open.

"You wait here a minute," the sheriff said.

Emily watched him get out and walk slowly toward the front of the house. She got more nervous when she saw him put his hand on his gun. He walked up onto the porch and peered in cautiously. She heard him yell, "Mrs. Slayton?" And then again, "Mrs. Slayton?"

He disappeared inside the door and Emily sat there in the car, her heart pounding. He was gone for a couple of minutes before he came out and then walked around to the back of the house. When he came back he waved for her to come out and join him.

They met near the front porch. "Seems they're gone, Doc."

197

***

George Hansen poured the coffee into two cups on his desk. He handed one to his friend, Jonathan McKendry who sat across his desk from him. "How's Emily?" he asked.

"She was better this morning, but she needs another day or so of bed rest."

"Good luck holding her down," George said and laughed.

"Damn, George, that sonofabitch could have really hurt her badly."

"And the sheriff hasn't been able to find him yet?"

"No, and Agnes insisted that she and her little girl go home yesterday. Emily is sick worrying about them."

"I don't blame her," George said.

"George, I'm starting to get a little heat about Sammy," Jonathan said.

"What do you mean?"

"One of my biggest customers came in yesterday, Tom Fitzgibbons, started threatening me about having Sammy back on the job."

"Yeah, I'm not surprised." George replied. "These damn summer people, I'm getting the same treatment for defending the boy. Can't seem to convince anyone that it's my damn job! The thing is, this kid's innocent and the half the town wants to lock him away regardless."

"Well, frankly I don't give a shit about Fitzgibbons, or any of his crowd," Jonathan said. "We can manage."

"You don't want to lose too many of those boat contracts, friend."

"Like I said, we can manage," Jonathan answered. "What's happening on Sammy's case?"

"Well, you know the charges came down and we'll go to trial here in a couple of weeks."

"What can we do to help this kid? No way this should go to trial!" Jonathan said.

"Yeah, I know. I just don't know what else we can do at this point, unless one of these kids changes their story, or their memories miraculously come back."

"Did I tell you that Connor Harris came by our house the other day?"

"You're kidding?"

"Said he was checking on Emily after the Slayton thing, but he was really after her to influence you on Sammy's case."

"That sonofabitch!" George said, standing and walking around the desk. "He's been in my face twice now about this and I'm about ready to smack the bastard!"

"I can't believe the judge would take this to trial," Jonathan repeated in frustration.

"The court of public opinion is pretty strong on this. I don't see how the judge could just drop the charges. He's got to live in this town, too and there's an election this fall."

Jonathan sat shaking his head, looking down into his coffee. "We've got to help this boy, George."

"I know."

"I was thinking about taking him out fishing tonight. Get his mind off all this," Jonathan said. "You want to come?"

"Not a bad idea."

"We haven't chased those trout down at Horton Creek since the *opener* back in April."

"Think they're waiting for us?" George asked, smiling.

"I think they're damn lonely. Meet me down at our dock around seven tonight."

***

Jennifer Harris parked the family's big sedan in the clearing by the beach. She kicked off her shoes and stepped out of the car. It was late morning and the sand was still cool beneath her feet. She started walking down the narrow foot trail through the woods, the beach grasses slapping at her bare legs, the sand squishing up between her toes. The sound of waves rolling up on the beach could be heard up ahead. Light from the sun overhead broke through the heavy tree cover in dappled patterns along the ground.

It had been almost a week since that night she had last been out to this beach at Fisherman's Island and still her heart beat heavily in her chest and the shame and guilt of what had happened then and since continued to haunt her. She had asked her mother if she could borrow the car to run a few errands, but she needed to see this place again.

The path broke out into low mounds of sand dunes going off in all directions. Clusters of cottonwood trees and low scrub brush could be seen across the landscape. She came over a rise and the broad blue expanse of Lake Michigan presented itself before her, big waves crashing up onto the beach from the brisk wind blowing out of the west. The wind felt good on her face and cooled the sweat drops breaking out on her forehead from the walk down from the car.

She turned left along another trail and soon came to a clearing with the burned remnants of the big bonfire from that night. Driftwood logs had been pulled around for people to sit near the fire and an old red metal chair that had started to rust after being left too long on the beach, rested nearby in the tall grass. There were still paper and beer cans left lying in the sand. Jennifer walked over and sat down in the chair and it was already hot from the morning sun. The smell of the fire was still there in the ashes and her mind went back to that night; the sounds of kids laughing and telling jokes, some going off into the dunes to make-out, the beer and whiskey bottles being passed around. She closed her eyes and it was dark again and she was back here on that night and she shivered as she thought of the liquor and then the lost moments that were causing pain for so many.

When she opened her eyes again, the sun's reflection off the sand was blinding and she held her hand up over her eyes for a moment to let them adjust again. She looked out across the lake, endless waves coming onshore. Sandpipers ran in little clusters along the beach and a few gulls flew overhead looking for dead fish washed up for an easy meal.

She stood up and looked around at the trails and footprints leading away from the fire. A trail leading off to the south held some recognition for her and she started walking up into the dunes. The sand was loose and it was hard to walk. More beer bottles littered the trail as she walked on and then she came over a small rise and stopped suddenly, looking down at an area hidden in behind some bushes. She moved slowly down the backside of the dune and over toward the bushes and she saw an empty whiskey bottle thrown up into the scrub brush. Reaching down with her hands behind her she sat on the side of the dune and looked at the place where she was sure this had all taken place. There were footprints in the sand and a flat area where a blanket or towel had packed the surface smooth. Fragments of images flashed in her brain and the sounds of the night came back to her again; the wild laughter, playful screams from the other girls when the boys touched them or chased them.

Jennifer put her head between her knees and closed her eyes and prayed for all of the haunting images to come back to her.

***

Mary Truegood sat in a pew in the tiny church, her eyes closed, her hands folded tightly in prayer. The chapel was empty and quiet and light filtered in through stained glass windows on the southern wall.

She prayed to the God that had brought her so much comfort over the years, during times that had not always been easy. She prayed now for her son and for her God to stand by him and see him through this time.

She heard someone walk up next to her and sit down. When she looked up she could see that it was the pastor and she closed her eyes again to continue her prayer. She felt his hand on her shoulder and was reassured that she and Sammy were not in this alone.

***

Sheriff Willy Potts had promised that he would continue to have his men search for Agnes and Sara Slayton. Emily couldn't stop worrying about the little girl. She pulled into the parking area in front of her husband's business and went into the office where Tracy greeted her.

"Dr. McKendry, are you feeling better?"

"I'm fine, Tracy. I saw Jonathan's truck out front. Is he around?"

"He went back out to the shop a few minutes ago."

"Thanks," she said and then walked out the back door into the yard where Jonathan stored new and used boats. She walked through the boats up on cradles and over to the big boathouse and saw Jonathan walking out. He saw her and got an immediate disapproving look across his face.

201

"I thought we agreed that you needed another day in bed," he said as he came up to her.

She put her arms around him and fell into the familiar comfort of his embrace. "Jonathan, I'm so afraid for the Slayton's."

"I know, honey."

"I just went out to the farm with Willy to check on them and they're gone."

Jonathan tensed and stood back. "You went out there!"

"With the sheriff, but they're gone, Jonathan. Agnes and Sara are gone."

"Let's go inside where you can sit down. You really shouldn't be out today."

"I'm fine," she said. "We have to find them, Jonathan. He's taken them and there's no one to protect them," she continued, the panic clear in her voice.

They entered Jonathan's office and he had her sit in his big leather chair behind the desk. He went out and brought back two glasses of water.

"What did the sheriff say he was going to do?" he asked, sitting down next to her.

"They're just going to keep looking, but they could be anywhere," she said. "Jonathan, what if he hurts them again?"

Jonathan looked at his wife's face and it pained him again to see the bruises and then the panic. Her eyes were moist and she looked at him as if he might actually have a solution. He felt helpless and frustrated and furious all at the same time. He should have gone after Slayton yesterday when he had a chance, he thought. He could have come back through the woods with his own shotgun and taken him by surprise.

"Where would he take them, Jonathan?" he heard his wife ask.

An idea came to him and he reached for her hand. "Let's go, I think I might know someone who can help."

A few minutes later Jonathan parked his truck downtown and he got out and went around to help Emily down. They were parked in front of the Helm, an old bar that Jonathan's brother used to frequent much too often back before he died.

Jonathan led Emily into the darkly lit bar. The stale smells of sweat and old beer came back to him. He looked over at the bar that had become the regular place for his brother to drink away a life that had betrayed him. Emily had been here before as well when she and George Hansen had confronted Luke McKendry about the death of George's sister, Catherine. It was a flood of sad memories that came back to both of them as they walked over to the bar.

The old bartender, Bud, looked up when he saw them. He was in his seventy's now and time had not been kind to him from the smoke and the booze and late hours.

"Well I'll be damned," he said. "That you, Jonathan?"

He nodded and sat down on one of the stools, helping Emily to do the same.

"How're you doing, Bud?" Jonathan asked.

"Good as can be expected."

"You remember my wife, Emily."

"Sure do. That was a damn scary night in here when old Luke came after you, mam. You're a doctor now, ain't you?"

"Yes," Emily said and she was thinking back to that night when Luke sat right where they were now and in his drunken state, as much as admitted to her and George that he had killed Catherine Hansen before he lashed out and attacked George with a bottle and then threatened to cut her with it before he ran out. The memories of it all made her shiver.

Jonathan tried to push the memories of his brother aside and said, "Bud, maybe you can help us. You ever see a man in here named Harold Slayton?"

The old man looked up and shook his head with a disgusted look. "More than I'd damn well like," he said.

Jonathan and Emily sat forward on their chairs. "You know Harold Slayton?" she asked.

"Yeah, the bastard... sorry mam. Yeah, he's in here a couple of times a week. He's a nasty drunk. Have to throw him out all the time," the old bartender said.

"He's disappeared with his family," Jonathan said. "Any idea where he might go?"

The old man reached for a mug on the bar and took a drink. Jonathan could smell that it was whiskey, not coffee. He put it back down and scratched the stubble on his unshaven face.

"You know, son, he talks now and then about this old hunting shack he's got up in the hills over past Boyne Falls."

"You know where it is?" Emily asked.

"Yeah, he's told me. Let me think, somewhere over off the Lake Louise road, right along Bear Creek I think."

"If he comes in here, Bud, you need to call the sheriff right away."

"What's he done now?"

"He's been beating his wife and daughter," Emily said, "and he came after me the other day."

Bud squinted in the dim light and saw the bruises on her face. "Yeah, just possible he'd go out there."

Emily looked over at Jonathan with a hopeful expression.

"Thanks Bud."

"Can I buy you all a drink? Hell, it's close to noon."

"Another time, Bud."

Chapter Twenty-three

The icy cold of the river knifed at his bare legs as he lowered himself down into the pull of the current. With just a pair of shorts on, Will Truegood felt his feet touch the soft sandy bottom of the creek, the long grasses along the high bank tickling at his back. He was taking a swim to clear his head and wash off the sweat and dirt from chopping wood all morning.

This part of the river was about twenty feet across and only two or three feet deep in most places. Old cedar stumps and logs lay under the surface in a patchwork of shapes. Tiny brook trout hid out in the quiet recesses, protected from the current and other predators.

He reached for a bar of soap on the bank and started to lather it in his hands under the water, suds flushing out and carried downstream. He washed his face and the cold water was shocking and satisfying at the same time. He dipped all the way under the surface of the clear river and the chill gripped at his lungs and he could feel his heartbeat pounding. He couldn't stop from shivering, but he kept washing his body with the bar of soap. He finished and threw the soap back up on the bank and then turned to drop back under the surface. His eyes were open and he could see the sandy bottom and logs and rocks. When he came up he turned back to the bank and pulled himself up, reaching over to get his towel.

Sitting by the riverbank he toweled off and felt the rush of blood back into his extremities as his body warmed. Hearing a small splash he looked over to see the ring of a trout's rise along the far shore. He continued to watch the run in the creek knowing that the fish would come up

205

again as soon as the next bug floated by. There was a hatch of small mayflies swirling over the creek and as they landed to lay their eggs the eager trout would make short work of most of them. The fish rose again and this time Will saw the open mouth come slowly up out of the water and sip in the little mayfly. He could tell it was a good fish because it rose slowly and confidently, knowing it could take the bug on its own terms. The smaller trout would fly out of the water in panic chasing the bug, unsure of their ability to catch their next meal.

Thou shalt not mimic or mock the mountains or the rivers...

These words from his people came back to him at times like this when he sat alone by the creek, or out in the fields. The whisper of the current over the rocks and fallen trees was a comforting sound that put him to sleep at night through the open windows of his cabin, followed him as he stalked a trout in behind a protected lie; that stayed with him when he was away and wanted to be back.

The smell and touch of Megan Clark eased back into his thoughts and he remembered the kiss from the night before. A sadness came over him because he knew that there was no future for him with this girl from the city and from a life so different from his own.

***

Megan Clark waited in the coffee shop down on Bridge Street after she had called Rick on his cell phone to come down to meet her. She had been back in town for an hour after the lunch with her father and Sally down at the Landings. She knew she had to talk to Rick and get all of this out between them.

A plastic cup of iced coffee sat in front of her on the table. The shop was busy and most tables were filled with shoppers taking a break, or locals on break from work catching up with friends.

The bell on the door jingled and Megan looked up to see her friend, Rebecca, coming through the door. They were both surprised to see each other and Rebecca came over and gave her a hug.

"Hi stranger," Rebecca said. "Where have you been?"

"I was out for lunch with Dad and Sally and I'm waiting for Rick."

"Let me get a drink first," Rebecca said and went over to the counter to order. When she came back and sat down she said, "Okay, all the dirt, please."

Megan took her time and told her friend Becca all the details of the past day's events with Will and Melissa's stolen car and then the confrontation last night with Rick and Will, and then the kiss.

"You let Will Truegood kiss you!"

"I kissed him back."

"Megan Clark, what am I going to do with you? Rick is going to be furious."

Megan heard the door chime ring again and looked over thinking it might be Rick coming in. It was a mother with two small children. "I don't see much future for me and Rick Brandtley."

"Megan, don't say that, this will work itself out."

Megan got irritated at her friends clueless attitude. "Becca, this won't work itself out. I've seen a side to Rick that I don't care to see anymore, and I can tell you that he's about had it with me, too."

The bell rang again and this time it was Rick Brandtley. He saw Megan and Rebecca right away and came over to the table. Megan felt a familiar attraction and then sadness as she realized that all of that was behind them now.

Rebecca stood up, "Hey Rick." She gave him a hug and a kiss on the cheek. "I was just heading out to run some more errands. I'll see you guys later. Megan, call me."

Megan nodded as her friend walked out the door. Rick stood there a while longer looking down at her. The look on his face was strangely different, no longer friendly and welcoming. "Sit down, Rick," she finally said.

He pulled a chair up next to her and sat down.

"Rick…"

"No, wait a minute, Megan. Let me start. First, I'm sorry about last night. Jimmy and I were way out of line and I'm sorry."

Megan didn't answer when he paused to wait for her response.

"But, I do have to say that I'm really fed up with you and whatever's going on with this Indian kid."

Megan felt her temper flare and she couldn't help lashing back, "Rick, that's enough!"

People around their table looked up in surprise.

He seemed startled as well and just looked back at her.

"Rick, whatever happens between me and Will Truegood, or anyone else for that matter, is no longer any of your business."

"Megan…"

"No, you and I are through and I'm sorry, but this just won't work anymore."

"What's gotten into you this summer, Clark?" he asked, his own anger coming forward.

"I think you should ask yourself that same question," she said.

"What?"

"Rick, whatever you're doing to get Will in trouble needs to stop; Melissa's car, whatever."

"Megan Clark, you are one crazy woman," he said.

"Rick, listen to me. I'm serious about this. I don't want to go to the police about this, but I will if I have to."

He shook his head in disgust. "You're willing to alienate all of your friends up here for some stupid local kid who lives in a shack in the woods?"

"I don't have to explain myself to you, or anyone else up here," Megan said, trying to keep her voice down from the other people in the shop.

He reached out to take her hand, but she pulled it away.

"This is over, Rick," she said, "and you need to make this right for Will on Melissa's car."

Rick Brandtley stood up shaking his head. "You have no idea what you're doing. You've lost your damn mind." He turned and walked out of the shop.

***

Anna Bataglia was working on the deck of the *EmmaLee* when Sally and Alex returned from lunch. She had papers spread out on a table in front of her and her cell phone to her ear. Half a sandwich lay uneaten on a plate and what looked like iced tea was half gone. She waved when she saw them come onboard. She finished her call and flipped her phone closed.

"Welcome back. How was the cruise?" she asked.

"We had a nice run down to the South Arm to get some lunch with Megan," Alex said.

"You look like you're feeling better," Sally said.

"The miracles of modern chemistry," Anna replied. "Alex, you and I need to spend some time before I catch the plane back to the city."

He looked over at Sally. "Now's probably as good a time as any. Can you excuse us for a while, honey?"

"Sure, I'm going to run up into town and visit with a few old friends. Take all the time you need." She looked down at Anna and the woman looked away, searching through some papers.

Alex kissed Sally on the cheek. "I'll see you in a while, honey. We'll get a nice dinner somewhere in town tonight."

"Sounds good," Sally said and turned to leave.

Alex pulled up a chair to the table. "What's happening?"

Anna took a drink from her glass. "Do you know a man named Alberto Manta?"

"Sure, he's one of our investors."

"Do you know what he does for a living?"

Alex seemed confused. "I don't know, trucking I think. Louis brought him in as a major investor in this last deal we did."

"You know I've had a couple of investigators digging deep on all of this, particularly on Louie. Well, they've found a few things that are quite interesting."

"Okay," he responded.

"First of all, Louis Kramer is in severe financial difficulties. He's basically on the edge of bankruptcy."

Alex seemed shocked. "You've got to be kidding. Are you sure about your sources?"

"Very."

"I knew that Lou was running into some difficulties with some of his other deals and companies, but I had no idea it was this bad."

209

"Well, it seems this investor, Alberto Manta, has been investing with Louis for a long time, including the money he put into your new venture."

"Right."

"Alex, Manta has some nasty connections. This is real dirty money."

"Oh shit!" was all Alex could manage.

Anna continued. "I don't know how the guy has stayed out of prison. The authorities have been trying to build a case against him for years. And now he shows up as a major investor with Alex Clark and Louis Kramer."

"Anna, I had no idea."

"That's what I figured. The problem is, the Feds won't care and this makes everything look just that much worse."

Alex sighed and looked out across the water. "God, what next?"

"Well, there's more. Apparently Manta is facing some difficult financial issues of his own and according to one of the contacts my people came across, he's leaning heavily on Louis to get his money back."

"Well, he's just going to have to be patient. The stock's frozen and he wouldn't want to sell it at this depressed price anyway."

"He doesn't want to sell any stock, Alex. He just wants his money back."

"And Louis doesn't have any money?"

"That would be correct," Anna said. "Sounds like a bad combination of circumstances for our friend, Mr. Kramer."

***

Connor Harris and his son Dylan drove along the north road through the hills along the lake between Charlevoix and Boyne City. Dylan was at the wheel of the long white Mercedes convertible. The car rolled smoothly through the curves in the road; heavy forest whirring by at times, open farm fields at others; occasionally a glimpse of the blue lake off to the right. Connor held a set of plans in his lap, looking down and paying little attention to the spectacular scenery speeding by.

"So you and your team go before the approval committee again on Tuesday?" he asked.

"Yeah."

"We need to know what the answer is going to be before we get you into that room."

"I know, Dad, dammit! My people are in touch with everyone on the committee. I think we'll still have trouble with one vote that will be the tie-breaker."

"And I assume you're taking steps to correct that problem?"

"It will be taken care of. We still have a couple days. I'm more concerned about the neighborhood association and the environmentalists that live out there."

"Build them a fucking pool or something!" Connor said. "Everyone has a fucking price."

Dylan rubbed his face in frustration. "You think we aren't working through all that?"

"These damn tree huggers!" Connor said in frustration. "What is so damned important about that swamp, or *wetlands*? It's a damn swamp for chrissakes!"

***

Megan Clark moved slowly down along the docks on Round Lake among the boat people and the tourists looking at the boats. She walked almost in a daze, not really noticing the people around her, tears running in slow trickles down her cheek.

A woman bumped into her. "Are you okay, dear?" she said

Megan looked at her and just nodded her head *yes* and then continued on. She had left the coffee shop and as she crossed the street into East Park up above the Round Lake public docks, it occurred to her that she had cast herself adrift, away from her friends, away from a boy that she had thought she really cared for.

As she continued on along the docks, the emotions and sense of loss overwhelmed her and she questioned herself for the stand she was taking and what she was trying to do to help another friend. Her cell phone rang in her purse and she started to reach for it and then decided to just let it ring.

Chapter Twenty-four

Jonathan and I never did get out to Horton Creek that night with Sammy Truegood. He and Emily were hell bent on finding Harold Slayton and his wife and daughter. It was a damn good thing they were.

***

Dr. Emily McKendry sat at the small table in their kitchen, a cup of tea steaming in front of her. Jonathan was on the phone with the sheriff's office discussing the news about Harold Slayton's hunting cabin. She heard Jonathan hang up the phone and come back into the room.

"He's going to meet me downtown with a couple of his men."

"I'm going, too, Jonathan," she said, standing up and coming over to him.

He reached out and took her in his arms. "Emily, the sheriff and I agreed that you need to stay here and rest. It's too soon for you to be out, particularly for something like this. Besides, you know very well that this guy is dangerous."

"Then we should just let the sheriff take care of it," she said.

"Willy agreed to let me go because I think I know where this place is. George and I used to hunt out that way."

Emily pulled him in and held him closely. "You let them do their jobs, but please watch out for Agnes and Sara. I can't stand the thought of them getting hurt anymore."

"I know, honey." He lifted her chin and kissed her goodbye.

***

ON PAST HORTON CREEK

Sammy Truegood finished work and got on his bike to head home. The shop foreman, Pete Borders stopped him before he left.

"Sammy, wait up a minute."

"Yeah Pete?"

"Some of the boys around the shop here have been talking stupid today. You probably heard some of it. I told them I'd have their heads if they kept on with it. Point is, there's folks in this town that have already convicted you and they're not feeling too good about you still being out on the street."

"You know I didn't do this, Pete?"

"Yeah I know, son, but you need to be careful. There's people that don't want to listen to the truth. You need to be careful and not let any of this get under your skin. It'll only make things worse."

He thanked his friend and got on his bike and pedaled out of the boatyard up onto the main road into Charlevoix. His mom would have dinner ready when he got home and Jonathan had mentioned going fishing, but then called and said he might not get back from something over in Boyne Falls in time tonight. Sammy had told him how much he appreciated what Jonathan and his friend George Hansen were doing for him.

He braked as he came down the big hill on Bridge Street, the little downtown district of Charlevoix before him, the docks and Round Lake off to the right. Traffic was backed up as usual for the drawbridge opening on the half hour to let boats through. He slowed to make his way between the traffic lane and parked cars. He noticed a family stop ahead on the sidewalk and the father pointed at him as he passed. The man yelled something at him, but he couldn't understand what he was saying. He put his head down, feeling the shame that all of this was bringing on himself and his family. Further up near the movie theatre he saw Andy Welton and his friend Josh Knowles walking up the sidewalk joking with two other boys.

Sammy knew that there was no use in trying to avoid them and then they saw him and stopped. Welton put his arm out in front of the others and stared back at Sammy with a look that had nothing but hate and malice. Sammy tried not to even flinch as he rode by, just returning the intense glare of Andy Welton and his friends. He was surprised that none of them said anything as he passed and as he continued on across the bridge and up the next hill he looked back and saw that they were still staring at him.

He turned up along Michigan and then the beach road out to their house near North Point. When he pulled into the dirt drive back to their house he immediately realized something was terribly wrong. His mother was sitting on the front porch of the little cottage tucked back in the woods, her head in her hands and she was sobbing uncontrollably. His little brother Jonas sat next to her playing with a toy. Sammy threw his bike down and ran over to her.

"Momma, what's…?"

"Oh Sammy," she cried out.

"What's happened?"

"I just got back from work," she paused to sniff back the tears and blow her nose on a handkerchief that she pulled from her purse. "I just got home a few minutes ago. Someone has broken into the house."

Sammy got up and ran through the front door and immediately stopped. The house had been ransacked. Everything had been knocked off shelves and tables, furniture was turned over and cushions ripped with knives. He walked into the kitchen and all of the cupboards had been emptied and jars and boxes of food smashed on the worn linoleum floor. Dishes and glasses lay smashed and broken all across the floor and into the back hall.

As he stood and looked at the wreckage that was his family's home, a rage grew up within him and he clenched his fists to keep from yelling out. He turned and walked slowly back through the debris and out onto the porch with his mother. He sat down next to her and put his arm around her shoulders. She turned her face into his shoulder and the sobs intensified as he tried to just hold her and comfort her.

"Momma, I'm so sorry about all this."

She shook her head against the sleeve of his shirt.

"We'll make this right, Momma. I swear to you I will make this right!" he said slowly, his anger almost overwhelming.

***

Jennifer Harris and her friend Elaine drove slowly through town looking for a parking place. They had planned to go to a movie. There was a new picture in town that had won an Academy Award, *The Greatest Show on Earth*. She saw an empty space up ahead and slowly pulled the big sedan into position. At the same time she saw Andy Welton and his pack of friends coming up on the sidewalk. Andy spotted her and they all came over to the car. Elaine rolled down her window by the curb.

"Hello gentleman," Elaine said.

Andy and Josh Knowles both stuck there head's through the open window.

"Ladies," Andy said.

"Hi Andy," Jennifer replied, still feeling embarrassed about being around him.

"Seen our friend Sammy lately?" Josh asked.

"No, why?" Jennifer replied.

"Well, you shouldn't have to worry about him anymore," Andy said.

"What do you mean?" Jennifer asked.

"Well, for one, he's going to be real busy for a while, and then his ass will be rotting in jail."

Josh laughed and said, "Yeah, I bet he's going to be real busy."

Jennifer was alarmed and said, "What have you done?"

"Nothing he didn't deserve," Josh said and laughed again.

She could hear the boys behind them laughing, too and saw them pushing each other around.

"Andy, you need to leave him alone. You're only causing more trouble," Jennifer said.

"You don't need to worry about anything," Andy said.

"I swear Andy, if you've hurt him…"

Elaine turned and looked at her friend with a puzzled expression, "Jennifer!"

"Don't tell me you're worried about this damn Indian kid after what he did to you?" Andy said, anger showing across his face.

Josh pulled away from the window, a look of disgust on his face and joined the other boys. Andy came around to the other side of the car and Jennifer rolled down her window.

He leaned in and said, "This is all going to be over soon and we can get back to how it used to be."

"How did it *used to be*, Andy?"

He looked at her with a confused stare and then said, "You and me, like we were last summer."

All Jennifer could think about was the second beach party when he had shown up drunk with his friends again after he had promised there wouldn't be any more drinking. "I don't know, Andy, I just don't know," she said.

He backed away from the window and rejoined his friends on the sidewalk. Jennifer and Elaine got out of the car. As Andy walked away with the others following he turned and looked back at Jennifer. "Don't start feeling sorry for this damn Indian kid, Jennifer. Don't even start."

***

Jonathan McKendry rode in the front seat of the patrol car with Sheriff Willy Potts. Two deputies followed in another car. They had just driven through Boyne City and were on their way across the Boyne Falls road. It was late afternoon and long shadows spilled across the road and light from the sun would occasionally break through the tall trees and shine in his eyes. The sheriff had a radio station playing music so low you couldn't make out what the song was, just a steady noise in the background. They came out of the forest and up ahead on the right he could see the bare grass hills of the ski resort at Boyne Mountain.

The crossed over the bridge at the Boyne River and then turned north on Highway 131. There wasn't much traffic in either direction and the little village of Boyne Falls was quiet as usual.

"What are you thinking, McKendry?" the sheriff said, breaking the lull in the conversation.

Jonathan looked over at him. "Just frustrated, I guess. We can bring this guy in and he might even do a little time in jail, but he'll be out again and his family and my wife will be in danger again."

"I know," Potts said. "It's a damn shame we can't do more."

Jonathan continued to direct them up the Lake Louise road and then had them turn on a small dirt road that ran along Bear Creek. "Could be anywhere along here, Sheriff. Old Bud wasn't entirely sure, but he said he didn't think it was very far down this road," Jonathan said.

A hundred yards ahead they could see a narrow two-track road turning off to the right. The sheriff slowed and came to a stop, the other car rolling up behind him.

"Not sure if this is the place, but we should probably walk on in there so we don't spook him," Potts said.

He gave directions to his deputies, one to stay with the cars and watch the road, the other to come with him and Jonathan. Sheriff Potts and his deputy both took 12 gauge shotguns out of the trunk of the first car. "Jonathan, you stay behind us now," he said.

They started up the narrow road that was not much more than two tire tracks with a high grassy mound down the middle. Tall thick cedars lined both sides and Jonathan walked behind the Sheriff and his deputy. They walked for nearly a quarter mile before they saw a clearing up ahead and all of them slowed and pressed against the edge of the trees for cover. Proceeding slowly along the tree line, a small unpainted shack came into view, not much larger than one room; a small window on the front wall and a stove pipe coming out of the sagging roof.

The three men knelt behind the cover of the trees and listened and watched. Harold Slayton's old truck could be seen parked on the far side of the shack. There was no other sign of people. After several minutes the sheriff whispered to Jonathan to stay where he was and then the two law officers slowly started moving closer to the house. Still there was no sign of occupants inside the shack.

Potts and his deputy took cover behind the trunks of two large oak trees. The sheriff looked back at Jonathan for a moment and then pumped two shells into the chamber of his shotgun. The deputy did the same.

The sheriff's voice startled Jonathan as it broke the stillness. "Harold Slayton, you in there?" he yelled.

There was no response and all Jonathan could hear was a blue jay squawking in a tree above them.

"Slayton, you need to come out now," the sheriff yelled again.

Jonathan thought he heard a muffled sob and the sheriff apparently heard it too and turned to look back at Jonathan. He waved his deputy forward to the far right side of the shack and he made his way slowly toward the front door, the shotgun aimed waist high in front of him. He came up to the side of the door and stopped to listen again.

"Slayton, come out now and there won't be anymore trouble, you hear me?"

Still no response.

The sheriff used the barrel of his gun to reach over and push on the door. It wasn't latched and swung open into the darkness of the small shack. Jonathan watched him look around the doorjamb and disappear inside. He couldn't help but hold his breath as he watched the sheriff disappear inside. Then he heard him yell out.

"McKendry, Jurgenson, get in here!"

Jonathan jumped up and started running and he saw Deputy Jurgenson run into the house in front of him. As he came through the door the light was so dim that he couldn't see at first, only the shadowy outline of Potts and Jurgenson over in a corner to the left. His heart was pounding and a terrible sense of dread made him tremble.

"Sheriff?" he said.

"Over here Jonathan," and he saw the big sheriff kneeling down slowly. He came up beside him and as his eyes adjusted he saw Agnes Slayton lying on the floor by a small black iron stove, her arms and legs splayed out at odd, unnatural angles.

"Ohmigod!" Jonathan said, falling to his knees next to the sheriff. Then he could see that there was blood on her face from a bad cut on her cheek and a pool of blood spread out from the back of her head across the worn wooden floor.

"That sonofabitch!" Jonathan yelled and he stood up looking around.

"Jonathan, just settle down," he heard the sheriff say and he watched as the man held his hand to Agnes Slayton's neck checking for a pulse.

Sheriff Potts shook his head and stood and then turned to look at Jonathan. "She's dead, Jonny."

Jonathan stood there in panic fighting back the urge to vomit, not sure what to do, or what to say. And then he thought of little Sara. "We need to find the girl!" he said.

They looked around and the shack was only one room and no one else was inside.

"Jurgenson, you run back to the road and bring the cars up. Jonathan, you come with me."

They walked back out into the sunlight and Jonathan shielded his eyes from the bright sun still just above the tree line to the west. Jurgenson ran back up the road and Jonathan followed the sheriff around the side of the shack. The old truck sat there, windows rolled down. Potts brought his shotgun up to firing position as they approached.

They both heard a soft sob coming from inside the truck and they quickened their pace, the sheriff out ahead. Jonathan saw him look into the side window and when he came up he saw that Sara Slayton was sitting on the floor of the truck, her head down between her knees, sobbing quietly.

Chapter Twenty-five

The sign above the gallery had changed and it always seemed odd for Sally to see it now. She had owned the shop as the *Thomason Gallery* for so many years. Her partner in the business, Gwen Roberts, had taken it over when Sally left that summer with Alex. The sign now read *The Charlevoix Gallery*. She pushed open the familiar front door and walked into the shop. Gwen's new partner, Tara Peterson, was standing behind a counter going through some paperwork. She looked up when she heard Sally come in.

"Well hello Sally, it's nice to see you," Tara said.

"Good morning, Tara," Sally said, looking around the shop. "You have some beautiful pieces.

"Thank you, we've brought in a whole new collection of work this summer."

"It's really wonderful, do you mind if I just look around a little?"

"No, not at all. Gwen is in the back. Do you want me to get her?" Tara offered.

"That would be great, thanks." Sally walked over to the far wall to look at several northern landscapes similar to her own style.

She heard Gwen's familiar voice, "What a nice surprise, the prodigal daughter returns home." Gwen came over and gave Sally a hug. "The nice weather is agreeing with you, Sal."

"It's been beautiful," Sally said. "The shop looks wonderful, what a nice selection you've brought in."

"Oh thanks, Tara and I were all over this winter trying to find new talent and Tara's work has been doing great."

"You've done really well."

Tara came out from the back room and went over behind the counter to finish up her paperwork.

"Tara, do you mind if Sally and I take a break and run next door to get a cup of coffee?" Gwen asked.

"No, go ahead. I'll hold down the fort."

Sally and Gwen walked down the street and ordered two lattes at the coffee shop and then found an empty table and two chairs out on the sidewalk. They sat down and watched the summer crowds flow by for a few moments.

Sally turned to Gwen. "So how are things up here in the cold north," Sally asked.

"It's been fine, Sal. You know, when you left I really thought for a long time about getting back to New York and starting over there, but I went back a couple times and it just didn't feel like home anymore. All of my old friends were either gone, or had changed so much I barely knew them anymore."

"I really miss the old town, too," Sally said. "It's been great to come back for a few weeks every summer with the boat, but I just miss the pace up here. It's so crazy in New York with Alex and Megan's schedules and the travel we've been doing."

"Are you doing alright?" Gwen asked, reaching over to touch her arm.

"I'm fine," she said.

"Why do I sense that's not completely true?" Gwen asked.

"No really, my marriage has turned out to be so much more than I had even hoped. Alex is really exactly what you see, just a truly nice man and Megan and I have become very close. She's just a great kid."

"So what's the problem?"

"Well, Alex has some serious issues with his business. I can't get into the details, but you know Louis Kramer, his partner?"

"Oh yeah, *Mr.* Mary Alice Gregory," Gwen said and then they both laughed.

221

"Yeah, what a pair," Sally said. "The thing is, Louis has pulled some pretty serious and apparently illegal stunts with the business and he and Alex are in a lot of trouble with the SEC and the Attorney General of New York."

"Oh Sally, I had no idea."

"Alex truly had no part in any of this, I'm sure, but as president of the company he's responsible and he may even be charged with some of this," Sally said.

"Honey, I'm so sorry. How long has this been going on?"

"Several months now. Alex has a top law firm in New York working for him and at least he *seems* pretty confident about the whole thing."

"But not so for Louis Kramer?"

"No, I think Louie is in a bunch of trouble."

"Well, I'm really sorry to hear that, even for Louis. He's kind of a lovable old guy."

"Not so lovable anymore," Sally said. "And then Alex has this hot Italian number as his lead attorney, Anna Bataglia."

"I hope she's good at what she does?" Gwen asked.

"Alex says she's one of the best. She's been here in town for a couple of days working with Alex and staying out on the ship."

"Well, isn't that convenient," Gwen said.

Sally sighed and took a sip from her coffee. "You should have seen her last night. Anna had more than a little too much wine with dinner and it was all too clear that she has a thing for Alex and I just can't get it out of my mind. They're spending so much time together…"

"You trust Alex, don't you?"

"Of course I do. I've never had any reason to feel otherwise, but this woman is quite a package and she obviously has something going on for Alex."

"Does he know?"

"I've talked to him about it and he's reassured me that they've worked together for years and nothing has ever happened."

"You send her up here and I'll talk to her!"

Sally laughed. "Too bad she doesn't like girls."

"Maybe she does!" Gwen said, laughing again.

"Well she's headed back to New York tonight, but Alex will be going back in a day or so, too. They have a preliminary hearing coming up."

"It's easy for me to say, honey," Gwen said, "but I doubt you have anything to worry about with Alex."

Sally just nodded, looking out at the people walking by, most with large bags full of clothing and other shopping treasures. She turned back to Gwen. "How are you and Tara doing? She seems really nice."

"She's a marvelous person, Sal, I really love her."

"That's wonderful," Sally said. "I'm truly happy for you." She took another sip from her coffee and then said, "Oh, I meant to tell you that they have a suspect in George's death."

"A suspect!" Gwen said surprised. "You mean he was murdered?"

"That's what the police think and they have a suspect in custody. The sheriff called us yesterday with an update on the whole mess."

"Who would want to hurt George Hansen?"

Sally shook her head and said, "I can't imagine, but apparently they found a knife in the lake and it looks like someone forced him underwater until he was dead and then pulled him back up into the boat. I just want to cry every time I think about George being gone and possibly killed in such a terrible way."

"Who is this guy?

"His name is Slayton."

Gwen grimaced and said, "Oh that Slayton family is nothing but trouble. They're in the paper all the time for some nonsense or another."

"Yeah, I know. Any idea why this guy would have something against George?" Sally asked.

Gwen thought for a few moments. "Maybe George was defending him for one of their many crimes. I know he was still handling a few cases."

"No it doesn't appear so. The sheriff has been over to George's law offices and checked all the files with his old partner."

"I hope they hang the guy," Gwen said.

***

223

Alex Clark was driving the Jeep up the street toward the little municipal airport on the outskirts of Charlevoix. Anna Bataglia sat next to him in the passenger's seat, her briefcase on her lap.

"Thanks for the lift, Alex."

"Sure, the boys said they'd be touching down about 4:30, so we should be right on time," he said, looking at the clock in the dashboard.

"Great, when are you planning to come back to the city," Anna asked.

"Probably just a day or so, unless you need me sooner. Just let me know."

"Okay," Anna said, looking out the side window at the sights of Charlevoix going by. "Alex, this is all going to work itself out."

He looked over at her. "I'm glad you're so sure."

"Really, I'm feeling better about the case they're going to be able to bring against Louis, particularly with all of his financial difficulties."

"And what about all of this documentation of my involvement that he's fabricated?" Alex asked.

"Again, I don't think you need to worry. Out team thinks we can tear Kramer's testicles out when we question him on the stand about any of that nonsense."

"Nice choice of words," Alex said, laughing.

They pulled into the airport drive and Alex parked the Jeep by the gate into the area where the private planes were lined up. Several jets and twin-engine prop planes stood tied down on the tarmac.

"Here comes the plane," Alex said pointing to the sky out to the east over Lake Charlevoix. He pulled her bag out of the back seat and they walked into the small terminal building. They watched the plane land and taxi up in front of the terminal.

Alex opened the door and followed her out as the pilots cut back the engines on his big Falcon jet, a *Clark Industries* logo on the tail. The door opened and one of the pilots came down and took Anna's bag.

"Good afternoon, Alex, Ms. Bataglia," he said.

"Hi Joey, take good care of the counselor here on the way back to the big city," Alex said."

"Will do, boss," the pilot said and he went back up into the plane with the bag.

"Anna turned to Alex. "Thank you for putting me up and for this ride home."

"No, thank you for all you're doing on this case. You're making me feel a lot better about the whole mess."

"It's so wonderful up here, Alex."

"I know, I have to drag myself out of here every time we have to leave."

She looked at him and smiled and then suddenly moved forward and kissed him on the mouth and then hugged him. They both pulled back and the look on Anna's face was as surprised as Alex's.

There was an awkward silence before Alex said unevenly, "Well counselor, have a nice trip."

She just looked at him for a moment and then climbed the stairs into the plane. The pilot closed the door and soon the engines were powered back up and the big jet was pulling away.

Alex stood there on the tarmac, the feel of her kiss still fresh on his lips with a dazed, confused feeling. *What the hell was that?*

***

Sheriff Elam Stone stood behind a door with a small window and watched Vince Slayton sitting in his cell. The man wore the standard issue jail jumpsuit and open-toed slippers. Stone looked away, shaking his head and walked back toward his office. He thought to himself that he was running out of ideas in connecting Slayton to George Hansen, other than a knife at the bottom of a lake that just happened to be found under Hansen's dead body, but no blood or other evidence on the knife that tied it to Hansen. *Where's the link and the damn motive?!*

He sat down behind his desk and looked at the papers strewn in disarray. Someone had dropped this week's copy of the *Charlevoix Courier* among the clutter and he happened to notice the lead article about the controversy over the proposed new condominium development down in Horton Bay. The headline read, *Chicago Developers to Make Second Appeal for Horton Creek Project.*

225

The sheriff knew that this project had been debated for months and the locals were putting up quite a stink. He read the article and reminded himself of the details. There was a large parcel of vacant land just west of Horton Bay that these developers, the Harris Company, had secured. They planned to build a large condominium complex with an equestrian center, pool and tennis courts, all the bells and whistles. The property had water access rights and they were talking about putting in a hundred or so slips for big boats. The hang-up was the building permit approval because of some encroachment on wetlands with the initial site plan. They were going back for approval of revised plans next week.

Stone had lived in the area for most of his life and the continuing development always frustrated him. There was so much disposable income among the wealthy these days that it seemed as if no price was too extravagant to get their little piece of the North Country. Cottages that had been built 30 years ago and still in perfectly fine shape were being purchased for seven figures only to be torn down to make room for a new 10,000 square foot summer home these people might use twice a year. And there were the condo developers who tried to squeeze as many people onto as little acreage as possible to maximize profits. He shook his head in disgust and threw the paper on a pile in his inbox.

***

Louis Kramer was cruising along the shoreline in Oyster Bay in one of his wife's boats. He had a cold vodka and tonic in the cup holder beside him. His cell phone rang in the clip on his belt and he pulled it out. He looked at the message display.

"Shit!" He knew it was Manta and he also knew that he had to answer it.

Nervously he flipped open the cover of the phone. "Kramer here," he said.

"Louis, I haven't heard from you. I thought we agreed you would get back to me by now?" Alberto Manta said on the other end of the line.

"Hey Berto, my friend," Louis answered.

"I'm not your friend, Louis," Manta said ominously, "and I want my fucking money!"

"I know, Berto. I have the wheels in motion, but I need a little more time."

"How long does it take to have your people wire the money to my account?"

"It's not as simple as that, Berto," Louis said.

"Look you asshole, I don't care where you get this money, but I want it in my account by tomorrow at noon, or we'll have a serious issue to deal with."

Kramer swallowed hard, trying to keep the phone from shaking next to his ear. "Alberto, I need more time!" Louis pleaded.

"You got a pencil?" Manta asked.

Louis reached for his planner book that he took everywhere with him sitting on the other front seat. "Yeah."

"Here's the number for my accountant in New York. He'll take care of the wire transfer to my account in the Caymans."

Louis wrote down the number. "I really need a couple more days to put that kind of money together."

He heard the phone click on the other end.

Chapter Twenty-six

Harold Slayton had run off into the woods that night when he heard Jonathan and the sheriff approaching. Fortunately they arrived before little Sara was physically injured again, but the emotional scars of seeing her mother beaten and killed when her head fell and hit the iron stove would be with her forever.

When Emily found out about Agnes Slayton she felt responsible for letting them go back. Nothing anyone said could help her through the guilt she was feeling.

***

Emily Compton got the call that they had taken Sara Slayton to the hospital in Charlevoix for an examination. When Jonathan told her about Agnes she dropped the phone and screamed out into the night, her grief ripping at her soul. When he came home she insisted that he take her back to the hospital to see Sara. George Hansen was there as well when they arrived.

Emily ran into the room where they were checking out the little girl and sat down next to her on the bed and wrapped her in her arms. Sara seemed almost in shock, not crying or talking, just staring straight ahead.

"Sara, I'm so sorry about this," Emily said. "You need to know that there are people in this world who love you and will take care of you." Emily looked over at Jonathan and George who were standing at the foot of the bed. Both men had tears in their eyes. They were whispering back and forth to each other but she couldn't hear what they were saying.

"He must have run out the back when we were coming up the road," Jonathan said. "The sheriff is sending more men out there tonight to look for him. He can't go far without his truck."

228

"This is just so sad," George said. "The poor little girl will have no family when her father is put away."

"Jonathan, Sara is going to stay with us," Emily said. It wasn't a question.

He looked back at his wife and nodded, knowing there was no use in even discussing other options with her.

***

Harold Slayton had run down an old deer trail that he knew when he saw the sheriff coming to get him. He had been on the move for over an hour, doubling back to get to the main road. The pint bottle of whiskey in his pocket was almost gone and he stopped to finish it. In his present state of drunkenness he felt only anger at his wife for arguing with him and threatening to take Sara away from him again. He was pretty sure he had hurt her more than he meant to, but she'd get over it, he figured. She always did.

He knew there was a farmhouse up ahead on the Bear Creek road. He could see the lights on now through the trees. It was close to dark, but he could still see enough to walk through the heavy woods on the perimeter of the property.

After he was sure that no one was outside the house he snuck up to an old truck sitting by the barn. When he looked inside he could see that the keys were in the ignition which was typical for people in this part of the country. He opened the door quietly and started the truck. It fired immediately and he backed up and drove out the driveway past the house. No one came out. It was determined later that the farm owner thought it was one of his son's going into town.

***

Jennifer and Elaine came out of the movie house and the sky above was dark with stars showing in a sparkling array. Jennifer stood by the curb and took in the fresh smells of the night after being cooped up in the tiny theatre.

"What do you want to do tonight, Jen?" her friend asked.

"I don't know, probably get some dinner. I need more than that bag of popcorn." She had to jump back when a car pulled up quickly almost running up on the curb. It was Andy and his friends and Josh Knowles leaned out the window. "Hi ladies! We're heading out to the beach at North Point for a fire. Come on, hop in."

Andy leaned over to look out the window. "Josh get in the back and let the girls sit up here," he said.

Josh immediately climbed over the seat and joined the other two boys and one girl in the back, a friend that both Jennifer and Elaine knew.

Jennifer's first reaction was to say *no*. She'd had more than enough of beach fires already this summer, but then she started feeling badly about how she had treated Andy earlier. She looked over at Elaine.

"Let's go," her friend said.

The two girls climbed in and Andy slammed down the accelerator and squealed the tires as he pulled away. As soon as Jennifer was in the car she could smell the alcohol on their breaths and she immediately regretted the decision. "Andy, maybe you should drop me off, I'm really not up for this tonight," she said.

"Come on, Jen, you need to lighten up and have a little fun," he said.

A whiskey bottle was passed up from the back seat. Andy reached for it and took a long drink. He handed it to Jennifer sitting next to him, but she shook her head *no*. Elaine grabbed the bottle and put her head back as she took a long pull. When she finished she said, "We have a little catching up to do."

The kids in the back cheered her on, but Jennifer just had a sinking feeling that this had been a big mistake. "Andy, really I need to go home," she said.

"I'll make sure you get home," Andy said. "Just come out to the beach for a little while. We've got some food and even some Cokes if you don't want to drink. It's fine."

She took a deep breath and settled back into the seat.

***

Sammy Truegood and his mother had been working all night on cleaning the mess in their house. A couple of neighbors had come over to help, but they had hardly made a dent in the devastation. His anger continued to simmer all night as he worked on the wreckage of their home.

230

In his mind he had little doubt that it was Andy Welton and his gang of summer punks. As he swept and cleaned he thought about a hundred different ways that he would get revenge.

George Hansen had warned him so many times to stay away from those people; that it would only jeopardize the case against him. He was at a point where that didn't matter anymore. These boys had crossed the line and there was no way they were going to get away with it.

***

Emily sat up with little Sara Slayton until well into the evening waiting for her to fall asleep. The grandfather clock ticking downstairs in their living room sounded deafening in the quiet house when normally she wouldn't have even paid attention to it. They had all been relieved to find out that Sara had not been hurt physically this time by Harold Slayton, but clearly she was emotionally scarred from what she had experienced. She hadn't spoken a word since she had been found in the truck. Emily had read her numerous stories but she just looked off vacantly, holding her worn doll and not responding.

Emily felt her heart breaking as she looked down at the helpless little girl. At the same time she was trying to subdue an ever growing rage aimed at this girl's father. *How can he even be considered her father!*

Jonathan came in to the small guest bedroom with two glasses of water, but he could see that Sara had finally fallen asleep. Emily eased her arm out from behind Sara's head and gently got up from the bed. She made sure that the little girl was covered and resting comfortably and then they both backed out quietly, leaving the lights on in case she woke up and wondered where she was.

When they were downstairs in the kitchen Emily picked up a wooden spoon that was lying on the counter and then turned and threw it as hard as she could against the far wall of cabinets. Jonathan looked up with a startled expression as it crashed against the cabinet door and then fell to the floor.

Emily wanted to scream, but knew it would wake up Sara. Jonathan came over and took her in his arms, trying to offer some type of comfort.

"I'm so sorry, honey."

231

"At least you brought her back before she was hurt anymore, but I just can't get the thought of Agnes out of my mind."

"I know, I will never get this out of my head either. It was really awful," he said.

"Where can that animal be?" she asked.

"A lot of people are out looking for him, but until morning it's going to be pretty hard. He can't get too far, but there's a lot of state forest out there to get lost in."

"Until he's behind bars I don't think I'll be able to sleep again."

"Without a car there's not much chance he'll get back to Charlevoix any time soon," Jonathan said.

Chapter Twenty-seven

Dylan Harris stepped in a soft boggy area on the property they had purchased and his expensive leather loafer sunk completely from view. He cursed loudly and struggled to free his foot from the oozing earth. Connor came up behind him and helped him out. The shoe was dripping with soft black mud that continued up his white khaki pants nearly to his shin.

"Shit!" he said, hanging on to his father's shoulder and shaking his foot to flick off some of the mud.

"That's what it looks like," his father said, laughing.

Dylan didn't seem to appreciate the joke.

The property was over 200 acres of mostly flat farmland, with a few dozen acres of heavily wooded land closer to the lake, most of which bordered protected wetlands near Horton Creek that were preventing them from moving forward with their project.

"What do you expect to find out here?" he asked his father. "We've been here a dozen times."

Connor was surveying the perimeter of the property and the area running along the wetlands. "We need access to this piece of the property," Connor said. "Otherwise we can't get enough units in here to make the numbers work."

Dylan stopped shaking his foot and started shaking his head in disgust. "We've been through this a thousand times, Dad. I know the projections."

Connor turned to look at his son. "What you should also remember is that if this damn project doesn't come together we are fucking done! We've got everything tied up in this *piece of crap* property!"

"I don't need reminding," Dylan said.

***

Sally found Alex back down at the *EmmaLee* sitting in his office below decks going through a Fed Ex package full of mail from New York. He didn't hear her walk in and she crept up behind him and kissed him on the ear. He flinched back and turned around quickly in the heavily padded leather desk chair.

"Oh honey, it's you," he said.

Sally teased him with a sexy smile and said, "Who else would be kissing you on the ear?"

Alex blew out a deep breath. "Well, interesting that you should ask."

"What?" Sally asked, pulling a chair up next to him.

"Now I don't want you to go all crazy about this, but I need to tell you what happened when I took Anna to the airport."

"What now?"

"Well, we were standing there while Joey was loading the plane, finishing up our discussion about next steps on the case and Anna was turning to leave and she came up and hugged me and then she kissed me."

Sally tried to remain calm. "Is this how you always say goodbye to your attorney?"

"Ahhh…no, this would be the first time," Alex said, "and you don't have to say *I told you so.*"

Sally sat forward in her chair and tried as hard as she could to keep from grabbing everything on Alex' desk and throwing it. Of course she knew the woman had these feelings for her husband, but after the discussion they had just had this morning, Sally was finding it hard to believe that she was being this brazen. "Alex, I really don't know *what* to say. Of course I'm not surprised, but…"

"I'm telling you this not to upset you, but to make sure you realize that I'm not trying to hide anything about this either."

"That's why I love you, Alex Clark," she said and leaned forward and kissed him on the cheek this time.

"I was so surprised when it happened that I really didn't know what to do, or say."

"You didn't kiss her back, did you?"

Alex chuckled and tossed the pile of mail in his lap back on the desk. "Obviously I need to have a few words with my attorney."

"Obviously," Sally echoed.

***

Megan saw Will Truegood standing on the beach near the road that came down to the lake at Horton Bay. She had called him out at his cabin to say that she wanted to see him. He said again that he didn't want her to be seen with him in Charlevoix, so they agreed to meet out at the quiet bay and she had asked Sally if she could take the little Chris Craft, *EmmaLee II*.

Will waded out into the water and caught the boat as she eased it up toward shore. "Hop in."

He jumped up onto the bow, pushing off and Megan turned and backed the boat out into the lake. Will sat down next to her. "What was so important that we couldn't talk on the phone?"

"I don't know, I just needed to see you." She turned the boat south across the bay and then she pressed the throttle down and boat sped out across the open lake. Fifteen minutes later they slowed as the little Chris Craft approached the Ironton Ferry, keeping the boat just above idle speed to obey the *No Wake* area through the narrows. They rode in silence for a while and Will looked hard at her, trying to read what this was all about. Megan just kept looking straight ahead, maneuvering in the boat traffic through the channel.

They passed the last buoy in the *No Wake* zone and Megan pressed the throttle down again and the boat sped up and came quickly on plane across the surface of the South Arm. She sat up on the back of the seat to let the wind blow in her face and Will joined her. He watched the joy in her eyes as she steered the little runabout down the lake. She looked over and smiled at him.

After they had gone a mile or so down the lake, Megan turned the boat in toward the bridge over to Holy Island. She slowed until they were only about 50 yards out from the bridge and then she turned off the engine. The *EmmaLee II* drifted slowly to a stop off shore.

"Sally told me a story about her father, Jonathan McKendry, when he was a boy up here," Megan said.

"My family knew the McKendry's very well. I was just a young kid when Jonathan and his wife and granddaughter were killed in the accident down off the Manitou's."

"We have the picture of her little daughter, Ellen, hanging in the house up in Charlevoix. She was the most beautiful little girl."

"Everyone's missed them all a lot up here," Will said. "So what's the story?"

"Oh I guess when Jonathan was 10 or 12 years old, he came down here to Holy Island with his older brother, Luke and Uncle George. They came in a boat similar to this and when they got to the island, Luke dared the two younger boys to do a back flip off the Holy Island bridge."

"What, into the sand?" Will said. "It's dry as a bone under the bridge. Look up there."

"I know, but back in the '30's the lake was a lot higher and there was plenty of water under the bridge. Luke had a bad leg and surprised both Jonathan and Uncle George when he did a perfect back flip off the rail of the bridge. But, he didn't come up and they both panicked and jumped in after him. Luke had gone back under the bridge and snuck back up behind and jumped down on top of them, scaring them half to death again."

Will laughed at the story, looking over at the old bridge, trying to imagine the scene all those years ago.

"I also wanted to tell you that I broke up with Rick this afternoon," she said suddenly, looking over at him to see his reaction.

Will looked down and grimaced, shaking his head and then said, "Megan, I didn't want any of this to come between you and your friends. I'm awful sorry."

Megan looked at him and said, "You don't have to be sorry for anything. These so-called friends of mine… well, I guess I didn't know them as well as I thought I did."

"Still, I'm sorry. I know this has to be really hard for you."

Megan nodded her head slowly, putting her feelings for Rick behind her and waiting for some clarity to come on how she felt about Will Truegood. He was just the most natural and easy person to be around and she knew right at that moment, sitting with him here on this quiet bay of the lake with the sun going down behind her, that she wanted him to kiss her again.

Will looked back trying to read the look on her face. "Megan?"

She slid over next to him. "Oh, just shut up," and then she pulled him close and pulled his mouth down to hers. She closed her eyes and let the feelings flow between them.

***

Sheriff Elam Stone had little patience for attorneys and the court appointed attorney for Vince Slayton was giving him further cause. He sat across the table from the two of them, the District Attorney for the county, Nelson Teague, sat at the head of the table.

Teague spoke, "Mr. Slayton, your attorney tells me that you are interested in sharing some information in this case in exchange for a plea agreement. Is that true?"

Slayton looked over at his lawyer. His greasy hair was slicked back behind his ears and he hadn't shaved since he'd been arrested. The lawyer was a young kid fresh out of law school from Petoskey named Ulrich. He had a cleaned and pressed blue suit on with a starched white shirt and red striped tie and was quite a contrast to Slayton sitting next to him.

Ulrich looked over at the prosecutor. "We need to have certain assurances."

"Off course you do," Teague said. "And would you mind sharing with us what those *assurances* might include?"

Ulrich leaned close to Vince Slayton and whispered something in his ear. Slayton nodded back. Teague looked over at the sheriff with a disgusted and impatient look and then took a sip from the bad coffee that Stone had brought him in a Styrofoam cup.

"My client will cooperate in this investigation in exchange for complete immunity," the young lawyer said confidently.

Teague choked and spit his coffee back into the cup. First he looked at Sheriff Elam Stone and then back at Slayton. "You've got to be fucking kidding me?"

Slayton looked over at his lawyer to say something. Ulrich didn't falter. "Those are our terms," he said.

"Well, you can take your terms right back into that jail cell, because immunity is totally out of the question here. We're talking capital murder, son!"

Ulrich whispered something to his client again and Slayton said something back to him in agreement. "This is by no means an admission of guilt in these charges against my client," Ulrich said, "but I can tell you that he has relevant information in this case that will implicate others."

Chapter Twenty-eight

Sammy Truegood was abandoned by almost everyone that summer of 1952. His friends, the community and many of his people assumed the worst and condemned him, even before all the facts were out. In spite of his best intentions he just wasn't able to let the system run its course. He kept making the situation worse by trying to take matters into his own hands.

***

The bonfire roared high up into the night sky, sparks floating up and then fizzling out, dry driftwood crackling and spitting down in the hot red coals. Jennifer Harris sat on a small log with Andy Welton. Elaine was across from them sitting with Josh Knowles and another boy. More beer and whiskey had appeared and everyone except Jennifer was close to stumbling drunk, including Elaine. Jennifer sat there silently, thinking about walking home.

In the firelight she could see on her watch that it was just after eleven o'clock which happened to be her curfew since the night she ended up in the hospital. She had asked Andy twice to take her home and he continued to put her off, asking for just a few more minutes. She had tried to get his keys, but he had gotten angry and told her to sit down and wait

"Andy, if you don't get me home now, my mother won't let me out again for the rest of the summer!" she said. "Do you understand me?"

He looked at her with a dazed expression and his head was weaving as he tried to focus on what she had said. Someone yelled something that was supposed to be funny from across the fire and Andy turned and started laughing, ignoring Jennifer's request. She got up and started walking away.

Andy almost didn't notice until Elaine yelled out, "Jennifer, where you going?"

Jennifer didn't turn back. She was determined to just walk home, even if it took her an hour. Her mother would just have to understand.

Andy jumped up and staggered after her. He caught up and grabbed her arm. "Come on, Jennifer, I'm sorry, we'll leave soon. Come on back."

She pulled her arm away and kept on up the trail into the woods. Andy stayed with her and this time pulled her around to stop her. "Jennifer…!"

"Andy, no! Just shut-up!" she screamed. "I knew this was a bad idea."

"Settle down…"

"No, I won't settle down and I'm leaving now! You're too drunk to drive anyway."

"I'm fine," he said and then repeated with a slurred mumble, "I'm fine Jennifer, just wait a minute."

She turned and walked away again.

***

Sammy Truegood was carrying more trash outside to put in the cans when he smelled smoke coming from over the dunes at North Point beach. His first thought was that it was kids burning a bonfire. It was fairly common out this way on the beach. But then he thought that it could also be a brush fire from some careless smoker and their house was too close to the woods to risk not checking it out. He went inside and told his mother he would be back in a few minutes. He left her sitting at the kitchen table with her head in her hands, too tired to answer him.

He walked down the road to where the trail led down to the beach. There were no street lights this far out of town, but there was half a moon overhead and when he got closer he could see two cars parked off the road under the trees. There were no people around so he continued on down the path through the woods. He heard someone coming towards him and made a quick decision that he didn't need to be seen, so he just slid quietly off the trail behind a tree.

There were two people coming, the first was a girl followed by a man who seemed to be staggering in the loose sand on the path. Then he heard the man call out.

"Jennifer, dammit, would you please stop for a minute!"

Sammy's senses were instantly on alert.

"Jennifer!" the man yelled out again.

The girl was closer now and in the soft light of the moon through the trees he could see that it was Jennifer Harris. The man ran to catch up with her, stumbling once and then grabbing her and spinning her around. "Please just wait up, I'll drive you home."

Sammy's heart started pounding and his mouth went dry when he saw that it was Andy Welton. He watched as Jennifer Harris struggled to get her arm free.

She started crying and screamed out, "You let me go now, or I'll…"

"Jennifer, stop it!" Andy yelled back.

Sammy reacted without thinking about what was right or wrong, only that he wasn't going to let anyone hurt Jennifer Harris again. He ran out from behind the tree and pushed himself between the two of them. Both were frightened by his sudden appearance and Jennifer even screamed.

"Welton, leave her alone," Sammy said and pushed him away from her. Andy lost his balance and fell back in the sand. He sat there for a few moments collecting himself and then struggled to get up again. Then he realized who had jumped out at them.

"Why you sonofabitch, it's the damn Indian kid," he said.

"Sammy, what are doing out here?" Jennifer asked, still with panic in her voice.

He turned to look at her. "I smelled smoke and was just coming out to check…"

Before he could finish he felt a stunning pain from a blow to the back of his head and it caused him to fall to his knees.

Jennifer screamed as she saw Andy standing there with a big stick in his hands. "Andy, please no!" She watched as Andy staggered backwards in his drunkenness, trying to find his balance.

Sammy got up holding his head, feeling a warm sticky wetness seep into his fingers. His rage from all that had happened to him and his family's home these past days overwhelmed him and he turned and ran at Welton, screaming wildly. The boy couldn't react in time and Sammy rammed him in the chest with his shoulder and fell to the ground on top of him. Welton tried to get up and took a swing at Sammy's face. He blocked the blow and then swung down as hard as he could with his fist on Welton's face. He forgot about the broken bones under the bandages on his right hand from hitting Connor Harris and when he connected with the forehead of Andy Welton he screamed out as he felt the bones breaking apart again.

Welton tried again to get up and this time Sammy swung hard with his left hand and caught him square in the nose. Blood gushed out across Welton's face and he cried out in pain. Sammy lost all sense of control and swung again. He heard Jennifer screaming and pulling at his shirt from behind. He swung again and again and he saw Welton try to cover his face with his arms and then breathless, he finally stopped and fell over in the sand. Jennifer dropped to her knees next to him, crying. His head was spinning and the fury was still racing through his brain as he tried to catch his breath. Andy Welton continued to lie on his back on the path, a low moaning sound coming from him, muffled by his arms over his face.

Sammy sat up and tried to gather his thoughts. Finally his mind began to clear and he knew he had to get Jennifer out of there. "Do you have a car?" he asked her.

She shook her head no, still sobbing and then got up and went over to Andy Welton and kneeled down next to him. Reaching into his pants pocket she pulled out a key ring and then looked over at Sammy.

"You need to go," he said.

She stared at him blankly for a moment in the semi-darkness and then got up and ran down the path toward the cars.

Sammy struggled to his feet, feeling a helpless sense of exhaustion numbing his body. Blood from the back of his head trickled down through his hair and onto his neck. Andy Welton continued to lie on the ground in a drunken and beaten stupor, moaning and rolling slowly from one side to another.

Sammy left him there and started back up the path. He heard a car start and then drive away.

***

Jonathan heard a knock at the door and left Emily at the kitchen table with a cup of tea. He looked out a sidelight window next to the door and saw George Hansen standing there in the porch light. He opened the door for his friend.

"Good thing we didn't go fishing tonight," George said as he walked through the door.

They walked together into the kitchen and George sat down across from Emily.

"Sara's finally asleep," Jonathan said.

"Would you like some tea, George?" Emily asked.

"No, thank you. I just wanted to check on everyone and to let you know that I finally got in touch with someone from the Public Health department. They agreed that it was okay to let Sara stay with you for a while, at least until they can get the case processed and look for a foster home or some responsible relatives."

"A foster home!" Emily said. "She needs people who will love her and take care of her."

"Emily, I know how you feel, but we need to let the system take its course here," George said.

"A lot of good that's done up 'til now," she replied.

Jonathan leaned against the counter by the sink. "No sign of Slayton yet?"

"No, I saw Potts when I left the hospital and nothing yet."

"What's gonna happen here, George?" Jonathan asked.

"When they find him, I'm sure he'll be charged with at least third degree murder. Not much question that he did this. I doubt there will be any bail, so he may be locked up for the rest of his life, or damned close to it."

"Thank God," Emily said.

***

MICHAEL LINDLEY

Harold Slayton drove through the little town of Boyne City past the Dilworth Hotel and the row of small shops on the main street. He saw the neon sign for the Boyne River Inn and was tempted to stop for a drink. His pint bottle was dry and he needed a drink badly, but he also was coherent enough to realize that he couldn't be seen in public. He kept on through town and turned right at the lake on the road back to Charlevoix.

Chapter Twenty-nine

Louis Kramer got up from the dinner table with his wife. The cook came in to clear dishes and they both took unfinished glasses of wine out onto the front deck of the house. The breeze off the lake was still blowing gently and with only an hour of light left, the low sun washed everything in the soft glow of the fading day. Louis looked out across the lake with a vacant stare, sipping on his wine.

"Lou, you haven't said two words all through dinner," Mary Alice said.

He didn't hear her, or chose not to respond.

"Louis!"

He turned his head slowly as she came up next to him by the deck rail. "I'm sorry, what did you say?"

"What the hell is the matter?" she said.

"What do you think is the matter?" he said with disgust and then started walking down the steps to the front lawn.

"Louis, where are you going?"

"I need to take a ride."

"We have people coming over to play cards in an hour."

He held up his hand and waved as he walked down to the lake. She kept yelling at him, but he wasn't listening. His mind was locked on his last phone conversation with Alberto Manta. There was no way in hell he was going to have the money to wire to Manta's accounts by tomorrow morning. He was in debt up to his neck in his other businesses. His personal investments had all been used to help fund this latest business. Mary Alice had a trust fund and her parents had money, but nothing close to what he needed. *Alex Clark sure as hell won't bail me out!*

He walked out onto the dock and two swans that had been feeding nearby on the bottom of the lake moved slowly away, hissing when he first approached. Putting his empty wine glass down on the top of one of the dock posts he jumped over the side of the big cruiser and went below to the bar. When he opened the cabinet for the liquor he was faced with a number of choices. An unopened bottle of vodka caught his eye and he grabbed it and walked quickly back up on deck. He had planned to take the cruiser out because it had the most liquor on board, but decided that was too much work to get underway.

He climbed out and went over to the little ski boat and hit the button for the power hoist to lower it down into the lake. A few minutes later he was steering out into Lake Charlevoix, the bottle of vodka now open on his lap. With no destination in mind he pushed the throttle down to three quarter speed and the little boat quickly sped away into the glare of the setting sun. Steering with his left hand, he took a long slow drink from the bottle and then choked as it burned down his throat. Then he took another.

***

The hostess at the Argonne Supper Club led Alex and Sally to a table out on the side porch. They sat down and Alex ordered drinks while Sally looked quickly through the menu. Then she wondered why she was even bothering because she knew they always ordered their oysters and shrimp.

She was still upset about Anna kissing her husband goodbye at the airport. At least Alex was noble enough to tell me about it, she thought. In a way she knew that she shouldn't worry about it. Alex could take care of it and she trusted him to deal with it. But something about this woman continued to make her uneasy. She obviously was not a woman who liked to take *no* for an answer and she and Alex would be spending a lot of time together in the coming weeks back in New York. *While I'm sitting here in sleepy Charlevoix.*

"I hope you're not still stewing about Anna?" Alex said.

She looked at him and smiled. "Of course not."

"You know, I'm worried about Megan seeing this Will kid with the stolen car and all," he said.

The waitress brought their drinks and placed them down on cocktail napkins. Alex ordered the house specialty with family style orders of steamed and batter-fried shrimp. The girl took the menus and headed back to the kitchen.

"I truly doubt that Will Truegood would steal a car and leave it in front of his house," she said. "It's just too bad that Megan's caught in the middle with her old friends. If Rick really did take this car to set Will up, Megan's better off without him, but I just can't believe he would be that stupid."

"Jealousy has a strange way with people," he said looking at her with a smirk on his face.

She threw a small piece of bread at him and said, "I'm not jealous!"

"I know, I'm just kidding. I'm sorry," he said and tried to stop laughing. "I don't know this Rick very well. He seemed like a nice enough kid last summer when we spent some time with him and his parents, but teenage boys can be a handful. I know, I used to be one."

"At times, I think you still are," she said and he threw the piece of bread back at her.

"Alright, peace," she said, holding up her hands. "I just wish there was something we could do to help Megan."

"Well thank you for that. I love that you care so much for my daughter."

"You know I love her like my own," she said and then immediately thoughts of her lost daughter, Ellen, came back to her.

Alex could see the look on her face and he had come to know his wife very well. "You must be thinking of Ellen?"

Sally nodded and reached for her drink, her eyes growing moist.

"We knew that Megan would never totally fill that space in your heart, but I'm glad that you both have each other now," he said.

"It's been wonderful having Megan to love and care for and worry about," Sally said and tried unsuccessfully to laugh her tears away.

***

Megan had dropped Will at the beach in Horton Bay earlier and had returned to Charlevoix. After she had tied the boat up at the city shopping

247

docks she met Rebecca who she had called earlier to come down to pick her up.

"Thanks for coming," Megan said.

"I hope you know what you're doing. Rick is really pissed," Rebecca said.

Megan didn't answer as they got into Rebecca's car.

"Actually, everyone's pissed at you. No one can believe you're accusing Rick of taking this car and then taking Will's side against him."

"Becca, I know," Megan said. "Can you please just take me up to Melissa's house?"

"Is she there?"

"I called her before you picked me up."

Rebecca pulled into the drive at the Wainwright's house and pulled to a stop. The lights were on in most of the rooms in the big summer house. Melissa's red convertible was parked in a pull-off to the side.

"You can just drop me, thanks," Megan said. "I can walk back to Sally's house later."

"What are you planning to pull with Ms. Melissa?" Rebecca asked.

"I think I'll beat the crap out of her!"

"Megan!"

"I'm kidding." She got out and closed the door and her friend pulled away. Melissa came out on the front porch to meet her. She must not want Momma and Daddy to hear this conversation, Megan thought.

"Hey Megan."

She didn't return the greeting and simply said, "Let's take a walk."

They walked together down the drive and then turned right on the sidewalk going down Dixon Avenue. Tall oaks lined the street on both sides forming a giant canopy. Lights were on in most of the big houses along the sides of the street.

They had gone almost a block before Melissa broke the silence. "Megan, I really don't want to talk about this car thing anymore. I told you what happened."

Megan stopped and turned to face the girl, grabbing her by both arms. "Alright, let's cut the bull here, Melissa," she said, letting her voice rise in anger. "I've had enough of you all trying to hurt Will and I've gone to the police."

"You did what!"

Megan didn't have much practice lying, but she continued on as best she could. "They should be up to question you first thing in the morning."

"Have you lost your mind?" Melissa said, the panic in her face clear in the light from a nearby street lamp.

"Melissa, they're really upset about all of you lying about this. It's a crime to provide a false police report."

Melissa pulled away and started walking again. Megan caught up and said, "You do not want to go to jail, Melissa."

The girl stopped suddenly and looked at Megan for a moment, breathing hard. "They said it was going to be a joke."

Megan could have jumped out of her skin, but she tried to remain calm and impassive. "A joke?"

"Rick and Jimmy said they wanted to play a joke on this Indian kid that had been hanging around you," Melissa said. "I'm sorry, Megan. I guess I thought it would be funny."

"Funny!"

"I guess I just didn't think. I'm sorry."

"You can't be serious!" Megan said. "Do you have any idea what you've done?"

"I said *I'm sorry*, Megan!"

Megan took her arm again and started leading her back toward her house. "You and I are going down to the police station right now and get this cleared up," Megan said.

"What are they going to do?"

"*You* are going to drop the charges."

"Will they arrest me?"

"Not if you tell them the truth and I'm going to be right there to make sure that you do!"

***

Connor Harris was smoking a cigar out on the front porch of their summer house. He watched a couple stroll by under the street lamp and he reached out to flick some ashes down into the bushes. *Can't even smoke in my own damn house anymore.*

His mind was spinning with a desperation that was almost making him nauseous. Since he had been released from jail for his past sins, he had tried to help his son get the business back on track, but every move they had made over the past few years seemed to have turned out wrong and they were now hanging by a thin string. *Even the summer house here in Charlevoix has a damn mortgage!*

He thought about his son Dylan and he knew that the man wasn't capable of pulling this new deal together. *I've helped him as much as I could up until now, more than he will ever know, actually.*

Chapter Thirty

Connor Harris always had a blind eye for the truth and I'm not sure I ever met a more stubborn man, certainly none more angry.

***

Jennifer Harris returned home and pulled into the driveway in Andy Welton's car. It was just past eleven o'clock and she hoped everyone in her house would be asleep. During the short ride home her mind had been spinning about Sammy Truegood. Tears continued to run down her face. *Why was he there? Why did he beat Andy so badly? Why had he helped her?*

She walked through the back door into the kitchen as quietly as she could and then stopped suddenly when she saw her brother Connor was sitting at the kitchen table with a newspaper. He looked up when she came in and immediately noticed the tears streaking her face and then stood up quickly and walked over to her.

"What the hell's happened now?"

"Connor, just leave me alone. I need to go to bed."

He grabbed her arm to stop her from passing. "First you're going to tell me what's going on."

She pulled her arm away and looked up at her brother and realized he would find out by morning anyway. It occurred to her that Andy might be hurt badly and maybe someone should go back to find him. She also knew that her family would be furious with her for going down to another drunken beach party.

The look on her brother's face grew deathly serious. "Jennifer?"

She started to worry about Andy. It could be hours before the rest of the kids at the beach came up the trail to go home, or what if he rolled over into the woods and passed out? They would never see him. "There was a fight down at the beach."

"Who was fighting?"

Jennifer hesitated for a moment, quickly trying to figure out how best to tell the story and how to reveal as little as possible about the details. "It was Andy, down at North Point," she finally said.

"Andy and who else?"

Jennifer felt her stomach churn; she didn't want to open all the trouble with Sammy Truegood again, but she knew it was just a matter of time until everyone knew. "It was Sammy," she said quietly.

Connor immediately tensed and grabbed her arm again. "What has that little shit done now?"

Jennifer still wasn't sure what had happened, or why, but she knew she had to tell the truth as best she could. "He was trying to help me."

"Help you!"

"Andy was drunk and he wouldn't bring me home and he kept trying to stop me on the trail and then all of a sudden, Sammy was there and he tried to get Andy to let me go." She couldn't hold back her tears. "I think Andy might be hurt."

"How bad?" Connor said, the look on his face growing more furious.

"I don't know," she said, "I just don't know."

"Why did you leave him down there?"

"I just wanted to get home. I was supposed to be home by eleven."

Connor shook her to get her to look at him. "Where were the other kids down there?"

"Down at the beach. Everyone was drinking and I just wanted to get out of there and Andy wouldn't take me home."

"Why was the Truegood kid there?" Connor asked.

"I said *I don't know!*" she cried out.

252

Connor went to the counter and picked up a set of keys. "You and I are going down there. I'll leave a note for Mother, so she won't worry about you if she wakes up."

***

Sammy Truegood opened the side door to his house and tried to enter quietly but he tripped over a pail that had been used for mopping up the mess. He heard his mother coming back to the kitchen. He watched her mouth drop when she saw him. He could only imagine what he looked like after the fight with Andy Welton and when he pulled his hand down from the back of his head, blood had run down the length of his arm to his elbow, some still wet and shining in the dim light of the kitchen. His mother gasped and held her hands up to her mouth, and then rushed over to him.

"Sammy, what's happened?"

He walked by her over to the sink and started trying to rinse the blood off his hands.

"Sammy?" his mother asked again and when she came up behind him she saw the blood caked on the back of his hair. "Ohmigod, son!"

"I'll be okay."

"Sammy, you tell me what's happened," she said as she started to delicately look through the mat of his hair to check the wound.

He flinched away when she touched the raw gash that had opened from Welton's attack.

"We need to get you to a doctor."

"No!" he said abruptly. "I said I'll be alright." He had rinsed as much of the blood away from his hands as he could without further scrubbing, the bandages on his right hand were soaked and the knuckles beneath were throbbing in pain. "Momma, just do what you can to put something on this," he said reaching up to the back of his head with his other hand.

She hurried out of the room to get something and he sat down on a chair at the small table in the kitchen. He looked around at the mess that had yet to be cleaned up in their house and the fury returned as he thought about Andy Welton and his friends. He shuddered when he remembered how enraged he had become just moments ago in the fight with Welton and then a cold fear rushed through him when he thought about what all of this would do with the charges that were already hanging over him.

His mother came back into the kitchen with towels and some bandages and she started dabbing at the wound on his head. "Sammy, you need to tell me what's happened here."

He knew that the truth would break her heart again and he said quietly, "Somebody jumped me down on the trail to the beach."

She came around to look at him and pulled his chin up. "Who would do that?"

He hesitated for a moment and then just shook his head, looking back down at the floor.

***

Harold Slayton had driven slowly through town trying not to attract any attention. He didn't think that reports of a stolen truck would have reached there yet, but he didn't want to draw unnecessary attention to himself. He knew he needed to get back out to his farm and if the cops weren't there he was going to get some food and a gun and some ammunition. Memories of the events that had led up to the fight with his wife were fuzzy in his brain from the whiskey, but he remembered Agnes screaming at him to stop and then he pushed her and she fell and hit her head and didn't move again. Sara had run out of the cabin and then he heard the men coming up the drive and he had hurried out the back door and watched from the woods as the sheriff and that McKendry fellow had come up to the old shack.

He thought again about his little girl, Sara, and a dark, irrational anger washed over him. They had taken his daughter away from him again, he thought, mindless to the fact that he had just killed the girl's mother.

***

"I need to get home," George said to Emily and Jonathan.

It was close to midnight on the little wall clock in the kitchen. Jonathan got up to walk him to the door. When they were down the hall away from Emily, he whispered, "What's going to happen to the little girl?"

"They'll process this through the courts and they'll start looking for a temporary foster home. There may be other family involved, too. I don't know," George said.

"They need to find that sonofabitch and put him away for good," Jonathan said.

"I'll follow up with the Public Health folks again in the morning and let you know," George said.

"Thanks buddy," Jonathan replied, shaking his hand as he walked out the front door.

George turned on the front porch and said, "You keep an eye on Emily tonight. I'm worried about how she's taking all this."

"I know, thanks," Jonathan said and he watched his friend walk away down the front sidewalk to his car.

He went back into the kitchen and Emily was gone, so he walked quietly up to their bedroom and found her sitting on the bed, her head down in her hands. He walked up and sat down gently next to her, putting his arm around her shoulders and pulling her close to him. She turned and buried her face in the front of his shirt and he could feel the quiet sobs racking her body.

***

Connor and Jennifer drove up to the clearing in the woods at North Point where the other car was parked and he pulled over and turned off the car. The moon was up behind them now, leaving soft shadows through the trees on the ground as they walked down the sandy path.

"Where was he," Connor asked.

"Just up there," she said and pointed.

Around a small bend in the trail they almost tripped over the body of Andy Welton. He was lying on his side and motionless. Connor knelt beside him and pushed him over on his back and there was still no movement. He could smell the liquor on him and he shook him gently, trying to wake him up. "Andy, hey Andy."

After a little more prodding the boy started to respond, shaking his head slowly and letting out a low, soft moaning sound. Even in the darkness

Connor could see the blood all over his face and down the front of his white shirt.

"We need to get him down to the hospital," Connor said.

Jennifer just stood there, a helpless feeling and fear consuming her.

"Help me out here!" Connor yelled.

***

The phone rang in the dark bedroom of Sheriff Willy Potts. He reached over and turned on a lamp by his bed. His wife pulled the covers up over her head and turned away from the light. He could see that it was just past midnight on the little alarm clock sitting on the nightstand. The phone rang again.

"Shit!" he whispered as he picked up the receiver. Immediately he heard the voice of Connor Harris yelling at him on the other end of the line. He listened without responding until Connor had relayed the whole story.

"I'll be down in twenty minutes."

***

Mary Truegood took the bloody towels over to the sink and started rinsing them. She hadn't spoken during the time she had worked to clean the wound on her son's head. Her mind raced with the fear of what might have happened that her son wasn't telling her and she could only think that this would be bad for him with the trial coming up and she started to cry.

Sammy came up and put his arms around her and tried to comfort her. He had never felt so hopeless.

Chapter Thirty-one

Megan Clark drove through the dark on the road along the north shore of Lake Charlevoix. She crossed the small bridge over Horton Creek and then turned left at the next road. A half mile later a mailbox was coming up on the left and she slowed the Jeep until she could read the name *Truegood* on the side. She turned in on the narrow two track road and drove on slowly until the cabin came into view in her headlights around the final turn.

Will came out barefoot, dressed in jeans and a gray t-shirt. He stood on the porch as she got out and walked up to the cabin.

"What are you doing out here in the wilderness, City Girl," he said with a smile.

She walked up the wood steps onto the porch and surprised him by coming up and hugging him and planting a big kiss on his mouth.

"Well, hello to you, too," he said, returning her kiss.

She stood back and smiled at him, bursting to tell him what had happened.

"What?" he asked, looking at her with a confused expression.

"I have some news for you," she said, trying to contain her excitement.

"What kind of news?"

"Well, you're a free man!"

"A free man?" he asked.

"I went to see my so-called *friend*, Melissa Wainwright tonight and we had a long talk about her stolen car."

"What about it?" Will asked, taking her hand and sitting down with her on the steps. The light from inside the house streamed out through the screened door onto the porch.

"Seems I was able to finally convince her to remember what really happened that night."

"And how did you do that?" he asked.

Megan giggled. "A little friendly persuasion."

***

Sally and Alex walked up to her house on Michigan and took the mail and papers out of the mailbox. They went inside and turned on the lights and then walked into the kitchen. Sally threw the mail down on the counter and then noticed the story on the cover of the Charlevoix paper.

"*Suspect Charged in the Murder of George Hansen.*"

"Alex, look at this," she said, handing him the paper. They've finally pressed charges and released something to the papers. I'm surprised nothing's come out earlier."

She watched as Alex picked up the *Courier* and started reading. He stopped after the first few paragraphs, handing it back to Sally. "Well, this should get the town talking."

Sally looked down at the page with a picture of George Hansen taken at a much younger age. Her heart ached again as she thought about the loss of her close friend. She read the whole article and then Alex came around and took her in his arms. "I'm sorry, honey," he said. "I know how you feel about George."

She put the paper down and looked up at Alex and said, "How about a walk down on the beach. I think I need a little fresh air."

They walked out the back door of the sun porch, kicking off their shoes and continued on across the lawn. The rumble of waves on the beach below greeted them as they made their way slowly down the trail through the dunes. The sand was cool beneath their feet and out on the blackness of the lake a few lights glimmered on distant boats. Up above a billion stars were shining brightly in the clear sky.

They held each other's hand and walked down to the water line. The beach was dark and deserted, except for a bonfire burning far to the north.

They headed in that direction and Sally was closest to the water and her feet splashed along when a bigger wave would roll in. She kept thinking of George and Elizabeth and how much she would miss her favorite *uncle.*

"I need to go back to New York tomorrow," Alex said, splitting the silence.

Sally stopped and looked at him in the darkness. "Why so soon?"

"My *attorney* called while you were in the restroom at the restaurant."

"What's the rush?"

"Apparently the Attorney General has pushed up a preliminary hearing. It's the day after tomorrow. We need to prepare."

Sally thought about Anna Bataglia and tried to control her anger. "What else did the lovely Ms. Bataglia have to say?"

"Actually, she said she was sorry for the scene at the airport."

Sally just looked back at him, the outlines of his face shadowed in the darkness.

"She said she didn't know what had come over her, that maybe she was still drunk from the night before."

"Hardly," Sally said.

"She's asked the managing partner of the firm to take over the case."

"You're kidding?"

"No, she said she thought it would be better to get Dick involved."

"How do you feel about that?" she asked.

"He's one of the best attorneys in the country. I couldn't be in better hands."

They continued on along the beach, Sally thinking about her husband and his *former* lawyer. "You're sure this won't disrupt your defense?"

"I'm sure they wouldn't let that happen," he answered.

Sally took his hand and led him up across the beach to a low sand dune. Tall pines and dunes rose up behind them into the dark sky. She sat down and pulled him down next to her and they looked out at the lake. A big freighter was on its way to the north a few miles out, a small city of lights.

Alex said, "Now I know that this is one of your favorite places to make out, if I remember correctly. What do you have in mind, Mrs. Clark?"

She reached over and put her hand behind his back and pulled him close. "Just come over here, will you."

***

Louis Clark tipped the bottle of vodka back as far as it would go and the few remaining drops moistened his lips. He looked at the bottle in the light of the dashboard of the little ski boat and then threw it over the side into the lake.

His head was aching from the liquor and he tried to focus his eyes on what was ahead in the lake. He had come out through the channel into Lake Michigan an hour ago to watch the sun go down and drink and think about his fate with Alberto Manta. As the liquor went down his desperation had grown and now he sat in quiet resignation.

"What the hell," he mumbled, as the little boat rocked in the waves. He could just make out lights on shore at the pier back into Charlevoix. He thought about his business and his life with Mary Alice and the choices he had made. They all came together in his mind in a drunken blur. Then he thought about his partner, Alex Clark and the trouble he had caused him and a profound sadness swept over him as he thought of the mess he had created.

Louis looked down on the dash to find the ignition key and images of the lights and dials blurred in his brain. He finally found the key and the engine came to life and idled softly. Reaching out for the throttle he pushed it forward slowly and the boat surged up into a following wave. The boat gained speed and splashed hard down into the waves, the spray of water coming over the windshield and in his face. He pressed the throttle forward again and the boat roared up into the night.

Louis was tossed around in his seat as the boat flew off the top of one wave and into the next, the engine whining as it came up out of the water. He yelled out as loud as he could over the roar of the engine, screaming out in some wild, unintelligible wail and the wind and water blew in his face.

He pushed the throttle lever down as far as it would go and the engine roared even louder, crashing through the surf, Louis holding on to the steering wheel to keep from being thrown out of the boat. Ahead through the ripples of water streaming up over the windshield he could see lights

260

coming; red and green and the bright flash of the lighthouse every few moments. The sounds of the engine were deafening in his ears and he couldn't even hear his own screams as the boat bore on.

The lights came closer and in the fuzziness of his brain he remembered a time at school when he first met Alex Clark and they had gone sailing together one weekend at his parent's house. A smile came across his face as he remembered his friend.

***

Alex and Sally both sat up on the beach as they heard the roar of a boat engine racing toward the channel into Round Lake. "What is that idiot doing?" Alex said.

"Too many crazy drunks with big toys around here," Sally said and then she pushed him back down on his back, easing herself up on top of him. As she leaned down to kiss him again the sound of an explosion echoed down the beach and she fell over on her side in surprise. They both looked down toward the pier as a large fireball rose up into the night illuminating the north pier into the channel.

"Oh my God, Alex!" Sally screamed.

They both got up and started running back along the beach, buttoning buttons and tucking in shirts. "Do you have your phone?" she yelled as they ran toward the pier.

Chapter Thirty-two

Sometimes there's a very thin line between obsession and madness. With Harold Slayton there was very little question.

***

The moon was low in the western sky and the slightest of breezes rustled the trees. The light of the coming morning to the east was just starting to show. Harold Slayton had parked his car down the street and walked through back yards to the McKendry house. He crouched in a cluster of shrubs in their backyard and looked at the house. All of the lights were off and in the adjoining houses as well.

When he had gone out to his farm earlier he left the truck a quarter mile up the road and had walked through the woods to his house. When he was sure that there were no police he had gone inside and packed the supplies that he needed and then quickly left. As he was going out the back door he saw the old doll that Sara liked to play with and he had thrown it in the bag.

As he knelt motionless in the bushes his legs started to ache and he laid down to stretch out for a minute. He knew that his daughter would be brought back here and he reached to his side and felt the cold metal from the barrel of his shotgun.

***

Jonathan had been awake most of the night looking up at the ceiling. Emily was asleep beside him, finally dozing off a little over an hour ago. The sound of the old alarm clock ticking next to the bed seemed louder than normal and he kept thinking about the sight of Agnes Slayton on the floor in the pool of her own blood.

Sara had cried out a few minutes ago and he had gone quietly down the hall to check on her. She was still asleep and he smiled as he pulled the blanket back up over her. He had almost started to cry and had to wipe the moisture out of his eyes.

As he lay there in the bed he looked over at the face of his wife Emily, illuminated in the moonlight coming in through the window. Even asleep he could see the pain in her face and he wondered what dream was haunting her.

A noise down on the first floor startled him and he sat up and listened again. He felt the cold prickly sensations of fear rush through him and he strained to listen for another sound. There was nothing but the ticking of the clock and then he heard another scraping sound. He could feel his heart beating faster in his chest and he pushed the covers away and got out of bed, trying not to wake Emily.

He walked as quietly as he could over to the closet on the far wall and pulling the door open he reached inside and pulled out the shotgun that he used for duck hunting with George and some other friends. There was a box of shells in a bag on the floor and he reached around in the dark until he found it. He loaded one shell and the noise was so loud that he looked over at Emily. He put two more shells in the pocket of his pajamas.

His fear turned to a quiet fury as he held the gun in his hands and looked at his wife sleeping unaware. He moved as quietly as he could out of the bedroom and down the hall to the top of the stairs. A loose board creaked and he stopped and backed up against the wall, listening again.

Now he could hear the relentless ticking of the big grandfather clock down in the living room. He flinched when the chimes began to ring out through the house and the noise seemed deafening as he tried to listen for other sounds of an intruder. He counted the chimes without thinking. It was five o'clock.

He stood there for another minute, listening, trying to keep calm and willing his heart to slow down. There were no other sounds below and he started down the steps slowly, trying not to make a noise. He clicked the safety off behind the trigger of the shotgun. The front door at the bottom of the stairs had narrow windows on each side and he could see the light coming from a street lamp reflecting on the dark stained oak floor.

He thought the noise had come from the back of the house and when he got to the bottom of the stairs he crouched low and listened again. Only the sound of the big clock broke the stillness. He looked around into the living room and saw nothing amiss and then moved slowly down the hall toward the kitchen and the back of the house.

Then he heard a board creaking upstairs and he saw Emily's legs coming down the steps.

"Jonathan, where are you?" she said in the darkness.

He felt a moment of panic and didn't know what to do or say.

"Jonathan?" she called out softly, trying not to wake Sara.

He moved quickly back over to the bottom of the stairs and when she saw the gun in his hands her eyes grew wide and her mouth fell open. Jonathan quickly held a finger up to his lips to keep her from speaking. He signaled for her to go back upstairs, but she didn't move.

She came down the last stair and whispered, "Jonathan…"

He could sense the fear in her voice and his hands began to shake grasping the big gun. "Just go back upstairs," he whispered as quietly as he could. "Go make sure Sara's okay."

She nodded and he watched as she started to back slowly up the stairs. When she was gone he looked back down the hallway and started to move toward the back of the house. He walked up to the doorway into the little dining room and he peered around the corner of the doorjamb until he was sure there was no one there. He continued on down the hall and his bare feet on the cold wood floor kept squeaking softly beneath him. As he reached the end of the hall he could see into the kitchen now and out through the back window. He stopped and tried his best to will his body to stop shaking and he took several deep breaths.

With the first step he took into the kitchen in a low crouch, he knew something was wrong. Before he could turn, he felt rather than saw the rushing motion of something coming at his face and in that split second before he could respond a crushing blow landed just above his right eye and pain shot out through his head and he staggered back, dropping his shotgun. He knew he was falling and he tried to grab for something as he realized that he was blacking out.

The last thing he heard was a shrill cry of "Jonathan!" coming from upstairs and a terrifying helpless feeling surged through him as he fell back onto the floor and lost consciousness.

***

Sammy Truegood had tried to sleep, but knew that the sheriff would be knocking at the door at any time. He got up from his bed and quietly slipped on his pants and a jacket and then carried his boots back through the house. He knew there was no sense trying to run. There was no place to go and he would never run from his problems anyway. Out in the back yard he sat on the porch and then laced up his boots. His bike was leaning against the back of the house and he walked it out to the street and then got on.

He rode down the quiet dirt street in the darkness, the moon and stars clear in the sky above him through the tree limbs hanging out over the road. The lights were out in the few houses that he passed. A dog came running out from one of the houses barking at him and Sammy called to him softly as he came out into the street, "Sonny, you go back." The big dog slowed and then ran alongside Sammy, its tail wagging. "Sonny, go on!" Sammy said, pointing back toward the dog's yard. Finally it broke away and trotted back.

Sammy turned on the road into town, not sure exactly where he was going, but certain in his mind that only trouble lay ahead in the coming day.

***

Jennifer Harris woke with the first light of morning through her bedroom window and as her mind cleared, the memories of the past night came back to her and she turned and buried her head in her pillow. She had been up most of the night thinking about Andy as they took him into the hospital. He could barely walk and his face was a swollen bloody mess. She and her brother Connor had left him with the nurses and Connor had gone out to call his parents. The sheriff had come down a bit later and gone into the room where they were working on Andy.

Her brother, Connor, had gotten into an argument with the big sheriff when he was trying to leave. She was sitting down the hall and couldn't hear everything they were saying, but as the sheriff walked by her to leave he turned back to her brother and said, "I told you, I'll go out and talk to him in the morning!"

She knew that he had been talking about Sammy and she rolled over on her back in bed as she thought about Sammy Truegood and all that had happened. The scattered memories of that first night at the beach that had started all of this bounced around in her brain and she closed her eyes trying to shut all of it out. Every day it seemed some new fragment of memory would come back to her about that night, but mostly she felt the enduring shame and emptiness that had stayed with her and haunted her.

Then she threw the covers back and with some strange sense of purpose that she didn't try to understand, she got up out of bed and went over to her closet and threw some clothes on. As quietly as she could she went down the stairs and out the back door taking the keys to her mother's car.

When she turned the engine on, she flinched at the noise and looked up at the big house expecting her brother to come running out after her. She put the transmission in reverse and backed out of the drive and then turned to head down into town. Turning left on Belvedere she headed west down the quiet street, cars parked along each side, no one else up yet in the early hour. Down to the right she could see Round Lake and a few boats anchored off. A low mist hung over the harbor, but the sky above was clear after the rains from yesterday.

She pulled up to the stop at Bridge Street and looked to her left up the hill. A big truck with its headlights still on came slowly down and passed her and then she pulled out and drove slowly down through the little town's shopping district. The streetlights were still on but there were very few cars along the curb. And then up ahead on the right along the sidewalk at the park she saw someone sitting on a bench. As she came closer she slowed and saw a bike on the ground next to the bench and then she could see that it was Sammy and she pulled quickly over to the curb.

He looked up as she got out of the car and came around to sit next to him. She could see a rough bandage on the back of his head and the dirty bloodstained bandages on his right hand. His face was worn and tired looking, as if he hadn't slept. He didn't say anything at first and turned back to look down at the lake.

"Sammy," she finally said, breaking the silence. "Are you okay?" He looked back at her and she winced when she saw the pain in his eyes. "Sammy, what is happening?" she said with desperation in her voice.

He just shook his head slowly and looked down at the ground.

"We went back and got Andy, Connor and me. He was hurt pretty badly and we took him down to the hospital."

Sammy looked up and just stared at her for a moment. He stood up and reached for her hand. "I'd like to take you somewhere."

***

George Hansen was on his way down to his office and as he drove by the McKendry's house he decided to stop for a moment and see if they were up and how Sara and Emily were doing. It was only seven o'clock, but he knew that neither of them slept very late. He parked the car at the curb and went up the front walk. As he got to the door he looked through the sidelight before he knocked.

He had a sinking feeling as he looked again and saw someone lying on the floor in the hallway. He tried the doorknob, but it was locked and then he ran around the side of the house to the back. Emily's car was parked in the drive. When he came around the back of the house he could see that the back door had been left open and he ran up the steps into the back entry and then into the kitchen. Jonathan was lying motionless at the opening into the hall; the right side of his face was swollen and covered in dried blood.

George rushed over and knelt beside his friend, shaking him gently, "Jonathan, Jonathan!" There was no response. He ran over to the sink and ran water on a towel and went back over to Jonathan and wiped softly at his brow and the ugly wound.

Jonathan's eyelids started to move and then he opened his eyes and looked blankly up at the ceiling and then over at George kneeling beside him.

"Jonathan, what in hell's happened?"

His friend just continued to lie there for a few moments and then George could see a sense of recognition come over his face which turned suddenly to fear. Jonathan tried to sit up and then moaned and fell back holding his head.

George tried to help ease his head back down on the hard wood floor.

"Emily," Jonathan whispered weakly.

George looked toward the stairs and his heart sank as he thought about what might have happened. "You wait here, I'll be right back." He stood up and walked apprehensively toward the stairwell and then up the stairs. There were no sounds in the house except for the incessant ticking of the grandfather clock.

When he got to the top of the stairs he stopped and listened. The doors to all three bedrooms were open and he walked slowly forward and looked into the first on the left. It was Jonathan and Emily's room and the bed was empty and the sheets and blankets were rumpled in disarray.

"Emily?" he called out softly. A nauseous fear almost overwhelmed him and his knees started to shake as he walked down the hall to the back bedrooms. The next room on the right had a bed that hadn't been disturbed and he went to the last door and cautiously looked in. There were two single beds coming out from the back wall. One had been slept in and two books lay on the bedspread at the foot of the bed, but there was no one in the room. He turned and looked down the hallway with the frightening realization of what must have happened and then he saw Jonathan struggling to come up the stairs.

Their eyes met and Jonathan yelled out, "Where's Emily?"

Chapter Thirty-three

Sally and Alex ran along the sand and then climbed up onto the north pier of the channel. The wreckage of the flaming boat was still floating in pieces out at the end of the pier. Alex had used his cell phone to call for the Coast Guard and the Sheriff's Marine Patrol. A few other people were out ahead of them, scurrying around, framed in the bright hot glow of the flames.

They ran as fast as they could and they heard yelling and screaming up ahead. They came out to the rail and they could see only parts of wreckage floating on the surface engulfed in flames, any part of the boat totally indistinguishable.

Sally turned and saw Alex's face lit brightly by the flames and she came to him and put her head on his shoulder. "Those poor people."

***

When they got back to the house Megan was there sitting at the island in the kitchen reading the paper. She had tears in her eyes as she looked down at the picture of her Uncle George. Sally came over and gave her a hug and kissed her on the top of the head.

"I know, honey," she said.

"So they've caught the guy at least," she said.

"Well, according to Elam, the sheriff, they think others may be involved," Alex said.

"I just can't believe this," Megan said and she went to the refrigerator and pulled out a soft drink. "I do have some better news."

"That's good," said Sally, "because we just came up from the beach and there was a terrible accident. Someone ran full speed into the end of the north pier. There was a huge explosion and fire and it looks pretty certain that everyone was lost."

"Oh, that's awful," Megan said. She opened her can of soda and sat down at the island. "And you saw it happen?"

Alex nodded, "We tried to help, but there was nothing left but burning wreckage." He looked at Megan with a sad smile and said, "Let's hear your *good* news."

"I just came back from seeing Will."

"Oh great," her father said.

"You won't believe what's happened."

"I can only imagine," said Sally.

Megan told them the story of Melissa and Rick and their so-called prank.

"I can't believe they would do that!" Sally said. "Have they lost their minds?"

"That's what I asked Melissa when she finally owned up to all of this," said Megan.

What did the sheriff's office say?" Alex asked.

"They're going to call all of them in tomorrow, Melissa and Rick and his friend, Jimmy, and hopefully scare the crap out of them," Megan said with a wry smile.

"I'm sorry about Rick, kiddo," Alex said. "I know you really cared for him."

"Well, I thought I did. I can't believe what a jerk he is."

"Yes," Sally said, "sometimes men can be more than we girls can ever understand," and then she looked over at her husband with a smile.

***

The phone by the bed rang and Sally opened her eyes to a soft light coming in through the window streaked with rain, heavy dark clouds drifting by outside. The phone rang again and she reached over and picked up the receiver. Alex was still asleep next to her.

"Hello."

She heard the quiet voice of Mary Alice Gregory on the other end of the line. She listened for a minute and the shocked realization of what had happened last night at the boat accident swept over her.

"Mary Alice, I'm so terribly sorry," she said. She listened again and then said softly, "Okay, I'd like to come out to see you later this morning." She heard Mary Alice say something else that she couldn't understand and then the line went dead. Sally looked over at her husband, oblivious to the death of his friend and partner.

***

The cook brought out a tray filled with coffee and croissants and the papers that Connor Harris liked to read each morning. He sat them down on a small table next to Connor's chair on the front veranda of the house. Rain dripped heavily off the eaves of the roof and thunder roared in the distance every few minutes. He didn't bother to acknowledge the servant and just reached for the coffee.

The front page headline of the *Charlevoix Courier* stuck out in the pile of newspapers under the *Wall Street Journal*. He picked up the local paper and read the story of the arrest of Vince Slayton in the death of George Hansen. He read every word and then put the paper slowly back down on the pile.

A bolt of lightning flashed out over the lake and he squinted as the bright light blinded him for the briefest of moments. The roaring rumble of thunder followed and rattled the coffee cup on the saucer next to him.

He was thinking of George Hansen and the run-ins they had shared over the many years; those summers back in the '40's when he had been doing George's sister before her death, just to spite McKendry's brother, Luke; and in '52, or whenever it was when his own sister, Jennifer had been raped and Hansen defended the Indian kid that was charged.

He picked up the paper again and looked at the picture of George Hansen. The anger and conflicts of those many years rushed back into his brain and he ripped the front page off and crumbling it into a ball, threw it out into the rain on the front yard.

***

Sally brought juice and coffee up to the bedroom for Alex with a copy of the *New York Times* that had just been delivered on the front porch.

271

He was sitting up reading an email message on his cell phone, the small lamp on the table beside him turned on. A clap of thunder outside startled them both. She came over and sat next to him on his side of the bed and put the tray on the night stand.

Alex looked up and saw the sad expression on his wife's face. "What's the matter? Gloomy day, gloomy mood?"

She shook her head *no*. "Mary Alice Gregory called a while ago," she said and paused a moment.

"What did she need?" he said sarcastically.

"It's Louis," she said. "It was Louis in the boat crash last night."

Alex sat up quickly and threw the book over to his side. "What?"

"He's dead, Alex. They retrieved the body this morning." She watched her husband's expression change and he rubbed his whiskered face trying to absorb the information. Then he looked back at her and shook his head slowly.

"I just can't believe this and we saw it happen," he said, a helpless tone in his voice.

"I know it's been bad between you and Louis these past months…" Sally said.

"But, he was my friend," Alex said, completing her thought.

Sally handed him the glass of orange juice. "I know this probably isn't the most respectful time to say this, honey, but what will this do to the investigation of the business?"

Alex looked out the window at the rain pelting down and then said. "You know, I have no idea. Certainly their list of *bad guys* just got shorter."

***

Sally knocked on the big ornate door at the summer home of Mary Alice Gregory and her family. She heard footsteps coming and the door opened and a servant let her in. The front foyer opened into a wide hallway that led down to a large room with windows all across the front looking out at Lake Charlevoix. Sally took off her wet coat and handed it to the woman.

"Thank you, my name is Sally Clark and I would like to speak with Mary Alice for a moment."

272

The woman nodded and hung the coat in the front closet. "Would you like to take a seat out in the front room?" she asked.

"Sure, thank you."

Sally followed her out to the front of the house and walked up to the wall of windows and looked out at the lake through the streaming rain. She heard footsteps behind her on the wooden floor and turned to see Mary Alice coming into the room from a back hallway. She was still dressed in a robe and her feet were bare. Sally had never seen her without make-up and her face was pale and dark circles stood out under her eyes. Her black hair was pulled back in a simple pony tail and hung lifeless down her back. She stopped for a moment and looked at Sally and seemed to be considering the situation.

Sally finally said, "I just wanted to come out and personally say how sorry Alex and I are about Louis and what's happened."

Mary Alice continued to look at her with little change in her expression.

"I know that Louis and Alex were having some serious problems," Sally said, "but even Alex said this morning that you need to put that aside at times like this, at least for a while, and remember a person for what they've meant in your life."

Mary Alice nodded and walked down into the room. She came up to Sally and stood there for a moment in front on her. "Thank you," she said softly.

Sally stepped forward and held out her arms and Mary Alice hesitated for a moment, but then reached out as well and the two women embraced. They stood there together for some time just holding each other.

Mary Alice said, "Thank you. Thank you for coming."

Mary Alice stepped back and Sally could see the trails of tears coming down her face and she couldn't help but think how devastated she would be if this had been Alex.

"Would you like some coffee, or anything?" Mary Alice offered.

"No thank you."

"Please sit down," she said, pointing to a sofa behind Sally.

Sally sat down and watched as Mary Alice walked over to the big stone fireplace against the far wall. She reached up and took an envelope from the mantel and then came back over and sat down. She fumbled with the envelope for a few moments and then took a piece of paper out and handed it to Sally.

"Louis wrote this note to Alex. I found it on his desk this morning,"

Sally looked back at Mary Alice Gregory with a confused expression and then looked down at the piece of paper. She unfolded it and started to read.

Hey Alex,

It's been a good ride, hasn't it partner. I know I've made a bit of a mess of things lately, but you need to know it broke my heart to have any of this hurt you.

I've sent a letter off to your attorney today with a complete explanation of what really happened here, with full documentation that you had nothing to do with the decisions that were made and the actions that were taken that got us into all this trouble.

I'm sorry that I couldn't have been a better friend to the end.

L. Kramer

Sally placed the note down on her lap and looked up at Mary Alice. Her tears were coming freely now and Sally reached over and took her hand.

Chapter Thirty-four

Is there really such a thing as coincidence in this world? Many believe that none of us is here by accident and that every breath we take and every day that we live has purpose and order.

***

George Hansen stopped the car on the street in front of the sheriff's office and looked over at Jonathan who was holding a wet towel against the side of his face. He had tried to call Sheriff Potts earlier but he wasn't in yet and when George had explained what had happened the desk clerk had told him to come down to the station and they would get the sheriff.

"You should wait here," George said.

"Jonathan didn't answer, but turned and opened his door to get out.

George watched him struggle to walk, holding on to the car as he came around. "Maybe somebody inside can patch you up."

Jonathan nodded, a pained looked showing from behind the bloody towel.

George took his arm and was helping him up the walk when he saw Connor Harris rushing out of the front door. He saw George right away and a strange and angry look came across his face and he rushed at George and Jonathan.

"That fucking kid has done it again, Hansen!" Connor screamed.

George was caught by surprise and wasn't sure what he meant at first. "Get out of the way, Harris!" he said.

Connor reached out and stopped him, not even looking at the condition of Jonathan. "It's that damn Truegood kid. He almost killed Andy Welton last night."

George stood back and looked at the furious face of Connor Harris. He hesitated only a moment and then said with a growing fury, "Harris, I don't know what's happened, but I do know that if you don't get out of my way right now, I'm going to rip your ugly face off!"

Harris backed off a step, surprised and then quickly regained some sense of composure. "A deputy's headed out to pick up that little sonofabitch right now!"

George started up the sidewalk with Jonathan, but Harris grabbed him again. George let go of Jonathan's arm and turned and reached for Connor Harris with both hands on the top of his shirt and with his face two inches away from Harris', said, "I told you to back off you ignorant asshole and I mean it!"

He pushed him away and Connor stumbled backwards into the grass on his bad leg. "I swear, Hansen…" he yelled as George and Jonathan continued up the walk and into the sheriff's office.

***

Harold Slayton stood looking out the small window on the side of the old chapel in the woods. He had been out this way before, working on a county road crew and he knew very few people ever found their way back here. He had hidden Jonathan McKendry's truck around back. The dirt road that led past the heavy stand of trees was pocked with puddles from the previous day's rain. He heard a muffled sound behind him and he turned to see Emily McKendry sitting in a front pew. Her mouth was bound and she stared at him with frightened eyes. His little daughter Sara was sitting in a chair over in a corner behind the small preacher's pulpit. She was looking down at her doll and not making a sound.

Slayton walked down the narrow aisle between the pews and came around to face Emily. She sat there with her hands tied behind her and her legs bound at the ankles. He thought back to the previous night and wondered why he hadn't just killed the bitch and her husband. After Jonathan had fallen and wouldn't get up, he had run up the stairs with his gun

276

in front of him. Emily had come out of the back bedroom and screamed. He pointed the shotgun at her and told her to shut up. She kept screaming at him and he clicked the safety on the top of the gun and aimed straight at her face. She stopped yelling and he pushed her with the barrel of the gun back into the bedroom.

He remembered the look of horror in his daughter's eyes when she woke up and saw him holding the gun in the face of this woman. For a moment he wanted to go to her and try to explain what had happened with her mother, but Emily yelled at him again.

"You get the hell out of here!" she screamed, tears streaming down her red face. "Do you hear me, get out now!"

Sara pushed the blankets away and crawled quickly out of bed, running to a corner of the room away from her father. She sat down cowering and crying. He reached in his coat pocket and pulled out the little doll and threw it at her. Sara quickly picked it up and held it closely to her chest.

When he had looked back at the McKendry woman she was starting to come toward him. "What have you done with my husband!" she shrieked.

He had put the end of the gun barrel right on her nose and pushed her back against the wall. He remembered his finger trembling on the trigger and then Sara had screamed out, "Daddy!"

He turned and saw his daughter there in the corner and for just a moment he felt a terrible sadness as he tried to imagine how all of this had gotten so far out of control.

He looked back at the woman and told her to lie face down on the bed. There was a cloth belt around her robe and he stripped it off and tied her hands tightly behind her back with it. He looked around the room and then finally took a pillow case off the pillow and tied it around her mouth to keep her from screaming anymore.

Sara had run up behind him and started hitting him on his back and in a fury he turned and slapped her with the back of his hand, knocking her down across the floor. Emily had cried out again in a muffled wail as she watched.

He had managed to get both of them down the stairs and into McKendry's truck. The keys had been lying on the kitchen counter. He knew he couldn't go home, or back to the hunting camp and he had thought of this old chapel out in the woods. He figured it would give him time until he could decide what to do with this bitch doctor and where he could take his daughter.

He thought he heard something outside and he ran back to the window. A long green car was coming slowly around the bend, splashing through the puddles.

***

Jennifer Harris pulled the car over into a small clearing. She could see an old log chapel across a field next to the tree line and a small cemetery in the back. There didn't seem to be anyone around. She turned to Sammy Truegood sitting next to her on the front seat. "What is this place?"

Sammy didn't answer, but opened his door and got out. He came around the front of the car and she met him there. It was then that she noticed the circle of bent trees off across the meadow. They were large trees planted in a near circle, but curiously bent over parallel to the ground at about six feet up and then curved upward again toward the sky.

"Sammy, where are we?"

He took her hand and led her off the road into the high grass toward the trees. She looked back at the chapel behind them and felt a chill run through her. They walked in silence across the field and then slowly into the center of the trees. She felt an ominous sense of uncertainty as she dropped his hand and turned slowly, looking at all of the trees.

Sammy finally spoke in a soft voice. "This is where my people have come for many generations to make peace with others and with themselves."

Jennifer looked at his face and saw a curious mixture of sadness and contentment in his expression. Then she looked around again and turned slowly, looking at all of the trees. A breeze blew up and the leaves rattled in a rustling soft flurry. She watched as Sammy looked into the treetops, listening to the rush of the wind.

"Why did you bring me here?" she said

278

He walked over to her and took her hands in his. "I could never lie to you in this place. You need to believe me when I tell you that I didn't hurt you that night. I didn't even come near you, or see you after you left the fire."

"Sammy…"

"You have to believe me!"

"Sammy, I'm so sorry," she whispered, choking back tears and then she fell into his arms and hugged him as she started to cry. They stood there for a few moments, neither saying a word. Jennifer could feel her tears wet against his cheek.

Then a muffled cry came from somewhere far away, just barely heard above the sound of the wind in the trees and they both looked up in the direction of the chapel.

***

Slayton turned and ran back to Emily and slapped her hard across the face with his hand. She fell back on the pew and Sara screamed out.

"Shut up," he hissed, turning to his daughter. He went over to her and knelt down and said again, "You be quiet, girl," and then he held his hand up like he was going to hit her. She whimpered and pulled herself up into a ball on the chair, her doll held protectively in her arms.

He looked back at the window and thought for a moment about what he should do. He could get out the side door with Sara and just drive away, but those two kids out there would surely see the truck and find the woman. He went back over to the window with his shotgun in his hand. They were coming.

***

Sammy and Jennifer walked through the tall grass toward the chapel. He looked around and then pointed for Jennifer to see the back of a pick-up truck over behind the chapel. Then they heard another scream from inside and they both stopped.

"You go over to the car and wait there," Sammy said. She hesitated at first, but then walked slowly backwards and stood behind the car. He continued toward the chapel and then he stopped to listen. All he could hear was the wind in the trees and he closed his eyes and listened again for the

279

voices of his people. He felt a soothing calmness come over him and he opened his eyes and continued toward the little front door. He stood outside for just a moment looking at the rustic old wooden door and then he reached for the handle and pulled back the door.

As he walked through he crouched suddenly when he saw the barrel of a man's shotgun aimed at his face down at the end of an aisle of pews. Then he saw Dr. McKendry tied up next to him and a little girl hiding in the back corner.

"You just stay right there," the man said.

Sammy felt the hair on the back of his neck rise up as he looked at the end of the barrel of the shotgun. And then in a sudden flurry of motion, he watched as Emily McKendry jumped to her feet and lunged at the man, knocking him down in the aisle. Sammy heard the little girl scream again and the man curse as he fell to the floor. Without another thought he started running up the aisle toward the man and things suddenly seemed to be moving in slow motion and his legs felt like they were heavy and slow and the man came up to his knees and picked up the gun.

Sammy heard himself yelling as he ran, but it sounded distant and wild. He watched as the barrel of the gun came up again and an explosion of smoke roared out of it, echoing through the rafters of the little church. The blast hit him hard in the chest knocking him backwards, his head landing hard on the wood planking of the floor.

He laid there for a moment and closed his eyes. He could hear the little girl screaming, but it sounded more like an echo. He was thinking that there should be pain, but he felt only a heaviness and coldness in his body and he opened his eyes again and looked up into the rafters of the church. The wind blew through the open door and then he smiled weakly as he finally heard the words of his people. They were with him now.

***

Jennifer heard the explosion of the shotgun blast and fell down to her knees in shock behind the car. Panic ripped through her and she started shaking uncontrollably. Slowly she rose up and looked through the windows of the car at the chapel across the field.

"Sammy!" she yelled out as loudly as she could. "Sammy!" she shrieked again and she waited and there was no answer. She started to run around the car, but then the fear grabbed her and she knew she had to get help. She ran back to the door and jumped in. The keys were still in the ignition and she tried to steady her hands and she reached for them and turned the key.

The car rumbled to life and she threw the shift gear forward and pressed down as hard as she could on the accelerator. The big sedan lurched forward onto the road, wheels spinning and gravel flying out behind. She looked back for just a moment in the rearview mirror and only saw the black emptiness behind the open door of the chapel.

Chapter Thirty-five

Megan Clark sat waiting for her friend Rebecca in the small coffee shop down in Charlevoix. Her hair was soaked and dripping after running through the downpour of rain from her car out at the curb. The hot coffee steamed in the big mug and she breathed in a big whiff. The bell on the door jangled and Megan looked up to see Rebecca coming in, trying to close an umbrella she was carrying.

Megan said, "Morning, got you a decaf latte."

Rebecca sat down and brushed her hair back. "Thanks," she said. She took the coffee and sipped it to see how hot it was. "Perfect."

"Becca, I just wanted to see you…" Megan started to say.

Rebecca interrupted. "No Megan, after you told me what happened this morning on the phone with Rick and Melissa and the rest of those idiots, I just felt so badly about how I've been treating you and Will."

Megan smiled and looked back at her friend.

Rebecca started laughing and said, "You didn't really beat the crap out of Melissa Wainwright, did you?"

Megan just laughed and leaned over to give her friend a hug.

***

Sally pulled in the drive at her house on Michigan Avenue and turned the car off to get out. The rain had stopped in the past few minutes and she could see breaks in the clouds coming in from far across Lake Michigan. She went inside and looked and listened for Alex. She heard him upstairs and walked up to find him packing clothes into a bag on their bed. He turned when he saw her come in and smiled and came over to give her a hug.

"How is Mary Alice doing?" he asked.

Sally sighed and looked up at her husband. "Well, she's not doing very well at all, but I'm glad I went to see her."

"That had to be hard for you after the history with you two."

"No," Sally said, "I really wanted to go and actually, we had a very interesting time."

Alex looked at her with a puzzled expression.

Sally handed him the note that she had been holding in her hand.

Alex sat down on the bed and quickly read the message from his old friend and business partner, Louis Kramer. Sally stood and watched the expression on his face change as he finished the note.

***

The rain had stopped when Megan was driving down the road along Horton Creek. She turned now into the road back to Will's cabin. As she pulled up he came out of the pole barn back behind his cabin. He had an old denim work shirt on and a ball cap on his head to keep his hair back.

"Morning!" he said with a big smile across his face.

She came up and gave him a hug, "Good morning to you, Will Truegood."

"What brings you out to the wilds this early?" he asked.

She smiled and said, "Do I need a reason?"

"No, of course not."

She lifted up on her toes and kissed him.

He stepped back and looked down at his dirty clothes. He had been splitting wood and stacking it in the barn. "You're going to get this mess all over you," he said.

"It doesn't matter," she replied laughing and then held up a newspaper she had been holding on to. "I wanted you to see this story about Uncle George."

He reached for the paper and said, "I saw it yesterday, at least they got one of the bastards."

"I know he's been a good friend to you and your family for a long time."

283

Will nodded, thinking back on the years and the stories he had been told. "George and I used to fish together these past few years."

"I know."

"He showed me a lot of his *secret spots*," Will said. "Hey, looks like the weather's breaking. I had been thinking about taking a break and running down to the creek. The brook trout always like to come out after a big rain washes some juicy food into the stream."

"How about one of George's *secret spots*," Megan said.

Chapter Thirty-six

The glorious sense of redemption can be so sweet, but tempered quickly by the often staggering realities of our lives.

***

Jonathan sat with George Hansen in a small room at the sheriff's department, a towel pressed against his head. He was frantic about his wife and Sheriff Potts had been trying to calm him down.

"We have to do something!" Jonathan said.

"We've got men checking the farmhouse and the hunting camp again, Jonathan," the sheriff explained. "We just can't go out running around blind."

There was a commotion in the hallway and they looked up to see Jennifer Harris rushing by the desk clerk.

***

The sheriff drove the first car with George in the front and Jonathan in the back holding a towel full of ice over his eye. They sped over the hills around the north side of Lake Charlevoix, another car with two deputies behind them.

Jennifer Harris had breathlessly explained what had happened out at Bent Trees and Jonathan had listened in horror as she described the chapel and the pick-up truck and then the shotgun blast. Then nothing when she called for Sammy. His worst nightmares flashed in his brain and he tried with all his will to keep from going mad with fear.

The cars turned on the old dirt road up to the chapel and Potts sped as fast as he could up the winding road. As the car bumped along Jonathan held the ice tighter against his head trying to ease the pain.

The chapel came into view and Jonathan looked over the dash and could see the old wooden church and the door open to inside. He felt a nauseous emptiness inside and as soon as the car stopped he threw open the door and tried his best to get out quickly. Potts stopped him with his big arm, a shotgun in the other.

"Just wait a minute," the old sheriff said.

The other car skidded up in the loose stones and the deputies got out. Both had shotguns that they were loading. They all stood behind the cars and looked across the grassy field to the chapel. Potts whispered to his men and they both went off running low in opposite directions. The sheriff watched quietly as the men got into position on the far sides of the church and then he turned to Jonathan and George. "You two need to stay right here."

"You'll have to lock me up," Jonathan said. "No way I'm staying back here."

Jonathan looked at the face of Sheriff Potts for some sign of response and then the old man nodded.

"You stay close behind me," he said and they started around the cars, staying low. The sheriff signaled for his men to move forward and Jonathan watched as they both started moving slowly toward the sides of the chapel. He looked over at George and they exchanged frantic looks.

"It's going to be okay, Jonathan," he heard his friend George whisper to him. "I know it's going to be okay."

Jonathan could only feel a cold fear and the pounding ache in his head as they walked slowly through the grass. They stopped behind a large oak tree. The sheriff looked around and saw that his men were still moving forward.

"Slayton!" the sheriff yelled out. "Slayton, you in there?" For a moment there was no sound and then they heard a yell from over behind the little church.

"Sheriff, back here, quick!" a deputy yelled from behind the chapel.

The sheriff moved out slowly, his gun pointed at the open door. Jonathan and George followed closely behind.

When they came around the corner Jonathan saw his truck parked and the deputy was standing there looking into the open driver's side door. Then he saw the blood splattered around a large hole in the back window of the truck and he ran as best he could past the sheriff, terror ripping at his brain. He pushed the deputy aside and then stopped suddenly and staggered back. George came up beside him.

On the front seat of his truck, Harold Slayton lay there on his side. The shotgun had fallen to the floor and as Jonathan slowly moved up to look in he could see that most of the man's head had been blown away and the bloody remains leaked out onto the seat of the truck.

Jonathan felt the bile in his gut rising up in his throat and he staggered back trying to keep from retching. Then a new terror gripped him as he thought of his wife and he started walking slowly toward the side door of the chapel. He could sense a dull roar growing in his brain and tears starting to flow down his cheeks.

He stumbled to the door and reached out to the doorjamb to catch himself. As his eyes quickly adjusted to the dark interior of the chapel he first saw little Sara Slayton crouched in the far corner, clutching her doll and shaking uncontrollably. He took one step inside and heard a low moan and he ran forward and saw Emily lying on the floor between the pews, tied up and shaking, her sobs barely heard through the cloth around her mouth.

Jonathan ran to her and she looked up and saw him and her eyes opened wide. He pulled the cloth loose from her mouth.

"Oh Jonathan, thank God, Jonathan," she cried out.

He worked with trembling hands to free her hands and feet and then helped her sit up on the pew. She fell into his arms and sobbed and then she kissed him.

"Oh Jonathan."

"Are you okay?" he finally managed to say weakly.

She just nodded and he buried his face in her hair and felt his tears flowing and the most wonderful sense of relief coming over him. He noticed George and the sheriff walking by him and then down the aisle toward the front of the church. They both knelt down out of sight and then he heard his friend George cry out.

**

Jennifer Harris was sitting in the kitchen with her mother and brother, Connor. Coffee cups were spread in front of them. There was a knock at the back door and Connor got up to see who it was. Jennifer was still trembling thinking about what had happened out at the church. She saw her friend, Elaine Howard, come past Connor followed by the big sheriff Elaine had obviously been crying and she ran to Jennifer and hugged her.

"I'm really so sorry, Jenn," she said sobbing.

Jennifer looked up at the sheriff, confused and afraid of what he was going to say. Connor came up and stood next to him.

"Folks, I'm sorry to say that Sammy Truegood was shot and killed this morning out at the chapel at Bent Trees."

"No!" Jennifer wailed and her mother came around the table to hold her. In her mind she knew that Sammy was gone, but she had been holding the slightest glimmer of hope. She looked over at her brother and was disgusted to see him smiling.

"The bastard got what he deserved," Connor said.

Jennifer jumped up and ran across the kitchen screaming, "You're the stupid bastard, Connor!" She started punching at him and he grabbed her arms and she felt someone pulling her away. It was the sheriff and he helped her back and sat her down at the table.

"It was a man named Harold Slayton," the sheriff said. "We've been looking for him for the murder of his wife. He kidnapped Dr. McKendry and his little girl last night and you and Sammy happened to come across him hiding out at the chapel. Thank goodness you were able to get away, miss."

"And Sammy's really dead?" she said quietly, knowing the answer.

"Yes, I'm afraid he was gone by the time we got out there," Potts said. "Slayton took his own life. We found him outside. He used his shotgun."

"Oh my Lord!" Jennifer's mother gasped.

Jennifer sat there, a dull numbness overcoming her.

"There's something more your friend here wants to tell you," she heard the sheriff say.

Jennifer looked up and Elaine was standing in front of her and she could see that she was shaking. Her face was a mess of tears and smeared makeup.

"Go ahead, miss," the sheriff said.

Elaine took a deep breath and sighed as she let the air out. "Jennifer, I'm so sorry, but last night…" She couldn't finish.

"What is it?" Jennifer asked.

"Last night out at the beach, after you left." Again she stopped and rubbed her dripping nose with the back of her hand.

"Elaine, just tell me," Jennifer said, trying to choke back her own tears.

Elaine breathed deep again to try to calm herself. "Last night out at the beach, I was with Josh, Josh Knowles."

Jennifer nodded. "Yes."

"Well Josh was really getting drunk and we were… well I had been drinking, too and we were back in the dunes, you know kissing and stuff." She looked around the room at everyone watching her. "Well Josh was really drunk and he started pulling at my clothes and I tried to get him to stop and he wouldn't and he just got rougher with me and he tore my blouse." She had to stop and gather herself.

"Elaine, what happened?" Jennifer said.

"Well, he wouldn't stop," she sobbed. "He wouldn't let me up and he started ripping at my jeans and I was punching him and he pinned me down and just started laughing at me."

"Oh Elaine!" Mrs. Harris said, going over to comfort the girl.

Jennifer watched her friend lean against her mother crying. Then she looked back and said, "Josh was laughing at me and he had this wild look in his eyes and then he said he was going to have me just like he did you, Jenn!"

Jennifer sat back in shock as the realization of what had happened came over her. She saw the frightened look on Elaine's face and then looked over at her brother, Connor, who stood there with a stupid, stunned expression on his face.

"Sammy told me again this morning that he didn't do anything," Jennifer said and cried out loud again.

"What did you do," Connor asked Elaine, his voice shaking.

"He kept ripping at my clothes and I finally kicked him in the groin as hard as I could with my knee and he rolled off me," Elaine said. "I ran all the way home. I was so ashamed of what had happened. My mother finally forced me to tell her this morning and then she took me down to the police."

Jennifer looked up at her brother and he stood there with a dazed and angry expression. She watched as he turned to look back at her for a moment and then he spun around and hurried out of the room and she heard him going up the steps and then the door to his room slamming. She got up and went over to her friend and put her arms around her. They both sobbed quietly and held onto each other for support. Jennifer's mind couldn't block out the memories of Sammy this morning and his final words of truth.

Chapter Thirty-seven

Sally was in the kitchen making sandwiches to eat before Alex left for the airport when she heard a knock on the front door. She rinsed her hands in the sink and grabbed a towel as she walked down the hall. Through the sidelight window she could see a woman standing on the porch.

When she opened the door she was greeted by the sweet smile of a woman in her sixties, her hair nearly white and cut short all over.

"Hello Sally," the woman said quietly.

"Oh Sara, I'm so glad you stopped by."

The older woman nodded and held out her arms to give Sally a hug. Sally stepped down onto the porch and embraced the woman. Sara Slayton Moore had been friends with her parents and with George for many years, and Sally had first met her when she was a young girl and Sara would come up to Charlevoix with her family to visit.

Sally had heard the stories many times about Sara's childhood and the horrible deaths of her parents and young Sammy Truegood. She knew how much her mother, Emily, had done to help her and how much she had loved her. Sara's mother, Agnes, had a sister that lived in Saginaw and they had adopted Sara after her parents were gone.

"It's so good to see you, Sara," Sally said. "I'm sorry we didn't have more time to talk down at George's service the other day. Come in, please." She walked with her into the kitchen. "We were just getting ready to have some lunch. You'll have to join us."

"That would be nice," Sara said, "if you're sure it won't be too much trouble?"

"No, of course not."

Alex walked down the steps and into the kitchen. "Well hello," he said in surprise when he saw the woman standing next to Sally.

"Oh honey, you have to meet an old friend of our family. This is Sara Moore, she knew my parents very well," Sally said.

"Nice to meet you, Sara," Alex said, holding out his hand.

"Hello Alex," said Sara. "Actually, Sally's parents saved my life many years ago."

Sally stopped working on the sandwiches and looked at her old friend and smiled. The two women exchanged knowing glances that acknowledged the history and tragedies their families had shared.

"Here, sit down please," Alex said, taking her over to a chair at the kitchen table.

"So how have you been, Sara?" Sally asked.

"Well dear, we've been staying with family for a few days after the funeral, but I really need to speak with you about something."

"Of course, what is it?" said Sally coming over to join her at the table. Alex sat down as well and they watched as Sara reached down into her large purse and pulled out a newspaper. It was the Charlevoix paper and she spread it out on the table.

"I saw in the paper that they think George Hansen was murdered," Sara said. "I hadn't heard about it until I saw this story."

"Yes," Sally said, reaching out to take her small hand. "It's been a terrible shock to think that anyone would want to hurt George."

Sara nodded at her in sad agreement and said, "You know this fellow they have in jail, this Vince Slayton, well he's a distant relative from my dad's side of the family."

"Yes, I know," Sally said. She looked at the woman's kind face and could only imagine how badly her father had treated her.

"Well, I had the strangest experience last night and seeing this story, I just had to come and see you."

"What happened?" Sally asked.

Sara hesitated for a moment and then looked at both Alex and Sally. "It was this dream I had last night, but it was almost too real to be a dream. George Hansen came to see me and we sat and talked."

"Oh Sara," Sally said, rubbing the back of her hand. "That must have been so unnerving!"

She smiled sadly and said, "Well, we talked about when I was a little girl and how your mother loved me and that she would have adopted me if my mother's sister hadn't come to take care of me." She started to cry and reached into her purse for a Kleenex.

Sally felt the tears welling up in her eyes, too. "I know my mother loved you so much, Sara."

"It was such a terrible day when I heard that they had been lost with your little girl," Sara said.

Sally nodded, looking down at the table.

"Well, George and I seemed to talk for the longest time last night and at the end he said the strangest thing."

"In this dream?" Alex asked.

"Yes, but it was like he was there with me in my room and when I woke up this morning, I had the strangest sensation that he had *really* been there."

Sally and Alex sat and listened to Sara and her story and the more she revealed about her *visit* and conversation with George Hansen the night before the more shocked the expression on their faces became. When Sara finished she looked at both of them as if hoping for some explanation of what had happened.

Sally turned to look at her husband. "We really need to go talk to Elam."

***

Connor Harris and his son, Dylan were coming out of the back door of the house to drive into town when the sheriff's car pulled in and blocked the drive. Connor was really having trouble with his bad leg and struggled to get down the stairs. His thin gray hair was oily and unwashed and slicked back on his head.

Sheriff Elam Stone slowly climbed out of the car and then Alex and Sally Clark opened doors on the other side and came out to join the sheriff. Another patrol car pulled in and several uniformed deputies got out. Connor looked up with an uneasy expression.

"What the hell is this all about?" Connor said as he limped over to lean against his car. Dylan stood back behind him with a bewildered look on his face.

Sheriff Stone walked up in front of Harris. "We received some information this morning that is a little troubling, Mr. Harris." Sally and Alex came up and stood behind the sheriff.

Connor struggled to remain calm and to keep his hands from shaking. "Go ahead," he said with what he hoped would sound like defiance and not fear.

"This project you're trying to get approval for out at Horton Creek," the sheriff said.

"Yeah, what about it," Dylan Harris said, coming up to stand next to his father.

Elam Stone said, "Seems that George Hansen was one of your biggest obstacles to getting this deal done. He was on the approval commission and wouldn't back down."

Connor felt like his legs were going to melt out from under him and he held on to the car to steady himself. "He sure as hell wasn't the only one," Connor said slowly.

"We've been told that he had been moving quickly to expose the environmental mess that you two were going to create out there along old Horton Creek and that he was working hard to get all of the information to the rest of the commission."

"What's this all about?" Connor heard his son ask.

"Mr. Harris," Stone said, looking at Connor, "we think you know a man named Vince Slayton that we have down at the jail."

Connor didn't answer. He was focused on trying to stop his stomach from turning over and the sheriff's words suddenly seemed a muffled echo.

"Mr. Harris!" the sheriff said more loudly.

Connor looked back at the sheriff and at Alex and Sally Clark with a blank stare. He tried to hide the panic on his face, but he knew that there was no longer any point. He turned to look at his son who was standing there with a dazed and confused look on his face. "Dylan, I was only trying to help," he said, the defeat in his voice clear to everyone.

***

Megan Clark thought that she had never seen a more beautiful place, standing in the shallow currents of Horton Creek, the crystalline water darting among moss and grass covered banks and deadfalls, tall green cedars pointing up into a bright blue sky. Will Truegood was at her side and silently motioned to the rise of a fish just across and downstream in a quiet eddy. She saw the tiny circle of water expanding as it moved away with the current. He pointed to where he wanted her to cast the little fly and she nodded, feeling her heart beat just a little faster.

She felt him reach around and put his hand on the fly rod's cork handle just above hers. Feeling him guide the rod up and back, the line came off the water below them with a quick snap and a million little droplets of water flew off the line in a brilliant mist of colors in the sunlight. The green line sailed back behind them until she felt his arm press forward and she watched as the line flowed out smoothly in front of them until the tiny yellow fly landed quietly just a few feet above where the fish had come up moments before. Holding her breath and watching the fly move slowly down to the fish, she felt Will's arm around her, calm and comforting, but ready to lift at the first sign of the rise of the fish.

"There!" he said and she gasped as she felt the rod strike quickly in their hands and come tight to the fish as it sipped in the fly and dove back for the bottom of the river.

Will let go and she stood there alone with the fish, a thumping pull on the tip of the long fly rod. The fish ran fast downstream from her and the reel whined as the fish took line and then she felt Will behind her again and reaching to hold her hand, pulling the rod low and away from the fish.

"Okay, you take it now," he said and backed a step away.

The fish slowed and she began reeling and then it flew up out of the water down below them. She screamed out as it bucked and flipped over in the air, water splashing in all directions.

"It's a fine trout," she heard him say. "Keep after it now."

She kept reeling and then the fish would run again and take back line.

"Lay your rod over to the other side," he told her.

She knew she was gaining on the fish and the quick runs grew shorter. A drop of sweat hung from the end of her nose and she wiped it away with her free hand. When she looked back at Will he was smiling at her.

"Watch the fish!" he said.

Then his arms were around her waist and he was pulling her gently backwards toward the near bank. They moved slowly through the current making sure of their steps in the loose bottom of the river. When they stopped in the slower current she reeled fast against the fish and felt the elation of seeing it come close in the clear water, lying over on its side. The brilliant green colors of the fish sparkled in the flow of the water, a bright shock of orange behind its gills. As it came closer, Will stepped around and reached slowly down with the small wooden net and she pulled up on the rod to steer the fish until he lifted it up free of the current.

"Wow!" was all she could manage to say as they both looked down at the beautiful fish. Will held the net low to let the flow of the river wash over it and Megan watched the fish breathe hard, its gills pulsing in the current. "It's so beautiful," she said.

He took the rod from and her and placed a small pair of forceps in her hand. "I'll let you get the fly. She could see it stuck in the corner of the fish's mouth and she reached down and flicked it away, the fish flopping in protest. She handed the fly back to Will and then reached down into the net and placed her hand under the belly of the fish, feeling the cool and wetness of it in the stream. She lifted it out and watched the colors of it shine in the sunlight. She turned to look back at Will and then the fish squirmed and leapt out of her hand up into the air, splashing down into the clear water and away before she could even react.

"Oh no!" she screamed and she heard Will laughing behind her. When she turned he was sitting on the bank, a big smile across his face, the fly rod pointing away at his side.

"Nicely done," he said.

"But, I wanted a picture," she said with a pouting grin as she splashed over to sit beside him.

"You will always have a picture of that fish in your mind, Megan," he said and she knew that he was right. She knew that she would never forget this day, or this spot, or the feel of that fish. She felt him put his arm around her and she rested her head on the side of his shoulder, looking out across the clear flow of the river to the far bank.

Later they drove back into Charlevoix to meet Alex and Sally for dinner. Megan told Will that she would like to go on through town to stop at the little cemetery. She turned the Jeep in and they bumped along the narrow trail through the tall trees and grassy fields covered with stone markings and colorful flowers. She looked over at him. "I'd like to say one last goodbye to Uncle George and tell him there's still a few nice trout out at Horton Creek."

He nodded and she pulled the Jeep over in the grass and parked. They got out and walked together across the lawn through the headstones, holding hands. Birds darted away through the branches and two black squirrels chased one another around the trunk of a tall oak.

They walked slowly around a large granite headstone and stood quietly, looking down. Megan felt Will squeeze her hand. She took a deep breath and felt the moisture of her tears welling up in the corners of her eyes. A swirl of wind swept up above them and the leaves in the tall branches rustled and then were still.

Megan and Will read the words etched into the stone and silently said their goodbyes.

George Adam Hansen

1923 – 2007

***

Moving on is a time of bringing closure and accountability. In those few precious moments before our eternal rest, we look to those we have loved to help guide their paths and those who have strayed to bring deliverance.

G.Hansen

THE END

ON PAST HORTON CREEK